"POWERFUL!"
—*Los Angeles Times*

NOELLE PAGE, the French actress famous for her beauty and notorious for her sensual appetites . . .

CONSTANTIN DEMIRIS, whose wealth, cunning, power and supreme vindictiveness made him one of the most feared men in the world . . .

LARRY DOUGLAS, the handsome playboy-pilot who always found he could get anything he wanted from a woman . . .

CATHERINE, his adoring young American wife, who woke to terror from a dream of love, as she began to suspect the hellish truth about these three people and the Greek island paradise where she was prisoner . . .

The Other Side of Midnight

"Fast-paced, sophisticated, erotic . . . with a climax as startling as any you will find!"—*Sunday Oregonian* . . . "Sex and intrigue laced together in a never-fail pattern!"—*Pittsburgh Post-Gazette* . . . "Superior, first rate entertainment!"—*Nashville Tennessean*

By the author of **The Naked Face**

The Other Side of Midnight

Sidney Sheldon

A DELL BOOK

Published by
DELL PUBLISHING CO., INC.
1 Dag Hammarskjold Plaza
New York, New York 10017

Dell ® TM 681510, Dell Publishing Co., Inc.
Reprinted by arrangement with
William Morrow & Company, Inc.
Printed in the United States of America
First Dell printing—February 1975
Second Dell printing—March 1975
Third Dell printing—March 1975
Fourth Dell printing—March 1975
Fifth Dell printing—April 1975
Sixth Dell printing—May 1975
Seventh Dell printing—May 1975
Eighth Dell printing—June 1975
Ninth Dell printing—July 1975
Tenth Dell printing—July 1975
Eleventh Dell printing—August 1975
Twelfth Dell printing—August 1975
Thirteenth Dell printing—August 1975
Fourteenth Dell printing—September 1975
Fifteenth Dell printing—September 1975
Sixteenth Dell printing—October 1975
Seventeenth Dell printing—October 1975
Eighteenth Dell printing—October 1975
Nineteenth Dell printing—November 1975
Twentieth Dell printing—December 1975
Twenty-first Dell printing—December 1975
Twenty-second Dell printing—February 1976
Twenty-third Dell printing—February 1976

Acknowledgments

I wish to express my gratitude to those who generously helped me color the mosaic of this novel with the tiles of their knowledge, expertise and memories.

In a few instances where I felt it would enhance the narrative, I have taken literary license; but any factual errors are my responsibility alone.

My grateful thanks go to the following:

In London:

Ms. V. Shrubsall, Air Historical Branch, British Ministry of Defense, for invaluable information on the Eagle Squadron, the group of American pilots who flew with the RAF before the United States entered World War II.

Earl Boebert, for additional material on the Eagle Squadron.

In Paris:

André Weil-Curiel, former Vice-Mayor of Paris, for helpful suggestions and recollections of Paris under the German occupation.

Madame Chevaulet, Head Archivist for the Comédie Française, for allowing me access to her files on the history of the French theater.

Claude Baigneres, journalist for *Le Figaro,* for his assistance in helping me track down sources of firsthand information about the French occupation.

In Athens:

Mrs. Aspa Lambrou, who magically opened all doors and was unfailingly and generously helpful.

Jean Pierre de Vitry D'Avaucourt, personal pilot to Aristotle Onassis, for his technical advice and suggestions.

Costas Efstathiades, distinguished attorney, for his assistance on Greek criminal law procedures.

In Los Angeles:

Raoul Aglion, Conseiller Economique of the Banque Nationale de Paris, for sharing his knowledge of French history and French customs.

Except for the mention of various historical world leaders, all characters in this book are fictional.

PROLOGUE
Athens: 1947

Through the dusty windshield of his car Chief of Police
Georgios Skouri watched the office buildings and hotels
of downtown Athens collapse in a slow dance of disintegration, one after the other like rows of giant pins in
some cosmic bowling alley.

"Twenty minutes," the uniformed policeman at the
wheel promised. "No traffic."

Skouri nodded absently and stared at the buildings.
It was an illusion that never ceased to fascinate him.
The shimmering heat from the pitiless August sun en-
veloped the buildings in undulating waves that made
them seem to be cascading down to the streets in a
graceful waterfall of steel and glass.

It was ten minutes past noon, and the streets were
almost deserted, but even the few pedestrians abroad
were too lethargic to give more than a passing curious
glance at the three police cars racing east toward Hellenikon, the airport that lay twenty miles from the center of Athens. Chief Skouri was riding in the first car.
Under ordinary circumstances, he would have stayed in
his comfortable, cool office while his subordinates went
out to work in the blazing noon heat, but these circumstances were far from ordinary and Skouri had a two-
fold reason for being here personally. First, in the
course of this day planes would be arriving carrying
VIPs from various parts of the globe, and it was necessary to see that they were welcomed properly and
whisked through Customs with a minimum of bother.
Second, and more important, the airport would be

crowded with foreign newspaper reporters and newsreel cameramen. Chief Skouri was not a fool, and it
had occurred to him as he had shaved that morning
that it would do no harm to his career if he were
shown in newsreels as he took the eminent visitors into
his charge. It was an extraordinary stroke of fate that
had decreed that a worldwide event as sensational as
this one had occurred in his domain, and he would be
stupid not to take advantage of it. He had discussed it
in great detail with the two people in the world closest
to him: his wife and his mistress. Anna, a middle-aged,
ugly, bitter woman of peasant stock, had ordered him
to keep away from the airport and stay in the background so that he could not be blamed if anything went
wrong. Melina, his sweet, beautiful young angel, had
advised him to greet the dignitaries. She agreed with
him that an event like this could catapult him into instant fame. If Skouri handled this well, at the very least
he would get a raise in salary and—God willing—
might even be made Commissioner of Police when the
present Commissioner retired. For the hundredth time
Skouri reflected on the irony that Melina was his wife
and Anna was his mistress, and he wondered again
where he had gone wrong.

Now Skouri turned his thoughts to what lay ahead.
He must make certain that everything went perfectly at
the airport. He was bringing with him a dozen of his
best men. His main problem, he knew, would be con-
trolling the press. He had been astonished by the number of important newspaper and magazine reporters
that had poured into Athens from all over the world.
Skouri himself had been interviewed six times—each
time in a different language. His answers had been
translated into German, English, Japanese, French,
Italian and Russian. He had just begun to enjoy his
new celebrity when the Commissioner had called to inform him that he felt it was unwise for the Chief of Police to comment publicly on a murder trial that had not

yet taken place. Skouri was sure that the Commissioner's real motivation was jealousy, but he had prudently decided not to press the issue and had refused all further interviews. However, the Commissioner certainly could not complain if he, Skouri, happened to be at the airport at the center of activity while the newsreel cameras were photographing the arriving celebrities.

As the car sped down Sygrou Avenue and swung left at the sea toward Phaleron, Skouri felt a tightening in his stomach. They were now only five minutes from the airport. He mentally checked over the list of celebrities who would be arriving in Athens before nightfall.

Armand Gautier was suffering from airsickness. He had a deep-seated fear of flying that stemmed from an excessive love of himself and his life and that, combined with the turbulence usually found off the coast of Greece in summer, had made him violently nauseous. He was a tall, ascetically thin man with scholarly features, a high forehead and a perpetually sardonic mouth. At twenty-two Gautier had helped create *La Nouvelle Vague* in France's struggling movie industry and in the years that followed had gone on to even bigger triumphs in the theater. Now acknowledged as one of the world's greatest directors, Gautier lived his role to the hilt. Until the last twenty minutes it had been a most pleasant flight. The stewardesses recognizing him had catered to his needs and had let him know they were available for other activities. Several passengers had come up to him during the flight to say how much they admired his films and plays, but he was most interested in the pretty English University student who was attending St. Anne's at Oxford. She was writing a thesis on the theater for her master's and had chosen Armand Gautier as her subject. Their conversation had gone well until the girl had brought up the name of Noelle Page.

"You used to be her director, didn't you?" she said. "I hope I can get into her trial. It's going to be a circus."

Gautier found himself gripping the sides of his seat, and the strength of his reaction surprised him. Even after all these years the memory of Noelle evoked a pain in him that was as sharp as ever. No one had ever touched him as she had, and no one ever would again. Since Gautier had read of Noelle's arrest three months earlier, he had been able to think of nothing else. He had cabled her and written her, offering to do whatever he could to help, but he had never received a reply. He had had no intention of attending her trial, but he knew he could not stay away. He told himself that it was because he wanted to see whether she had changed since they had lived together. And yet he admitted to himself there was another reason. The theatrical part of him had to be there to view the drama, to watch Noelle's face as the judge told her whether she was to live or die.

The metallic voice of the pilot came over the intercom to announce that they would be landing in Athens in three minutes, and the excitement of the anticipation of seeing Noelle again made Armand Gautier forget his airsickness.

Dr. Israel Katz was flying to Athens from Capetown, where he was the resident neurosurgeon and chief of staff at Groote Schuur, the large new hospital that had just been built. Israel Katz was recognized as one of the leading neurosurgeons in the world. Medical journals were filled with his innovations. His patients included a prime minister, a president and a king.

He leaned back in the seat of the BOAC plane, a man of medium height, with a strong, intelligent face, deep-set brown eyes and long, slender, restless hands. Dr. Katz was tired, and because of that he began to feel the familiar pain in a right leg that was no longer

there, a leg amputated six years earlier by a giant with
an ax.

It had been a long day. He had done predawn sur-
gery, visited half a dozen patients and then walked out
of a Board of Directors' meeting at the hospital in order to fly to Athens for the trial. His wife, Esther, had
tried to dissuade him.

"There is nothing you can do for her now, Israel."

Perhaps she was right, but Noelle Page had once
risked her life to save his and he owed her something.
He thought of Noelle now, and he felt the same in-
describable feeling that he had felt whenever he had
been with her. It was as though the mere memory of
her could dissipate the years that separated them. It
was romantic fantasy, of course. Nothing could ever
bring those years back. Dr. Israel Katz felt the plane
shudder as the wheels were lowered and it started its
descent. He looked out the window and spread out below him was Cairo, where he would transfer to a TAE
plane to Athens, and Noelle. Was she guilty of murder? As the plane headed for the runway he thought
about the other terrible murder she had committed in
Paris.

Philippe Sorel stood at the railing of his yacht
watching the harbor of Piraeus moving closer. He had
enjoyed the sea voyage because it was one of the rare
opportunities he had to escape from his fans. Sorel was
one of the few sure box-office attractions in the world,
and yet the odds against his ever rising to stardom had
been tremendous. He was not a handsome man. On the
contrary. He had the face of a boxer who had lost his
last dozen matches, his nose had been broken several
times, his hair was thin and he walked with a slight
limp. None of these things mattered, for Philippe Sorel
had sex appeal. He was an educated, soft-spoken man,
and the combination of his innate gentleness and
truck-driver's face and body drove the women frantic

and made men look up to him as a hero. Now as his
yacht approached the harbor, Sorel wondered again
what he was doing here. He had postponed a movie
that he had wanted to make in order to attend Noelle's
trial. He was only too well aware of what an easy target he would be for the press as he sat in the courtroom every day, completely unprotected by his press
agents and managers. The reporters were certain to
misunderstand his attendance and think that it was a
bid to reap publicity from the murder trial of his
former mistress. Any way he looked at it, it was going
to be an agonizing experience, but Sorel had to see Noelle again, had to find out if there was some way in
which he could help her. As the yacht began to slide
into the white-stoned breakwater of the harbor, he
thought about the Noelle he had known, lived with and
loved, and he came to a conclusion: Noelle was perfectly capable of murder.

As Philippe Sorel's yacht was approaching the coast
of Greece, the Special Assistant to the President of the
United States was in a Pan American Clipper, one hundred air miles northwest of the Hellenikon Airport.
William Fraser was in his fifties, a handsome gray-
haired man with a craggy face and an authoritative
manner. He was staring at a brief in his hand, but he
had not turned a page or stirred for more than an hour.
Fraser had taken a leave of absence to make this journey, even though it had come at a most inconvenient
time, in the midst of a congressional crisis. He knew
how painful the next few weeks were going to be for
him, and yet he felt that he had no choice. This was a
journey of vengeance, and the thought filled Fraser
with a cold satisfaction. Deliberately Fraser forced his
thoughts away from the trial that would begin tomorrow and looked out the window of the plane. Far below he could see an excursion boat bobbing its way
toward Greece, its coast looming in the distance.

* * *

Auguste Lanchon had been seasick and terrified for three days. He was seasick because the excursion boat which he had boarded in Marseille had been caught in the tail end of a mistral, and he was terrified because he was afraid that his wife would find out what he was doing. Auguste Lanchon was in his sixties, a fat, bald-headed man with small stumpy legs and a pockmarked face with porcine eyes and thin lips that constantly had a cheap cigar clamped between them. Lanchon owned a dress shop in Marseille and he could not afford—or at least that is what he constantly told his wife—to take a vacation like rich people. Of course, he remind-ed himself, this was not truly a vacation. He had to see his darling Noelle once again. In the years since she had left him, Lanchon had followed her career avidly in the gossip columns, in newspapers and maga-zines. When she had starred in her first play, he had taken the train all the way to Paris to see her, but No-elle's stupid secretary had kept them apart. Later he had watched Noelle's movies, seeing them again and again and remembering how she had once made love to him. Yes, this trip would be expensive, but Auguste Lanchon knew that it would be worth every sou of it. His precious Noelle would remember the good times they used to have together, and she would turn to him for protection. He would bribe a judge or some other official—if it did not cost too much—and Noelle would be freed, and he would set her up in a little apartment in Marseille where she would always be available to him when he wanted her.

If only his wife did not find out what he was doing.

In the city of Athens Frederick Stavros was working in his tiny law office on the second floor of an old run-down building in the poor Monastiraki section of the city. Stavros was an intense young man, eager and am-bitious, struggling to make a living from his chosen profession. Because he could not afford an assistant, he was forced to do all the tedious background legal research himself. Ordinarily he hated this part of his work, but this time he did not mind because he knew that if he won this case his services would be in such demand that he would never have to worry again for the rest of his life. He and Elena could be married and begin to raise a family. He would move into a suite of luxurious offices, hire law clerks and join a fashionable club like the Athenee Lesky, where one met affluent potential clients. The metamorphosis had already begun. Every time Frederick Stavros walked out into the streets of Athens, he was recognized and stopped by someone who had seen his picture in the newspaper. In a few short weeks he had jumped from anonymity to the attorney who was defending Larry Douglas. In the privacy of his soul Stavros admitted to himself that he had the wrong client. He would have preferred to be defending the glamorous Noelle Page instead of a nonentity like Larry Douglas, but he himself was a nonentity. It was enough that he, Frederick Stavros, was a major participant in the most sensational murder case of the century. If the accused were acquitted, there would be enough glory for everyone. There was only one thing that plagued Stavros, and he thought about it constantly. Both defendants were charged with the same crime, but another attorney was defending Noelle Page. If Noelle Page was found innocent, and Larry Douglas was convicted . . . Stavros shuddered and tried not to think about it. The reporters kept asking him whether he thought the defendants were guilty. He smiled to himself at their naïveté. What did it matter whether they were guilty or innocent? They were entitled to the best legal defense that money could buy. In his case he admitted that the definition was stretched a bit. But in the case of Noelle Page's lawyer . . . ah, that was something else again. Napoleon Chotas had undertaken her defense, and there was no more brilliant criminal lawyer in the world. Chotas had never lost an important case. As he thought about that, Frederick Stavros smiled to himself. He would not have admitted it to anyone, but he was planning to ride to victory on Napoleon Chotas' talent.

While Frederick Stavros was toiling in his dingy law office, Napoleon Chotas was attending a black-tie dinner party at a luxurious home in the fashionable Kolonaki section of Athens. Chotas was a thin, emaciated-looking man with the large, sad eyes of a bloodhound in a corrugated face. He concealed a brilliant, incisive brain behind a mild, vaguely baffled manner. Now toying with his dessert, Chotas sat, preoccupied, thinking about the trial that would begin tomorrow. Most of the conversation that evening had centered around the forthcoming trial. The discussion had been a general one, for the guests were too discreet to ask him direct questions. But toward the end of the evening as the ouzo and brandy flowed more freely, the hostess asked, "Tell us, do you think they are guilty?"

Chotas replied innocently, "How could they be? One of them is my client." He drew appreciative laughter.

"What is Noelle Page really like?"

Chotas hesitated. "She's a most unusual woman," he replied carefully. "She's beautiful and talented—" To his surprise he found that he was suddenly reluctant to discuss her. Besides, there was no way one could capture Noelle with words. Until a few months ago he had only been dimly aware of her as a glamorous figure flitting through the gossip columns and adorning the covers of movie magazines. He had never laid eyes on her, and if he had thought of her at all, it had been with the kind of indifferent contempt he felt toward all actresses. All body and no brain. But, God, how wrong he had been! Since meeting Noelle he had fallen hopelessly in love with her. Because of Noelle Page he had broken his cardinal rule: never become emotionally involved with a client. Chotas remembered vividly the afternoon he had been approached to undertake her defense. He had been in the midst of packing for a three-week vacation trip that he and his mistress were going to make to Paris and London. Nothing, he had believed, could have stopped him from making that journey. But it had only taken two words. In his mind's eye he saw his butler walk into the bedroom, hand him the telephone and say, "Constantin Demiris."

The island was inaccessible except by helicopter and yacht, and both the airfield and the private harbor were patrolled twenty-four hours a day by armed guards with trained German shepherds. The island was Constantin Demiris' private domain, and no one intruded without an invitation. Over the years its visitors had included kings and queens, presidents and ex-presidents, movie stars, opera singers and famous writers and painters. They had all come away awed. Constantin Demiris was the third wealthiest, and one of the most powerful men in the world, and he had taste and style and knew how to spend his money to create beauty.

Demiris sat in his richly paneled library now, relaxed in a deep armchair, smoking one of the flat-shaped Egyptian cigarettes especially blended for him, thinking about the trial that would begin in the morning. The press had been trying to get to him for months, but he had simply made himself unavailable. It was enough that his mistress was going to be tried for murder, enough that his name would be dragged into the case, even indirectly. He refused to add to the furor by granting any interviews. He wondered what Noelle was feeling now, at this moment, in her cell in the Nikodemous Street Prison. Was she asleep? Awake? Filled with panic at the ordeal that lay before her? He thought of his last conversation with Napoleon Chotas. He trusted Chotas and knew that the lawyer would not fail him. Demiris had impressed upon the attorney that it did not matter to him whether Noelle was innocent or guilty. Chotas was to see to it that he earned every penny of the stupendous fee that Constantin Demiris was paying him to defend her. No, he had no reason to worry. The trial would go well. Because Constantin Demiris was a man who never forgot anything, he remembered that Catherine Douglas' favorite flowers were Triantafylias, the beautiful roses of Greece. He reached forward and picked up a note pad from his desk. He made a notation. *Triantafylias. Catherine Douglas.*

It was the least he could do for her.

Book One

CATHERINE
Chicago: 1919-1939

1

Every large city has a distinctive image, a personality that gives it its own special cachet. Chicago in the 1920's was a restless, dynamic giant, crude and without manners, one booted foot still in the ruthless era of the tycoons who helped give birth to it: William B. Ogden and John Wentworth, Cyrus McCormick and George M. Pullman. It was a kingdom that belonged to the Philip Armours and Gustavus Swifts and Marshall Fields. It was the domain of cool professional gangsters like Hymie Weiss and Scarface Al Capone.

One of Catherine Alexander's earliest memories was of her father taking her into a bar with a sawdust-covered floor and swinging her up to the dizzyingly high stool. He ordered an enormous glass of beer for himself and a Green River for her. She was five years old, and she remembered how proud her father was as strangers crowded around to admire her. All the men ordered drinks and her father paid for them. She recalled how she had kept pressing her body against his arm to make sure he was still there. He had only returned to town the night before, and Catherine knew that he would soon leave again. He was a traveling salesman, and he had explained to her that his work took him to distant cities and he had to be away from her and her mother for months at a time so that he could bring back nice presents. Catherine had desperately tried to make a deal with him. If he would stay with her, she would give up the presents. Her father had laughed and said what a precocious child she was and then had left town, and it was six months before she saw him again. During those early years her mother whom she saw every day seemed a vague, shapeless personality, while her father, whom she saw only on brief occasions, was vivid and wonderfully clear. Catherine thought of him as a handsome, laughing man, full of sparkling humor and warm, generous gestures. The occasions when he came home were like holidays, full of treats and presents and surprises.

When Catherine was seven, her father was fired from his job, and their life took on a new pattern. They left Chicago and moved to Gary, Indiana, where he went to work as a salesman in a jewelry store. Catherine was enrolled in her first school. She had a wary, arms-length relationship with the other children and was terrified of her teachers, who misinterpreted her lonely standoffishness as conceit. Her father came home to dinner every night, and for the first time in her life Catherine felt that they were a real family, like other families. On Sunday the three of them would go to Miller Beach and rent horses and ride for an hour or two along the sand dunes. Catherine enjoyed living in Gary, but six months after they moved there, her father lost his job again and they moved to Harvey, a suburb of Chicago. School was already in session, and Catherine was the new girl, shut out from the friendships that had already been formed. She became known as a loner. The children, secure in the safety of their own groups, would come up to the gangly newcomer and ridicule her cruelly.

During the next few years Catherine donned an armor of indifference, which she wore as a shield against the attacks of the other children. When the armor was pierced, she struck back with a trenchant, caustic wit. Her intention was to alienate her tormentors so that they would leave her alone, but it had an unexpectedly different effect. She worked on the school paper, and in her first review about a musical that her classmates had staged, she wrote, "Tommy Belden had a trumpet solo in the second act, but he blew it." The line was widely quoted, and—surprise of surprises—Tommy Belden came up to her in the hall the next day and told Catherine that he thought it was funny.

In English the students were assigned *Captain Horatio Hornblower* to read. Catherine hated it. Her book report consisted of one sentence: "His barque was worse than his bight," and her teacher, who was a weekend sailor, gave her an "A." Her classmates began to quote her remarks and in a short time she was known as the school wit.

That year Catherine turned fourteen and her body was beginning to show the promise of a ripening woman. She would examine herself in the mirror for hours on end, brooding about how to change the disaster she saw reflected. Inside she was Myrna Loy, driving men mad with her beauty, but her mirror—which was her bitter enemy—showed hopelessly tangled black hair that was impossible to manage, solemn gray eyes, a mouth that seemed to grow wider by the hour and a nose that was slightly turned up. Maybe she wasn't really *ugly,* she told herself cautiously, but on the other hand no one was going to knock down doors to sign her up as a movie star. Sucking in her cheeks and squinting her eyes sexily she tried to visualize herself as a model. It was depressing. She struck another pose. Eyes open wide, expression eager, a big friendly smile. No use. She wasn't the All-American type either. She wasn't anything. Her body was going to be all right, she dourly supposed, but nothing special. And that, of course, was what she wanted more than anything in the world: to be something special, to be Somebody, to be Remembered, and never, never, never, never, to die.

The summer she was fifteen, Catherine came across *Science and Health* by Mary Baker Eddy and for the next two weeks she spent an hour a day before her mirror, willing her reflection to become beautiful. At the end of that time the only change she could detect was a new patch of acne on her chin and a pimple on her forehead. She gave up sweets, Mary Baker Eddy and looking in the mirror.

Catherine and her family had moved back to Chicago and settled in a small, dreary apartment on the north side, in Rogers Park, where the rent was cheap. The country was moving deeper into an economic depression. Catherine's father was working less and drinking more, and he and her mother were constantly yelling at each other in a never-ending series of recriminations that drove Catherine out of the house. She would go down to the beach half a dozen blocks away and walk along the shore, letting the brisk wind give wings to her thin body. She spent long hours staring at the restless gray lake, filled with some desperate longing to which she could not put a name. She wanted something so much that at times it would engulf her in a sudden wave of unbearable pain.

Catherine had discovered Thomas Wolfe, and his books were like a mirror image of the bittersweet nostalgia that filled her, but it was a nostalgia for a future that had not happened yet, as though somewhere, sometime, she had lived a wonderful life and was restless to live it again. She had begun to have her periods, and while she was physically changing into a woman, she knew that her needs, her longings, this aching-wanting was not physical and had nothing to do with sex. It was a fierce and urgent longing to be recognized, to lift herself above the billions of people who teemed the earth, so everyone would know who she was, so when she walked by, they would say, "There goes Catherine Alexander, the great—" The great *what?* There was the problem. She did not know what she wanted, only that she ached desperately for it. On Saturday afternoons whenever she had enough money, she would go to the State and Lake Theater or to the McVickers or the Chicago, and see movies. She would completely lose herself in the wonderful, sophisticated world of Cary Grant and Jean Arthur, laugh with Wallace Beery and Marie Dressler and agonize over Bette Davis' romantic disasters. She felt closer to Irene Dunne than to her mother.

Catherine was in her senior year at Senn High School and her archenemy, the mirror, had finally become her friend. The girl in the mirror had a lively, interesting face. Her hair was raven black and her skin a soft, creamy white. Her features were regular and fine, with a generous, sensitive mouth and intelligent gray eyes. She had a good figure with firm, well-developed breasts, gently curving hips and shapely legs. There was an air of aloofness about her image, a hauteur that Catherine did not feel, as though her reflection possessed a characteristic that she did not. She supposed that it was part of the protective armor she had worn since her early school days.

The Depression had clutched the nation in a tighter and tighter vise, and Catherine's father was incessantly involved in big deals that never seemed to materialize. He was constantly spinning dreams, inventing things that were going to bring in millions of dollars. He devised a set of jacks that fitted above the wheels of an automobile and could be lowered by the touch of a button on the dashboard. None of the automobile manufacturers was interested. He worked out a continuously rotating electric sign to carry advertisements inside stores. There was a brief flurry of optimistic meetings and then the idea faded away.

He borrowed money from his younger brother, Ralph, in Omaha to outfit a shoe-repair truck to travel around the neighborhood. He spent hours discussing the scheme with Catherine and her mother. "It can't fail," he explained. "Imagine having the shoemaker coming to your door! No one's ever done it before. I have one Shoe-mobile out now, right? If it only makes twenty dollars a day, that's a hundred and twenty dol-

lars a week. Two trucks will bring in two hundred and
forty a week. Within a year I'll have twenty trucks.
That's two thousand four hundred dollars a week. A
hundred and twenty-five thousand a year. And that's
only the beginning. . . ." Two months later the shoemaker and the truck disappeared, and that was the end
of another dream.

Catherine had hoped to be able to go to Northwestern University. She was the top scholar in her
class, but even on a scholarship college would be difficult to manage, and the day was coming, Catherine
knew, when she would have to quit school and go to
work full time. She would get a job as a secretary, but
she was determined that she would never surrender the
dream that was going to give such rich, wonderful
meaning to her life; and the fact that she did not know
what either the dream or the meaning was made it all
the more unbearably sad and futile. She told herself
that she was probably going through adolescence.
Whatever it was, it was hell. *Kids are too young to
have to go through adolescence,* she thought bitterly.

There were two boys who thought they were in love
with Catherine. One was Tony Korman who was going
to join his father's law firm one day and who was a
foot shorter than Catherine. He had pasty skin and
myopic watery eyes that adored her. The other was
Dean McDermott, who was fat and shy and wanted to
be a dentist. Then of course, there was Ron Peterson,
but he was in a category by himself. Ron was Senn
High's football star, and everybody said he was a cinch
to go to college on an athletic scholarship. He was tall
and broad-shouldered, had the looks of a matinee idol
and was easily the most popular boy in school.

The only thing that kept Catherine from instantly
getting engaged to Ron was the fact that he was not
aware she was alive. Every time she passed him in the
school corridor, her heart would begin to pound wildly.
She would think up something clever and provocative

to say so he would ask her for a date. But when she approached him, her tongue would stiffen, and they would pass each other in silence. Like the *Queen Mary* and a garbage scow, Catherine thought hopelessly.

The financial problem was becoming acute. The rent was three months overdue, and the only reason they had not been evicted was that the landlady was captivated by Catherine's father and his grandiose plans and inventions. Listening to him, Catherine was filled with a poignant sadness. He was still his cheerful, optimistic self, but she could see behind the frayed facade. The marvelous, careless charm that had always given a patina of gaiety to everything he did had eroded. He reminded Catherine of a small boy in a middle-aged man's body spinning tales of the glorious future to hide the shabby failures of the past. More than once she had seen him give a dinner party for a dozen people at Henrici's and then cheerfully take one of his guests aside and borrow enough to cover the check plus a lavish tip, of course. Always lavish, for he had his reputation to maintain. But in spite of all these things and in spite of the fact that Catherine knew that he had been a casual and indifferent father to her, she loved this man. She loved his enthusiasm and smiling energy in a world of frowning, sullen people. This was his gift, and he had always been generous with it.

In the end, Catherine thought, he was better off with his wonderful dreams that would never materialize, than her mother who was afraid to dream.

In April Catherine's mother died of a heart attack. It was Catherine's first confrontation with death. Friends and neighbors filled the little apartment, offering their condolences, with the false, whispered pieties that tragedy invokes.

Death had diminished Catherine's mother to a tiny shriveled figure without juices or vitality, or perhaps life had done that to her, Catherine thought. She tried to recall memories that she and her mother had shared, laughter that they had had together, moments when their hearts had touched; but it was Catherine's father who kept leaping into her mind, smiling and eager and gay. It was as though her mother's life was a pale shadow that retreated before the sunlight of memory. Catherine stared at the waxen figure of her mother in her casket, dressed in a simple black dress with a white collar, and thought what a wasted life it had been. What had it all been for? The feelings Catherine had had years ago came over her again, the determination to be somebody, leave a mark on the world, so she would not end up in an anonymous grave with the world neither knowing nor caring that Catherine Alexander had ever lived and died and been returned to the earth.

Catherine's Uncle Ralph and his wife, Pauline, flew in from Omaha for the funeral. Ralph was ten years younger than Catherine's father and totally unlike his brother. He was in the vitamin mail-order business and very successful. He was a large, square man, square shoulders, square jaw, square chin, and, Catherine was sure, a square mind. His wife was a bird of a woman, all flutter and twitter. They were decent enough people, and Catherine knew that her uncle had loaned a great deal of money to his brother, but Catherine felt that she had nothing in common with them. Like Catherine's mother, they were people without dreams.

After the funeral, Uncle Ralph said that he wanted to talk to Catherine and her father. They sat in the tiny living room of the apartment, Pauline flitting about with trays of coffee and cookies.

"I know things have been pretty rough for you financially," Uncle Ralph said to his brother. "You're too much of a dreamer, always were. But you're my brother. I can't let you sink. Pauline and I talked it over. I want you to come to work for me."

"In Omaha?"

"You'll make a good, steady living and you and

Catherine can live with us. We have a big house."

Catherine's heart sank. Omaha! It was the end of all her dreams.

"Let me think it over," her father was saying.

"We'll be catching the six o'clock train," Uncle Ralph replied. "Let me know before we leave."

When Catherine and her father were alone, he groaned, "Omaha! I'll bet the place doesn't even have a decent barber shop."

But Catherine knew that the act he was putting on was for her benefit. Decent barber shop or no, he had no choice. Life had finally trapped him. She wondered what it would do to his spirit to have to settle down to a steady, dull job with regular hours. He would be like a captured wild bird beating his wings against his cage, dying of captivity. As for herself, she would have to forget about going to Northwestern University. She had applied for a scholarship but had heard nothing. That afternoon her father telephoned his brother to say that he would take the job.

The next morning Catherine went to see the principal to tell him that she was going to transfer to a school in Omaha. He was standing behind his desk and before she could speak, he said, "Congratulations, Catherine, you've just won a full scholarship to Northwestern University."

Catherine and her father discussed it thoroughly that night, and in the end it was decided that he would move to Omaha and Catherine would go to Northwestern and live in one of the dormitories on the campus. And so, ten days later, Catherine took her father down to the La Salle Street station to see him off. She was filled with a deep sense of loneliness at his departure, a sadness at saying good-bye to the person she loved the most; and yet at the same time she was eager for the train to leave, filled with a delicious excitement at the thought that she would be free, living her own life for the first time. She stood on the platform watching the face of her father pressing against the train window for a last look; a shabbily handsome man who still truly believed that one day he would own the world.

On the way back from the station Catherine remembered something and laughed aloud. To take him to Omaha, to a desperately needed job, her father had booked a Drawing Room.

Matriculation day at Northwestern was filled with an almost unbearable excitement. For Catherine it held a special significance that she could not put into words: It was the key that would unlock the door to all the dreams and nameless ambitions that had burned so fiercely within her for so long. She looked around the huge assembly hall where hundreds of students were lined up to register, and she thought: *Someday you'll all know who I am. You'll say, "I went to school with Catherine Alexander."* She signed up for the maximum number of allowed courses and was assigned to a dormitory. That same morning she found a job working afternoons as a cashier at the Roost, a popular sandwich and malt shop across from the campus. Her salary was fifteen dollars a week, and while it would not afford her any luxuries, it would take care of her school books and basic necessities.

By the middle of her sophomore year Catherine decided that she was probably the only virgin on the entire campus. During the years she was growing up, she had overheard random snatches of conversations as her elders discussed sex. It sounded wonderful, and her strongest fear was that it would be gone by the time she was old enough to enjoy it. Now it looked as though she had been right. At least as far as *she* was concerned. Sex seemed to be the single topic of conversation at school. It was discussed in the dormitories, in classrooms, in the washrooms and at the Roost. Catherine was shocked by the frankness of the conversations.

"Jerry is unbelievable. He's like King Kong."

"Are you talking about his cock or his brain?"

"He doesn't need a brain, honey. I came six times last night."

"Have you ever gone out with Ernie Robbins? He's small, but he's mighty."

"Alex asked me for a date tonight. What's the dope?"

"The dope is Alex. Save yourself the trouble. He took me out to the beach last week. He pulled down my pants and started to grope me, and I started to grope him, but I couldn't find it." Laughter.

Catherine thought the conversations were vulgar and disgusting and she tried not to miss a word. It was an exercise in masochism. As the girls described their sexual exploits, Catherine visualized herself in bed with a boy, having him make wild and frantic love to her. She would feel a physical ache in her groin and press her fists hard against her thighs, trying to hurt herself, to take her mind off the other pain. *My God,* she thought, *I'm going to die a virgin. The only nineteen-year-old virgin at Northwestern. Northwestern, hell, maybe even the United States! The Virgin Catherine. The Church will make me a Saint and they'll light candles to me once a year. What's the matter with me?* she thought. *I'll tell you,* she answered herself. *Nobody's asked you and it takes two to play. I mean, if you want to do it right, it takes two to play.*

The name that most frequently cropped up in the girls' sexual conversations was Ron Peterson. He had enrolled at Northwestern on an athletic scholarship and was as popular here as he had been at Senn High School. He had been elected freshman class president. Catherine saw him in her Latin class the day the term began. He was even better looking than he had been in high school, his body had filled out, and his face had taken on a rugged devil-may-care maturity. After class, he walked toward her, and her heart began to pound.

Catherine Alexander!

Hello, Ron.

Are you in this class?

Yes.

What a break for me.

Why?

Why? Because I don't know anything about Latin and you're a genius. We're going to make beautiful music. Are you doing anything tonight?

Nothing special. Do you want to study together?

Let's go to the beach where we can be alone. We can study any time.

He was staring at her.

"Hey! . . . er—?" trying to think of her name.

She swallowed, trying desperately to remember, herself. "Catherine," she said quickly. "Catherine Alexander."

"Yeah. How about this place! It's terrific, isn't it?"

She tried to put eagerness in her voice to please him, agree with him, woo him. "Oh yes," she gushed, "it's the most—"

He was looking at a stunning blond girl waiting at the door for him. "See you," he said, and moved away to join the girl.

And that was the end of the Cinderella and Prince Charming story, she thought. *They lived happily ever after, he in his harem and she in a windswept cave in Tibet.*

From time to time Catherine would see Ron walking along the campus, always with a different girl and sometimes two or three. *My God, doesn't he ever get tired?* she wondered. She still had visions that one day he would come to her for help in Latin, but he never spoke to her again.

At night lying in her lonely bed, Catherine would think about all the other girls making love to their boyfriends, and the boy who would always come to her was Ron Peterson. In her mind he would undress her and then she would slowly undress him, the way they always did it in romantic novels, taking off his shirt and gently running her fingers over his chest, then undoing his trousers and pulling down his shorts. He would pick her up and carry her toward the bed. At that point Catherine's comic sense would get the better of her and he would sprain his back and fall to the floor, moaning and groaning with pain. *Idiot,* she told herself, *you can't even do it right in your fantasies.* Maybe she should enter a nunnery. She wondered if nuns had sexual fantasies and if it was a sin for them to masturbate. She wondered if priests ever had sexual intercourse.

She was sitting in a cool, tree-shaded courtyard in a lovely old abbey outside Rome, trailing her fingers in the sun-warmed water of an ancient fish pond. The gate opened, and a tall priest entered the courtyard. He wore a wide-brimmed hat and a long black cassock and he looked exactly like Ron Peterson.

Ah, scusi, signorina, he murmured, *I did not know I had a visitor.*

Catherine quickly sprang to her feet. *I shouldn't be here,* she apologized. *It was just so beautiful I had to sit here and drink it in.*

You are most welcome. He moved toward her, his eyes dark and blazing. *Mia cara . . . I lied to you.*

Lied to me?

Yes. His eyes were boring into hers. *I knew you were here because I followed you.*

She felt a thrill go through her. *But—but you are a priest.*

Bella signorina, I am a man first and a priest afterward. He lurched forward to take her in his arms, and he stumbled on the hem of his cassock and fell into the fish pond.

Shit!

Ron Peterson came into the Roost every day after school and would take a seat at the booth in the far corner. The booth would quickly fill up with his friends and become the center of boisterous conversation. Catherine stood behind the counter near the cash register and when Ron entered, he would give her a pleasant, absent nod and move on. He never addressed her by name. *He's forgotten it,* Catherine mused.

But each day when he walked in, she gave him a big smile and waited for him to say hello, ask her for a date, a glass of water, her virginity, anything. She might as well have been a piece of furniture. Examining the girls in the room with complete objectivity she decided she was prettier than all but one girl, the fantastic looking Jean-Anne, the Southern blonde with whom Ron was most often seen, and she was certainly brighter than all of them put together. What in God's name then was wrong with her? Why was it that not one single boy asked her for a date? She learned the answer the next day.

She was hurrying south along the campus headed for the Roost when she saw Jean-Anne and a brunette whom she did not know, walking across the green lawn toward her.

"Well, it's Miss Big Brain," Jean-Anne said.

And Miss Big Boobs, Catherine thought enviously. Aloud she said, "That was a murderous Lit quiz, wasn't it?"

"Don't be condescending," Jean-Anne said coldly. "You know enough to teach the Lit course. And that's not all you could teach us, is it, honey?"

Something in her tone made Catherine's face begin to redden.

"I—I don't understand."

"Leave her alone," the brunette said.

"Why should I?" Jean-Anne asked. "Who the hell does she think she is?" She turned to Catherine. "Do you want to know what everyone says about you?"

God, no. "Yes."

"You're a lesbo."

Catherine stared at her, unbelievingly. "I'm a *what?*"

"A lesbian, baby. You're not fooling anybody with that holier-than-thou act."

"Th—that's ridiculous," Catherine stammered.

"Did you really think you could fool people?" Jean-Anne asked. "You're doing everything but carrying a sign."

"But I—I never—"

"The boys get it up for you, but you never let them put it in."

"Really—" Catherine blurted.

"Fuck off," Jean-Anne said. "You're not our type."

They walked away, leaving her standing there, numbly staring after them.

That night, Catherine lay in bed, unable to sleep.

How old are you, Miss Alexander?

Nineteen.

Have you ever had sexual intercourse with a man?

Never.

Do you like men?

Doesn't everyone?

Have you ever wanted to make love to a woman?

Catherine thought about it long and hard. She had had crushes on other girls, on women teachers but that had been part of growing up. Now she thought about making love to a woman, their bodies intertwining, her lips on another woman's lips, her body being caressed by soft, feminine hands. She shuddered. *No!* Aloud, she said, "I'm normal." But if she was normal, why was she lying here like this? Why wasn't she out somewhere getting laid like everyone else in the world? Perhaps she was frigid. She might need some kind of operation. A lobotomy, probably.

When the Eastern sky began to lighten outside the dormitory window, Catherine's eyes were still open, but she had made a decision. She was going to lose her virginity. And the lucky man was going to be every maiden's bedside companion, Ron Peterson.

NOELLE
Marseille-Paris: 1919-1939

2

She was born a Royal Princess.

Her earliest memories were of a white bassinet covered with a lace canopy, decorated with pink ribbons and filled with soft stuffed animals and beautiful dolls and golden rattles. She quickly learned that if she opened her mouth and let out a cry, someone would hurry to hold and comfort her. When she was six months old her father would take her out in the garden in her perambulator and let her touch the flowers and he would say, "They're lovely, Princess, but you're more beautiful than any of them."

At home she enjoyed it when her father lifted her up in his strong arms and carried her to a window where she could look out and see the roofs of the high buildings, and he would say, "That's your Kingdom out there, Princess." He would point to the tall masts of ships bobbing at anchor in the bay. "Do you see those big ships? One day they'll be yours to command."

Visitors would come to the castle to see her, but only a few special ones were permitted to hold her. The others would stare down at her as she lay in her crib and would exclaim over her unbelievably delicate features, and her lovely blond hair, her soft honey-colored skin, and her father would proudly say, "A stranger could tell she is a Princess!" And he would lean over her crib and whisper, "Someday a beautiful Prince will come and sweep you off your feet." And he would gently tuck the warm pink blanket around her and she would drift off to a contented sleep. Her whole world was a roseate dream of ships, tall masts and castles, and it was not until she was five years old that she understood that she was the daughter of a Marseille fishmonger, and that the castles she saw from the window of her tiny attic room were the warehouses around the stinking fish market where her father worked, and that her navy was the fleet of old fishing ships that set out from Marseille every morning before dawn and returned in the early afternoon to vomit their smelly cargo into the waterfront docks.

This was the kingdom of Noelle Page.

The friends of Noelle's father used to warn him about what he was doing. "You mustn't put fancy ideas in her head, Jacques. She'll think she's better than everybody else." And their prophecies came true.

On the surface Marseille is a city of violence, the town crowded with hungering sailors with money to spend and clever predators to relieve them of it. But unlike the rest of the French, the people of Marseille have a sense of solidarity that comes from a common struggle for survival, for the lifeblood of the town comes from the sea, and the fishermen of Marseille belong to the family of fishermen all over the world. They share alike in the storms and the calm days, the sudden disasters and the bountiful harvests.

So it was that Jacques Page's neighbors rejoiced at his good fortune in having such an incredible daughter. They too recognized the miracle of how, out of the dung of the dirty, ribald city, a true Princess had been spawned.

Noelle's parents could not get over the wonder of their daughter's exquisite beauty. Noelle's mother was a heavyset, coarse-featured peasant woman with sagging breasts and thick thighs and hips. Noelle's father was squat, with broad shoulders and the small suspicious eyes of a Breton. His hair was the color of the wet sand along the beaches of Normandy. In the beginning it had seemed to him that nature had made a mistake, that this exquisite blond fairy creature could not really belong to him and his wife, and that as Noelle grew older she would turn into an ordinary, plain-looking girl like all the other daughters of his friends. But the miracle continued to grow and flourish, and Noelle became more beautiful each day.

Noelle's mother was less surprised than her husband by the appearance of a golden-haired beauty in the family. Nine months before Noelle had been born, Noelle's mother had met a strapping Norwegian sailor just off a freighter. He was a giant Viking god with blond hair and a warm, seductive grin. While Jacques was at work, the sailor had spent a busy quarter of an hour in her bed in their tiny apartment.

Noelle's mother had been filled with fear when she saw how blond and beautiful her baby was. She walked around in dread, waiting for the moment that her husband would point an accusing finger at her and demand to know the identity of the real father. But, incredibly, some ego-hunger in him made him accept the child as his own.

"She must be a throwback to some Scandinavian blood in my family," he would boast to his friends, "but you can see that she has my features."

His wife would listen, nodding agreement, and think what fools men were.

Noelle loved being with her father. She adored his clumsy playfulness and the strange, interesting smells that clung to him, and at the same time she was terrified by the fierceness of him. She would watch wide-eyed as he yelled at her mother and slapped her hard across the face, his neck corded with anger. Her mother would scream out in pain, but there was something beyond pain in her cries, something animal and sexual and Noelle would feel pangs of jealousy and wish she were in her mother's place.

But her father was always gentle with Noelle. He liked to take her down to the docks and show her off to the rough, crude men with whom he worked. She was known up and down the docks as The Princess and she was proud of this, as much for her father's sake as for her own.

She wanted to please her father, and because he loved to eat, Noelle began cooking for him, preparing his favorite dishes, gradually displacing her mother in the kitchen.

At seventeen the promise of Noelle's early beauty had been more than fulfilled. She had matured into an exquisite woman. She had fine, delicate features, eyes a vivid violet color and soft ash-blond hair. Her skin was fresh and golden as though she had been dipped in honey. Her figure was stunning, with generous, firm, young breasts, a small waist, rounded hips and long shapely legs, with delicate ankles. Her voice was distinctive, soft and mellifluous. There was a strong, smoldering sensuality about Noelle, but that was not her magic. Her magic lay in the fact that beneath the sensuality seemed to lie an untouched island of innocence, and the combination was irresistible. She could not walk down the streets without receiving propositions from passersby. They were not the casual offers that the prostitutes of Marseille received as their daily currency, for even the most obtuse men perceived something special in Noelle, something that they had never seen before and perhaps would never see again, and each was willing to pay as much as he could afford to try to make it a part of himself, however briefly.

Noelle's father was conscious of her beauty, too. In fact, Jacques Page thought of little else. He was aware of the interest that Noelle aroused in men. Even though neither he nor his wife ever discussed sex with Noelle, he was certain she still had her virginity, a woman's little capital. His shrewd peasant mind gave long and serious thought to how he could best capitalize on the windfall that nature had unexpectedly bestowed upon him. His mission was to see that his daughter's beauty paid off as handsomely as possible for Noelle and for him. After all, he had sired her, fed her, clothed her, educated her—she owed him everything. And now it was time for him to be repaid. If he could set her up as some rich man's mistress, it would be good for her, and he would be able to live the life of ease to which he was entitled. Each day it was getting more and more difficult for an honest man to make a living. The shadow of war had begun to spread across Europe. The Nazis had marched into Austria in a lightning coup that had left Europe stunned. A few months later the Nazis had taken over the Sudeten area and then marched into Slovakia. In spite of Hitler's assurances that he was not interested in further conquest, the feeling persisted that there was going to be a major conflict.

The impact of events was felt sharply in France. There were shortages in the stores and markets, as the government began to gear for a massive defense effort. Soon, Jacques feared, they would even stop the fishing and then where would he be? No, the answer to his problem was in finding a suitable lover for his daughter. The trouble was that he knew no wealthy men. All his friends were piss-poor like himself, and he had no intention of letting any man near her who could not pay his price.

The answer to Jacques Page's dilemma was inadvertently supplied by Noelle herself. In recent months Noelle had become increasingly restless. She did well in her classes, but school had begun to bore her. She told her father that she wanted to get a job. He studied her silently, shrewdly weighing the possibilities.

"What kind of job?" he asked.

"I don't know," Noelle replied. "I might be able to work as a model, papa."

It was as simple as that.

Every afternoon for the next week Jacques Page went home after work, carefully bathed to get the smell of fish out of his hands and hair, dressed in his good suit and went down to the Canebière, the main street that led from the old harbor of the city to the richer districts. He walked up and down the street exploring all the dress salons, a clumsy peasant in a world of silk and lace, but he neither knew nor cared that he was out of place. He had but one objective and he found it when he reached the Bon Marché. It was the finest dress shop in Marseille, but that was not why he chose it. He chose it because it was owned by Monsieur Auguste Lanchon. Lanchon was in his fifties, an ugly bald-headed man with small stumpy legs and a greedy, twitching mouth. His wife, a tiny woman with the profile of a finely honed hatchet, worked in the fitting room, loudly supervising the tailors. Jacques Page took one look at Monsieur Lanchon and his wife and knew that he had found the solution to his problem.

Lanchon watched with distaste as the shabbily dressed stranger entered the door of his shop. Lanchon said rudely, "Yes? What can I do for you?"

Jacques Page winked, poked a thick finger in Lanchon's chest and smirked, "It is what I can do for *you,* Monsieur. I am going to let my daughter work for you."

Auguste Lanchon stared at the lout standing before him, an expression of incredulity on his face.

"You are going to *let—*"

"She will be here tomorrow, nine o'clock."

"I do not—"

Jacques Page had left. A few minutes later, Auguste Lanchon had completely dismissed the incident from his mind. At nine o'clock the next morning, Lanchon looked up and saw Jacques Page entering the shop. He was about to tell his manager to throw the man out, when behind him he saw Noelle. They were walking toward him, the father and his unbelievably beautiful daughter, and the old man was grinning, "Here she is, ready to go to work."

Auguste Lanchon stared at the girl and licked his lips.

"Good morning, Monsieur," Noelle smiled. "My father told me that you had a job for me."

Auguste Lanchon nodded his head, unable to trust his voice.

"Yes, I—I think we could arrange something," he managed to stammer. He studied her face and figure and could not believe what he saw. He could already imagine what that naked young body would feel like under him.

Jacques Page was saying, "Well, I will leave you two to get acquainted," and he gave Lanchon a hearty whack on the shoulder and a wink that had a dozen different significances, none of them leaving any doubt in Lanchon's mind about his intentions.

For the first few weeks Noelle felt that she had been transported to another world. The women who came to the shop were dressed in beautiful clothes and had lovely manners, and the men who accompanied them were a far cry from the crude, boisterous fishermen with whom she had grown up. It seemed to Noelle that for the first time in her life the stench of fish was out of her nostrils. She had never really been aware of it before, because it had always been a part of her. But now everything was suddenly changed. And she owed it all to her father. She was proud of the way he got along with Monsieur Lanchon. Her father would come to the shop two or three times a week and he and Monsieur Lanchon would slip out for a cognac or a beer and when they returned there would be an air of camaraderie between them. In the beginning Noelle had disliked Monsieur Lanchon, but his behavior toward her was always circumspect. Noelle heard from one of the girls that Lanchon's wife had once caught him in the stockroom with a model and had picked up a pair of shears and had barely missed castrating him. Noelle was aware that Lanchon's eyes followed her everywhere she went, but he was always scrupulously polite. "Probably," she thought, with satisfaction, "he is afraid of my father."

At home the atmosphere suddenly seemed much

brighter. Noelle's father no longer struck her mother and the constant bickering had stopped. There were steaks and roasts to eat, and after dinner Noelle's father would take out a new pipe and fill it with a rich smelling tobacco from a leather pouch. He bought himself a new Sunday suit. The international situation was worsening and Noelle would listen to discussions between her father and his friends. They all seemed to be alarmed by the imminent threat to their livelihood, but Jacques Page appeared singularly unconcerned.

On September 1, 1939, Hitler's troops invaded Poland and two days later Great Britain and France declared war against Germany.

Mobilization was begun and overnight the streets were filled with uniforms. There was an air of resignation about what was happening, a *déjà vu* feeling of watching an old movie that one had seen before; but there was no fear. Other countries might have reason to tremble before the might of the German armies but France was invincible. It had the Maginot Line, an impenetrable fortress that could protect France against invasion for a thousand years. A curfew was imposed and rationing was started, but none of those things bothered Jacques Page. He seemed to have changed, to have calmed. The only time Noelle saw him fly into a fury was one night when she was in the darkened kitchen kissing a boy whom she dated occasionally. The lights suddenly went on and Jacques Page stood in the doorway trembling with rage.

"Get out," he screamed at the terrified boy. "And keep your hands off my daughter, you filthy pig!"

The boy fled in panic. Noelle tried to explain to her father that they had been doing nothing wrong, but he was too furious to listen.

"I will not have you throw yourself away," he roared. "He is a nobody, he is not good enough for my Princess."

Noelle lay awake that night marveling at how much her father loved her and vowing that she would never do anything to distress him again.

One evening just before closing time a customer came into the shop and Lanchon asked Noelle to model some dresses. By the time Noelle finished, everyone had left the shop except Lanchon and his wife, who was working on the books in the office. Noelle went into the empty dressing room to change. She was in her bra and pants when Lanchon walked into the room. He stared at her and his lips began to twitch. Noelle reached for her dress, but before she could put it on Lanchon swiftly moved toward her and shoved his hand between her legs. Noelle was filled with revulsion, her skin beginning to crawl. She tried to pull away, but Lanchon's grip was strong and he was hurting her. "You are beautiful," he whispered. "Beautiful. I will see that you have a good time."

At that moment Lanchon's wife called out to him and he reluctantly let go of Noelle and scurried out of the room.

On the way home Noelle debated whether to tell her father what had happened. He would probably kill Lanchon. She detested him and could not bear to be near him, and yet she wanted the job. Besides, her father might be disappointed if she quit. She decided that for the moment she would say nothing and would find a way to handle it herself. The following Friday Madame Lanchon received a call that her mother was ill in Vichy. Lanchon drove his wife to the railroad station and then raced back to the shop. He called Noelle into his office and told her he was going to take her away for the weekend. Noelle stared at him, thinking at first that it was some kind of joke.

"We will go to Vienne," he babbled. "There is one of the great restaurants of the world there, La Pyramide. It is expensive, but it doesn't matter, I can be very generous to those who are good to me. How soon can you be ready?"

She stared at him. "Never" was all she could bring herself to say. "Never." And she turned and fled into

the front of the shop. Monsieur Lanchon looked after
her for a moment, his face mottled with fury, then
snatched the telephone on his desk. An hour later Noelle's father walked into the shop. He made straight for
Noelle and her face lit up with relief. He had sensed
that something was wrong and had come to rescue her.
Lanchon was standing at the door to his office. Noelle's
father took her arm and hurried her into Lanchon's office. He swung around to face her.

"I'm so glad you came, Papa," Noelle said. "I—"

"Monsieur Lanchon tells me that he made you a
splendid offer and you refused him."

She stared at him, bewildered. "Offer? He asked me
to go away with him for the weekend."

"And you said no?"

Before Noelle could answer, her father drew his
hand back and slapped her hard across the cheek. She
stood there in stunned disbelief, her ears ringing, and
through a filmy haze heard her father saying, "Stupid!
stupid! It's time you started thinking of someone besides yourself, you selfish little bitch!" And he hit her
again.

Thirty minutes later as her father stood at the curb
watching them drive off, Noelle and Monsieur Lanchon
left for Vienne.

The hotel room consisted of a large double bed,
cheap furniture and a washstand and basin in one corner. Monsieur Lanchon was not a man to throw away
his money. He gave the bellboy a small tip and the moment the bellboy left, Lanchon turned toward Noelle
and began to tear off her clothes. He cupped her
breasts in his hot, moist hands and squeezed them
hard.

"My God, you are beautiful," he panted. He pulled
down her skirt and pants and pushed her onto the bed.
Noelle lay there unmoving, uncaring, as though she
were suffering from some kind of shock. She had not
uttered one word driving down in the car. Lanchon

hoped that she was not ill. He could never explain it to the police or, God forbid, his wife. He hastily took off his clothes, throwing them on the floor and then moved onto the bed beside Noelle. Her body was even more splendid than he had anticipated.

"Your father tells me you have never been fucked." He grinned. "Well, I am going to show you what a man feels like." He rolled his plump belly on top of her and thrust his organ between her legs. He began to push harder and harder, forcing himself into her. Noelle felt nothing. In her mind she was listening to her father yelling, *You should be grateful to have a kind gentleman like Monsieur Lanchon wanting to take care of you. All you have to do is be nice to him. You will do it for me. And for yourself.* The whole scene had been a nightmare. She was sure that her father had somehow misunderstood, but when she started to explain, he had struck her again and begun screaming, "You will do as you are told. Other girls would be grateful for your chance." *Her chance.* She looked up at Lanchon, the squat ugly body, the panting animal face with its piggish eyes. This was the Prince to whom her father had sold her, her beloved father who cherished her and could not bear to let her waste herself on anyone unworthy. And she remembered the steaks that had suddenly appeared on the table and her father's new pipes and his new suit and she wanted to vomit.

It seemed to Noelle that in the next few hours she died and was born again. She had died a Princess, and she was reborn a slut. Slowly she had become aware of her surroundings and of what was happening to her. She was filled with a hatred such as she had not known could exist. She would never forgive her father for his betrayal. Oddly enough she did not hate Lanchon, for she understood him. He was a man with the one weakness common to all men. From now on, Noelle decided, that weakness was going to be her strength. She would learn to use it. Her father had been right all along. She *was* a Princess and the world did belong to her. And now she knew how to get it. It was so simple. Men ruled the world because they had the strength, the money and the power; therefore it was necessary to rule men, or at least one man. But in order to do that one had to be prepared. She had a great deal to learn. And this was the beginning.

She turned her attention to Monsieur Lanchon. She lay under him, feeling, experiencing how the male organ fit and what it could do to a woman.

In his frenzy at having this beautiful creature under his fat, bucking body, Lanchon did not even notice that Noelle simply lay there, but he would not have cared. Just feasting his eyes on her was enough to rouse him to heights of passion he had not felt in years. He was accustomed to the accordioned, middle-aged body of his wife and the tired merchandise of the whores of Marseille, and to find this fresh, young girl under him was like a miracle come into his life.

But the miracle was just beginning for Lanchon. After he had spent himself making love to Noelle for the second time, she spoke and said, "Lie still." She began to experiment on him with her tongue and her mouth and her hands, trying new things, finding the soft, sensitive areas of his body and working on them until Lanchon cried aloud with pleasure. It was like pressing a series of buttons. When Noelle did *this,* he moaned and when she did *this,* he writhed in ecstasy. It was so easy. This was her school, this was her education. This was the beginning of power.

They spent three days there and never once went to Le Pyramide, and during those days and nights, Lanchon taught her the little that he knew about sex, and Noelle discovered a great deal more.

When they drove back to Marseille, Lanchon was the happiest man in all France. In the past he had had quick affairs with shopgirls in a *cabinet particuliers,* a restaurant that had a private dining room with a couch; he had haggled with prostitutes, been niggardly with presents for his mistresses, and notoriously penurious with his wife and children. Now he found himself saying magnanimously, "I'm going to set you up in an apartment, Noelle. Can you cook?"

"Yes," Noelle replied.

"Good. I will come for lunch every day and we will make love. And two or three nights a week, I will come for dinner." He put his hand on her knee and patted it. "How does that sound?"

"It sounds wonderful," Noelle said.

"I will even give you an allowance. Not a large one," he added quickly, "but enough so you can go out and buy pretty things from time to time. All I ask is that you see no one but me. You belong to me now."

"As you wish, Auguste," she said.

Lanchon sighed contentedly, and when he spoke, his voice was soft. "I've never felt this way about anyone before. And do you know why?"

"No, Auguste."

"Because you make me feel young. You and I are going to have a wonderful life together."

They reached Marseille late that evening, driving in silence, Lanchon with his dreams, Noelle with hers.

"I will see you in the shop tomorrow at nine o'clock," Lanchon said. He thought it over. "If you are tired in the morning, sleep a little longer. Come in at nine-thirty."

"Thank you, Auguste."

He pulled out a fistful of francs and held them out.

"Here. Tomorrow afternoon you will look for an apartment. This will be a deposit to hold it until I can see it."

She stared at the francs in his hand.

"Is something wrong?" Lanchon asked.

"I want us to have a really beautiful place," Noelle said, "where we can enjoy being together."

"I'm not a rich man," he protested.

Noelle smiled understandingly and put her hand on his thigh. Lanchon stared at her a long moment and then nodded.

"You're right," he said. He reached into his wallet and began peeling off francs, watching her face as he did so.

When she seemed satisfied, he stopped, flushed with his own generosity. After all what did it matter? Lanchon was a shrewd businessman, and he knew that this would insure that Noelle would never leave him.

Noelle watched him as he drove happily away, then she went upstairs, packed her things and removed her savings from her hiding place. At ten o'clock that night, she was on a train to Paris.

When the train pulled into Paris early the next morning, the PLM Station was crowded with those travelers who had eagerly just arrived, and those who were just as eagerly fleeing the city. The din in the station was deafening as people shouted greetings and tearful farewells, rudely pushing and shoving, but Noelle did not mind. The moment she stepped off the train, before she had even had a chance to see the city, she knew that she was home. It was Marseille that seemed like a strange town and Paris the city to which she belonged. It was an odd, heady sensation, and Noelle reveled in it, drinking in the noises, the crowds, the excitement. It all belonged to her. All she had to do now was claim it. She picked up her suitcase and started toward the exit.

Outside in the bright sunlight with the traffic insanely whizzing around, Noelle hesitated, suddenly realizing that she had nowhere to go. Half a dozen taxis were lined up in front of the station. She got into the first one.

"Where to?"

She hesitated. "Could you recommend a nice inexpensive hotel?"

The driver swung around to stare at her appraisingly. "You're new in town?"

"Yes."

He nodded. "You'll be needing a job, I suppose."

"Yes."

"You're in luck," he said. "Have you ever done any modeling?"

Noelle's heart leaped. "As a matter of fact, I have," she said.

"My sister works for one of the big fashion houses," the driver confided. "Just this morning she mentioned that one of the girls quit. Would you like to see if the vacancy is still open?"

"That would be wonderful," Noelle replied.

"If I take you there, it will cost you ten francs."

She frowned.

"It will be worth it," he promised.

"All right." She leaned back in the seat. The driver put the taxi in gear and joined the maniacal traffic heading toward the center of town. The driver chattered as they drove, but Noelle did not hear a word he said. She was drinking in the sights of her city. She supposed that because of the blackout, Paris was more subdued than usual, but to Noelle it seemed a city of pure magic. It had an elegance, a style, even an aroma all its own. They passed Notre Dame and crossed the Pont Neuf to the Right Bank and swung toward Marshall Foch Boulevard. In the distance Noelle could see the Eiffel Tower, dominating the city. Through the rearview mirror, the driver saw the expression on her face.

"Nice, huh?"

"It's beautiful," Noelle answered quietly. She still could not believe she was here. It was a Kingdom fit for a Princess . . . for her.

The taxi pulled up in front of a dark, gray stone building on the rue de Provence.

"We're here," the driver announced. "That's two francs on the meter and ten francs for me."

"How do I know the job will still be open?" Noelle asked.

The driver shrugged. "I told you, the girl just left this morning. If you don't want to go in, I'll take you back to the station."

"No," Noelle said quickly. She opened her purse, took out twelve francs and handed them to the driver. He stared at the money, then looked at her. Embarrassed, she reached into her purse and handed him another franc.

He nodded, unsmiling, and watched her lift her suitcase out of the taxi.

As he started to drive away, Noelle asked, "What's your sister's name?"

"Jeanette."

Noelle stood on the curb watching the taxi disappear, then turned to look at the building. There was no identifying sign in front, but she supposed that a fashionable dress house did not need a sign. Everyone would know where to find it. She picked up her suitcase, went up to the door and rang the bell. A few moments later the door was opened by a maid wearing a black apron. She looked at Noelle blankly.

"Yes?"

"Excuse me," Noelle said. "I understand that there is an opening for a model."

The woman stared at her and blinked.

"Who sent you?"

"Jeanette's brother."

"Come in." She opened the door wider and Noelle stepped into a reception hall done in the style of the 1800's. There was a large Baccarat chandelier hanging from the ceiling, several more scattered around the hall, and through an open door, Noelle could see a sitting room filled with antique furniture and a staircase leading upstairs. On a beautiful inlaid table were copies of *Figaro* and *L'Echo de Paris.* "Wait here. I'll find out if Madame Delys has time to see you now."

"Thank you," Noelle said. She set her suitcase down and walked over to a large mirror on the wall. Her clothes were wrinkled from the train ride, and she suddenly regretted her impulsiveness in coming here before freshening up. It was important to make a good impression. Still, as she examined herself, she knew that she looked beautiful. She knew this without conceit, accepting her beauty as an asset, to be used like any other asset. Noelle turned as she saw a girl in the mirror coming down the stairs. The girl had a good figure and a pretty face, and was dressed in a long brown skirt and a high-necked blouse. Obviously the quality of models here was high. She gave Noelle a brief smile and went into the drawing room. A moment later Madame Delys entered the room. She was in her forties and was short and dumpy with cold, calculating eyes. She was dressed in a gown that Noelle estimated must have cost at least two thousand francs.

"Regina tells me that you are looking for a job," she said.

"Yes, ma'am," Noelle replied.

"Where are you from?"

"Marseille."

Madame Delys snorted. "The playpen of drunken sailors."

Noelle's face fell.

Madame Delys patted her on the shoulder. "It does not matter, my dear. How old are you?"

"Eighteen."

Madame Delys nodded. "That is good. I think my customers will like you. Do you have any family in Paris?"

"No."

"Excellent. Are you prepared to start work right away?"

"Oh, yes," Noelle assured her eagerly.

From upstairs came the sound of laughter and a moment later a red-headed girl walked down the stairs on the arm of a fat, middle-aged man. The girl was wearing only a thin negligee.

"Finished already?" Madame Delys asked.

"I've worn Angela out," the man grinned. He saw Noelle. "Who's this little beauty?"

"This is Yvette, our new girl," Madame Delys said. And without hesitation added, "She's from Antibes, the daughter of a Prince."

"I've never screwed a Princess," the man exclaimed. "How much?"

"Fifty francs."

"You must be joking. Thirty."

"Forty. And believe me, you'll get your money's worth."

"It's a deal."

They turned to Noelle. She had vanished.

Noelle walked the streets of Paris, hour after hour. She strolled along the Champs-Élysées, down one side and up the other, wandering through the Lido Arcade and stopping at every shop to gaze at the incredible cornucopia of jewelry and dresses and leather goods and perfumes, and she wondered what Paris was like when there were *no* shortages. The wares displayed in the windows were dazzling, and while one part of her felt like a country bumpkin, another part of her knew that one day these things would belong to her. She walked through the Bois and down the rue du Faubourg-St.-Honoré and along the avenue Victor-Hugo, until she began to feel tired and hungry. She had left her purse and suitcase at Madame Delys', but she had no intention of going back there. She would send for her things.

Noelle was neither shocked nor upset by what had happened. It was simply that she knew the difference between a courtesan and a whore. Whores did not change the course of history: courtesans did. Meanwhile she was without a cent. She had to find a way to survive until she could find a job the next day. Dusk was beginning to brush the sky, and the merchants and hotel doormen were busy putting up blackout curtains against possible air attacks. To solve her immediate problem, Noelle needed to find someone to buy her a good hot dinner. She asked directions from a gendarme and then headed for the Crillon Hotel. Outside, forbidding iron shutters covered the windows, but inside, the lobby was a masterpiece of subdued elegance, soft and understated. Noelle walked in confidently as if she belonged there and took a seat in a chair facing the elevator. She had never done this before, and she was a bit nervous. But she remembered how easy it had been to handle Auguste Lanchon. Men were really very uncomplicated. There was only one lesson a girl had to remember: A man was soft when he was hard and hard when he was soft. So it was only necessary to keep him hard until he gave you what you wanted. Now, looking around the lobby, Noelle decided that it would be a simple matter to catch the eye of an unattached male on his way, perhaps, to a lonely dinner.

"Pardon, Mademoiselle."

Noelle turned her head to look up at a large man in a dark suit. She had never seen a detective in her life, but there was no doubt whatever in her mind.

"Is Mademoiselle waiting for someone?"

"Yes," Noelle replied, trying to keep her voice steady. "I'm waiting for a friend."

She was suddenly acutely aware of her wrinkled dress, and the fact that she carried no purse.

"Is your friend a guest of this hotel?"

She felt a surge of panic rising in her "He—er—not exactly."

He studied Noelle a moment, then said in a hardened tone, "May I see your identification?"

"I—I don't have it with me." she stammered. "I lost it."

The detective said, "Perhaps Mademoiselle will come with me." He put a firm hand on her arm, and she rose to her feet.

And at that moment someone took her other arm and said, "Sorry I'm late, cherie, but you know how those damned cocktail parties are. You have to blast your way out. Been waiting long?"

Noelle swung around in astonishment to look at the speaker. He was a tall man, his body lean and hard-looking, and he wore a strange, unfamiliar uniform. He had blue-black hair with a widow's peak and eyes the color of a dark, stormy sea, with long, thick lashes. His features had the look of an old Florentine coin. It was an irregular face, the two profiles not quite matching, as though the minter's hand had slipped for an instant. It was a face that was extraordinarily alive and mobile so that you felt it was ready to smile, to laugh, to frown. The only thing that saved it from being femininely beautiful was a strong, masculine chin with a deep cleft in it.

He gestured toward the detective. "Is this man bothering you?" His voice was deep, and he spoke French with a very slight accent.

"N-no," Noelle said, in a bewildered voice.

"I beg your pardon, sir," the hotel detective was saying. "I misunderstood. We have been having a problem here lately with . . ." He turned to Noelle. "Please accept my apologies, Mademoiselle."

The stranger turned to Noelle. "Well now, I don't know. What do you think?"

Noelle swallowed and nodded quickly.

The man turned to the detective. "Mademoiselle's being generous. Just watch yourself in the future." He took Noelle's arm and they headed for the door.

When they reached the street, Noelle said, "I—I don't know how to thank you, Monsieur."

"I've always hated policemen." The stranger grinned. "Do you want me to get you a taxi?"

Noelle stared at him, the panic beginning to rise in her again, as she remembered her situation. "No."

"Right. Good night." He walked over to the stand and started to get into a taxi, turned around and saw that she was standing there, rooted, staring after him. In the doorway of the hotel was the detective watching. The stranger hesitated, then walked back to Noelle. "You'd better get out of here," he advised. "Our friend's still interested in you."

"I have nowhere to go," she replied.

He nodded and reached into his pocket.

"I don't want your money," she said quickly.

He looked at her in surprise. "What *do* you want?" he asked.

"To have dinner with you."

He smiled and said, "Sorry. I have a date, and I'm late already."

"Then go ahead," she said. "I'll be fine."

He shoved the bills back into his pocket. "Suit yourself, honey," he said. *"Au 'voir."* He turned and began walking toward the taxi again. Noelle looked after him, wondering what was wrong with her. She knew she had behaved stupidly, but she also knew that she could not have done anything else. From the first moment she had looked at him she had experienced a reaction that she had never felt before, a wave of emotion so strong that she could almost reach out and touch it. She did not even know his name, and would probably never see him again. Noelle glanced toward the hotel and saw the detective moving purposefully toward her. It was her own fault. This time she would not be able to talk her way out of it. She felt a hand on her shoulder, and as she turned to see who it was, the stranger took her arm and propelled her toward the taxi, quickly opened the door and climbed in beside her. He gave the driver an address. The taxi pulled away, leaving the detective at the curb, staring after them. "What about your date?" Noelle asked.

"It's a party," he shrugged. "One more won't make any difference. I'm Larry Douglas. What's your name?"

"Noelle Page."

"Where are you from, Noelle?"

She turned and looked into his brilliant dark eyes and said, "Antibes. I am the daughter of a Prince."

He laughed, showing even, white teeth.

"Good for you, Princess," he said.

"Are you English?"

"American."

She looked at his uniform. "America is not at war."

"I'm in the British RAF," he explained. "They've just formed a group of American flyers. It's called the Eagle Squadron."

"But why should you fight for England?"

"Because England's fighting for us," he said. "Only we don't know it yet."

Noelle shook her head. "I don't believe that. Hitler is a Boche clown."

"Maybe. But he's a clown who knows what the Germans want: to rule the world."

Noelle listened, fascinated, as Larry discussed Hitler's military strategy, the sudden withdrawal from the League of Nations, the mutual defense pact with Japan and Italy, not because of what he was saying but because she enjoyed watching his face as he talked. His dark eyes sparkled with enthusiasm as he spoke, blazing with an overpowering, irresistible vitality.

Noelle had never met anyone like him. He was— that rarity of rarities—a spendthrift with himself. He was open and warm and alive, sharing himself, enjoying life, making sure that everyone around him enjoyed it. He was like a magnet pulling into his orbit everyone who approached.

They arrived at the party, which was being given in a small flat on the rue Chemin Vert. The apartment was filled with a group of laughing, shouting people, most of them young. Larry introduced Noelle to the hostess, a predatory, sexy-looking redhead, and then was swallowed by the crowd. Noelle caught glimpses of him during the evening, surrounded by eager young girls, each trying to capture his attention. And yet there was no ego about him, Noelle thought. It was as though he were totally unaware of how attractive he was. Someone found a drink for Noelle and someone else offered to bring her a plate of food from the buffet, but she was suddenly not hungry. She wanted to be with the American, wanted him away from the girls who crowded around him. Men were coming up to her and trying to start conversations, but Noelle's mind was elsewhere. From the moment they had walked in, the American had completely ignored her, had acted as though she did not exist. *Why not?* Noelle thought. Why should he bother with her when he could have any girl at the party? Two men were trying to engage her in conversation, but she could not concentrate. The room had suddenly become unbearably hot. She looked around for a means of escape.

A voice said in her ear, "Let's go," and a few moments later she and the American were out on the street, in the cool night air. The city was dark and quiet against the invisible Germans in the sky, and the cars glided through the streets like silent fish in a black sea.

They could not find a taxi, so they walked, had dinner in a little bistro on the place des Victoires and Noelle found that she was starved. She studied the American sitting across from her, and she wondered what it was that had happened to her. It was as though he had touched some wellspring deep within her that she had never even known existed. She had never felt happiness like this before. They talked about everything. She told him about her background, and he told her that he came from South Boston and was Boston Irish. His mother had been born in Kerry County.

"Where did you learn to speak French so well?" Noelle asked.

"I used to spend my summers at Cap D'Antibes when I was a kid. My old man was a stock-market tycoon until the bears got him."

"Bears?"

So Larry had to explain to her about the arcane ways of the stock market in America. Noelle did not care what he talked about, so long as he kept talking.

"Where are you living?"

"Nowhere." She told him about the taxi driver and Madame Delys and the fat man believing she was a Princess and offering to pay forty francs for her, and Larry laughed aloud.

"Do you remember where the house is?"

"Yes."

"Come on, Princess."

When they arrived at the house on the rue de Provence, the door was opened by the same uniformed maid. Her eyes lit up as she saw the handsome young American, then darkened when she saw who was with him.

"We want to see Madame Delys," Larry said. He and Noelle walked into the reception hall. There were several girls in the drawing room beyond. The maid left and a few minutes later Madame Delys entered. "Good evening, Monsieur," she said to Larry. She turned to Noelle, "Ah, I hope you have changed your mind."

"She hasn't," said Larry, pleasantly. "You have something that belongs to the Princess."

Madame Delys looked at him questioningly.

"Her suitcase and purse."

Madame Delys hesitated a moment, then left the room. A few minutes later the maid returned, carrying Noelle's purse and suitcase.

"*Merci,*" Larry said. He turned to Noelle. "Let's go, Princess."

That night Noelle moved in with Larry, to a small, clean hotel on the rue Lafayette. There was no discussion about it, it was inevitable for both of them. When they made love that night, it was more exciting than anything Noelle had ever known, a wild primitive explosion that shook them both. She lay in Larry's arms all night, holding him close, happier than she had ever dreamed possible.

The next morning they awoke, made love, and went out to explore the city. Larry was a wonderful guide, and he made Paris seem a lovely toy for Noelle's amusement. They had lunch in the Tuileries, spent the afternoon at Mal Maison and spent hours wandering around the place des Vosges at the end of Notre Dame, the oldest section of Paris, built by Louis XIII. He showed her places that were off the beaten track of the tourists, the place Maubert with its colorful street market and the quai de la Mégisserie with its cages of brightly hued birds and squeaky animals. He took her through the Marché de Buci and they listened to the din of the hawkers, pitching the merits of their bins of fresh tomatoes, their seaweed-bedded oysters, their neatly labeled cheeses. They went to the Du Pont, on Montparnasse. They had dinner on the Bateau Mouche and finished up by having onion soup at four in the morning at Les Halles with the butchers and truck drivers. Before they were through Larry had collected a large group of friends, and Noelle realized that it was because he had the gift of laughter. He had taught her to laugh and she had not known that laughter was within her. It was like a gift from a god. She was grateful to Larry and very much in love with him. It was dawn when they returned to their hotel room. Noelle was exhausted, but Larry was filled with energy, a restless dynamo. Noelle lay in bed watching him as he stood at the window looking at the sun rise over the rooftops of Paris.

"I love Paris," he said. "It's like a temple to the best things that men have ever done. It's a city of beauty and food and love." He turned to her and grinned, "Not necessarily in that order."

Noelle watched as he took off his clothes and climbed into bed beside her. She held him, loving the feel of him, the male smell of him. She thought of her father and how he had betrayed her. She had been wrong to judge all men by him and Auguste Lanchon. She knew now that there were men like Larry Douglas. And she also knew that there could never be anyone else for her.

"Do you know who the two greatest men who ever lived were, Princess?" he was asking.

"You," she said.

"Wilbur and Orville Wright. They gave man his real freedom. Have you ever flown?" She shook her

head. "We had a summer place in Montauk—that's at
the end of Long Island—and when I was a kid I used
to watch the gulls wheel through the air over the
beach, riding the current, and I would have given my
soul to be up there with them. I knew I wanted to be a
flyer before I could walk. A friend of the family took
me up in an old biplane when I was nine, and I took
my first flying lesson when I was fourteen. That's when
I'm really alive, when I'm in the air."

And later:

"There's going to be a world war. Germany wants to
own it all."

"It won't get France, Larry. No one can cross the
Maginot Line."

He snorted: "I've crossed it a hundred times." She
looked at him puzzled. "In the air, Princess. This is
going to be an air war . . . my war."

And later, casually:

"Why don't we get married?"

It was the happiest moment of Noelle's life.

Sunday was a relaxed, lazy day. They had breakfast
at a little outdoor café in Montmartre, went back to
the room and spent almost the entire day in bed. Noelle could not believe anyone could be so ecstatic. It
was pure magic when they made love, but she was just
as content to lie there and listen to Larry talk and
watch him as he moved restlessly about the room. Just
being near him was enough for her. It was odd, she
thought, how things worked out. She had grown up
being called Princess by her father, and now, even
though it had happened as a joke, Larry was calling
her Princess. When she was with Larry, she *was* something. He had restored her faith in men. He was her
world, and Noelle knew that she would never need
anything more, and it seemed incredible to her that she
could be so lucky, that he felt the same way about her.

"I wasn't going to get married until this war was
over," he told her. "But to hell with that. Plans are

made to be changed, right, Princess?"

She nodded, filled with a happiness that threatened to burst inside her.

"Let's get married by some *maire* in the country," Larry said "Unless you want a big wedding?"

Noelle shook her head. "The country sounds wonderful."

He nodded. "Deal. I have to report back to my Squadron tonight. I'll meet you here next Friday. How does that sound?"

"I—I don't know if I can stand being away from you that long." Noelle's voice was shaky.

Larry took her in his arms and held her. "Love me?" he asked.

"More than my life," Noelle replied simply.

Two hours later Larry was on his way back to England. He did not let her drive to the airport with him. "I don't like good-byes," he said. He gave her a large fistful of franc notes. "Buy yourself a wedding gown, Princess. I'll see you in it next week." And he was gone.

Noelle spent the next week in a state of euphoria, going back to the places she and Larry had been, spending hours dreaming about their life together. The days seemed to drag by, the minutes stubbornly refusing to move, until Noelle thought she would go out of her mind.

She went to a dozen shops looking for her wedding dress, and finally she found exactly what she wanted, at Madeleine Vionett. It was a beautiful white organza with a high-necked bodice, long sleeves with a row of six pearl buttons, and three crinoline petticoats. It cost much more than Noelle had anticipated, but she did not hesitate. She used all the money that Larry had given her and nearly all her own savings. Her whole being was centered on Larry. She thought about ways to please him, she searched through her mind for memories that might amuse him, anecdotes that would entertain him. She felt like a schoolgirl.

And so it was that Noelle waited for Friday to come, in an agony of impatience, and when it finally arrived she was up at dawn and spent two hours bathing and dressing, changing clothes and changing again, trying to guess which dress would please Larry most. She put on her wedding gown, but quickly took it off again, afraid that it might bring bad luck. She was in a frenzy of excitement.

At ten o'clock Noelle stood in front of the pier glass in the bedroom, and she knew that she had never looked as beautiful. There was no ego in her appraisal; she was simply pleased for Larry, glad that she could bring him this gift. By noon he had not appeared, and Noelle wished that he had told her what time he expected to arrive. She kept phoning the desk for messages every ten minutes and kept picking up the phone to make sure it was working. By six o'clock that evening, there was still no word from him. By midnight he had not called, and Noelle sat huddled in a chair, staring at the phone, willing it to ring. She fell asleep, and when she woke, it was dawn, Saturday. She was still in the chair, stiff and cold. The dress she had so carefully chosen was wrinkled, and there was a run in her stocking.

Noelle changed clothes and stayed in the room all that day, stationing herself in front of the open window, telling herself that if she stayed there, Larry would appear; if she left, something terrible would happen to him. As Saturday morning lengthened into afternoon, she began to be filled with the conviction that there had been an accident. Larry's plane had crashed, and he was lying in a field or in a hospital, wounded or dead. Noelle's mind was filled with ghastly visions. She sat up all night Saturday, sick with worry, afraid to leave the room and not knowing how to reach Larry.

When Noelle had not heard from him by Sunday noon, she could stand it no longer. She had to telephone him. But how? With a war on it was difficult to place an overseas call and she was not even certain where Larry was. She knew only that he flew with the RAF in some American squadron. She picked up the telephone and spoke to the switchboard operator.

"It is impossible," the operator said flatly.

Noelle explained the situation, and whether it was her words or the frantic despair in her voice she never knew, but two hours later she was talking to the War Ministry in London. They could not help her, but they transferred her to the Air Ministry at Whitehall who put her through to Combat Operations, where she was disconnected before she could get any information. It was four more hours before Noelle was reconnected, and by then she was on the verge of hysteria. Air Operations could give her no information and suggested she try the War Ministry.

"I've talked to them!" Noelle screamed into the phone. She began to sob, and the male English voice at the other end of the phone said in embarrassment, "Please, miss, it can't be that bad. Hold on a moment."

Noelle held the receiver in her hand, knowing that it was hopeless, certain that Larry was dead and that she would never know how or where he died. And she was about to replace the receiver when the voice spoke in her ear again and said cheerfully, "What you want, miss, is the Eagle Squadron. They're the Yanks, based in Yorkshire. It's a bit irregular, but I'm going to put you through to Church Fenton, their airfield. Their chaps will be able to help you." And the line went dead.

It was eleven o'clock that night before Noelle could get the call through again. A disembodied voice said, "Church Fenton Air Base," and the connection was so bad that Noelle could barely hear him. It was as though he were speaking from the bottom of the sea. He was obviously having difficulty hearing her. "Speak up, please," he said. By now, Noelle's nerves were so frayed that she could hardly control her voice.

"I'm calling"—she did not even know his rank.

Lieutenant? Captain? Major? "I'm calling Larry Douglas. This is his fiancée."

"I can't hear you, miss. Can you speak louder, please?"

On the edge of panic Noelle screamed out the words again, sure that the man at the other end of the phone was trying to conceal from her that Larry was dead. For a miraculous instant the line cleared, and she heard the voice saying as though he were in the next room, "Lieutenant Larry Douglas?"

"Yes," she said, holding on tightly to her emotions.

"Just a moment, please."

Noelle waited for what seemed an eternity and then the voice came back on the line and said, "Lieutenant Douglas is on weekend leave. If it's urgent, he can be reached at the Hotel Savoy ballroom in London, General Davis' party." And the line went dead.

When the maid came in to clean the room the next morning, she found Noelle on the floor, semiconscious. The maid stared at her a moment, tempted to mind her own business and leave. Why did these things always have to happen in *her* rooms? She went over and touched Noelle's forehead. It was burning hot. Grumbling, the maid waddled down the hall and asked the porter to send up the manager. One hour later an ambulance pulled up outside the hotel and two young interns carrying a stretcher were directed to Noelle's room. Noelle was unconscious. The young intern in charge raised her eyelid, put a stethoscope to her chest and listened to the rales as she breathed. "Pneumonia," he said to his companion. "Let's get her out of here."

They lifted Noelle onto the stretcher and five minutes later the ambulance was racing toward the hospital. She was rushed into an oxygen tent, and it was four days before she was fully conscious. She dragged herself reluctantly up from the murky green depths of oblivion, subconsciously knowing something terrible had happened and fighting not to remember what it was. As the awful thing floated closer and closer to the surface of her mind, and she struggled to keep it from herself, it suddenly came to her clear and whole. Larry Douglas. Noelle began to weep, racked with sobs until she finally drifted off into a half-sleep. She felt a hand gently holding hers, and she knew that Larry had come back to her, that everything was all right. Noelle opened her eyes and stared at a stranger in a white uniform, taking her pulse. "Well! Welcome back," he announced cheerfully.

"Where am I?" Noelle asked.

"L'Hotel-Dieu, the City Hospital."

"What am I doing here?"

"Getting well. You've had double pneumonia. I'm Israel Katz." He was young, with a strong, intelligent face and deep-set brown eyes.

"Are you my doctor?"

"Intern," he said. "I brought you in." He smiled at her. "I'm glad you made it. We weren't sure."

"How long have I been here?"

"Four days."

"Would you do me a favor?" she asked weakly.

"If I can."

"Call the Hotel Lafayette. Ask them—" she hesitated. "Ask them if there are any messages for me."

"Well, I'm awfully busy—"

Noelle squeezed his hand fiercely. "Please. It's important. My fiancé is trying to get in touch with me."

He grinned. "I don't blame him. All right. I'll take care of it," he promised. "Now you get some sleep."

"Not until I hear from you," she said.

He left, and Noelle lay there waiting. Of course Larry had been trying to get in touch with her. There had been some terrible misunderstanding. He would explain it all to her and everything would be all right again.

It was two hours before Israel Katz returned. He walked up to her bed and set down a suitcase. "I brought your clothes. I went to the hotel myself," he said.

She looked up at him, and he could see her face tense.

"I'm sorry," he said, embarrassed. "No messages."

Noelle stared at him for a long time, then turned her face to the wall, dry-eyed.

Noelle was released from the hospital two days later. Israel Katz came to say good-bye to her. "Do you have any place to go?" he asked. "Or a job?"

She shook her head.

"What work do you do?"

"I'm a model."

"I might be able to help you."

She remembered the taxi driver and Madame Delys. "I don't need any help," she said.

Israel Katz wrote a name on a piece of paper. "If you change your mind, go there. It's a small fashion house. An aunt of mine owns it. I'll talk to her about you. Do you have any money?"

She did not answer.

"Here." He pulled a few francs out of his pocket and handed them to her. "I'm sorry I don't have more. Interns aren't very well paid."

"Thank you," Noelle said.

She sat at a small street café sipping a coffee and deciding how to pick up the pieces of her life. She knew that she had to survive, for she had a reason to live now. She was filled with a deep and burning hatred that was so all-consuming that it left no room for anything else. She was an avenging Phoenix rising from the ashes of the emotions that Larry Douglas had murdered in her. She would not rest until she had destroyed him. She did not know how, or when, but she knew that one day she would make it happen.

Now she needed a job and a place to sleep. Noelle opened her purse and took out the piece of paper that the young intern had given her. She studied it a moment and made up her mind. That afternoon she went to see Israel Katz's aunt and was given a job modeling in a small, second-rate fashion house on the rue Boursault.

Israel Katz's aunt turned out to be a middle-aged, gray-haired woman with the face of a harpy and the soul of an angel. She mothered all her girls and they adored her. Her name was Madame Rose. She gave Noelle an advance on her salary and found her a tiny apartment near the salon. The first thing Noelle did when she unpacked was to hang up her wedding dress. She put it in the front of the closet so that it was the first thing she saw in the morning and the last thing she saw when she undressed at night.

Noelle knew that she was pregnant before there were any visible signs of it, before any tests had been made, before she missed her period. She could sense the new life that had formed in her womb, and at night she lay in bed staring at the ceiling thinking about it, her eyes glowing with wild animal pleasure.

On her first day off Noelle phoned Israel Katz and made a date to meet him for lunch.

"I'm pregnant," she told him.

"How do you know? Have you had any tests?"

"I don't need any tests."

He shook his head. "Noelle, a lot of women think they are going to have babies when they are not. How many periods have you missed?"

She pushed the question aside, impatiently. "I want your help."

He stared at her. "To get rid of the baby? Have you discussed this with the father?"

"He's not here."

"You know abortions are illegal. I could get into terrible trouble."

Noelle studied him a moment. "What's your price?"

His face tightened angrily. "Do you think everything has a price, Noelle?"

"Of course," she said simply. "Anything can be bought and sold."

"Does that include you?"

"Yes, but I'm very expensive. Will you help me?"

There was a long hesitation. "All right. I'll want to make some tests first."

"Very well."

The following week Israel Katz arranged for Noelle to go to the laboratory at the hospital. When the test results were returned two days later, he telephoned her at work. "You were right," he said. "You're pregnant."

"I know."

"I've arranged for you to have a curettage at the hospital. I've told them that your husband was killed in an accident and that you are unable to have the baby. We'll do the operation next Saturday."

"No," she said.

"Is Saturday a bad day for you?"

"I'm not ready for the abortion yet, Israel. I just wanted to know that I could count on you to help me."

Madame Rose noticed the change in Noelle, not merely a physical change, but something that went much deeper, a radiance, an inner glow that seemed to fill her. Noelle walked around with a constant smile, as though hugging some wonderful secret.

"You have found a lover," Madame Rose said. "It shows in your eyes."

Noelle nodded. "Yes, Madame."

"He is good for you. Hold onto him."

"I will," Noelle promised. "As long as I can."

Three weeks later Israel Katz telephoned her. "I haven't heard from you," he said. "I was wondering if you had forgotten?"

"No," Noelle said. "I think of it all the time."

"How do you feel?"

"Wonderful."

"I've been looking at the calendar. I think that we had better go to work."

"I'm not ready yet," Noelle said.

Three weeks passed before Israel Katz telephoned her again.

"How about having dinner with me?" he asked.

"All right."

They arranged to meet at a cheap café on the rue de Chat Qui Peche. Noelle had started to suggest a better restaurant when she remembered what Israel had said about interns not having much money.

He was waiting for her when she arrived. They chatted aimlessly through dinner and it was not until the coffee arrived that Israel discussed what was on his mind.

"Do you still want to have the abortion?" he asked.

Noelle looked at him in surprise. "Of course."

"Then you must have it right away. You're more than two months pregnant."

She shook her head. "No, not yet, Israel."

"Is this your first pregnancy?"

"Yes."

"Then let me tell you something, Noelle. Up until three months, an abortion is usually an easy matter. The embryo has not been fully formed and all you need is a simple curettage, but after three months"—he hesitated—"it's another kind of operation, and it becomes dangerous. The longer you wait, the more dangerous it becomes. I want you to have the operation now."

Noelle leaned forward. "What's the baby like?"

"Now?" He shrugged. "Just a lot of cells. Of course, all the nuclei are there to form a complete human being."

"And after three months?"

"The embryo starts to become a person."

"Can it feel things?"

"It responds to blows and loud noises."

She sat there, her eyes locked onto his. "Can it feel pain?"

"I suppose so. But it is protected with an amniotic sac." He suddenly felt an uneasy stirring. "It would be pretty hard for anything to hurt it."

Noelle lowered her eyes and sat staring at the table, silent and thoughtful.

Israel Katz studied her a moment and then said shyly, "Noelle, if you want to keep this baby and are afraid to because it will have no father . . . well, I would be willing to marry you and give the baby a name."

She looked up in surprise. "I have already told you. I don't want this baby. I want to have an abortion."

"Then, for Christ's sake, have it!" Israel shouted. He lowered his voice as he realized that other patrons were staring at him. "If you wait much longer, there isn't a doctor in France who will do it. Don't you understand? If you wait too long, you could die!"

"I understand," Noelle said quietly. "If I were going to have this baby, what kind of diet would you put me on?"

He ran his fingers through his hair, bewildered. "Lots of milk and fruit, lean meat."

That night on her way home Noelle stopped at the corner market near her apartment and bought two quarts of milk and a large box of fresh fruit.

Ten days later Noelle went into Madame Rose's office and told her that she was pregnant and asked for a leave of absence.

"For how long?" Madame Rose asked, eyeing Noelle's figure.

"Six or seven weeks."

Madame Rose sighed. "Are you sure what you are doing is the best thing?"

"I'm sure," Noelle replied.

"Is there anything I can do?"

"Nothing."

"Very well. Come back to me as soon as you can. I will ask the cashier to give you an advance on your salary."

"Thank you, Madame."

For the next four weeks Noelle never left her apartment, except to buy groceries. She felt no hunger and ate very little for herself, but she drank enormous quantities of milk for the baby and crammed her body with fruit. She was not alone in the apartment. The baby was with her and she talked to him constantly. She knew it was a boy just as she had known she was pregnant. She had named him Larry.

"I want you to grow to be big and strong," she said as she drank her milk. "I want you to be healthy . . . healthy and strong when you die." She lay in bed every day plotting her vengeance against Larry and his son. What was in her body was not a part of her. It belonged to him and she was going to kill it. It was the only thing of his that he had left her, and she was going to destroy it just as he had tried to destroy her.

How little Israel Katz had understood her! She was not interested in a formless embryo that knew nothing. She wanted Larry's spawn to feel what was going to happen to him, to suffer, as she had suffered. The wedding dress was hanging near her bed now, always in sight, a talisman of evil, a reminder of his betrayal. *First, Larry's son, then Larry.*

The phone rang often, but Noelle lay in bed, lost in her dreams until it stopped. She was sure that it was Israel Katz trying to reach her.

One evening there was a pounding on the door. Noelle lay in bed, ignoring it, but finally when the pounding continued, she dragged herself up and opened the door.

Israel Katz was standing there, his face filled with concern. "My God, Noelle, I've been calling you for days."

He looked at her bulging stomach. "I thought you might have had it done somewhere else."

She shook her head. "No. You're going to do it."

Israel stared at her. "Haven't you understood anything I told you? It's too late! No one's going to do it."

He saw the empty bottles of milk and the fresh fruit on the table, then looked back at her. "You *do* want the baby," he said. "Why won't you admit it?"

"Tell me, Israel, what's he like now?"

"Who?"

"The baby. Does he have eyes and ears? Does he have fingers and toes? Can he feel pain?"

"For Christ's sake, Noelle, stop it. You talk as if . . . as if . . ."

"What?"

"Nothing." He shook his head in despair. "I don't understand you."

She smiled softly. "No. You don't."

He stood there a moment, making up his mind.

"All right, I'm putting my ass in a sling for you, but if you're really determined to have an abortion, let's get it over with. I have a doctor friend who owes me a favor. He'll . . ."

"No."

He stared at her.

"Larry's not ready yet," she said.

Three weeks later at four o'clock in the morning, Israel Katz was awakened by a furious concierge pounding on his door. "Telephone, Monsieur Night Owl!" he yelled. "And tell your caller that it is the middle of the night, when respectable people are asleep!"

Israel stumbled out of bed and sleepily made his way down the hall to the telephone, wondering what crisis had arisen. He picked up the receiver.

"Israel?"

He did not recognize the voice at the other end of the phone.

"Yes?"

"Now . . ." It was a whisper, disembodied and anonymous.

"Who is this?"

"Now. Come now, Israel . . ."

There was an eeriness to the voice, an unearthly quality that sent a chill down his spine. "Noelle?"

"Now . . ."

"For Christ's sake," he exploded. "I won't do it. It's too late. You'll die, and I'm not going to be responsible. Get yourself to a hospital."

There was a click in his ear, and he stood there holding the phone. He slammed the receiver and went back to his room, his mind churning. He knew that he could not do any good now, no one could. She was five and a half months pregnant. He had warned her time and time again, but she had refused to listen. Well, it was her responsibility. He wanted to have no part of it.

He began to dress as fast as he could, his bowels cold with fear.

When Israel Katz walked into her apartment, Noelle was lying on the floor in a pool of blood, hemorrhaging. Her face was dead white, but it showed no sign of the agony that must have been racking her body. She was wearing what appeared to be a wedding dress. Israel knelt at her side. "What happened?" he asked. "How did—?" He stopped, as his eyes fell on a bloody, twisted wire coat hanger near her feet.

"Jesus Christ!" He was filled with a rage and at the same time a terrible frustrating feeling of helplessness. The blood was pouring out faster now, there was not a moment to lose.

"I'll call an ambulance," and he started to rise.

Noelle reached up and grabbed his arm with surprising strength, and pulled him back down to her.

"Larry's baby is dead," she said, and her face was lit with a beautiful smile.

A team of six doctors worked for five hours trying to save Noelle's life. The diagnosis was septic poisoning, perforated womb, blood poisoning and shock. All the doctors agreed that there was little chance that she could live. By six o'clock that night Noelle was out of danger and two days later, she was sitting up in bed able to talk. Israel came to see her.

"All the doctors say that it is a miracle you're alive, Noelle."

She shook her head. It was simply not her time to die. She had taken her first vengeance on Larry, but it was only the beginning. There was more to come. Much more. But first she had to find him. It would take time. But she would do it.

CATHERINE
Chicago: 1939-1940

3

The growing winds of war that were blowing across Europe were reduced to no more than gentle, warning zephyrs when they reached the shores of the United States.

On the Northwestern campus, a few more boys joined the ROTC, there were student rallies urging President Roosevelt to declare war on Germany and a few seniors enlisted in the Armed Forces. In general, however, the sea of complacency remained the same, and the underground swell that was soon to sweep over the country was barely perceptible.

As she walked to her cashier's job at the Roost that October afternoon, Catherine Alexander wondered whether the war would change her life, if it came. She knew one change that she had to make, and she was determined to do it as soon as possible. She desperately wanted to know what it was like to have a man hold her in his arms and make love to her, and she knew that she wanted it partly because of her physical needs, but also because she felt she was missing out on an important and wonderful experience. My God, what if she got run over by a car and they did a post mortem on her and discovered she was a virgin! No, she had to do something about it. Now.

Catherine glanced around the Roost carefully, but she did not see the face she was looking for. When Ron Peterson came in an hour later with Jean-Anne, Catherine felt her body tingle and her heart begin to pound. She turned away as they walked past her, and out of the corner of her eye she saw the two make their way to Ron's booth and sit down. Large banners were strung around the room, "TRY OUR DOUBLE HAMBURGER SPECIAL" . . . "TRY OUR LOVER'S DELIGHT" . . . "TRY OUR TRIPLE MALT."

Catherine took a deep breath and walked over to the booth. Ron Peterson was studying the menu, trying to make up his mind. "I don't know what I want," he was saying.

"How hungry are you?" Jean-Anne asked.

"I'm starved."

"Then try this." They both looked up in surprise. It was Catherine standing over the booth. She handed Ron Peterson a folded note, turned around and walked back to the cash register.

Ron opened the note, looked at it and burst into laughter. Jean-Anne watched him coolly.

"Is it a private joke or can anyone get in on it?"

"Private," Ron grinned. He slipped the note into his pocket.

Ron and Jean-Anne left shortly afterward. Ron didn't say anything as he paid his check, but he gave Catherine a long, speculative look, smiled and walked out with Jean-Anne on his arm. Catherine looked after them, feeling like an idiot. She didn't even know how to make a successful pass at a boy.

When her shift was up, Catherine got into her coat, said good night to the girl coming in to relieve her and went outside. It was a warm autumn evening with a cooling breeze skipping in off the lake. The sky looked like purple velvet with soft, far-flung stars just out of reach. It was a perfect evening to—what? Catherine made a list in her mind.

I can go home and wash my hair.

I can go to the library and study for the Latin exam tomorrow.

I can go to a movie.

I can hide in the bushes and rape the first sailor who comes along.

I can go get myself committed.

Committed, she decided.

As she started to move along the campus toward the library, a figure stepped out from behind a lamp post.

"Hi, Cathy. Where you headed?"

It was Ron Peterson, smiling down at her, and Catherine's heart started to pound until it began to burst out of her chest. She watched as it took off on its own, beating its way through the air. She became aware that Ron was staring at her. No wonder. How many girls did he know who could do that heart trick? She desperately wanted to comb her hair and fix her makeup and check the seams of her stockings, but she tried to let none of her nervousness show. Rule one: Keep calm.

"Blug," she mumbled.

"Where are you headed?"

Should she give him her list? God, no! He'd think she was insane. This was her big chance and she must not do a single thing to destroy it. She looked up at him, her eyes as warm and inviting as Carole Lombard's in *Nothing Sacred.*

"I didn't have any special plans," she said invitingly.

Ron was studying her, still not sure of her, some primeval instinct making him cautious. "Would you *like* to do something special?" he said.

This was it. The Proposition. The point of no return. "Name it," she said, "and I'm yours." And cringed inwardly. It sounded so corny. No one said, "Name it and I'm yours" except in bad Fannie Hurst novels. He was going to turn on his heel and walk away in disgust.

But he didn't. Incredibly, he smiled, took her arm and said, "Let's go."

Catherine walked along with him, stunned. It had been as simple as that. She was on her way to getting laid. She began to tremble inside. If he found out she was a virgin, she would be finished. And what was she going to talk about when she was in bed with him? Did people talk when they were actually doing it, or did they wait until it was over? She didn't want to be rude, but she had no idea what the rules were.

"Have you had dinner?" Ron was asking.

"Dinner?" She stared up at him, trying to think. Should she have had dinner? If she said yes, then he could take her right to bed and she could get it over with. "No," she said quickly, "I haven't." *Now why did I say that? I've ruined everything.* But Ron did not seem upset.

"Good. Do you like Chinese food?"

"It's my favorite." She hated it, but the gods certainly weren't going to count a little yellow lie on the biggest night of her life.

"There's a good Chinese joint over on Estes. Lum Fong's. Do you know it?"

No, but she would never forget it as long as she lived.

What did you do the night you lost your cherry?

Oh, I went to Lum Fong's first and had some Chinese food with Ron Peterson.

Was it good?

Sure. But you know Chinese food. An hour later, I was sexy again.

They had reached his car, a maroon Reo convertible. Ron held the door open for Catherine, and she sat in the seat where all the other girls she envied had once sat. Ron was charming, handsome, a top athlete. And a sex maniac. It would make a good title for a movie. *The Sex Maniac and the Virgin.* Maybe she should have held out for a nicer restaurant like Henrici's in the Loop and then Ron would have thought, *This is the kind of girl I want to take home to Mother.*

"A penny for your thoughts," he said.

Oh, great! All right, so he wasn't the most brilliant conversationalist in the world. But that wasn't why she was here, was it? She looked up at him sweetly. "I was just thinking about you." She snuggled against him.

He grinned. "You really had me fooled, Cathy."

"I did?"

"I always thought you were pretty standoffish—I mean, not interested in men."

The word you're fumbling for is lesbian, Catherine thought, but aloud she said, "I just like to pick my time and place."

"I'm glad you picked me."

"So am I." And she was. She really was. She could be certain that Ron was a good lover. He had been factory-tested and approved by every horny coed within a radius of a hundred and fifty miles. It would have been humiliating to have had her first sexual experience with someone as ignorant as she was. With Ron she was getting a master. After tonight she would not be calling herself Saint Catherine any longer. Instead she would probably be known as "Catherine the Great." And this time she would know what the "Great" stood for. She would be fantastic in bed. The trick was not to panic. All the wonderful things she had read about in the little green books she used to keep hidden from her mother and father were about to happen to her. Her body was going to be an organ filled with exquisite music. Oh, she knew it would hurt the first time; it always did. But she would not let Ron know. She would move her behind around a lot because men hated for a woman to just lie there, motionless. And when Ron penetrated her, she would bite her lip to conceal the pain and cover it up with a sexy cry.

"What?"

She turned to Ron, appalled, and realized she had cried aloud. "I—I didn't say anything."

"You gave a kind of funny cry."

"Did I?" She forced a little laugh.

"You're a million miles away."

She analyzed the line and decided it was bad. She must be more like Jean-Anne. Catherine put her hand on his arm and moved closer. "I'm right here," she said.

She tried to make her voice throaty, like Jean Arthur in *Calamity Jane.*

Ron looked down at her, confused, but the only thing he could read in her face was an eager warmth.

Lum Fong's was a dreary-looking, run-of-the-mill Chinese restaurant located under the Elevated. All through dinner they could hear the rumble of the trains as they ran overhead rattling the dishes. The restaurant looked like a thousand other anonymous Chinese restaurants all over America, but Catherine carefully absorbed the details of the booth they were seated in, committing to memory the cheap, spotted wallpaper, the chipped china teapot, the soy-sauce stains on the table.

A little Chinese waiter came up to the table and asked if they wanted a drink. Catherine had tasted whiskey a few times in her life and hated it, but this was New Year's Eve, the Fourth of July, the End of her Maidenhood. It was fitting to celebrate.

"I'll have an old-fashioned with a cherry in it." *Cherry! Oh, God!* It was a dead giveaway.

"Scotch and soda," Ron said.

The waiter bowed himself away from the table. Catherine wondered if it were true that Oriental women were built slantwise.

"I don't know why we never became friends before," Ron was saying. "Everyone says you're the brightest girl in the whole goddamned university."

"You know how people exaggerate."

"And you're damned pretty."

"Thank you." She tried to make her voice sound like Katherine Hepburn in *Alice Adams* and looked meaningfully into his eyes. She was no longer Catherine Alexander. She was a sex machine. She was about to join Mae West, Marlene Dietrich, Cleopatra. They were all going to be sisters under the foreskin.

The waiter brought the drink and she finished it in one quick nervous gulp. Ron watched her in surprise.

"Easy," he warned. "That's pretty potent stuff."

"I can handle it," Catherine assured him, confidently.

"Another round," he told the waiter. Ron reached across the table and caressed her hand. "It's funny. Everybody at school had you wrong."

"Wrong. No one at school's had me."

He stared at her. *Careful, don't be clever.* Men preferred to bed girls who had excessively large mammary glands and gluteus maximus muscles and exceedingly small cerebrums.

"I've had a—thing for you for a long time," she said, hurriedly.

"You sure kept it a secret." Ron pulled out the note she had written and smoothed it out. "Try our Cashier," he read aloud, and laughed. "So far I like it better than the Banana Split." He ran his hands up and down Catherine's arm and his touch sent tiny ripples down her spine, just like the books said it would. Perhaps after tonight she would write a manual on sex to instruct all the poor, dumb virgins who didn't know what life was all about. After the second drink Catherine was beginning to feel sorry for them.

"It's a pity."

"What's a pity?"

She had spoken aloud again. She decided to be bold. "I was feeling sorry for all the virgins in the world," she said.

Ron grinned at Catherine. "I'll drink to that." He lifted his glass. She looked at him sitting across from her obviously enjoying her company. She had nothing to worry about. Everything was going beautifully. He asked if she would like another drink, but Catherine declined. She did not intend to be in an alcoholic stupor when she was deflowered. *Deflowered? Did people still use words like deflowered?* Anyway, she wanted to remember every moment, every sensation. *Oh, my*

God! She wasn't wearing anything! Would he? Surely a man as experienced as Ron Peterson would have something to put on, some protection so she wouldn't get pregnant. What if he was expecting the same thing? What if he was thinking that a girl as experienced as Catherine Alexander would surely have some protection? Could she come right out and ask him? She decided that she would rather die first, right at the table. They could carry her body away and give her a ceremonial Chinese burial.

Ron ordered the dollar seventy-five six-course dinner, and Catherine pretended to eat it, but it might as well have been Chinese cardboard. She was beginning to get so tense she couldn't taste anything. Her tongue was suddenly dry and the roof of her mouth felt strangely numb. *What if she had just had a stroke?* If she had sex right after a stroke, it would probably kill her. Perhaps she should warn Ron. It would hurt his reputation if they found a dead girl in his bed. Or maybe it would enhance it.

"What's the matter?" Ron asked. "You look pale."

"I feel great," Catherine said, recklessly. "I'm just excited about being with you."

Ron looked at her approvingly, his brown eyes taking in every detail of her face and moving down to her breasts and lingering there. "I feel the same way," he replied.

The waiter had taken the dishes away, and Ron had paid the check. He looked at her, but Catherine couldn't move.

"Do you want anything else?" Ron asked.

Do I? Oh, yes! I want to be on a slow boat to China. I want to be in a cannibal's kettle being boiled for dinner. I want my mother!

Ron was watching her, waiting. Catherine took a deep breath. "I—I can't think of anything."

"Good." He drew the syllable out, long and lastingly so that it seemed to put a bed on the table between them. "Let's go." He stood up and Catherine followed.

The euphoric feeling from the drinks had completely vanished and her legs began to tremble.

They were outside in the warm night air when a sudden thought hit Catherine and filled her with relief. *He's not going to take me to bed tonight. Men never do that with a girl on the first date. He's going to ask me out to dinner again and next time we'll go to Henrici's and we'll get to know each other better. Really know each other. And we'll probably fall in love— madly—and he'll take me to meet his parents and then everything will be all right . . . and I won't feel this stupid panic.*

"Do you have any preference in motels?" Ron asked.

Catherine stared up at him, speechless. Gone were the dreams of a genteel musicale evening with his mother and father. The bastard was planning to take her to bed in a motel! Well, that was what she wanted, wasn't it? Wasn't that the reason she had written that insane note?

Ron's hand was on Catherine's shoulder now, sliding down her arm. She felt a warm sensation in her groin. She swallowed and said, "If you've seen one motel, you've seen them all."

Ron looked at her strangely. But all he said was, "OK. Let's go."

They got into his car and started driving west. Catherine's body had turned into a block of ice, but her mind was racing at a feverish pitch. The last time she had stayed in a motel was when she was eight and was driving across country with her mother and father. Now she was going to one to go to bed with a man who was a total stranger. What did she know about him anyway? Only that he was handsome, popular and knew an easy lay when he saw one.

Ron reached over and took her hand. "Your hands are cold," he said.

"Cold hands, hot legs." *Oh, Christ,* she thought. *There I go again.* For some reason, the lyrics of "Ah,

Sweet Mystery of Life" started to go through Catherine's head. Well she was about to solve it. She was on her way to finding out what everything was all about. The books, the sexy advertisements, the thinly veiled love lyrics—"Rock Me in the Cradle of Love," "Do It Again," "Birds Do It." *OK,* she thought. *Now Catherine is going to do it.*

Ron turned south onto Clark Street.

Ahead on both sides of the street were huge blinking red eyes, neon signs that were alive in the night, screaming out their offers of cheap and temporary havens for impatient young lovers. "EASY REST MOTEL," "OVERNIGHT MOTEL," "COME INN," *(Now that had to be Freudian!)* "TRAVELER'S REST." The paucity of imagination was staggering, but on the other hand the owners of these places were probably too busy bustling fornicating young couples in and out of bed to worry about being literary.

"This is about the best of them," Ron said, pointing to a sign ahead.

"PARADISE INN—VACANCY."

It was a symbol. There was a vacancy in Paradise, and she, Catherine Alexander, was going to fill it.

Ron swung the car into the courtyard next to a small whitewashed office with a sign that read: RING BELL AND ENTER. The courtyard consisted of about two dozen numbered wooden bungalows.

"How does this look?" Ron asked.

Like Dante's Inferno. Like the Colosseum in Rome when the Christians were about to be thrown to the lions. Like the Temple of Delphi when a Vestal Virgin was about to get hers.

Catherine felt that excited feeling in her groin again. "Terrific," she said, "Just terrific."

Ron smiled knowingly. "I'll be right back." He put his hand on Catherine's knee, sliding it up toward her thigh, gave her a quick, impersonal kiss and swung out of the car and went into the office. She sat there, looking after him, trying to make her mind blank.

She heard the wail of a siren in the distance. *Oh, my God,* she thought wildly, *it's a raid! They're always raiding these places!*

The door to the manager's office opened and Ron came out. He was carrying a key and apparently was deaf to the siren which was coming closer and closer. He walked over to Catherine's side of the car and opened the door.

"All set," he said. The siren was a screaming banshee moving in on them. Could the police arrest them for merely being in the courtyard?

"Come on," Ron said.

"Don't you hear that?"

"Hear what?"

The siren passed them and went ululating down the street away from them, receding into the distance. Damn! "The birds," she said weakly.

There was a look of impatience on Ron's face.

"If there's anything wrong——" he said.

"No, no," Catherine cut in quickly. "I'm coming." She got out of the car and they moved toward one of the bungalows. "I hope you got my lucky number," she said brightly.

"What did you say?"

Catherine looked up at him and suddenly realized no words had come out. Her mouth was completely dry. "Nothing," she croaked.

They reached the door and it said number thirteen. It was exactly what she deserved. It was a sign from heaven that she was going to get pregnant, that God was out to punish Saint Catherine.

Ron unlocked the door and held it open for her. He flicked on the light switch and Catherine stepped inside. She could not believe it. The room seemed to consist of one enormous bed. The only other furniture was an uncomfortable-looking easy chair in a corner, a small dressing table with a mirror over it, and next to the bed, a battered radio with a slot for feeding it quarters. No one would ever walk in here and mistake this room for anything but what it was: a place where a boy brought a girl to screw her. You couldn't say, Well, here we are in the ski lodge, or the war games room, or the bridal suite at the Ambassador. No. What this was was a cheap love nest. Catherine turned to see what Ron was doing and he was throwing the bolt on the door. *Good. If the Vice Squad wanted them, they'd have to break down the door first.* She could see herself being carried out in the nude by two policemen while a photographer snapped her picture for the front page of the *Chicago Daily News*.

Ron moved up to Catherine and put his arms around her. "Are you nervous?" he asked.

She looked up at him and forced a laugh that would have made Margaret Sullavan proud. "Nervous? Ron, don't be silly."

He was still studying her, unsure. "You've done this before, haven't you, Cathy?"

"I don't keep a scorecard."

"I've had a strange feeling about you all evening."

Here it comes. He was going to throw her out on her virgin ass and tell her to get lost in a cold shower. Well, she wasn't going to let that happen. Not tonight. "What kind of feeling?"

"I don't know." Ron's voice was perplexed. "One minute you're kind of sexy and, you know, *with* it, and the next minute your mind is way off somewhere and you're as frigid as ice. It's like you're two people. Which one is the real Catherine Alexander?"

Frigid as ice, she automatically said to herself. Aloud she said, "I'll show you." She put her arms around him and kissed him on the lips and she could smell egg foo young.

He kissed her harder and pulled her close to him. He ran his hands over her breasts, caressing them, pushing his tongue into her mouth. Catherine felt a hot moisture deep down inside her and she could feel her pants dampen. *Here I go,* she thought. *It's really going to happen! It's really going to happen!* She clung to him harder, filled with a growing, almost unbearable excitement.

"Let's get undressed," Ron said hoarsely. He stepped back from her and started to take off his jacket.

"No," she said. "Let me." There was a new confidence in her voice. If this was the night of nights, she was going to do it right. She was going to remember everything she had ever read or heard. Ron wasn't going back to school to snicker to the girls about how he had made love to a dumb little virgin. Catherine might not have Jean-Anne's bust measurement, but she had a brain ten times as useful, and she was going to put it to work to make Ron so happy in bed he wouldn't be able to stand it. She took off his jacket and laid it on the bed, then reached for his tie.

"Hold it," Ron said. "I want to see you undress."

Catherine stared at him, swallowed, slowly reached for her zipper and got out of her dress. She was standing in her bra, slip, pants, shoes and stockings.

"Go on."

She hesitated a moment, then reached down and stepped out of her slip. *Lions, 2—Christians, 0,* she thought.

"Hey, great! Keep going."

Catherine slowly sat down on the bed and carefully removed her shoes and stockings, trying to make it look as sexy as she could. Suddenly she felt Ron behind her, undoing her bra. She let it fall to the bed. He lifted Catherine to her feet and started sliding her pants down. She took a deep breath and closed her eyes, wishing that she were in another place with another man, a human being who loved her, whom she loved, who would father splendid children to bear his name, who would fight for her and kill for her and for whom she would be an adoring helpmate. *A whore in his bed, a great cook in his kitchen, a charming hostess in his living room . . .* a man who would kill a son of a bitch like Ron Peterson for daring to bring her to this tacky, degrading room. Her pants fell to the floor. Catherine opened her eyes.

Ron was staring at her, his face filled with admiration. "My God, Cathy, you're beautiful," he said. "You're really beautiful." He bent down and kissed her breast. She caught a glimpse in the dressing-table mirror. It looked like a French farce, sordid and dirty. Everything inside her except the hot pain in her groin told her that this was dreary and ugly and wrong, but there was no way to stop it now. Ron was whipping off his tie and unbuttoning his shirt, his face flushed. He undid his belt and stripped down to his shorts, then sat down on the bed and started to take off his shoes and socks. "I mean it, Catherine," he said, his voice tight with emotion. "You're the most beautiful goddamn thing I've ever laid eyes on."

His words only increased Catherine's panic. Ron stood up, a broad, anticipatory grin on his face, and let his shorts drop to the floor. His male organ was standing out stiffly, like an enormous, inflated salami with hair around it. It was the largest, most incredible thing Catherine had ever seen in her life.

"How do you like that?" he said, looking down at it proudly.

Without thinking, Catherine said, "Sliced on rye. Hold the mustard and lettuce."

And she stood there, watching it go down.

In Catherine's sophomore year there was a change in the atmosphere of the campus.

For the first time there was a growing concern about what was happening in Europe and an increasing feeling that America was going to get involved. Hitler's dream of the thousand-year rule of the Third Reich was on its way to becoming a reality. The Nazis had occupied Denmark and invaded Norway.

Over the past six months the talk on campuses across the country had shifted from sex and clothes and proms to the ROTC and the draft and lend-lease. More and more college boys were appearing in army and navy uniforms.

One day Susie Roberts, a classmate from Senn, stopped Catherine in the corridor. "I want to say good-bye, Cathy. I'm leaving."

"Where are you going?"

"The Klondike."

"The *Klondike?*"

"Washington, D.C. All the girls are striking gold there. They say for every girl there are at least a hundred men. I like those odds." She looked at Catherine. "What do you want to stick around this place for? School's a drag. There's a whole big world waiting out there."

"I can't leave just now," Catherine said. She was not sure why: She had no real ties in Chicago. She corresponded regularly with her father in Omaha and talked to him on the telephone once or twice a month and each time he sounded as though he were in prison.

Catherine was on her own now. The more she thought about Washington, the more exciting it seemed. That evening she phoned her father and told him she wanted to quit school and go to work in Washington. He asked her if she would like to come to Omaha, but Catherine could sense the reluctance in his voice. He did not want her to be trapped, as he had been.

The next morning Catherine went to the dean of women and informed her she was quitting school. Catherine sent a telegram to Susie Roberts and the next day she was on a train to Washington, D.C.

NOELLE
Paris: 1940

4

On Saturday, June 14, 1940, the German Fifth Army marched into a stunned Paris. The Maginot Line had turned out to be the biggest fiasco in the history of warfare and France lay defenseless before one of the most powerful military machines the world had ever known.

The day had begun with a strange gray pall that lay over the city, a terrifying cloud of unknown origin. For the last forty-eight hours sounds of intermittent gunfire had broken the unnatural, frightened silence of Paris. The roar of the cannons was outside the city, but the echoes reverberated into the heart of Paris. There had been a flood of rumors carried like a tidal wave over the radio, in newspapers and by word of mouth. The Boche were invading the French coast . . . London had been destroyed . . . Hitler had reached an accord with the British government . . . The Germans were going to wipe out Paris with a deadly new bomb. At first each rumor had been taken as gospel, creating its own panic, but constant crises finally exert a soporific effect, as though the mind and body, unable to absorb any further terror, retreat into a protective shell of apathy. Now the rumor mills had ground to a complete halt, newspaper presses had stopped printing and radio stations had stopped broadcasting. Human instinct had taken over from the machines, and the Parisians sensed that this was a day of decision. The gray cloud was an omen.

And then the German locusts began to swarm in.

Suddenly Paris was a city filled with foreign uniforms and alien people, speaking a strange, guttural tongue, speeding down the wide, tree-lined avenues in large Mercedes limousines flying Nazi flags or pushing their way along the sidewalks that now belonged to them. They were truly the *über Mensch,* and it was their destiny to conquer and rule the world.

Within two weeks an amazing transformation had taken place. Signs in German appeared everywhere. Statues of French heroes had been knocked down and the swastika flew from all state buildings. German efforts to eradicate everything Gallic reached ridiculous proportions. The markings on hot and cold water taps were changed from *chaud* and *froid* to *heiss* and *kalt.* The place de Broglie in Strasbourg became Adolf Hitler Platz. Statues of Lafayette, Ney and Kleber were dynamited by squadrons of Nazis. Inscriptions on the monuments for the dead were replaced by "GEFALLEN FUR DEUTSCHLAND."

The German occupation troops were enjoying themselves. While French food was too rich and covered with too many sauces, it was still a pleasant change from war rations. The soldiers neither knew nor cared that Paris was the city of Baudelaire, Dumas and Molière. To them Paris was a garish, eager, overpainted whore with her skirts pulled up over her hips and they raped her, each in his own way. The Storm-troopers forced young French girls to go to bed with them, sometimes at the point of a bayonet, while their leaders like Goering and Himmler raped the Louvre and the rich private estates they greedily confiscated from the newly created enemies of the Reich.

If French corruption and opportunism rose to the surface in the time of France's crisis, so did the heroism. One of the underground's secret weapons was the *Pompiers,* the fire department, which in France is under the jurisdiction of the army. The Germans had confiscated dozens of buildings for the use of the army, the Gestapo and various ministries, and the location of these buildings was of course no secret. At an underground resistance headquarters in St. Remy resistance leaders pored over large maps detailing the location of each building. Experts were then assigned their targets, and the following day a speeding car or an innocent-looking bicyclist would pass by one of the buildings and fling a homemade bomb through the window. Up to that point the damage was slight. The ingenuity of the plan lay in what followed next.

The Germans would call in the *Pompiers* to put out the fire. Now it is instinctive in all countries that when there is a conflagration the firemen are in complete charge: And so it was in Paris. The *Pompiers* raced into the building while the Germans stood meekly aside and watched them destroy everything in sight with high-pressure hoses, axes and—when the opportunity presented itself—their own incendiary bombs. In this way the underground managed to destroy priceless German records locked away in the fortresses of the Wehrmacht and the Gestapo. It took almost six months for the German high command to figure out what was happening, and by that time irreparable damage had been done. The Gestapo could prove nothing, but every member of the *Pompiers* was rounded up and sent to the Russian front to fight.

There was a shortage of everything from food to soap. There was no gasoline, no meat, no dairy products. The Germans had confiscated everything. Stores that carried luxury goods stayed open, but their only customers were the soldiers who paid in occupation marks which were identical with the regular marks except that they lacked the white strip at the edge and the printed promise to pay was not signed.

"Who will redeem these?" the French shopkeepers moaned.

And the Germans grinned, "The Bank of England."

Not all Frenchmen suffered, however. For those

with money and connections there was always the Black Market.

Noelle Page's life was changed very little by the occupation. She was working as a model at Chanel's on rue Canbon in a hundred-and-fifty-year-old graystone building that looked ordinary on the outside, but was very smartly decorated within. The war, like all wars, had created overnight millionaires, and there was no shortage of customers. The propositions that came to Noelle were more numerous than ever; the only difference was that most of them were now in German. When she was not working, she would sit for hours at small outdoor cafés on the Champs-Élysées, or on the Left Bank near the Pont Neuf. There were hundreds of men in German uniforms, many of them with young French girls. The French civilian men were either too old or lame, and Noelle supposed that the younger ones had been sent to camps or conscripted for military duty. She could tell the Germans at a glance, even when they were not in uniform. They had a look of arrogance stamped on their faces, the look that conquerors have had since the days of Alexander and Hadrian. Noelle did not hate them, nor did she like them. They simply did not touch her.

She was filled with a busy inner life, carefully planning out each move. She knew exactly what her goal was, and she knew that nothing could stop her. As soon as she was able to afford it, she engaged a private detective who had handled a divorce for a model with whom she worked. The detective's name was Christian Barbet, and he operated out of a small, shabby office on the rue St. Lazare. The sign on the door read:

ENQUÊTES
PRIVÉES ET COMMERCIALES
RECHERCHES
RENSEIGNEMENTS

CONFIDENTIELS
FILATURES
PREUVES

The sign was almost larger than the office. Barbet was short and bald with yellow, broken teeth, narrow squinting eyes and nicotine-stained fingers.

"What can I do for you?" he asked Noelle.

"I want information about someone in England."

He blinked suspiciously. "What kind of information?"

"Anything. Whether he's married, who he sees. Anything at all. I want to start a scrapbook on him."

Barbet gingerly scratched his crotch and stared at her.

"Is he an Englishman?"

"An American. He's a pilot with the Eagle Squadron of the RAF."

Barbet rubbed the top of his head, uneasily. "I don't know," he grumbled. "We're at war. If they caught me trying to get information out of England about a flyer—"

His voice trailed off and he shrugged expressively. "The Germans shoot first and ask questions afterward."

"I don't want any military information," Noelle assured him. She opened her purse and took out a wad of franc notes. Barbet studied them hungrily.

"I have connections in England," he said cautiously, "but it will be expensive."

And so it began. It was three months before the little detective telephoned Noelle. She went to his office, and her first words were: "Is he alive?" and when Barbet nodded, her body sagged with relief and Barbet thought, *It must be wonderful to have someone love you that much.*

"Your boyfriend has been transferred," Barbet told her.

"Where?"

He looked down at a pad on his desk. "He was attached to the 609th Squadron of the RAF. He's been transferred to the 121st Squadron at Martlesham East, in East Anglia. He's flying Hurri—"

"I don't care about that."

"You're paying for it," he said. "You might as well get your money's worth." He looked down at his notes again. "He's flying Hurricanes. Before that he was flying American Buffaloes."

He turned over a page and added, "It becomes a little personal here."

"Go on," Noelle said.

Barbet shrugged. "There's a list of girls he is sleeping with. I didn't know whether you wanted—"

"I told you—everything."

There was a strange note in her voice that baffled him. There was something not quite normal here, something that did not ring true. Christian Barbet was a third-rate investigator handling third-rate clients, but because of that he had developed a feral instinct for truth, a nose for smelling out facts. The beautiful girl standing in his office disturbed him. At first Barbet had thought she might be trying to involve him in some kind of espionage. Then he decided that she was a deserted wife seeking evidence against her husband. He had been wrong about that, he admitted, and now he was at a loss to figure out what his client wanted or why. He handed Noelle the list of Larry Douglas' girl friends and watched her face as she read it. She might have been reading a laundry list.

She finished and looked up. Christian Barbet was totally unprepared for her next words. "I'm very pleased," Noelle said.

He looked at her and blinked rapidly.

"Please call me when you have something more to report."

Long after Noelle Page had gone, Barbet sat in his

office staring out the window, trying to puzzle out what his client was really after.

The theaters of Paris were beginning to boom again. The Germans attended to celebrate the glory of their victories and to show off the beautiful Frenchwomen they wore on their arms like trophies. The French attended to forget for a few hours that they were an unhappy, defeated people.

Noelle had attended the theater in Marseille a few times, but she had seen sleazy amateur plays acted out by fourth-rate performers for indifferent audiences. The theater in Paris was something else again. It was alive and sparkling and filled with the wit and grace of Molière, Racine and Colette. The incomparable Sacha Guitry had opened his theater and Noelle went to see him perform. She attended a revival of Büchner's *La Morte de Danton* and a play called *Asmodée* by a promising new young writer named François Mauriac. She went to the Comédie Française to see Pirandello's *Chacun La Verité* and Rostand's *Cyrano de Bergerac*. Noelle always went alone, oblivious of the admiring stares of those around her, completely lost in the drama taking place on the stage. Something in the magic that went on behind the footlights struck a responsive chord in her. She was playing a part just like the actors on stage, pretending to be something that she wasn't, hiding behind a mask.

One play in particular, *Huis Clos* by Jean Paul Sartre, affected her deeply. It starred Philippe Sorel, one of the idols of Europe. Sorel was ugly, short and beefy, with a broken nose and the face of a boxer. But the moment he spoke, a magic took place. He was transformed into a sensitive handsome man. *It's like the story of the Prince and the Frog,* Noelle thought, watching him perform. *Only he is both.* She went back to watch him again and again, sitting in the front row studying his performance, trying to learn the secret of his magnetism.

One evening during intermission an usher handed Noelle a note. It read, "I have seen you in the audience night after night. Please come backstage this evening and let me meet you. P.S." Noelle read it over, savoring it. Not because she gave a damn about Philippe Sorel, but because she knew that this was the beginning she had been looking for.

She went backstage after the performance. An old man at the stage door ushered her into Sorel's dressing room. He was seated before a makeup mirror, wearing only shorts, wiping off his makeup. He studied Noelle in the mirror. "It's unbelievable," he said finally. "You're even more beautiful up close."

"Thank you, Monsieur Sorel."

"Where are you from?"

"Marseille."

Sorel swung around to look at her more closely. His eyes moved to her feet and slowly worked their way up to the top of her head, missing nothing. Noelle stood there under his scrutiny, not moving. "Looking for a job?" he asked.

"No."

"I never pay for it," Sorel said. "All you'll get from me is a pass to my play. If you want money, fuck a banker."

Noelle stood there quietly watching him. Finally Sorel said, "What *are* you looking for?"

"I think I'm looking for you."

They had supper and afterward went back to Sorel's apartment in the beautiful rue Maurice-Barres, overlooking the corner where it became the Bois de Boulogne. Philippe Sorel was a skillful lover, surprisingly considerate and unselfish. Sorel had expected nothing from Noelle but her beauty, and he was astonished by her versatility in bed.

"Christ!" he said. "You're fantastic. Where did you learn all that?"

Noelle thought about it a moment. It was really not

a question of learning. It was a matter of feeling. To her a man's body was an instrument to be played on, to explore to its innermost depths, finding the responsive chords and building upon them, using her own body to help create exquisite harmonies.

"I was born with it," she said simply.

Her fingertips began to lightly play around his lips, quick little butterfly touches, and then moved down to his chest and stomach. She saw him starting to grow hard and erect again. She arose and went into the bathroom and returned a moment later and slid his hard penis into her mouth. Her mouth was hot, filled with warm water.

"Oh, Christ," he said.

They spent the entire night making love, and in the morning, Sorel invited Noelle to move in with him.

Noelle lived with Philippe Sorel for six months. She was neither happy nor unhappy. She knew that her being there made Sorel ecstatically happy, but this did not matter in the slightest to Noelle. She regarded herself as simply a student, determined to learn something new every day. He was a school that she was attending, a small part in her large plan. To Noelle there was nothing personal in their relationship, for she gave nothing of herself. She had made that mistake twice, and she would never make it again. There was room for only one man in Noelle's thoughts and that was Larry Douglas. Noelle would pass the place des Victoires or a park or restaurant where Larry had taken her, and she would feel the hatred well up within her, choking her, so it became difficult to breathe, and there was something else mixed in with the hatred, something Noelle could not put a name to.

Two months after moving in with Sorel, Noelle received a call from Christian Barbet.

"I have another report for you," the little detective said.

"Is he all right?" Noelle asked quickly.

Again Barbet was filled with that sense of uneasiness. "Yes," he said.

Noelle's voice was filled with relief. "I'll be right down."

The report was divided into two parts. The first dealt with Larry Douglas' military career. He had shot down five German planes and was the first American to become an Ace in the war. He had been promoted to Captain. The second part of the report interested her more. He had become very popular in London's wartime social life and had become engaged to the daughter of a British Admiral. There followed a list of girls that Larry was sleeping with, ranging from show girls to the wife of an under-secretary in the Ministry.

"Do you want me to keep on with this?" Barbet asked.

"Of course," Noelle replied. She took an envelope from her purse and handed it to Barbet. "Call me when you have anything further."

And she was gone.

Barbet sighed and looked up at the ceiling. *"Folle,"* he said thoughtfully. *"Folle."*

If Philippe Sorel had had any inkling of what was going on in Noelle's mind, he would have been astonished. Noelle seemed totally devoted to him. She did everything for him: cooked wonderful meals, shopped, supervised the cleaning of his apartment and made love whenever the mood stirred him. And asked for nothing. Sorel congratulated himself on having found the perfect mistress. He took her everywhere, and she met all his friends. They were enchanted with her and thought Sorel a very lucky man.

One night as they were having supper after the show, Noelle said to him, "I want to be an actress, Philippe."

He shook his head. "God knows you're beautiful enough, Noelle, but I've been up to my ass in actresses all my life. You're different, and I want to keep you that way. I don't want to share you with anyone." He patted her hand. "Don't I give you everything you need?"

"Yes, Philippe," Noelle replied.

When they returned to the apartment that night, Sorel wanted to make love. When they finished, he was drained. Noelle had never been as exciting, and Sorel congratulated himself that all she needed was the firm guidance of a man.

The following Sunday was Noelle's birthday, and Philippe Sorel gave a dinner party for her at Maxim's. He had taken over the large private dining room upstairs, decorated with plush red velvet and deep dark wood paneling. Noelle had helped write the guest list, and there was one name she included without mentioning it to Philippe. There were forty people at the party. They toasted Noelle's birthday and gave her lavish gifts. When dinner was over, Sorel rose to his feet. He had drunk a good deal of brandy and champagne and he was a little unsteady, his words a bit slurred.

"My friends," he said, "we've all drunk to the most beautiful girl in the world and we've given her lovely birthday presents, but I have a present for her that's going to be a *big* surprise." Sorel looked down at Noelle and beamed, then turned to the crowd. "Noelle and I are going to be married."

There was an approving cheer and the guests raced up to clap Sorel on the back and wish luck to the bride-to-be. Noelle sat there smiling up at the guests, murmuring her thank-yous. One of the guests had not risen. He was seated at a table at the far end of the room, smoking a cigarette in a long holder and viewing the scene sardonically. Noelle was aware that he had been watching her during dinner. He was a tall, very thin man, with an intense, brooding face. He seemed amused by everything that was happening around him, more an observer at the party than a guest.

Noelle caught his eye and smiled.

Armand Gautier was one of the top directors in France. He was in charge of the French Repertory Theater, and his productions had been acclaimed all over the world. Having Gautier direct a play or a motion picture was an almost certain guarantee of its success. He had the reputation of being particularly good with actresses and had created half a dozen important stars.

Sorel was at Noelle's side, talking to her. "Were you surprised, my darling?" he asked.

"Yes, Philippe," she said.

"I want us to be married right away. We'll have the wedding at my villa."

Over his shoulder Noelle could see Armand Gautier watching her, smiling that enigmatic smile. Some friends came and took Philippe away and when Noelle turned, Gautier was standing there.

"Congratulations," he said. There was a mocking note in his voice. "You hooked a big fish."

"Did I?"

"Philippe Sorel is a great catch."

"For someone perhaps," Noelle said indifferently.

Gautier looked at her in surprise. "Are you trying to tell me you're not interested?"

"I'm not trying to tell you anything."

"Good luck." He turned to go.

"Monsieur Gautier . . ."

He stopped.

"Could I see you tonight?" Noelle asked quietly. "I would like to talk to you alone."

Armand Gautier looked at her for a moment, then shrugged. "If you wish."

"I will come to your place. Will that be satisfactory?"

"Yes, of course. The address is—"

"I know the address. Twelve o'clock?"

"Twelve o'clock."

Armand Gautier lived in a fashionable old apartment building on rue Marbeuf. A doorman escorted Noelle into the lobby and an elevator boy took her to the fourth floor and indicated Gautier's apartment. Noelle rang the bell. A few moments later the door was opened by Gautier. He wore a flowered dressing gown.

"Come in," he said.

Noelle walked into the apartment. Her eye was untrained, but she sensed that it was done in beautiful taste and that the objets d'art were valuable.

"Sorry I'm not dressed," Gautier apologized. "I've been on the telephone."

Noelle's eyes locked onto his. "It will not be necessary for you to be dressed." She moved over to the couch and sat down.

Gautier smiled. "That was the feeling I had, Miss Page. But I'm curious about something. Why me? You're engaged to a man who is famous and wealthy. I am sure that if you are looking for some extracurricular activities, you could find men more attractive than I, and certainly richer and younger. What is it you want from me?"

"I want you to teach me to act," Noelle said.

Armand Gautier looked at her a moment, then sighed. "You disappoint me. I expected something more original."

"Your business is working with actors."

"With actors, not amateurs. Have you ever acted?"

"No. But you will teach me." She took off her hat and her gloves. "Where is your bedroom?" she asked.

Gautier hesitated. His life was full of beautiful women wanting to be in the theater, or wanting a bigger part, or the lead in a new play, or a larger dressing room. They were all a pain. He knew that he would be a fool to get involved with one more. And yet there was no need to get involved. Here was a beautiful girl throwing herself at him. It would be a simple matter to take her to bed and then send her away. "In there," he said, indicating a door.

He watched Noelle as she walked toward the bedroom. He wondered what Philippe Sorel would think if he knew that his bride-to-be was spending the night here. Women. Whores, all of them. Gautier poured himself a brandy and made several phone calls. When he finally went into the bedroom, Noelle was in his bed, naked, waiting for him. Gautier had to admit that she was an exquisite work of nature. Her face was breathtaking, and her body was flawless. Her skin was the color of honey, except for the triangle of soft golden hair between her legs. Gautier had learned from experience that beautiful girls were almost invariably narcissistic, so preoccupied with their own egocentricities that they were lousy lays. They felt their contribution to lovemaking was simply conferring their presence in a man's bed, so that the man ended up making love to an unmoving lump of clay and was expected to be grateful for the experience. Ah, well, perhaps he could teach this one something.

As Noelle watched him, Gautier undressed, leaving his clothes carelessly strewn on the floor, and moved toward the bed. "I'm not going to tell you you are beautiful," he said. "You've heard it too many times already."

"Beauty is wasted," Noelle shrugged, "unless it is used to give pleasure."

Gautier looked at her in quick surprise, then smiled. "I agree. Let's use yours." He sat down beside her.

Like most Frenchmen, Armand Gautier prided himself on being a skilled lover. He was amused by the stories he had heard of Germans and Americans whose idea of making love consisted of jumping on top of a girl, having an instant orgasm, and then putting on their hat and departing. The Americans even had a phrase for it. "Wham, bam, thank you ma'am." When Armand Gautier was emotionally involved with a woman, he used many devices to heighten the enjoyment of lovemaking. There was always a perfect dinner, the right wines. He arranged the setting artistically so that it was pleasing to the senses, the room was delicately scented and soft music was playing. He aroused his women with tender sentiments of love and later the coarse language of the gutter. And Gautier was adept at the manual foreplay that preceded sex.

In Noelle's case he dispensed with all of these. For a one-night stand there was no need for perfume or music or empty endearments. She was here simply to get laid. She was indeed a silly fool if she thought that she could trade what every woman in the world carried between her legs for the great and unique genius that Armand Gautier possessed in his head.

He started to climb on top of her. Noelle stopped him.

"Wait," she whispered.

As he watched, puzzled, she reached for two small tubes that she had placed on the bedside table. She squeezed the contents of one into her hand and began to rub it onto his penis.

"What is this all about?" he asked.

She smiled. "You'll see." She kissed him on the lips, her tongue darting into his mouth in quick bird-like movements. She pulled away and her tongue started moving toward his belly, her hair trailing across his body like light, silky fingers. He felt his organ begin to rise. She moved her tongue down his legs to his feet and began to suck gently on his toes. His organ was stiff and hard now and she mounted him as he lay there. As he felt himself penetrating her, the warmth of her vagina acted on the cream she had put on his penis and the sensation became unbearably exciting. As she rode him, moving up and down, her left hand was caressing his testicles and they began to grow hot. There was menthol in the cream on his penis and the sensation of the cold while inside her warmth, and the heat of his testicles, drove him into an absolute frenzy.

They made love all night long and each time Noelle made love to him differently. It was the most incredibly sensuous experience he had ever had.

In the morning Armand Gautier said, "If I can get

up enough energy to move, I'll get dressed and take you out to breakfast."

"Lie there," Noelle said. She walked over to a closet, selected one of his robes and put it on. "You rest. I'll be back."

Thirty-five minutes later Noelle returned with a breakfast tray. On it were freshly squeezed orange juice, a delicious sausage-and-chive omelet, heated, buttered croissants and jam and a pot of black coffee. It tasted extraordinarily good.

"Aren't you having anything?" Gautier asked.

Noelle shook her head. "No." She was seated in an easy chair watching him as he ate. She looked even more beautiful wearing his dressing gown open at the top, revealing the curves of her delicious breasts. Her hair was tousled and carefree.

Armand Gautier had radically revised his earlier estimate of Noelle. She was not any man's quick lay; she was an absolute treasure. However, he had met many treasures in his career in the theater, and he was not about to spend his time and talent as a director on a starry-eyed amateur who wanted to break into the theater, no matter how beautiful she might be, or how skilled in bed. Gautier was a dedicated man who took his art seriously. He had refused to compromise it in the past, and he was not about to start now.

The evening before, he had planned to spend the night with Noelle and send her packing in the morning. Now as he ate his breakfast and studied her, he was trying to figure out a way to hold onto Noelle as a mistress until he got bored with her, without encouraging her as an actress. He knew that he had to hold out some bait. He felt his way cautiously. "Are you planning to marry Philippe Sorel?" he asked.

"Of course not," Noelle replied. "That is not what I want."

Now it was coming. "What do you want?" Gautier asked.

"I told you," Noelle said quietly. "I want to be an actress."

Gautier bit into another croissant, stalling for time. "Of course," he said. Then he added, "There are many fine dramatic coaches I could send you to, Noelle, who would . . ."

"No," she said. Noelle was watching him pleasantly, warmly, as though eager to accede to anything he suggested. And yet Gautier had a feeling that inside her was a core of steel. There were many ways she could have said "no." With anger, reproach, disappointment, sulking, but she had said it with softness. And absolute finality. This was going to be more difficult than he had anticipated. For a moment Armand Gautier was tempted to tell her, as he told dozens of girls every week, to go away, that he had no time to waste on her. But he thought of the incredible sensations he had experienced during the night and he knew he would be a fool to let her go so soon. She was surely worth a slight, a very slight, compromise.

"Very well," Gautier said. "I will give you a play to study. When you have memorized it, you will read it to me and we will see how much talent you have. Then we can decide what to do with you."

"Thank you, Armand," she said. There was no triumph in her words, nor even any pleasure that he could detect. Just a simple acknowledgment of the inevitable. For the first time Gautier felt a small twinge of doubt. But that of course was ridiculous. He was a master at handling women.

While Noelle was getting dressed, Armand Gautier went into his book-lined study and scanned the familiar-looking worn volumes on the shelves. Finally, with a wry smile, he selected Euripides' *Andromache*. It was one of the most difficult classics to act. He went back into the bedroom and handed the play to Noelle.

"Here you are, my dear," he said. "When you have memorized the part, we shall go over it together."

"Thank you, Armand. You will not be sorry."

The more he thought about it, the more pleased Gautier was with his ploy. It would take Noelle a week or two to memorize the part, or what was even more likely, she would come to him and confess that she was unable to memorize it. He would sympathize with her, explain how difficult the art of acting was, and they could assume a relationship untainted by her ambition. Gautier made a date to have dinner with Noelle that evening, and she left.

When Noelle returned to the apartment she shared with Philippe Sorel, she found him waiting for her. He was very drunk.

"You bitch," he yelled. "Where have you been all night?"

It would not matter what she said. Sorel knew that he was going to listen to her apologies, beat her up, then take her to bed and forgive her.

But instead of apologizing Noelle merely said, "With another man, Philippe. I've come to pick up my things."

And as Sorel watched her in stunned disbelief, Noelle walked into the bedroom and began to pack.

"For Christ's sake, Noelle," he pleaded. "Don't do this! We love each other. We're going to get married." He talked to her for the next half hour, arguing, threatening, cajoling, and by that time Noelle had finished packing and had left the apartment and Sorel had no idea why he had lost her, for he did not know that he had never possessed her.

Armand Gautier was in the middle of directing a new play that was to open in two weeks and he spent all day at the theater in rehearsals. As a rule when Gautier was in production, he thought of nothing else. Part of his genius was the intense concentration he was able to bring to his work. Nothing existed for him but the four walls of the theater and the actors he was working with. This day however was different. Gautier found his mind constantly wandering to Noelle and the incredible night they had had together. The actors would go through a scene and then stop and wait for his comments, and Gautier would suddenly realize that he had been paying no attention. Furious with himself he tried to focus his attention on what he was doing, but thoughts of Noelle's naked body and the amazing things it had done to him would keep coming back. In the middle of one dramatic scene he found that he was walking around the stage with an erection, and he had to excuse himself.

Because Gautier had an analytical mind he tried to figure out what it was about this girl that had affected him like this. Noelle was beautiful, but he had slept with some of the most beautiful women in the world. She was consummately skilled at lovemaking but so were other women to whom he had made love. She seemed intelligent but not brilliant; her personality was pleasant but not complex. There was something else, something the director could not quite put his finger on. And then he remembered her soft "no" and he felt that it was a clue. There was some force in her that was irresistible, that would obtain anything she wanted. There was something in her that was untouched. And like other men before him Armand Gautier felt that though Noelle had affected him more deeply than he cared to admit to himself, he had not touched her at all, and this was a challenge that his masculinity could not refuse.

Gautier spent the day in a confused state of mind. He looked forward to the evening with tremendous anticipation, not so much because he wanted to make love to Noelle but because he wanted to prove to himself that he had been building something out of nothing. He wanted Noelle to be a disappointment to him so that he could dismiss her from his life.

As they made love that night, Armand Gautier made himself consciously aware of the tricks and devices and artifices Noelle used so he would realize that it was all

mechanical, without emotion. But he was mistaken.
She gave herself to him fully and completely, caring
only about bringing him pleasure such as he had never
known before and reveling in his enjoyment. When
morning came Gautier was more firmly bewitched by
her than ever.

Noelle prepared breakfast for him again, this time
delicate crêpes with bacon and jam, and hot coffee,
and it was magnificent.

"All right," Gautier told himself. "You have found a
young girl who is beautiful to look at, who can make
love and cook. Bravo! But is that enough for an intelligent man? When you are through making love and
eating, you must talk. What can she talk to you
about?" The answer was that it didn't really matter.

There had been no more mention of the play and
Gautier was hoping that Noelle had either forgotten
about it or had been unable to cope with memorizing
the lines. When she left in the morning, she promised
to have dinner with him that evening.

"Can you get away from Philippe?" Gautier asked.

"I've left him," Noelle said simply. She gave Gautier
her new address.

He stared at her for a moment. "I see."

But he did not. Not in the least.

They spent the night together again. When they
were not making love, they talked. Or rather Gautier
talked. Noelle seemed so interested in him that he
found himself talking about things he had not discussed
in years, personal things that he had never revealed to
anyone before. No mention was made of the play he
had given her to read, and Gautier congratulated himself on having solved his problem so neatly.

The following night when they had had dinner and
were ready to retire, Gautier started toward the bedroom.

"Not yet," Noelle said.

He turned in surprise.

"You said you would listen to me do the play."

"Well, of—of course," Gautier stammered, "whenever you're ready."

"I am ready."

He shook his head. "I don't want you to read it, cherie," he said. "I want to hear it when you have memorized it so that I can really judge you as an actress."

"I have memorized it," Noelle replied.

He stared at her in disbelief. It was impossible that she could have learned the entire part in only three days.

"Are you ready to hear me?" she asked.

Armand Gautier had no choice. "Of course," he said. He gestured toward the center of the room. "That will be your stage. The audience will be here." He sat down on a large comfortable settee.

Noelle began to do the play. Gautier could feel the gooseflesh begin to crawl, his own personal stigmata, the thing that happened to him when he encountered real talent. Not that Noelle was expert. Far from it. Her inexperience shone through every move and gesture. But she had something much more than mere skill: She had a rare honesty, a natural talent that gave every line a fresh meaning and color.

When Noelle finished the soliloquy, Gautier said warmly, "I think that one day you will become an important actress, Noelle. I really mean that. I am going to send you to Georges Faber, who is the best dramatic coach in all of France. Working with him, you will—"

"No."

He looked at her in surprise. It was that same soft "no" again. Positive and final.

" 'No' what?" Gautier asked in some confusion. "Faber does not take on anyone but the biggest actors. He will only take you because I tell him to."

"I am going to work with you," Noelle said.

Gautier could feel the anger mounting in him. "I don't coach anyone," he snapped. "I am not a teacher.

I direct professional actors. When you are a professional actor, then I will direct you." He was fighting to check the anger in his voice. "Do you understand?"

Noelle nodded. "Yes, I understand, Armand."

"Very well then."

Mollified, he took Noelle in his arms and received a warm kiss from her. He knew now that he had worried unnecessarily. She was like any other woman, she needed to be dominated. He would have no further problem with her.

Their lovemaking that night surpassed anything that had gone before, possibly, Gautier thought, because of the added excitement of the slight quarrel they had had.

During the night he said to her, "You really can be a wonderful actress, Noelle. I'm going to be very proud of you."

"Thank you, Armand," she whispered.

Noelle fixed breakfast in the morning, and Gautier left for the theater. When he telephoned Noelle during the day, she did not answer, and when he arrived home that night she was not there. Gautier waited for her to return, and when she did not appear he lay awake all night wondering if she could have been in an accident. He tried to phone Noelle at her apartment, but there was no answer. He sent a telegram that went undelivered, and when he stopped at her apartment after rehearsal, no one answered his ring.

During the week that followed, Gautier was frantic. Rehearsals were turning into a shambles. He was screaming at all the actors and upsetting them so badly that his stage manager suggested they stop for the day and Gautier agreed. After the actors had left, he sat on the stage alone, trying to understand what had happened to him. He told himself that Noelle was just another woman, a cheap ambitious blonde with the heart of a shopgirl who wanted to be a star. He denigrated her in every way he could think of, but in the end he knew it was no use. He had to have her. That night he wandered the streets of Paris, getting drunk in small bars where he was unknown. He tried to think of ways to reach Noelle but to no avail. There was no one he could even talk to about her, except Philippe Sorel, and that, of course, was out of the question.

A week after Noelle had disappeared, Armand Gautier arrived home at four o'clock in the morning, drunk, opened the door and walked into the living room. All the lights were on. Noelle was curled up in an easy chair dressed in one of his robes, reading a book. She looked up as he entered, and smiled.

"Hello, Armand."

Gautier stared at her, his heart lifting, a feeling of infinite relief and happiness flooding through him. He said, "We'll begin working tomorrow."

CATHERINE
Washington: 1940

5

Washington, D.C., was the most exciting city that Catherine Alexander had ever seen. She had always thought of Chicago as the heartland, but Washington was a revelation. Here was the real core of America, the pulsating center of power. At first, Catherine had been bewildered by the variety of uniforms that filled the streets: Army, Navy Air Corps, Marines. For the first time Catherine began to feel the grim possibility of war as something real.

In Washington the physical presence of war was everywhere. This was the city where war, if it came, would begin. Here it would be declared and mobilized and masterminded. This was the city that held in its hand the fate of the world. And she, Catherine Alexander, was going to be a part of it.

She had moved in with Susie Roberts, who was living in a bright and cheery fourth floor walk-up apartment with a fair-sized living room, two small adjoining bedrooms, a tiny bathroom and a kitchenette built for a midget. Susie had seemed glad to see her. Her first words were:

"Hurry and unpack and get your best dress steamed out. You have a dinner date tonight."

Catherine blinked. "What took you so long?"

"Cathy, in Washington, it's the *girls* who have the little black books. This town is so full of lonely men, it's pitiful."

They had dinner that first evening at the Willard

Hotel. Susie's date was a congressman from Indiana and Catherine's date was a lobbyist from Oregon, and both men were in town without their wives. After dinner they went dancing at the Washington Country Club. Catherine had hoped that the lobbyist might be able to give her a job. Instead she got the offer of a car and her own apartment, which she declined with thanks.

Susie brought the congressman back to the apartment, and Catherine went to bed. A short time later she heard them go into Susie's bedroom, and the bedsprings began to creak. Catherine pulled a pillow over her head to drown out the sound, but it was impossible. She visualized Susie in bed with her date making wild, passionate love. In the morning when Catherine got up for breakfast, Susie was already up, looking bright and cheerful, ready to go to work. Catherine searched for telltale wrinkles and other signs of dissipation on Susie, but there were none. On the contrary she looked radiant, her skin absolutely flawless. *My God,* Catherine thought, *she's a female Dorian Gray. One day she's going to come in looking great, and I'll look a hundred and ten years old.*

A few days later at breakfast Susie said, "Hey, I heard about a job opening that might interest you. One of the girls at the party last night said she's quitting to go back to Texas. God knows why anyone who ever got away from Texas would want to go back there. I remember I was in Amarillo a few years ago and . . ."

"Where does she work?" Catherine interrupted.

"Who?"

"The girl," Catherine said patiently.

"Oh. She works for Bill Fraser. He's in charge of public relations for the State Department. *Newsweek* did a cover story on him last month. It's supposed to be a cushy job. I just heard about it last night, so if you get over there now, you should beat all the other girls to it."

"Thanks," Catherine said gratefully. "William Fraser, here I come."

Twenty minutes later Catherine was on her way to the State Department. When she arrived, the guard told her where Fraser's office was and she took the elevator upstairs. *Public Relations. It sounded exactly like the sort of job she was looking for.*

Catherine stopped in the corridor outside the office and took out her hand mirror to check her makeup. She would do. It was not yet nine-thirty so she should have the field to herself. She opened the door and walked in.

The outer office was packed with girls standing, sitting, leaning against the wall, all seemingly talking at once. The frantic receptionist behind the beleaguered desk was vainly trying to bring order into the scene. "Mr. Fraser's busy right now," she kept repeating. "I don't know when he can see you."

"Is he interviewing secretaries or isn't he?" one of the girls demanded.

"Yes, but . . ." She looked around desperately at the mob. "My God! This is ridiculous!"

The corridor door opened and three more girls pushed their way in, shoving Catherine to one side.

"Is the job filled yet?" one of them asked.

"Maybe he'd like a harem," another girl suggested. "Then we can all stay."

The door to the inner office opened, and a man came out. He was just a little under six feet, and had the almost-slim body of a nonathlete who keeps in shape at the athletic club three mornings a week. He had curly blond hair graying at the temples, bright blue eyes and a strong, rather forbidding jaw line. "What in hell's going on here, Sally?" His voice was deep and authoritative.

"These girls heard about the vacancy, Mr. Fraser."

"Jesus! I didn't hear about it myself until an hour ago." His eyes swept over the room. "It's like jungle drums." As his eyes moved toward Catherine, she stood up straight and gave him her warmest I'll-be-a-great-secretary smile, but his eyes passed right over her and went back to the receptionist. "I need a copy of *Life*," he told her. "An issue that came out three or four weeks ago. It has a picture of Stalin on the cover."

"I'll order it, Mr. Fraser," the receptionist said.

"I need it now." He started back toward his office.

"I'll call the Time-Life Bureau," the receptionist said, "and see if they can dig up a copy."

Fraser stopped at the door. "Sally, I have Senator Borah on the line. I want to read him a paragraph from that issue. You have two minutes to find a copy for me." He went into his office and closed the door.

The girls in the room looked at one another and shrugged. Catherine stood there, thinking hard. She turned and pushed her way out of the office.

"Good. That's one down," one of the girls said.

The receptionist picked up the telephone and dialed information. "The number for the Time-Life Bureau," she said. The room grew silent as the girls watched her. "Thank you." She replaced the receiver, then picked it up and dialed again. "Hello. This is Mr. William Fraser's office in the State Department. Mr. Fraser needs a back issue of *Life* immediately. It's the one with Stalin on the cover . . . You don't keep any back issues there? Who could I talk to? . . . I see. Thank you." She hung up.

"Tough luck, honey," one of the girls said.

Another added: "They sure come up with some beauties, don't they? If he wants to come over to my place tonight, I'll read to him." There was a laugh.

The intercom buzzed. She flipped down the key. "Your two minutes are up," Fraser's voice said. "Where's the magazine?"

The receptionist drew a deep breath. "I just talked to the Time-Life Bureau, Mr. Fraser, and they said it would be impossible to get . . ."

The door opened and Catherine hurried in. In her hand was a copy of *Life* with a picture of Stalin on the cover. She pushed her way through to the desk and placed the magazine in the receptionist's hand. The receptionist stared at it incredulously. "I . . . I have a copy of it here, Mr. Fraser. I'll bring it right in." She rose, gave Catherine a grateful smile and hurried into the inner office. The other girls turned to stare at Catherine with suddenly hostile eyes.

Five minutes later the door to Fraser's office opened, and Fraser and the receptionist appeared. The receptionist pointed to Catherine. "That's the girl."

William Fraser turned to regard Catherine speculatively. "Would you come in, please?"

"Yes, sir." Catherine followed Fraser into his office, feeling the eyes of the other girls stabbing into her back. Fraser closed the door.

His office was the typical, bureaucratic Washington office, but he had decorated it in style, stamping it with his personal taste in furniture and art.

"Sit down, Miss . . ."

"Alexander, Catherine Alexander."

"Sally tells me that you came up with the *Life* magazine."

"Yes, sir."

"I assume you didn't just happen to have a three-week-old issue in your purse."

"No, sir."

"How did you find it so quickly?"

"I went down to the barber shop. Barber shops and dentists' offices always have old issues lying around."

"I see." Fraser smiled, and his craggy face seemed less formidable. "I don't think that would have occurred to me," he said. "Are you that bright about everything?"

Catherine thought about Ron Peterson. "No, sir," she replied.

"Are you looking for a job as a secretary?"

"Not really." Catherine saw his look of surprise. "I'll take it," she added hastily. "What I'd really like to be is your assistant."

"Why don't we start you out as a secretary today?" Fraser said dryly. "Tomorrow you can be my assistant."

She looked at him hopefully. "You mean I have the job?"

"On trial." He flicked down the intercom key and leaned toward the box. "Sally, would you please thank the young ladies. Tell them the position is filled."

"Right, Mr. Fraser."

He flicked the button up. "Will thirty dollars a week be satisfactory?"

"Oh yes, sir. Thank you, Mr. Fraser."

"You can start tomorrow morning, nine o'clock. Have Sally give you a personnel form to fill out."

When Catherine left the office, she walked over to the *Washington Post*. The policeman at the desk in the lobby stopped her.

"I'm William Fraser's personal secretary," she said loftily, "over at the State Department. I need some information from your morgue."

"What kind of information?"

"On William Fraser."

He studied her a moment and said, "That's the weirdest request I've had all week. Has your boss been bothering you, or something?"

"No," she said disarmingly. "I'm planning to write an exposé on him."

Five minutes later, a clerk was showing her into the morgue. He pulled out the file on William Fraser, and Catherine began to read.

One hour later Catherine was one of the world's foremost authorities on William Fraser. He was forty-five years old, had been graduated from Princeton summa cum laude, had started an advertising agency, Fraser Associates, which had become one of the most successful agencies in the business, and had taken a leave of absence a year ago at the request of the President, to work for the government. He had been married to Lydia Campion, a wealthy socialite. They had been divorced for four years. There were no children. Fraser was a millionaire and had a home in Georgetown and a summer place at Bar Harbor, Maine. His hobbies were tennis, boating and polo. Several of the news stories referred to him as "one of America's most eligible bachelors."

When Catherine arrived home and told Susie her good news, Susie insisted that they go out to celebrate. Two rich Annapolis cadets were in town.

Catherine's date turned out to be a pleasant enough boy, but all evening she kept mentally comparing him to William Fraser, and compared to Fraser the boy seemed callow and dull. Catherine wondered whether she was going to fall in love with her new boss. She had not felt any girlish tingly feeling when she had been with him, but there was something else, a liking for him as a person and a feeling of respect. She decided that the tingly feeling probably existed only in French sex novels.

The cadets took the girls to a small Italian restaurant on the outskirts of Washington where they had an excellent dinner, then went to see *Arsenic and Old Lace,* which Catherine enjoyed tremendously. At the end of the evening the boys brought them home, and Susie invited them in for a nightcap. When it appeared to Catherine that they were starting to settle down for the night, she excused herself and said she had to go to bed.

Her date protested. "We haven't even gotten started yet," he said. "Look at them."

Susie and her escort were on the couch, locked in a passionate embrace.

Catherine's escort clutched her arm. "There could be a war soon," he said earnestly. Before Catherine could stop him, he took her hand and placed it against the hardness between his legs. "You wouldn't send a man into battle in this condition, would you?"

Catherine withdrew her hand, fighting not to be angry. "I've given it a lot of thought," she said evenly, "and I've decided to sleep only with the walking wounded." She turned and went into her bedroom, locking the door behind her. She found it difficult to go to sleep. She lay in bed thinking about William Fraser, her new job and the male hardness of the boy from Annapolis. An hour after she had gone to bed, she heard Susie's bedsprings creaking wildly. From then on sleep was impossible.

At eight-thirty the next morning Catherine arrived at her new office. The door was unlocked, and the light in the reception office was on. From the inner office she heard the sound of a man's voice and she walked inside.

William Fraser was at his desk, dictating into a machine. He looked up as Catherine entered and snapped off the machine. "You're early," he said.

"I wanted to look around and get my bearings before I began work."

"Sit down." There was something in his tone that puzzled her. He seemed angry. Catherine took a seat. "I don't like snoops, Miss Alexander."

Catherine felt her face redden. "I—I don't understand."

"Washington's a small town. It's not even a town. It's a goddamn village. There's nothing that goes on here that everybody doesn't know about in five minutes."

"I still don't—"

"The publisher of the *Post* phoned me two minutes after you arrived there to ask why my secretary was doing research on me."

Catherine sat there stunned, not knowing what to say.

"Did you find out all the gossip you wanted to know?"

She felt her embarrassment swiftly changing to anger. "I wasn't snooping," Catherine said. She rose to her feet. "The only reason I wanted information on you was so that I would know what kind of man I was working for." Her voice was trembling with indignation. "I think a good secretary should adapt to her employer, and I wanted to know what to adapt to."

Fraser sat there, his expression hostile.

Catherine stared at him, hating him, on the verge of tears. "You don't have to worry about it anymore, Mr. Fraser. I quit." She turned and started toward the door.

"Sit down," Fraser said, his voice like a whiplash. Catherine turned, in shock. "I can't stand goddamn prima donnas."

She glared at him. "I'm not a . . ."

"OK. I'm sorry. Now, will you sit down. Please?" He picked up a pipe from his desk and lit it.

Catherine stood there not knowing what to do, filled with humiliation. "I don't think it's going to work," she began. "I . . ."

Fraser drew on the pipe and flicked out the match. "Of course it'll work, Catherine," he said reasonably. "You can't quit now. Look at all the trouble I'd have breaking in a new girl."

Catherine looked at him and saw the glint of amusement in his bright blue eyes. He smiled, and reluctantly her lips curved into a small smile. She sank into a chair.

"That's better. Did anyone ever tell you you're too sensitive?"

"I suppose so. I'm sorry."

Fraser leaned back in his chair. "Or maybe I'm the one who's oversensitive. It's a pain in the ass being called 'one of America's most eligible bachelors.'"

Catherine wished he would not use words like that. *But what bothered her most?* she wondered. *Ass or bachelor?*

Maybe Fraser was right. Perhaps her interest in him was not as impersonal as she thought. Perhaps subconsciously . . .

". . . a target for every goddamned idiotic unmarried female in the world," Fraser was saying. "You wouldn't believe it if I told you how aggressive women can be."

Wouldn't she? Try our cashier. Catherine blushed as she thought of it.

"It's enough to turn a man into a fairy." Fraser sighed. "Since this seems to be National Research Week, tell me about you. Any boyfriends?"

"No," she said. "That is, no one special," she added quickly.

He looked at her quizzically. "Where do you live?"

"I share an apartment with a girl who was a classmate at college."

"Northwestern."

She looked at him in surprise, then realized he must have seen the personnel form she had filled out.

"Yes, sir."

"I'm going to tell you something about me that you didn't find in the newspaper morgue. I'm a tough sonofabitch to work for. You'll find me fair, but I'm a perfectionist. We're hard to live with. Do you think you can manage?"

"I'll try," Catherine said.

"Good. Sally will fill you in on the routine around here. The most important thing you have to remember is that I'm a chain coffee drinker. I like it black and hot."

"I'll remember." She got to her feet and started toward the door.

"And, Catherine?"

"Yes, Mr. Fraser?"

"When you go home tonight, practice saying some profanity in front of the mirror. If you're going to keep wincing every time I say a four-letter word, it's going to drive me up the wall."

He was doing it to her again, making her feel like a child. "Yes, Mr. Fraser," she said coldly. She stormed out of the office, almost slamming the door behind her.

The meeting had not gone anything like Catherine had expected. She no longer liked William Fraser. She thought he was a smug, dominating, arrogant boor. No wonder his wife had divorced him. Well she was here and she would start, but she made up her mind that she would begin looking for another job, a job working for a human being instead of a despot.

When Catherine walked out of the door, Fraser leaned back in his chair, a smile touching his lips. Were girls still that achingly young, that earnest and dedicated? In her anger with her eyes blazing and her lips trembling Catherine had seemed so defenseless that Fraser had wanted to take her in his arms and protect her. Against himself, he admitted ruefully. There was a kind of old-fashioned shining quality about her that he'd almost forgotten existed in girls. She was lovely and she was bright, and she had a mind of her own. She was going to become the best goddamn secretary that he had ever had. And deep down Fraser had a feeling that she was going to become more than that. How much more, he was not sure yet. He had been burned so often that an automatic warning system took over the moment his emotions were touched by any female. Those moments had come very seldom. His pipe had gone out. He lit it again, and the smile was still on his face. A little later when Fraser called her in for dictation, Catherine was courteous but cool. She waited for Fraser to say something personal so she could show him how aloof she was, but he was distant and businesslike. He had, Catherine thought, obviously wiped the incident of this morning from his mind. How insensitive could a man be?

In spite of herself Catherine found the new job fascinating. The telephone rang constantly, and the names of the callers filled her with excitement. During the first week the Vice-President of the United States called twice, half a dozen senators, the Secretary of State and a famous actress who was in town publicizing her latest picture. The week was climaxed by a telephone call from President Roosevelt, and Catherine was so nervous she dropped the phone and disconnected his secretary.

In addition to the telephone calls Fraser had a constant round of appointments at the office, his country club or at one of the better-known restaurants. After the first few weeks Fraser allowed Catherine to set up his appointments for him and make the reservations. She began to know who Fraser wanted to see and who he wanted to avoid. Her work was so absorbing that by the end of the month she had totally forgotten about looking for another job.

Catherine's relationship with Fraser was still on a very impersonal level, but she knew him well enough now to realize that his aloofness was not unfriendliness. It was a dignity, a wall of reserve that served as a shield against the world. Catherine had a feeling that Fraser was really very lonely. His job called for him to be gregarious, but she sensed that by nature he was a solitary man. She also sensed that William Fraser was out of her league. *For that matter so is most of male America,* she decided.

She double-dated with Susie every now and then but found most of her escorts were married sexual athletes, and she preferred to go to a movie or the theater alone. She saw Gertrude Lawrence and a new comedian named Danny Kaye in *Lady in the Dark,* and *Life with Father,* and *Alice in Arms,* with a young actor named Kirk Douglas. She loved *Kitty Foyle* with Ginger Rogers because it reminded her of herself. One night at a performance of *Hamlet* she saw Fraser sitting in a box with an exquisite girl in an expensive white evening gown that Catherine had seen in *Vogue.* She had no idea who the girl was. Fraser made his own personal dates, and she never knew where he was going or with whom. He looked across the theater and saw her. The next morning he made no reference to it until he had finished the morning's dictation.

"How did you like *Hamlet?*" he asked.

"The play's going to make it, but I didn't care much for the performances."

"I liked the actors," he said. "I thought the girl who played Ophelia was particularly good."

Catherine nodded and started to leave.

"Didn't you like Ophelia?" Fraser persisted.

"If you want my honest opinion," Catherine said carefully, "I didn't think she was able to keep her head above water." She turned and walked out.

When Catherine arrived at the apartment that night, Susie was waiting for her. "You had a visitor," Susie said.

"Who?"

"An FBI man. They're investigating you."

My God, thought Catherine. *They found out I'm a virgin, and there's probably some kind of law against it in Washington.* Aloud she said, "Why would the FBI be investigating me?"

"Because you're working for the government now."

"Oh."

"How's your Mr. Fraser?"

"My Mr. Fraser's just fine," Catherine said.

"How do you think he'd like me?"

Catherine studied her tall, willowy brunette roommate. "For breakfast."

As the weeks went by Catherine became acquainted with the other secretaries working in nearby offices. Several of the girls were having affairs with their bosses, and it did not seem to matter to them whether the men were married or single. They envied Catherine's working for William Fraser.

"What's Golden Boy really like?" one of them asked Catherine one day at lunch. "Has he made a pass at you yet?"

"Oh, he doesn't bother with that," Catherine said earnestly. "I just come in at nine o'clock every morning, we roll around on the couch until one o'clock, then we break for lunch."

"Seriously, how do you find him?"

"Resistible," Catherine lied. Her feelings toward William Fraser had mellowed considerably since their first quarrel. He had told her the truth when he said he was a perfectionist. Whenever she made a mistake, she was reprimanded for it, but she had found him to be fair and understanding. She had watched him take time out from his own problems to help other people, people who could do nothing for him, and he always arranged it so that he never took credit for it. Yes, she liked William Fraser very much indeed, but that was no one's business but her own.

Once when they had had a great deal of work to catch up on, Fraser had asked Catherine to have dinner with him at his home so that they could work late. Talmadge, Fraser's chauffeur, was waiting with the limousine in front of the building. Several secretaries coming out of the building watched with knowing eyes as Fraser ushered Catherine into the back seat of the car and slid in next to her. The limousine glided smoothly into the late afternoon traffic.

"I'm going to ruin your reputation," Catherine said.

Fraser laughed. "I'll give you some advice. If you ever want to have an affair with a public figure, do it out in the open."

"What about catching cold?"

He grinned. "I meant, take your paramour—if they still use that word—out to public places, well-known restaurants, theaters."

"Shakespearean plays?" Catherine asked innocently.

Fraser ignored it. "People are always looking for devious motives. They'll say to themselves, 'Uh-huh, he's taking so-and-so out in public. I wonder who he's seeing secretly.' People never believe the obvious."

"It's an interesting theory."

"Arthur Conan Doyle wrote a story based on deceiving people with the obvious," Fraser said. "I don't recall the name of it."

"It was Edgar Allen Poe. 'The Purloined Letter.'" The moment Catherine said it, she wished she hadn't.

Men did not like smart girls. But then what did it matter? She was not his girl, she was his secretary.

They rode the rest of the way in silence.

Fraser's home in Georgetown was something out of a picture book. It was a four-story Georgian house that must have been over two hundred years old. The door was opened by a butler in a white jacket. Fraser said, "Frank, this is Miss Alexander."

"Hello, Frank. We've talked on the phone," Catherine said.

"Yes, ma'am. It's nice to meet you, Miss Alexander."

Catherine looked at the reception hall. It had a beautiful old staircase leading to the second floor, its oak wood burnished to a sheen. The floor was marble, and overhead was a dazzling chandelier.

Fraser studied her face. "Like it?" he asked.

"Like it? Oh, yes!"

He smiled, and Catherine wondered if she had sounded too enthusiastic, like a girl who was attracted by wealth, like one of those aggressive females who were always chasing him. "It's . . . it's pleasant," she added lamely.

Fraser was looking at her mockingly, and Catherine had the terrible feeling that he could read her thoughts. "Come into the study."

Catherine followed him into a large book-lined room done in dark paneling. It had an aura of another age, the graciousness of an easier, friendlier way of life.

Fraser was studying her. "Well?" he asked gravely.

Catherine was not going to be caught again. "It's smaller than the Library of Congress," she said, defensively.

He laughed aloud. "You're right."

Frank came into the room carrying a silver ice bucket. He set it on top of the bar in the corner. "What time would you like dinner, Mr. Fraser?"

"Seven-thirty."

"I'll tell the cook." Frank left the room.

"What may I fix you to drink?"

"Nothing, thank you."

He looked over at her. "Don't you drink, Catherine?"

"Not when I'm working," she said. "I get my *p*'s and *o*'s mixed up."

"You mean *p*'s and *q*'s, don't you?"

"*P*'s and *o*'s. They're next to each other on the typewriter."

"I didn't know."

"You're not supposed to. That's why you pay me a king's ransom every week."

"What do I pay you?" Fraser asked.

"Thirty dollars and dinner in the most beautiful house in Washington."

"You're sure you won't change your mind about that drink?"

"No, thank you," Catherine said.

Fraser mixed a martini for himself, and Catherine wandered around the room looking at the books. There were all the traditional classic titles and, in addition, a whole section of books in Italian and another section in Arabic.

Fraser walked over to her side. "You don't really speak Italian and Arabic, do you?" Catherine asked.

"Yes. I lived in the Middle East for a few years and learned Arabic."

"And the Italian?"

"I went with an Italian actress for a while."

Her face flushed. "I'm sorry. I didn't mean to pry."

Fraser looked at her, his eyes filled with amusement, and Catherine felt like a schoolgirl. She was not sure whether she hated William Fraser or loved him. Of one thing she was sure. He was the nicest man she had ever known.

Dinner was superb. All the dishes were French with divine sauces. The dessert was Cherries Jubilee. No wonder Fraser worked out at the club three mornings a week.

"How is it?" Fraser asked her.

"It's not like the food in the commissary," she said and smiled.

Fraser laughed. "I must eat in the commissary one day."

"I wouldn't if I were you."

He looked at her. "Food that bad?"

"It's not the food. It's the girls. They'd mob you."

"What makes you think so?"

"They talk about you all the time."

"You mean they ask questions about me?"

"I'll say," she grinned.

"I imagine when they're through, they must feel frustrated by the lack of information."

She shook her head. "Wrong. I make up all kinds of stories about you."

Fraser was leaning back in his chair, relaxing over a brandy. "What kind of stories?"

"Are you sure you want to hear?"

"Positive."

"Well, I tell them that you're an ogre and that you scream at me all day long."

He grinned. "Not *all* day long."

"I tell them that you're a nut about hunting and that you carry a loaded rifle around the office while you dictate and I'm constantly afraid that it'll go off and kill me."

"That must hold their interest."

"They're having a fine time trying to figure out the real you."

"Have you figured out the real me?" Fraser's tone had become serious.

She looked into his bright blue eyes for a moment, then turned away. "I think so," she said.

"Who am I?"

Catherine felt a sudden tension within her. The bantering was over and a new note had crept into the conversation. An exciting note, a disturbing note. She did not answer.

Fraser looked at her for a moment, then smiled. "I'm a dull subject. More dessert?"

"No, thank you. I won't eat again for a week."

"Let's go to work."

They worked until midnight. Fraser saw Catherine to the door, and Talmadge was waiting outside to drive her back to the apartment.

She thought about Fraser all the way home. His strength, his humor, his compassion. Someone had once said that a man had to be very strong before he could allow himself to be gentle. William Fraser was very strong. This evening had been one of the nicest evenings of Catherine's life and it worried her. She was afraid that she might turn into one of those jealous secretaries who sits around the office all day hating every girl who telephones her boss. Well, she was not going to allow that to happen. Every eligible female in Washington was throwing herself at Fraser's head. She was not going to join the crowd.

When Catherine returned to the apartment, Susie was waiting up for her. She pounced on Catherine the moment she came in.

"Give!" Susie demanded. "What happened?"

"Nothing happened," Catherine replied. "We had dinner."

Susie stared at her incredulously. "Didn't he even make a pass at you?"

"No, of course not."

Susie sighed. "I should have known it. He was afraid to."

"What do you mean by that?"

"What I mean by that, sweetie, is that you come off like the Virgin Mary. He was probably afraid if he laid a finger on you, you'd scream 'rape' and faint dead away."

Catherine felt her cheeks redden. "I'm not interested in him that way," she said stiffly. "And I don't come off like the Virgin Mary." *I come off like the Virgin*

Catherine. Dear old Saint Catherine. All she had done was to move her holy headquarters to Washington. Nothing else had changed. She was still doing business at the same old church.

During the next six months Fraser was away a good deal. He made trips to Chicago and San Francisco and to Europe. There was always enough work to keep Catherine busy, and yet the office seemed lonely and empty with Fraser gone.

There was a constant stream of interesting visitors, most of them men, and Catherine found herself barraged with invitations. She had her choice of lunches, dinners, trips to Europe and bed. She accepted none of the invitations, partly because she was not interested in any of the men but mostly because she felt that Fraser would not approve of her mixing business with pleasure. If Fraser was aware of the constant opportunities she declined, he said nothing. The day after she had had dinner with him at his home he had given her a ten-dollar-a-week raise.

It seemed to Catherine that there was a change in the tempo of the city. People were moving faster, becoming more tense. The headlines screamed of a constant series of invasions and crises in Europe. The fall of France had affected Americans more deeply than the other swift-moving events in Europe, for they felt a sense of personal violation, a loss of liberty in a country that was one of the cradles of Liberty.

Norway had fallen, England was fighting for its life in the battle of Britain and a pact had been signed between Germany, Italy and Japan. There was a growing feeling of inevitability that America was going to get into the war. Catherine asked Fraser about it one day.

"I think it's just a question of time before we get involved," he said thoughtfully. "If England can't stop Hitler, we're going to have to."

"But Senator Borah says . . ."

"The symbol of the America Firsters should be an ostrich," Fraser commented angrily.

"What will you do if there's a war?"

"Be a hero," he said.

Catherine visualized him handsome in an officer's uniform going off to war, and she hated the idea. It seemed stupid to her that in this enlightened age people should still think they could solve their differences by murdering one another.

"Don't worry, Catherine," Fraser said. "Nothing will happen for a while. And when it does happen, we'll be ready for it."

"What about England?" she asked. "If Hitler decides to invade, will it be able to stand up against him? He has so many tanks and planes and they have nothing."

"They will have," Fraser assured her. "Very soon."

He had changed the subject, and they had gone back to work.

One week later the headlines were filled with the news of Roosevelt's new concept of lend-lease. So Fraser had known about it and had tried to reassure her without revealing any information.

The weeks went by swiftly. Catherine accepted an occasional date, but each time she found herself comparing her escort to William Fraser, and she wondered why she bothered going with anyone. She was aware that she had backed herself into a bad emotional corner, but she did not know how to get out of it. She told herself that she was merely infatuated with Fraser and would get over it, but meanwhile her feelings kept her from enjoying the company of other men because they all fell so far short of him.

Late one evening as Catherine was working, Fraser came back to the office unexpectedly after attending a play. She looked up, startled, as he walked in.

"What in hell are we running here?" he growled. "A slave ship?"

"I wanted to finish this report," she said, "so you

could take it with you to San Francisco tomorrow."

"You could have mailed it to me," he replied. He sat down in a chair opposite Catherine and studied her. "Don't you have better things to do with your evenings than get out dull reports?" he asked.

"I happened to be free this evening."

Fraser leaned back in the chair, folded his fingers together and dropped them under his chin, staring at her. "Do you remember what you said the first day you walked into this office?"

"I said a lot of silly things."

"You said you didn't want to be a secretary. You wanted to be my assistant."

She smiled. "I didn't know any better."

"You do now."

She looked up at him. "I don't understand."

"It's very simple, Catherine," he said quietly. "For the past three months, you've really been my assistant. Now I'm going to make it official."

She stared at him, unbelievingly. "Are you sure that you . . . ?"

"I didn't give you the title or a salary raise sooner because I didn't want it to scare you. But now you know you can do it."

"I don't know what to say," Catherine stammered. "I—you won't be sorry, Mr. Fraser."

"I'm sorry already. My assistants always call me Bill."

"Bill."

Later that night as Catherine lay in bed, she remembered how he had looked at her and how it had made her feel, and it was a long time before she was able to go to sleep.

Catherine had written to her father several times asking him when he was coming to Washington to visit her. She was eager to show him around the city and introduce him to her friends and to Bill Fraser. She had received no reply to her last two letters. Worried, she telephoned her uncle's house in Omaha. Her uncle answered the phone.

"Cathy! I—I was just about to call you."

Catherine's heart sank.

"How's father?"

There was a brief pause.

"He's had a stroke. I wanted to call you sooner but your father asked me to wait until he was better."

Catherine gripped the receiver.

"Is he better?"

"I'm afraid not, Cathy," her uncle's voice said. "He's paralyzed."

"I'm on my way," Catherine said.

She went in to Bill Fraser and told him the news.

"I'm sorry," Fraser said. "What can I do to help?"

"I don't know. I want to go to him right away, Bill."

"Of course." And he picked up a telephone and began to make calls. His chauffeur drove Catherine to her apartment, where she threw some clothes into a suitcase, and then took her to the airport, where Fraser had arranged a plane reservation for her.

When the plane landed at the Omaha airport, Catherine's aunt and uncle were there to meet her, and one look at their faces told her that she was too late. They drove in silence to the funeral parlor and as Catherine entered the building she was filled with an ineffable sense of loss, of loneliness. A part of her had died and could never be recovered. She was ushered into the small chapel. Her father's body was lying in a simple coffin wearing his best suit. Time had shrunk him, as though the constant abrasion of living had worn him down and made him smaller. Her uncle had handed Catherine her father's personal effects, the accumulations and treasures of a lifetime, and they consisted of fifty dollars in cash, some old snapshots, a few receipted bills, a wristwatch, a tarnished silver penknife and a collection of her letters to him, neatly tied with a

piece of string and dog-eared from constant reading. It
was a pitiful legacy for any man to have left, and
Catherine's heart broke for her father. His dreams
were so big and his successes so small. She remembered how alive and vital he had been when she was a
little girl and the excitement when he came home from
the road with his pockets full of money and his arms
full of presents. She remembered his wonderful inventions that never quite worked. It wasn't much to
remember, but it was all there was left of him. There
were suddenly so many things Catherine wanted to say
to him, so much she wanted to do for him; and it
would always be too late.

They buried her father in the small graveyard next
to the church. Catherine had planned on spending the
night with her aunt and uncle and taking the train back
the next day, but suddenly she could not bear to stay a
moment longer, and she called the airport and made a
reservation on the next plane to Washington. Bill
Fraser was at the airport to meet her, and it seemed
the most natural thing in the world for him to be there,
waiting for her, taking care of her when she needed
him.

He took Catherine to an old country inn in Virginia
for dinner, and he listened while she talked about her
father. In the middle of telling a funny story about
him, Catherine began to cry, but strangely she felt no
embarrassment in front of Bill Fraser.

He suggested that Catherine take some time off, but
she wanted to keep busy, wanted to keep her mind
filled with anything but the death of her father. She
slipped into the habit of having dinner with Fraser once
or twice a week, and Catherine felt closer to him than
ever before.

It happened without any planning or forethought.
They had been working late at the office. Catherine
was checking some papers and sensed Bill Fraser
standing in back of her. His fingers touched her neck,
slowly and caressingly.

"Catherine . . ."

She turned to look up at him and an instant later she was in his arms. It was as though they had kissed a thousand times before, as though this was her past as well as her future, where she had always belonged.

It's this simple, Catherine thought. *It's always been this simple, but I didn't know it.*

"Get your coat, darling," Bill Fraser said. "We're going home."

In the car driving to Georgetown they sat close together, Fraser's arm around Catherine, gentle and protective. She had never known such happiness. She was sure she was in love with him, and it did not matter if he was not in love with her. He was fond of her, and she would settle for that. When she thought of what she had been willing to settle for before—Ron Peterson—she shuddered.

"Anything wrong?" Fraser asked.

Catherine thought of the motel room with the dirty cracked mirror. She looked at the strong intelligent face of the man with his arm around her. "Not now," she said gratefully. She swallowed. "I have to tell you something. I'm a virgin."

Fraser smiled and shook his head in wonder. "It's incredible," he said. "How did I wind up with the only virgin in the city of Washington?"

"I tried to correct it," Catherine said earnestly, "but it just didn't work out."

"I'm glad it didn't," Fraser said.

"You mean you don't mind?"

He was smiling at her again, a teasing grin that lit up his face. "Do you know your problem?" he asked.

"I'll say!"

"You've been worrying too much about it."

"I'll say!"

"The trick is to relax."

She shook her head gently.

"No, darling. The trick is to be in love."

Half an hour later the car pulled up in front of his

house. Fraser led Catherine inside to the library.

"Would you like a drink?"

She looked at him. "Let's go upstairs."

He took her in his arms and kissed her hard. She held him fiercely, wanting to draw him into her. *If anything goes wrong tonight,* Catherine thought, *I'll kill myself. I really will kill myself.*

"Come on," he said. He took Catherine's hand.

Bill Fraser's bedroom was a large masculine-looking room with a Spanish highboy against one wall. At the far end of the room was an alcove with a fireplace and in front of it, a breakfast table. Against one wall was a large double bed. To the left was a dressing room and off that, a bathroom.

"Are you sure you wouldn't care for that drink?" Fraser asked.

"I don't need it."

He took her in his arms again and kissed her. She felt the male hardness of him, and a delicious warmth coursed through her body.

"I'll be back," he said.

Catherine watched him disappear into the dressing room. This was the nicest, most wonderful man she had ever known. She stood there thinking about him, then suddenly realized why he had left the room. He wanted to give her a chance to undress alone, so that she would not be embarrassed. Quickly Catherine began taking off her clothes. She stood there a minute later nude and looked down at her body and thought, *Good-bye, Saint Catherine.* She went over to the bed, pulled back the spread and crawled between the sheets.

Fraser walked in, wearing a cranberry moiré silk dressing gown. He came over to the bed and stared at her. Her black hair was fanned out against the white pillow, framing her beautiful face. It was all the more stirring because he knew that it was totally unplanned.

He slipped the robe off and moved into the bed beside her. She suddenly remembered.

"I'm not wearing anything," Catherine said. "Do you think I'll get pregnant?"

"Let's hope so."

She looked at him, puzzled, and opened her mouth to ask him what he meant, but he put his lips on hers and his hands began to move down her body, gently exploring, and she forgot everything except what was happening to her, her whole consciousness concentrated on one part of her body, feeling him try to enter her, hard and pulsing, forcing, an instant of sharp, unexpected pain, then sliding in, moving faster and faster, an alien body in her body, plunging deep inside her, moving with a rhythm that grew more and more frantic, and he said, "Are you ready?" She was not sure what she was supposed to be ready for, but she said, "Yes," and suddenly he cried, "Oh, Cathy!" and made one last sporadic thrust and lay still on top of her.

And it was all over, and he was saying, "Was it wonderful for you?" and she said, "Yes, it was wonderful," and he said, "It gets better as it goes along," and she was filled with joy that she was able to bring him this happiness, and she tried not to worry about what a disappointment it had been. Perhaps it was like olives. You had to acquire a taste for it. She lay in his arms, letting the sound of his voice wash over her, comforting her, and she thought *This is what is important, being together as two human beings, loving and sharing each other*. She had read too many lurid novels, heard too many promising love songs. She had been expecting too much. Or perhaps—and if this were true, she must face it—she was frigid. As though reading her thoughts, Fraser pulled her closer and said, "Don't worry if you're disappointed, darling. The first time is always traumatic."

When Catherine did not answer, Fraser raised himself up on an elbow and looked at her, concerned, and said, "How do you feel?"

"Fine," she said quickly. She smiled. "You're the best lover I ever had."

She kissed him and held him close, feeling warm and safe until finally the hard knot inside her began to dissolve, and a feeling of relaxation filled her, and she was content.

"Would you like a brandy?" he asked.

"No, thanks."

"I think I'll fix myself one. It isn't every night a man beds a virgin."

"Did you mind that?" she asked.

He looked at her with that strange, knowing look, started to say something and changed his mind. "No," he said. There was a note in his voice that she did not understand.

"Was I—?" she swallowed. "You know—all right?"

"You were lovely," he said.

"Truth?"

"Truth."

"Do you know why I almost didn't go to bed with you?" she asked.

"Why?"

"I was afraid that you wouldn't want to see me again."

He laughed aloud. "That's an old wives' tale fostered by nervous mothers who want to keep their daughters pure. Sex doesn't drive people apart, Catherine. It brings them closer together." And it was true. She had never felt so close to anyone. Outwardly she might look the same, but Catherine knew that she had changed.

The young girl who had come to this house earlier in the evening had vanished forever and in her place was a woman. William Fraser's woman. She had finally found the mysterious Holy Grail that she had been searching for. The quest was over.

Now even the FBI would be satisfied.

NOELLE
Paris: 1941

6

To some the Paris of 1941 was a cornucopia of riches and opportunity; to others it was a living hell. Gestapo had become a word of dread, and tales of their activities became a chief—if whispered—topic of conversation. The offenses against the French Jews, which had begun as almost a prankish breaking of a few shop windows, had been organized by the efficient Gestapo into a system of confiscation, segregation and extermination.

On May 29, a new ordinance had been issued. ". . . a six-pointed star with the dimensions of the palm of a hand and a black edge. It is to be made of yellow cloth and bear in black lettering the inscription JUDEN. It must be worn from the age of six visibly on the left side of the chest solidly sewn to the clothing."

Not all Frenchmen were willing to be stepped on by the German boot. The Maquis, the French underground resistance, fought cleverly and hard and when caught were put to death in ingenious ways.

A young Countess whose family owned a chateau outside Chartres was forced to quarter the officers of the local German Command in her downstairs rooms for six months, during which time she had five wanted members of the Maquis hidden on the upper floors of the chateau.

The two groups never met, but in three months the Countess' hair had turned completely white.

The Germans lived as befit the status of conquerors, but for the average Frenchman there was a shortage of everything except cold and misery. Cooking gas was rationed, and there was no heat. Parisians survived the winters by buying sawdust by the ton, storing it in one-half of their apartments and keeping the other half warm by means of special sawdust-burning stoves.

Everything was ersatz, from cigarettes and coffee to leather. The French joked that it did not matter what you ate; the taste was all the same. The French women—traditionally the most smartly dressed women in the world—wore shabby coats of sheepskin instead of wool and platform shoes of wood, so that the sound of women walking the streets of Paris resembled the clip-clop of horses' hooves.

Even baptisms were affected, for there was a shortage of sugar almonds, the traditional sweet for the baptismal ceremony, and candy shops displayed invitations to come in and register for sugar almonds. There were a few Renault taxis on the street, but the most popular form of transportation was the two-seater cabs with tandem bikes.

The theater, as always in times of prolonged crisis, flourished. People found escape from the crushing realities of everyday life in the movie houses and on the stages.

Overnight, Noelle Page had become a star. Jealous associates in the theater said that it was due solely to the power and talent of Armand Gautier, and while it was true that Gautier had launched her career, it is axiomatic among those who work in the theater that no one can make a star except the public, that faceless, fickle, adoring, mercurial arbiter of a performer's destiny. The public adored Noelle.

As for Armand Gautier, he bitterly regretted the part he had played in starting Noelle's career. Her need of him was now gone; all that held her to him was a whim, and he lived in constant dread of the day she would leave him. Gautier had worked in the theater most of his life, but he had never met anyone like Noelle. She was an insatiable sponge, learning everything he had to teach her and demanding more. It had been fantastic to watch the metamorphosis in her as she went from the halting, external beginnings of grasping a part to the self-assured inner mastery of the character. Gautier had known from the very beginning that Noelle was going to be a star—there was never any question about it—but what astonished him as he learned to know her better was that stardom was not her goal. The truth was that Noelle was not even interested in acting.

At first, Gautier simply could not believe it. Being a star was the top of the ladder, the *sine qua non*. But to Noelle acting was simply a stepping stone, and Gautier had not the faintest clue as to what her real goal was. She was a mystery, an enigma, and the deeper Gautier probed, the more the riddle grew, like the Chinese boxes that opened and revealed further boxes inside. Gautier prided himself on understanding people, particularly women, and the fact that he knew absolutely nothing about the woman he lived with and loved drove him frantic. He asked Noelle to marry him, and she said, "Yes, Armand," and he knew that she meant nothing by it, that it meant no more to her than her engagement to Philippe Sorel or God alone knew how many other men in her past life. He realized that the marriage would never take place. When Noelle was ready, she would move on.

Gautier was sure that every man who met her tried to persuade her to go to bed with him. He also knew from his envious friends that none of them had succeeded.

"You lucky son of a bitch," one of his friends had said, "You must be hung like *un taureau*. I offered her a yacht, her own chateau and a staff of servants in Cap d'Antibes, and she laughed at me."

Another friend, a banker, told him, "I have finally found the first thing money cannot buy."

"Noelle?"

The banker nodded. "That's right. I told her to

name her price. She was not interested. What is it you
have for her, my friend?"

Armand Gautier wished he knew.

Gautier remembered when he had found the first
play for her. He had read no more than a dozen pages
when he knew it was exactly what he was looking for.
It was a tour de force, a drama about a woman whose
husband had gone to war. A soldier appeared at her
home one day telling her that he was a comrade of her
husband with whom he had served on the Russian
Front. As the play developed, the woman fell in love
with the soldier, unaware that he was a psychopathic
killer and that her life was in danger. It was a great
acting role for the wife, and Gautier agreed to direct
it immediately, on condition that Noelle Page play the
lead. The backers were reluctant to star an unknown
but agreed to have her audition for them. Gautier hurried home to bring the news to Noelle. She had come
to him because she wanted to be a star and now he was
going to give her her wish. He told himself this would
bring them closer together, would make her really love
him. They would get married and he would possess
her, always.

But when Gautier had told her the news, Noelle had
merely looked up at him and said, "That is wonderful,
Armand, thank you." In exactly the same tone of voice
in which she might have thanked him for telling her the
correct time or lighting her cigarette.

Gautier watched her for a long moment, knowing
that in some strange way Noelle was sick, that some
emotion in her had either died, or had never been alive
and that no one would ever possess her. He knew this
and yet he could not really believe it, because what he
saw was a beautiful, affectionate girl who happily
catered to his every whim and asked for nothing in return. Because he loved her, Gautier put his doubts
aside, and they went to work on the play.

Noelle was brilliant at the audition and got the part

without question, as Gautier had known she would. When the play opened in Paris two months later, Noelle became, overnight, the biggest star in France. The critics had been prepared to attack the play and Noelle because they were aware that Gautier had put his mistress, an inexperienced actress, in the lead, and it was a situation too delicious for them to pass up. But she had completely captivated them. They searched for new superlatives to describe her performance and her beauty. The play was a complete sellout.

Every night after the performance, Noelle's dressing room was filled with visitors. She saw everyone: shoe clerks, soldiers, millionaires, shop girls, treating them all with the same patient courtesy. Gautier would watch in amazement. *It is almost as though she were a Princess receiving her subjects,* he thought.

Over a period of a year Noelle received three letters from Marseille. She tore them up, unopened, and finally they stopped coming.

In the spring, Noelle starred in a motion picture that Armand Gautier directed, and when it was released, her fame spread. Gautier marveled at Noelle's patience in giving interviews and being photographed. Most stars hated it and did it either to help increase their box office value or for reasons of ego. In Noelle's case, she was indifferent to both motivations. She would change the subject when Gautier questioned her about why she was willing to pass up a chance to rest in the South of France in order to stay in a cold, rainy Paris to do tiresome poses for *Le Matin, La Petite Parisienne* or *L'Illustration.* It was just as well, for Gautier would have been stunned if he had known her real reason. Noelle's motivation was very simple.

Everything she did was for Larry Douglas.

When Noelle posed for photographs, she visualized her former lover picking up a magazine and recognizing her picture. When she played a scene in a movie, she saw Larry Douglas sitting in a theater one night in some far-off country, watching her. Her work was a reminder to him, a message from the past, a signal that would one day bring him back to her; and that was all Noelle wanted, for him to come back to her, so that she could destroy him.

Thanks to Christian Barbet, Noelle had an ever-growing scrapbook on Larry Douglas. The little detective had moved from his shabby offices to a large, luxurious suite on the rue Richer, near the Folies-Bergère. The first time Noelle had gone to see him in his new offices, Barbet had grinned at her surprised expression and said, "I got it cheap. These offices were occupied by a Jew."

"You said you had some news for me," Noelle said curtly.

The smirk left Barbet's face. "Ah yes." He did have news. It was difficult getting information from England under the very nose of the Nazis, but Barbet had found ways. He bribed sailors on neutral ships to smuggle in letters from an agency in London. But that was only one of his sources. He appealed to the patriotism of the French underground, the humanity of the International Red Cross and the cupidity of black marketeers with overseas connections. To each of them he told a different story, and the flow of information kept coming in.

He picked up a report on his desk. "Your friend was shot down over the English Channel," he said without preamble. Out of the corner of his eye he watched Noelle's face, waiting for her aloof facade to crumble, taking enjoyment in the pain he was inflicting. But Noelle's expression never changed. She looked at him and said confidently, "He was rescued." Barbet stared at her and swallowed and answered reluctantly, "Well, yes. He was picked up by a British Rescue boat." And wondered how the devil she could have known.

Everything about this woman baffled him, and he hated her as a client and was tempted to drop her, but Barbet knew that that would have been stupid.

He had attempted once to make a pass at her, hinting that his services would be less expensive, but Noelle had rebuffed him in a manner that made him feel like a clumsy lout, and he would never forgive her for that. One day, Barbet promised himself quietly, one day this tight-assed bitch would pay.

Now, as Noelle stood in his office, a look of distaste on her beautiful face, Barbet hurriedly went on with the report, eager to get rid of her.

"His squadron has moved to Kirton, in Lincolnshire. They're flying Hurricanes and—" Noelle was interested in something else.

"His engagement to the Admiral's daughter," she said, "it's off, isn't it?"

Barbet looked up in surprise and mumbled, "Yes. She found out about some of his other women." It was almost as though Noelle had already seen the report. She had not, of course, but it did not matter. The bond of hatred that tied Noelle to Larry Douglas was so strong it seemed that nothing important could ever happen to him without her knowing it. Noelle took the report and left. When she returned home she read it over slowly, then carefully filed it among the other reports and locked it up where it could not be found.

One Friday night after a performance, Noelle was in her dressing room at the theater creaming off her makeup, when there was a knock at the door, and Marius, the elderly, crippled stage doorman, entered.

"Pardon, Miss Page, a gentleman asked me to bring these to you."

Noelle glanced up in the mirror and saw that he was carrying an enormous bouquet of red roses in an exquisite vase.

"Set it down there, Marius," Noelle said, and she watched as he carefully placed the vase of roses on a table.

It was late November and no one in Paris had seen roses for more than three months. There must have been four dozen of them, ruby red, long-stemmed, wet with dew. Curious, Noelle walked over and picked up the card. It read: "To the lovely Fräulein Page. Would you have supper with me? General Hans Scheider."

The vase that the flowers rested in was delft, intricately patterned and very expensive. General Scheider had gone to a great deal of trouble.

"He would like an answer," the stage doorman said.

"Tell him I never eat supper and take these home to your wife."

He stared at her in surprise. "But the General . . ."

"That is all."

Marius nodded his head, picked up the vase and hurried out. Noelle knew that he would rush to spread the story of how she had defied a German general. It had happened before with other German officials, and the French people regarded her as some kind of heroine. It was ridiculous. The truth of the matter was that Noelle had nothing against the Nazis, she was merely indifferent to them. They were not a part of her life or her plans, and she simply tolerated them, awaiting the day when they would return home. She knew that if she became involved with any Germans it would hurt her. Not now, perhaps, but it was not the present Noelle was concerned about; it was the future. She thought that the idea of the Third Reich ruling for one thousand years was *merde*. Any student of history knew that eventually all conquerors were conquered. In the meantime she would do nothing that would allow her fellow Frenchmen to turn on her when the Germans were finally ousted. She was totally untouched by the Nazi occupation and when the subject came up—as it constantly did—Noelle avoided any discussion about it.

Fascinated by her attitude, Armand Gautier often tried to draw her out on the subject.

"Don't you care that the Nazis have conquered France?" he would ask her.

"Would it matter if I cared?"

"That's not the point. If everyone felt as you do, we would be damned."

"We are damned anyway, are we not?"

"Not if we believe in free will. Do you think our life is ordained from the time we are born?"

"To some degree. We are given bodies, our birthplace and our station in life, but that does not mean that we cannot change. We can become anything we want to be."

"My point exactly. That is why we must fight the Nazis."

She looked at him. "Because God is on our side?"

"Yes," he replied.

"If there is a God," Noelle answered reasonably, "and He created them, then He must be on their side, also."

In October, the first anniversary of Noelle's play, the backers gave a party for the cast at Tour d'Argent. There was a mixture of actors, bankers and influential businessmen. The guests were mostly French, but there were a dozen Germans at the party, a few of them in uniform, all of them except one with French girls. The exception was a German officer in his forties, with a long, lean intelligent face, deep green eyes and a trim, athletic body. A narrow scar ran from his cheekbone to his chin. Noelle was aware that he had been watching her all evening although he had not come near her.

"Who is that man?" she casually asked one of the hosts.

He glanced over at the officer who was sitting alone at a table sipping champagne, then turned to Noelle in surprise. "It is strange you should ask. I thought he was a friend of yours. That is General Hans Scheider. He is on the General Staff." Noelle remembered the roses and the card. "Why did you think he was a friend of mine?" she asked.

The man appeared flustered. "I naturally assumed . . . I mean, every play and motion picture produced in France must be approved by the Germans. When the censor tried to stop your new movie from being made, the General personally stepped in and gave his approval."

At that moment Armand Gautier brought someone to meet Noelle and the conversation changed.

Noelle paid no further attention to General Scheider.

The next evening when she arrived at her dressing room, there was one rose in a small vase with a little card that said: "Perhaps we should start smaller. May I see you? Hans Scheider."

Noelle tore up the note and threw the flower into the wastebasket.

After that night Noelle became aware that at almost every party she and Armand Gautier attended, General Scheider was there. He always remained in the background watching her. It happened too often to be a coincidence. Noelle realized that he must be going to a great deal of trouble to keep track of her movements and to get himself invitations to places where she would be.

She wondered why he was so interested, but it was an idle speculation and it did not really bother her. Occasionally Noelle would amuse herself by accepting an invitation and not showing up, then checking with the hostess the next day to see if General Scheider had been there. The answer was always "Yes."

Despite the swift and lethal punishment meted out by the Nazis to anyone who opposed them, sabotage continued to flourish in Paris. In addition to the Maquis there were dozens of small groups of freedom-loving French who risked their lives to fight the enemy with whatever weapons were at hand. They murdered German soldiers when they could catch them off guard, blew up supply trucks and mined bridges and trains. Their activities were denounced in the controlled daily press as deeds of infamy, but to the loyal French the deeds of infamy were glorious exploits. The name of one man kept cropping up in the newspapers—he was nicknamed *Le Cafard,* the cockroach, because he seemed to scurry around everywhere, and the Gestapo was unable to catch him. No one knew who he was.

Some believed that he was an Englishman living in Paris; another theory held that he was an agent of General De Gaulle, the leader of the Free French Forces; and some even said that he was a disaffected German. Whoever he was, drawings of cockroaches were beginning to spring up all over Paris, on buildings, sidewalks, and even inside German Army headquarters. The Gestapo was concentrating its efforts on catching him. Of one fact there was no doubt. *Le Cafard* had become an instant folk hero.

On a rainy afternoon in December, Noelle attended the opening of an art exhibition of a young artist whom she and Armand knew. The exhibit was held in a gallery on the rue du Faubourg-St.-Honoré. The room was crowded. Many celebrities were in attendance and photographers were everywhere. As Noelle walked around, moving from painting to painting, she felt someone touch her arm. She turned and found herself looking into the face of Madame Rose. It took Noelle a moment to recognize her. The familiar, ugly face was the same, and yet it seemed twenty years older, as though through some alchemy in time she had become her own mother. She wore a big black cape, and somewhere in the back of Noelle's consciousness was the fleeting thought that she was not wearing the prescribed yellow JUDEN star.

Noelle started to speak, but the older woman stopped her by squeezing her arm.

"Could you meet me?" she asked in a barely audible voice. "Les Deux Magots."

Before Noelle could reply, Madame Rose melted into the crowd, and Noelle was surrounded by photographers. As she posed and smiled for them, Noelle was remembering Madame Rose and her nephew, Israel Katz. They had both been kind to her in a time of need. Israel had saved her life twice. Noelle wondered what Madame Rose wanted. Money, probably.

Twenty minutes later Noelle slipped away and took

a taxi to the place St. Germain des Prés. It had been raining on and off all day, and now the rain had started to turn into a cold, driving sleet. As her taxi pulled up in front of Les Deux Magots and Noelle stepped out into the biting cold, a man in a raincoat and wide-brimmed hat appeared at her side out of nowhere. It took Noelle a moment to recognize him. Like his aunt, he looked older, but the change went deeper than that. There was an authority, a strength that had not been there before. Israel Katz was thinner than when she had last seen him, and his eyes were hollowed, as though he had not slept in days. Noelle noticed that he was not wearing the yellow six-pointed Jewish star.

"Let's get out of the rain," Israel Katz said.

He took Noelle's arm and led her inside. There were half a dozen customers in the café, all French. Israel led Noelle to a table in a back corner.

"Would you like something to drink?" he asked.

"No, thank you."

He took off his rain-soaked hat, and Noelle studied his face. She knew instantly that he had not called her here to ask for money. He was watching her.

"You're still beautiful, Noelle," he said quietly. "I've seen all of your movies and plays. You're a great actress."

"Why didn't you ever come backstage?"

Israel hesitated, then grinned shyly. "I didn't want to embarrass you."

Noelle stared at him a moment before she realized what he meant. To her, "Juden" was just a word that appeared in newspapers from time to time, and it meant nothing in her life; but what must it be like to *live* that word, to be a Jew in a country sworn to wipe you out, exterminate you, particularly when it was your own motherland.

"I choose my own friends," Noelle replied. "No one tells me whom to see."

Israel smiled wryly. "Don't waste your courage," he

advised. "Use it where it can help."

"Tell me about you," she said.

He shrugged. "I live a very unglamorous life. I became a surgeon. I studied under Dr. Angibouste. Have you heard of him?"

"No."

"He's a great heart surgeon. He made me his protégé. Then the Nazis took away my license to practice medicine." He held up his beautifully sculptured hands and examined them as though they belonged to someone else. "So I became a carpenter."

She looked at him for a long moment. "Is that all?" she asked.

Israel studied her in surprise. "Of course," he said. "Why?"

Noelle dismissed the thought at the back of her mind.

"Nothing. Why did you want to see me?"

He leaned closer to her and lowered his voice. "I need a favor. A friend—"

At that moment, the door opened and four German soldiers in gray-green uniforms walked into the bistro, led by a corporal. The corporal called out in a loud voice: "*Achtung!* We wish to see your identity papers."

Israel Katz stiffened, and it was as though a mask fell into place. Noelle saw his right hand slide into the pocket of his overcoat. His eyes flickered toward the narrow passageway that led to an exit in the rear, but one of the soldiers was already moving toward it, blocking it. Israel said in a low urgent voice, "Get away from me. Walk out the front door. Now."

"Why?" Noelle demanded.

The Germans were examining the identification papers of some customers at a table near the entrance.

"Don't ask questions," he commanded. "Just go."

Noelle hesitated a moment, then rose to her feet and started toward the door. The soldiers were moving on to the next table. Israel had pushed his chair back to give himself more freedom. The movement attracted the attention of two of the soldiers. They walked over to him.

"Identity papers."

Somehow Noelle knew that it was Israel the soldiers were looking for and that he was going to try to escape and they would kill him. He had no chance.

She turned and called out to him, "François! We are going to be late for the theater. Pay the check and let's go."

The soldiers looked at her in surprise. Noelle started back toward the table.

Corporal Schultz moved to face her. He was a blond, apple-cheeked boy in his early twenties. "Are you with this man, Fräulein?" he asked.

"Of course I am! Haven't you anything better to do than pester honest French citizens?" Noelle demanded, angrily.

"I am sorry, my good Fräulein, but . . ."

"I am not your good Fräulein!" Noelle snapped. "I am Noelle Page. I am starring at the Variétés Théâtre, and this man is my costar. Tonight, when I am having supper with my dear friend, General Hans Scheider, I shall inform him of your behavior this afternoon and he will be furious with you."

Noelle saw the look of recognition come into the corporal's eyes, but whether it was a recognition of her name or General Scheider's, she could not be sure.

"I—I am sorry, Fräulein," he stammered. "Of course I recognize you." He turned to Israel Katz, who sat there silently, his hand in his coat pocket. "I do not recognize this gentleman."

"You would if you barbarians ever went to the theater," said Noelle with stinging contempt. "Are we under arrest or may we leave?"

The young corporal was aware of everyone's eyes on him. He had to make an instant decision. "Of course the Fräulein and her friend are not under arrest," he said. "I apologize if I have inconvenienced you. I—"

Israel Katz looked up at the soldier and said coolly, "It's raining outside, Corporal. I wonder if one of your men could find us a taxi."

"Of course. At once."

Israel got into the taxi with Noelle, and the German corporal stood in the rain watching as they drove away. When the taxi stopped for a traffic light three blocks away, Israel opened the door, squeezed Noelle's hand once and disappeared without a word into the night.

At seven o'clock that evening when Noelle walked into her theater dressing room, there were two men waiting for her. One of them was the young German corporal from the bistro that afternoon. The other was in mufti. He was an albino, completely hairless, with pink eyes, and he somehow reminded Noelle of an unformed baby. He was in his thirties, with a moon face. His voice was high-pitched and almost laughably feminine, but there was an ineffable quality, a deadliness about him that was chilling. "Miss Noelle Page?"

"Yes."

"I am Colonel Kurt Mueller, Gestapo. I believe you have met Corporal Schultz."

Noelle turned to the corporal, indifferently, "No, I don't believe I have."

"At the *kaffehause* this afternoon," the corporal said helpfully.

Noelle turned to Mueller. "I meet so many people."

The colonel nodded. "It must be difficult to remember everyone when you have so many friends, Fräulein."

She nodded. "Exactly."

"For example, this friend you were with this afternoon." He paused, watching Noelle's eyes. "You told Corporal Schultz that he is starring in the show with you?"

Noelle looked at the Gestapo man in surprise. "The

corporal must have misunderstood me."

"Nein, Fräulein," the corporal replied indignantly, "You said . . ."

The colonel turned to give him a freezing look, and the corporal's mouth snapped closed in mid-sentence.

"Perhaps," said Kurt Mueller amiably. "This kind of thing can happen so easily when one is trying to communicate in a foreign language."

"That is true," said Noelle quickly.

Out of the corner of her eye she saw the corporal's face redden with anger, but he kept his mouth shut.

"I'm sorry to have troubled you over nothing," Kurt Mueller said.

Noelle felt her shoulders relax and she suddenly realized how tense she had been.

"That's perfectly all right," she said. "Perhaps I can give you tickets for the play."

"I have seen it," the Gestapo man said, "and Corporal Schultz has already bought his ticket. But thank you."

He started toward the door, then paused. "When you called Corporal Schultz a barbarian, he decided to buy a ticket this evening to see your performance. When he looked at the actors' photographs in the lobby, he did not see the picture of your friend from the *kaffehause*. That is when he called me."

Noelle's heart began to beat faster.

"Just for the record, Mademoiselle. If he was not your costar, who was he?"

"A—a friend."

"His name?" The high-pitched voice was still soft, but it had become dangerous.

"What difference does it make?" Noelle asked.

"Your friend answers the description of a criminal we are looking for. He was reported seen in the vicinity of the place St. Germain des Prés this afternoon."

Noelle stood watching him, her mind racing.

"What is the name of your friend?" Colonel Mueller's voice was insistent.

"I—I don't know."

"Ah, then he was a stranger?"

"Yes."

He stared at her, his cold pink eyes drilling into hers. "You were sitting with him. You stopped the soldiers from looking at his papers. Why?"

"I felt sorry for him," Noelle said. "He came up to me . . ."

"Where?"

Noelle thought quickly. Someone could have seen them going into the bistro together. "Outside the café. He told me that the soldiers were looking for him because he had stolen some groceries for his wife and children. It seemed such a minor crime that I . . ." She looked up at Mueller appealingly, "I helped him."

Mueller studied her a moment and nodded his head admiringly. "I can understand why you are such a big star." The smile died from his face, and when he spoke again his voice was even softer. "Let me give you some advice, Mademoiselle Page. We wish to be on good terms with you French. We want you to be our friends as well as our allies. But anyone who helps our enemy becomes our enemy. We will catch your friend, Mademoiselle, and when we do, we will question him, and I promise you he will talk."

"I have nothing to be afraid of," Noelle said.

"You are wrong." She could barely hear him. "You have me to be afraid of." Colonel Mueller nodded to the corporal and started toward the door again. He turned once more. "If you hear from your friend, you will report it to me at once. If you fail to do so . . ." He smiled at her. And the two men were gone.

Noelle sank into a chair, drained. She was aware that she had not been convincing, but she had been caught completely off guard. She had been so sure that the incident had been forgotten. She remembered now some of the stories she had heard about the Gestapo, and a small chill went through her. Supposing they caught Israel Katz and he did talk. He could tell them that they were old friends, that Noelle had lied about not knowing him. But surely that could not be important. Unless . . . the name she had thought of in the restaurant popped into her mind again. *Le Cafard*.

Half an hour later when Noelle went on stage, she managed to put everything out of her mind but the character she was playing. It was an appreciative audience and as she took her curtain calls, she received a tremendous ovation. She could still hear the applause as she walked back to her dressing room and opened the door. Seated in a chair was General Hans Scheider. He rose to his feet as Noelle entered and said politely, "I was informed that we have a supper date this evening."

They had supper at Le Fruit Perdu along the Seine, about twenty miles outside of Paris. They had been driven there by the General's chauffeur in a shiny, black limousine. The rain had stopped, and the night was cool and pleasant. The General had made no reference to the day's incident until they had finished eating. Noelle's first impulse had been not to go with him, but she decided that it was necessary to learn how much the Germans really knew and how much trouble she might be in.

"I received a call from Gestapo headquarters this afternoon," General Scheider was saying. "They informed me that you told a Corporal Schultz that you were having supper with me this evening." Noelle watched him, saying nothing. He went on. "I decided that it would be most unpleasant for you if I said 'No,' and most pleasant for me if I said 'Yes.' " He smiled. "So here we are."

"This is all so ridiculous," Noelle protested. "Helping a poor man who stole some groc—"

"Don't!" The General's voice was sharp. Noelle looked at him in surprise. "Don't make the mistake of believing that all Germans are fools. And do not underestimate the Gestapo."

Noelle said, "They have nothing to do with me, General."

He toyed with the stem of his wine glass. "Colonel Mueller suspects you of having helped a man he wants very badly. If that is true, you are in a great deal of trouble. Colonel Mueller neither forgives nor forgets." He looked at Noelle. "On the other hand," he said carefully, "if you should not see your friend again, this whole thing could simply blow over. Would you like a cognac?"

"Please," Noelle said.

He ordered two Napoleon brandies. "How long have you been living with Armand Gautier?"

"I am sure you know the answer to that," Noelle replied.

General Scheider smiled. "As a matter of fact, I do. What I really wanted to ask you is why you refused to have dinner with me before. Was it because of Gautier?"

Noelle shook her head. "No."

"I see," he said stiffly. There was a note in his voice that surprised her.

"Paris is full of women," Noelle said. "I am sure you could have your pick."

"You don't know me," the General said quietly, "or you wouldn't have said that." He sounded embarrassed. "I have a wife and child in Berlin. I love them very much, but I have been away from them for more than a year now, and I have no idea when I will see them again."

"Who forced you to come to Paris?" Noelle asked cruelly.

"I was not making a bid for sympathy. I just wanted to explain myself a little. I am not a promiscuous man. The first time I saw you on the stage," he said, "something happened to me. I felt I wanted to know you very much. I would like us to be good friends."

There was a quiet dignity about the way he spoke.

"I can promise nothing," Noelle said.

He nodded. "I understand."

But of course he did not. Because Noelle intended never to see him again. General Scheider tactfully changed the conversation and they talked of acting and the theater, and Noelle found him surprisingly knowledgeable. He had an eclectic mind and a deep intelligence. Casually he ranged from topic to topic, pointing out the mutual interests that the two of them shared. It was a skillful performance and Noelle was amused. He had gone to a great deal of trouble to learn about her background. He looked every inch the German General in his olive-green uniform, strong and authoritative, but there was a gentleness that bespoke another kind of man altogether, an intellectual quality that belonged to the scholar rather than the soldier. And yet there was the scar running across his face.

"How did you get your scar?" Noelle asked.

He ran his finger along the deep incision. "I was in a duel many years ago," he shrugged. "In German, we call this *wildfleisch*—it means 'proud skin.' "

They discussed the Nazi philosophy.

"We are not monsters," General Scheider stated. "And we have no wish to rule the world. But neither do we intend to sit still and be punished any longer for a war we lost more than twenty years ago. The Treaty of Versailles is a bondage that the German people have finally broken out of."

They spoke of the occupation of Paris. "It was not the fault of your French soldiers that it was so easy for us," General Scheider said. "A good deal of the responsibility must fall on the shoulders of Napoleon the Third."

"You're joking," Noelle replied.

"I am perfectly serious," he assured her. "In the days of Napoleon, the mobs were constantly using the tangled, twisted streets of Paris for barricades and ambushes against his soldiers. In order to stop them, he commissioned Baron Eugene Georges Haussmann to straighten out the streets and fill the city with nice, wide boulevards." He smiled. "The boulevards down which our troops marched. I am afraid history will not be kind to planner Haussmann."

After dinner, driving back to Paris, he asked, "Are you in love with Armand Gautier?"

His tone was casual, but Noelle had the feeling that her answer was important to him.

"No," she said slowly.

He nodded, satisfied. "I did not think so. I believe I could make you very happy."

"As happy as you make your wife?"

General Scheider stiffened for a moment as though he had been struck and then turned to look at Noelle.

"I can be a good friend," he said quietly. "Let us hope that you and I are never enemies."

When Noelle returned to the apartment, it was almost 3:00 A.M., and Armand Gautier was waiting for her in a state of agitation.

"Where the hell have you been?" he demanded, as she walked in the door.

"I had an engagement." Noelle's eyes moved past him into the room. It looked as though a cyclone had struck. Desk drawers were open and the contents strewn around the room. The closets had been ransacked, a lamp had been overturned and a small table lay on its side, one leg broken.

"What happened?" Noelle asked.

"The Gestapo was here! My God, Noelle, what have you been up to?"

"Nothing."

"Then why would they do this?"

Noelle began to move around the room, straightening the furniture, thinking hard. Gautier grabbed her shoulders and turned her around. "I want to know what's happening."

She took a deep breath. "All right."

She told him of the meeting with Israel Katz, leaving

out his name and the conversation later with Colonel Mueller. "I don't know that my friend is *Le Cafard,* but it is possible."

Gautier sank into a chair, stunned. "My God!" he exclaimed. "I don't care *who* he is! I don't want you to have anything more to do with him. We could both be destroyed because of this. I hate the Germans as much as you do . . ." He stopped, not sure whether Noelle hated the Germans or not. He began again, "Cherie, as long as the Germans are making the rules, we must live under them. Neither of us can afford to get involved with the Gestapo. This Jew—what did you say his name was?"

"I didn't say."

He looked at her a moment. "Was he your lover?"

"No, Armand."

"Does he mean anything to you?"

"No."

"Well, then." Gautier sounded relieved. "I don't think we have anything to worry about. They can't blame you if you had one accidental meeting with him. If you don't see him again, they'll forget the whole thing."

"Of course they will," Noelle said.

On the way to the theater the next evening, Noelle was followed by two Gestapo men.

From that day on Noelle was followed everywhere she went. It first began as a feeling, a premonition that she was being stared at. Noelle would turn and see in a crowd a young Teutonic-looking man in civilian clothes who seemed to be paying no attention to her. Later, the feeling would return, and this time it would be another young Teutonic-looking man. It was always someone different and though they were in plain clothes, they wore a uniform that was distinctively theirs: an attitude of contempt, superiority and cruelty, and the emanations were unmistakable.

Noelle said nothing to Gautier about what was happening for she saw no point in alarming him any further. The incident with the Gestapo in the apartment had made him very nervous. He could talk of nothing but what the Germans could do to both his and Noelle's career if they wished to, and Noelle was aware that he was right. One had only to look at the daily newspapers to know that the Nazis showed no mercy to their enemies. There had been several telephone messages from General Scheider, but Noelle had ignored them. If she did not want the Nazis as an enemy, neither did she want them as a friend. She decided that she would remain like Switzerland: neutral. The Israel Katzes of the world would have to take care of themselves. Noelle was mildly curious about what he had wanted from her, but she had no intention of getting involved.

Two weeks after Noelle had seen Israel Katz, the newspapers carried a front-page story that the Gestapo had caught a group of saboteurs headed by *Le Cafard*. Noelle read all the stories carefully, but nothing was mentioned about whether *Le Cafard* himself had been captured. She remembered Israel Katz's face when the Germans had started to close in on him, and she knew that he would never let them take him alive. *Of course,* Noelle told herself, *it could be my fantasy. He is probably a harmless carpenter, as he said.* But if he was harmless, why was the Gestapo so interested in him? Was he *Le Cafard*? And had he been captured, or had he escaped? Noelle walked over to the window of her apartment that faced on the Avenue Martigny. Two black rain-coated figures stood under a streetlamp, waiting. For what? Noelle began to feel the sense of alarm that Gautier felt, but with it came a feeling of anger. She remembered Colonel Mueller's words: *You have me to be afraid of.* It was a challenge. Noelle had the feeling she was going to hear from Israel Katz again.

The message came the next morning from—of all

the unlikely people—her concierge. He was a small, rheumy-eyed man in his seventies, with a wizened, leathery face and no lower teeth, so that it was difficult to understand him when he spoke. When Noelle rang for the elevator he was waiting inside. They rode down together, and as they neared the lobby, he mumbled, "The birthday cake you ordered is ready at the bakery at rue de Passy."

Noelle stared at him a moment, not sure whether she had heard him correctly, then said, "I didn't order any cake."

"Rue de Passy," he repeated stubbornly.

And Noelle suddenly understood. Even then, she would have done nothing about it if she had not seen the two Gestapo agents waiting for her across the street. To be followed around like a criminal! The two men were in conversation. They had not seen her yet. Angrily Noelle turned to the concierge and said, "Where is the service entrance?"

"This way, Mam'selle."

Noelle followed him through a back corridor, down a flight of stairs to the basement and out to an alley. Three minutes later she was in a taxi, on her way to meet Israel Katz.

The bakery was an ordinary-looking shop in a run-down, middle-class neighborhood. The lettering on the window read *BOULANGERIE,* and the letters were flaked and chipped. Noelle opened the door and stepped inside. She was greeted by a small dumpling of a woman in a spotless white apron.

"Yes, Mademoiselle?"

Noelle hesitated. There was still time to leave, still time to turn back and not get involved in something dangerous that was none of her business.

The woman was waiting.

"You—you have a birthday cake for me," Noelle said, feeling foolish at the game-playing, as though somehow the gravity of what was happening was demeaned by the childish artifices that were employed.

The woman nodded. "It is ready, Miss Page." She put a *CLOSED* sign on the door, locked it and said, "This way."

He was lying on a cot in the small back room of the bakery, his face a mask of pain, bathed in perspiration. The sheet twisted around him was soaked in blood, and there was a large tourniquet around his left knee.

"Israel."

He moved to face the door, and the sheet fell away, revealing a sodden pulp of mashed bone and flesh where his knee had been.

"What happened?" Noelle asked.

He tried to smile but did not quite make it. His voice was hoarse and strained with pain. "They stepped on *Le Cafard,* but we're not easy to kill."

So she had been correct. "I read about it," Noelle said. "Are you going to be all right?"

Israel took a deep painful breath and nodded. His words came in labored gasps.

"The Gestapo is turning Paris upside down looking for me. My only chance is to get out of the city. . . . If I can get to Le Havre, I have friends who will help me get on a boat out of the country."

"Can't you get a friend to drive you out of Paris?" Noelle asked. "You could hide in the back of a truck—"

Israel shook his head weakly. "Road blocks. Not a mouse can get out of Paris."

Not even *un Cafard,* Noelle thought. "Can you travel with that leg?" she asked, stalling for time, trying to come to a decision.

His lips tightened in the rictus of a smile.

"I'm not going to travel with this leg," Israel said.

Noelle looked at him, not understanding, and at that moment the door opened and a large, heavy-shouldered, bearded man entered. In his hand he carried an ax. He walked up to the bed and pulled back the sheet, and Noelle felt the blood drain from her face. She thought of General Scheider and the hairless albino from the Gestapo and what they would do to her if they caught her.

"I will help you," Noelle said.

CATHERINE
Washington-Hollywood: 1941

7

It seemed to Catherine Alexander that her life had entered a new phase, as though somehow she had climbed to some higher emotional level, a heady and exhilarating peak. When Bill Fraser was in town, they had dinner together every night and went to concerts or the theater or the opera. He found a small, charming apartment for her near Arlington. He wanted to pay her rent, but Catherine insisted on paying it herself. He bought her clothes and jewelry. She had resisted at first, embarrassed by some deeply ingrained Protestant ethic, but it had given Fraser such obvious pleasure that finally Catherine had stopped arguing about it.

Whether you like it or not, she thought, *you're a mistress.* It had always been a loaded word for her, filled with connotations of cheap, slinky women in backstreet apartments, living out lives of emotional frustration. But now that it was happening to her, Catherine found that it was not really like that at all. It just meant that she was sleeping with the man she loved. It did not feel dirty or sordid, it felt perfectly natural. *It's interesting,* she thought, *how the things that other people do seem so horrible, and yet when you're doing them they seem so right. When you are reading about the sexual experiences of someone else, it's* True Confessions, *but when it's you it's the* Ladies' Home Journal.

Fraser was a thoughtful and understanding companion, and it was as though they had been together always. Catherine could predict his reactions to almost any situation and knew his every mood. Contrary to what Fraser had said, sex with him did not become more exciting, but Catherine told herself that sex was only a small part of a relationship. She was not a schoolgirl who needed constant titillation, she was a mature woman. *Give or take a little,* she thought, wryly.

Fraser's advertising agency was being run in his absence by Wallace Turner, a senior account executive. William Fraser tried to have as little to do with the business as possible, so he could devote himself to his job in Washington, but whenever a major problem arose at the agency and they needed his advice, Fraser got in the habit of discussing it with Catherine, using her as a sounding board. He found that she had a natural flair for the business. Catherine often came up with ideas for campaigns that proved very effective.

"If I weren't so selfish, Catherine," Fraser said one night at dinner, "I'd put you in the agency and turn you loose on some of our accounts." He covered her hand with his. "I'd miss you too much," he added. "I want you here with me."

"I want to be here, Bill. I'm very happy with things the way they are." And it was true. She had thought that if she were ever in a situation like this, she would want desperately to get married, but somehow there seemed no urgency about it. In every important way they were already married.

One afternoon as Catherine was finishing some work, Fraser walked into her office.

"How would you like to take a drive out to the country tonight?" he asked.

"Love it. Where are we going?"

"To Virginia. We're having dinner with my parents."

Catherine looked up at him in surprise. "Do they know about us?" she asked.

"Not everything," he grinned. "Just that I have a

fantastic young assistant and I'm bringing her to dinner."

If she felt a pang of disappointment, she did not let it show on her face. "Fine," she said. "I'll stop by the apartment and change."

"I'll pick you up at seven o'clock."

"Date."

The Frasers' house, set in the beautiful rolling hills of Virginia, was a large Colonial farmhouse with sixty acres of vivid green grass and farmland surrounding it. The house dated back to seventeen hundred.

"I've never seen anything like it," Catherine marveled.

"It's one of the best breeding farms in America," Fraser informed her.

The car drove past a corral filled with beautiful horses, past the neatly kept paddocks and the caretaker's cottage.

"It's like another world," Catherine exclaimed. "I envy your growing up here."

"Do you think you'd like living on a farm?"

"This isn't exactly a farm," she said dryly. "It's more like owning your own country."

They had arrived in front of the house.

Fraser turned to her. "My mother and father are a little formal," he warned, "but there's nothing for you to worry about. Just be yourself. Nervous?"

"No," Catherine said. "Panicky." And as she said it, she realized with a sense of astonishment that she was lying. In the classic tradition of all girls about to meet the parents of the man they loved, she should have been petrified. But she felt nothing except curiosity. There was no time to wonder about that now. They were getting out of the car and a butler in full livery was opening the door, greeting them with a welcoming smile.

Colonel Fraser and his lady could have been living

out of the pages of an ante-bellum story book. The first thing that struck Catherine was how old and fragile-looking they were. Colonel Fraser was a pale carbon of what had once been a handsome, vital man. He reminded Catherine very strongly of someone, and with a shock, she realized who it was: an old, worn-out version of his son. The colonel had sparse white hair and walked with a painful stoop. His eyes were pale blue and his once-powerful hands were gnarled with arthritis. His wife had the look of an aristocrat and still retained traces of a girlish beauty. She was gracious and warm to Catherine.

In spite of what Fraser had told her, Catherine had the feeling that she was there for their inspection. The colonel and his wife spent the evening questioning her. They were very discreet but thorough. Catherine told them about her parents and her childhood, and when she talked about moving from school to school, she made it sound like adventurous fun, rather than the agony it had been. As she talked she could see Bill Fraser proudly beaming at her. Dinner was superb. They dined by candlelight in a large, old-fashioned dining room with a real marble fireplace and liveried servants. *Old silver, old money and old wine.* She looked at Bill Fraser and a wave of warm gratitude went through her. She had the feeling that this kind of life could be hers if she wanted it. She knew that Fraser loved her, and she loved him. And yet there was something missing: a sense of excitement. *Possibly,* she thought, *I'm expecting too much. I've probably been warped by Gary Cooper, Humphrey Bogart and Spencer Tracy! Love isn't a knight in shining armor. It's a gentleman farmer in a gray tweed suit. Damn all those movies and books!* As she looked at the colonel, she could see Fraser twenty years hence, looking exactly the same as his father. She was very quiet during the rest of the evening.

On the way home Fraser asked, "Did you enjoy the evening?"

"Very much. I liked your parents."

"They liked you, too."

"I'm glad." And she was. Except for the vaguely disquieting thought in the back of her mind that somehow she should have been more nervous about meeting them.

The following evening, while Catherine and Fraser were having dinner at the Jockey Club, Fraser told her that he had to go to London for a week. "While I'm gone," he said, "I have an interesting job for you. They've asked our office to supervise an Army Air Corps recruiting film they're shooting at MGM studios in Hollywood. I'd like you to handle the picture while I'm gone."

Catherine stared at him incredulously. "Me? I can't even load a Brownie. What do I know about making a training film?"

"About as much as anyone else," Fraser grinned. "It's all pretty new, but you don't have to worry. They'll have a producer and everything. The Army plans to use actors in the film."

"Why?"

"I guess they feel that soldiers won't be convincing enough to play soldiers."

"That sounds like the Army."

"I had a long talk with General Mathews this afternoon. He must have used the word 'glamour' a hundred times. That's what they want to sell. They're starting a big recruitment drive aimed at the elite young manhood of America. This is one of the opening guns."

"What do I have to do?" Catherine asked.

"Just see that everything runs smoothly. You'll have final approval. You have a reservation to Los Angeles on a nine A.M. plane tomorrow."

Catherine nodded. "All right."

"Will you miss me?"

"You know I will," she replied.

"I'll bring you a present."

"I don't want any presents. Just come back safely."

She hesitated. "The situation's getting worse, isn't it, Bill?"

He nodded. "Yes," he said. "I think we're going to be at war soon."

"How horrible."

"It's going to be even more horrible if we *don't* get into it," he said quietly. "England got out of Dunkirk by a miracle. If Hitler decides to cross the Channel now, I don't think the British can stop him." They finished their coffee in silence, and he paid the check.

"Would you like to come to the house and spend the night?" Fraser asked.

"Not tonight," Catherine said. "You have to get up early, and so do I."

"All right."

After he had dropped her off at her apartment and she was getting ready for bed, Catherine asked herself why she had not gone home with Bill on the eve of his departure.

She had no answer.

Catherine had grown up in Hollywood even though she had never been there. She had spent hundreds of hours in darkened theaters, lost in the magic dreams manufactured by the film capital of the world, and she would always be grateful for the joy of those happy hours.

When Catherine's plane landed at the Burbank airport, she was filled with excitement. A limousine was waiting to drive her to her hotel. As they drove down the sunny, broad streets, the first thing Catherine noticed was the palm trees. She had read about them and had seen pictures of them, but the reality was overwhelming. They were everywhere, stretching tall against the sky, the lower part of their graceful trunks bare and the upper part beautiful and verdant. In the center of each tree was a ragged circle of fronds, like a dirty petticoat, Catherine thought, hanging unevenly below a green tutu.

They drove by a huge building that looked like a factory. A large sign over the entrance said "Warner Bros." and under it, "Combining Good Pictures with Good Citizenship." As the car went past the gate, Catherine thought of James Cagney in *Strawberry Blond,* and Bette Davis in *Dark Victory* and smiled happily.

They passed the Hollywood Bowl, which looked enormous from the outside, turned off Highland Avenue and went west on Hollywood Boulevard. They passed the Egyptian Theater and two blocks to the west, Grauman's Chinese, and Catherine's spirits soared. It was like seeing two old friends. The driver swung down Sunset Boulevard and headed for the Beverly Hills Hotel. "You'll enjoy this hotel, miss. It's one of the best in the world."

It was certainly one of the most beautiful that Catherine had ever seen. It was just north of Sunset, in a semicircle of sheltering palm trees surrounded by large gardens. A graceful driveway curved up to the front door of the hotel, painted a delicate pink. An eager young assistant manager escorted Catherine to her room, which turned out to be a lavish bungalow on the grounds behind the main building of the hotel. There was a bouquet of flowers on the table with the compliments of the management and a larger, more beautiful bouquet with a card that read: "Wish I were there or you were here. Love, Bill." The assistant manager had handed Catherine three telephone messages. They were all from Allan Benjamin, whom she had been told was the producer of the training film. As Catherine was reading Bill's card, the phone rang. She ran to it, picked up the receiver and said eagerly, "Bill?" But it turned out to be Allan Benjamin.

"Welcome to California, Miss Alexander," his voice shrilled through the receiver. "Corporal Allan Benjamin, producer of this little clambake."

A corporal. She would have thought that they would have put a captain or a colonel in charge.

"We start shooting tomorrow. Did they tell you that we're using actors instead of soldiers?"

"I heard," Catherine replied.

"We start shooting at nine in the morning. If you could get here by about eight, I'd like to have you take a look at them. You know what the Army Air Corps wants."

"Right," said Catherine briskly. She had not the faintest idea what the Army Air Corps wanted, but she supposed that if one used common sense and picked out types that looked like they might be pilots, that would be sufficient.

"I'll have a car there for you at seven thirty A.M.," the voice was saying. "It'll only take you half an hour to get to Metro. It's in Culver City. I'll meet you on Stage Thirteen."

It was almost four o'clock in the morning before Catherine fell asleep, and it seemed the moment her eyes closed, the phone was ringing and the operator was telling her that a limousine was waiting for her.

Thirty minutes later Catherine was on her way to Metro-Goldwyn-Mayer.

It was the largest motion picture studio in the world. There was a main lot consisting of thirty-two sound stages, the enormous Thalberg Administration Building which housed Louis B. Mayer, twenty-five executives, and some of the most famous directors, producers and writers in show business. Lot two contained the large standing outdoor sets which were constantly redressed for various movies. Within a space of three minutes, you could drive past the Swiss Alps, a western town, a tenement block in Manhattan and a beach in Hawaii. Lot three on the far side of Washington Boulevard housed millions of dollars' worth of props and flat sets and was used to shoot outdoor spectacles.

All this was explained to Catherine by her guide, a young girl who was assigned to take her to Stage 13. "It's a city in itself," she was saying proudly. "We produce our own electricity, make enough food in the commissary to feed six thousand people a day and build all our own sets right on the back lot. We're completely self-sufficient. We don't need anybody."

"Except an audience."

As they walked along the street, they passed a castle that consisted of a facade with two by fours propping it up. Across from it was a lake, and down the block was the lobby of a San Francisco theater. No theater, just the lobby.

Catherine laughed aloud, and the girl stared at her.

"Is there anything wrong?" she asked.

"No," Catherine said. "Everything is wonderful."

Dozens of extras walked along the street, cowboys and Indians chatting amiably together as they walked toward the sound stages. A man appeared unexpectedly from around a corner and as Catherine stepped back to avoid him, she saw that he was a knight in armor. Behind him walked a group of girls in bathing suits. Catherine decided that she was going to like her brief fling in show business. She wished her father could have seen this. He would have enjoyed it so much.

"Here we are," the guide said. They were in front of a huge, gray building. A sign on the side of it said "STAGE 13."

"I'll leave you here. Will you be all right?"

"Fine," Catherine said. "Thank you."

The guide nodded and left. Catherine turned back to the sound stage. A sign over the door read: "DO NOT ENTER WHEN RED LIGHT IS ON." The light was off, so Catherine pulled the handle of the door and opened it. Or tried to. The door was unexpectedly heavy, and it took all her strength to get it open.

When she stepped inside, Catherine found herself confronted by a second door as heavy and massive as the first. It was like entering a decompression chamber.

Inside the cavernous sound stage, dozens of people were racing around, each one busy on some mysterious errand. A group of men were in Air Corps uniforms, and Catherine realized that they were the actors who would appear in the film. At a far corner of the sound stage was an office set complete with desk, chairs and a large military map hanging on the wall. Technicians were lighting the set.

"Excuse me," she said to a man passing by. "Is Mister Allan Benjamin here?"

"The little corporal?" He pointed. "Over there."

Catherine turned and saw a slight, frail-looking man in an ill-fitting uniform with corporal's stripes. He was screaming at a man wearing a general's stars.

"Fuck what the casting director said," he yelled. "I'm up to my ass in generals. I need non-coms." He raised his hands in despair. "Everybody wants to be a chief, nobody wants to be an Indian."

"Excuse me," said Catherine, "I'm Catherine Alexander."

"Thank God!" the little man said. He turned to the others, bitterness in his voice. "The fun and games are over, you smart-asses. Washington's here."

Catherine blinked. Before she could speak, the little corporal said, "I don't know what I'm doing here. I had a thirty-five-hundred-dollar-a-year job in Dearborn editing a furniture trade magazine, and I was drafted into the Signal Corps and sent to write training films. What do I know about producing or directing? This is the most disorganized mess I've ever seen." He belched and touched his stomach. "I'm getting an ulcer," he moaned, "and I'm not even in show business. Excuse me."

He turned and hurried toward the exit, leaving Catherine standing there. She looked around, help-lessly. Everyone seemed to be staring at her, waiting for her to do something.

A lean, gray-haired man in a sweater moved toward her, an amused smile on his face. "Need any help?" he asked quietly.

"I need a miracle," Catherine said frankly. "I'm in

charge of this, and I don't know what I'm supposed to be doing."

He grinned at her. "Welcome to Hollywood. I'm Tom O'Brien, the A.D."

She looked at him, quizzically.

"The assistant director. Your friend, the corporal, was supposed to direct it, but I have a feeling he won't be back." There was a calm assurance about the man which Catherine liked.

"How long have you worked at Metro-Goldwyn-Mayer?" she asked.

"Twenty-five years."

"Do you think you could direct this?"

She saw the corner of his lips twist. "I could try," he said gravely. "I've done six pictures with Willie Wyler." His eyes grew serious. "The situation isn't as bad as it looks," he said. "All it needs is a little organization. The script's written, and the set's ready."

"That's a beginning," Catherine said. She looked around the sound stage at the uniforms. Most of them were badly fitted, and the men wearing them looked ill at ease.

"They look like recruiting ads for the Navy," Catherine commented.

O'Brien laughed appreciatively.

"Where did these uniforms come from?"

"Western Costume. Our Wardrobe Department ran out. We're shooting three war pictures."

Catherine studied the men critically. "There are only half a dozen that are really bad," she decided. "Let's send them back and see if we can't do better."

O'Brien nodded approvingly. "Right."

Catherine and O'Brien walked over to the group of extras. The din of conversation on the enormous stage was deafening.

"Let's hold it down, boys," O'Brien yelled. "This is Miss Alexander. She's going to be in charge here."

There were a few appreciative whistles and cat calls.

"Thanks," Catherine smiled. "Most of you look fine, but a few of you are going to have to go back to Western Costume and get different uniforms. Let's line up, so we can take a good look at you."

"I'd like to take a good look at *you*. What are you doing for dinner tonight?" one of the men called.

"I'm having it with my husband," Catherine said, "right after his match."

O'Brien formed the men into a ragged line. Catherine heard laughter and voices nearby and turned in annoyance. One of the extras was standing next to a piece of scenery, talking to three girls who were hanging on his every word and giggling hysterically at everything he said. Catherine watched a moment, then walked over to the man and said, "Excuse me. Would you mind joining the rest of us?"

The man turned slowly. "Are you talking to me?" he asked lazily.

"Yes," Catherine said. "We'd like to go to work." She walked away.

He whispered something to the girls which drew a loud laugh, then slowly moved after Catherine. He was a tall man, his body lean and hard-looking, and he was very handsome, with blue-black hair and stormy dark eyes. His voice, when he spoke, was deep and filled with insolent amusement. "What can I do for you?" he asked Catherine.

"Do you want to work?" Catherine replied.

"I do, I do," he assured her.

Catherine had once read an article about extras. They were a strange breed of people, spending their anonymous lives on sound stages, lending background atmosphere to crowd scenes in which stars appeared. They were faceless, voiceless people, inherently too ambitionless to seek any kind of meaningful employment. The man in front of her was a perfect example. Because he was outrageously handsome, someone from his hometown had probably told him that he could be a star, and he had come to Hollywood, learned that talent was necessary as well as good looks and had settled for being an extra. The easy way out.

"We're going to have to change some of the uniforms," Catherine said patiently.

"Is there anything wrong with mine?" he asked.

Catherine took a closer look at his uniform. She had to admit that it fitted perfectly, emphasizing his broad shoulders but not exaggerating them, tapering in at his lean waist. She looked at his tunic. On his shoulders were the bars of a captain. Across his breast he had pinned on a splash of brightly colored ribbons.

"Are they impressive enough, Boss?" he asked.

"Who told you you were going to play a captain?"

He looked at her, seriously, "It was my idea. Don't you think I'd make a good captain?"

Catherine shook her head. "No. I don't."

He pursed his lips thoughtfully. "First lieutenant?"

"No."

"How about second lieutenant?"

"I don't really feel you're officer material."

His dark eyes were regarding her quizzically. "Oh? Anything else wrong?" he asked.

"Yes," she said. "The medals. You must be terribly brave."

He laughed. "I thought I'd give this damned film a little color."

"There's only one thing you forgot," Catherine said crisply. "We're not at war yet. You'd have had to win those at a carnival."

The man grinned at her. "You're right," he admitted sheepishly. "I didn't think of that. I'll take some of them off."

"Take them all off," Catherine said.

He gave her that slow, insolent grin again. "Right, Boss."

She almost snapped, "Stop calling me boss," but thought, *the hell with him,* and turned on her heel to talk to O'Brien.

Catherine sent eight of the men back to change their

uniforms and spent the next hour discussing the scene with O'Brien. The little corporal had come back briefly and then had disappeared. It was just as well, Catherine thought. All he did was complain and make everyone nervous. O'Brien finished shooting the first scene before lunch, and Catherine felt it had not gone too badly. Only one incident had marred her morning. Catherine had given the infuriating extra several lines to read in order to humiliate him. She had wanted to show him up on the set to pay him back for his impertinence. He had read his lines perfectly, carrying off the scene with aplomb. When he had finished, he had turned to her and said, "Was that all right, Boss?"

When the company broke for lunch, Catherine walked over to the enormous studio commissary and sat at a small table in the corner. At a large table next to her was a group of soldiers in uniform. Catherine was facing the door, when she saw the extra walk in, the three girls hanging on him, each one pushing to get closer to him. Catherine felt the blood rush to her face. She decided it was merely a chemical reaction. There were some people you hated on sight, just as there were others you liked on sight. Something about his overbearing arrogance rubbed her the wrong way. He would have made a perfect gigolo and that was probably exactly what he was.

He seated the girls at a table, looked up and saw Catherine, then leaned over and said something to the girls. They all looked at her and then there was a burst of laughter. Damn him! She watched as he moved toward her table. He stared down at her, that slow, knowing smile on his face. "Mind if I join you a moment?" he asked.

"I—" but he was already seated, studying her, his eyes probing and amused.

"What is it you want?" Catherine asked stiffly.

His grin widened. "Do you really want to know?"

Her lips tightened with anger. "Listen—"

"I wanted to ask you," he said quickly, "how I did

this morning." He leaned forward earnestly. "Was I convincing?"

"You may be convincing to them," Catherine said, nodding toward the girls, "but if you want my opinion, I think you're a phony."

"Have I done something to offend you?"

"Everything you do offends me," she said evenly. "I don't happen to like your type."

"What is my type?"

"You're a fake. You enjoy wearing that uniform and strutting around the girls, but have you thought about enlisting?"

He stared at her incredulously. "And get shot at?" he asked. "That's for suckers." He leaned forward and grinned. "This is a lot more fun."

Catherine's lips were quivering with anger. "Aren't you eligible for the draft?"

"I suppose technically I'm eligible, but a friend of mine knows a guy in Washington and"—he lowered his voice—"I don't think they'll ever get me."

"I think you're contemptible," Catherine exploded.

"Why?"

"If you don't know why, I could never explain it to you."

"Why don't you try? At dinner tonight. Your place. Do you cook?"

Catherine rose to her feet, her cheeks flushed with anger. "Don't bother coming back to the set," she said. "I'll tell Mr. O'Brien to send you your check for this morning's work."

She turned to go, then remembered and asked, "What's your name?"

"Douglas," he said. "Larry Douglas."

Fraser telephoned Catherine from London the next night to find out how things had gone. She reported to him the day's happenings but made no mention of the incident with Larry Douglas. When Fraser returned to Washington, she would tell him about it, and they would laugh over it together.

Early the next morning as Catherine was getting dressed to go to the studio, the doorbell rang. She opened the bungalow door and a delivery boy stood there holding a large bouquet of roses.

"Catherine Alexander?" he asked.

"Yes."

"Sign here please."

She signed the form that he handed her. "They're lovely," she said, taking the flowers.

"That'll be fifteen dollars."

"I beg your pardon?"

"Fifteen dollars. They're C.O.D."

"I don't under—" her lips tightened. Catherine reached for the card attached to the flowers and pulled it out of the envelope. The card read: "I would have paid for these myself, but I'm not working. Love, Larry."

She stared at the card unbelievingly.

"Well, do you want 'em or not?" asked the delivery boy.

"Not," she snapped. She thrust the flowers back in his arms.

He looked at her, puzzled. "He said you'd laugh. That it was kind of a private joke."

"I'm not laughing," Catherine said. She slammed the door furiously.

All that day, the incident kept rankling her. She had met egotistical men but never anyone with the outrageous conceit of Mr. Larry Douglas. She was sure that he had had an endless succession of victories with empty-headed blondes and bosomy brunettes who couldn't wait to fling themselves into his bed. But for him to put her in that category made Catherine feel cheap and humiliated. The mere thought of him made her flesh crawl. She determined to put him out of her mind.

At seven o'clock that evening Catherine started to

leave the stage. An assistant came up to her, an envelope in his hand.

"Did you charge this, Miss Alexander?" he asked.

It was a charge slip from central casting and it read:

One uniform (captain)
Six service ribbons (assorted)
Six medals (assorted)

Actor's Name: Lawrence Douglas . . . (Personal Charge to Catherine Alexander—MGM).

Catherine looked up, her face flushed.

"No!" she said.

He stared. "What shall I tell them?"

"Tell them I'll pay for his medals if they're awarded posthumously."

The picture finished shooting three days later. Catherine looked at the rough-cut the following day and approved it. The film would not win any awards, but it was simple and effective. Tom O'Brien had done a good job.

On Saturday morning Catherine boarded a plane for Washington. She had never been so glad to leave a city. Monday morning she was back in her office trying to catch up on the work that had piled up during her absence.

Just before lunch, her secretary, Annie, buzzed her. "A Mr. Larry Douglas is on the phone from Hollywood, California, collect. Do you want to take the call?"

"No," she snapped. "Tell him that I—never mind, I'll tell him myself." She took a deep breath and pressed the phone button. "Mr. Douglas?"

"Good morning." His voice had the consistency of hot fudge. "I had a hard time tracking you down. Don't you like roses?"

"Mr. Douglas—" Catherine began. Her voice quavered with fury. She took a deep breath and said, "Mr. Douglas, I love roses. I don't like you. I don't like anything about you. Is that clear?"

"You don't know anything about me."

"I know more than I want to know. I think you're cowardly and despicable, and I don't want you ever to call me again." Trembling, she slammed down the receiver, her eyes filled with tears of anger. How dare he! She would be so glad when Bill returned.

Three days later Catherine received a ten by twelve photograph of Lawrence Douglas in the mail. It was inscribed, "To the boss, with love from Larry."

Annie stared at it in awe, and said, "My God! Is he real?"

"Fake," retorted Catherine. "The only real thing is the paper it's printed on." She savagely tore the picture to shreds.

Annie watched, dismayed. "What a waste. I've never seen one like that in the flesh."

"In Hollywood," Catherine said grimly, "they have sets that are all front—no foundation. You've just seen one."

During the next two weeks, Larry Douglas phoned at least a dozen times. Catherine instructed Annie to tell him not to call again and not to bother telling her about his calls. One morning while Annie was taking dictation, she looked up and said apologetically, "I know you told me not to bother you with Mr. Douglas' calls, but he called again, and he sounded so desperate and well . . . kind of lost."

"He *is* lost," Catherine said coldly, "and if you're smart, you won't try to find him."

"He sure sounds charming."

"He invented treacle."

"He asked a lot of questions about you." She saw Catherine's look. "But, of course," she added hastily, "I didn't tell him anything."

"That was very bright of you, Annie."

Catherine began to dictate again, but her mind was not on it. She supposed the world was full of Larry Douglases. It made her appreciate William Fraser all the more.

Bill Fraser returned the following Sunday morning, and Catherine went to the airport to meet him. She watched as he finished with Customs and came toward the exit where she was standing. His face lit up when he saw her.

"Cathy," he said. "What a surprise. I didn't expect you to meet me."

"I couldn't wait," she smiled and gave him a warm hug that made him look at her quizzically.

"You've missed me," he said.

"More than you know."

"How was Hollywood?" he asked. "Did it go well?"

She hesitated. "Fine. They're very pleased with the picture."

"So I hear."

"Bill, next time you go away," she said, "take me with you."

He looked at her, pleased and touched.

"It's a deal," Fraser said. "I missed you. I've been doing a lot of thinking about you."

"Have you?"

"Do you love me?"

"Very much, Mr. Fraser."

"I love you, too," he said. "Why don't we go out tonight and celebrate?"

She smiled. "Wonderful."

"We'll have dinner at the Jefferson Club."

She dropped Fraser at his house.

"I have a few thousand calls to make," he said. "Could you meet me at the club? Eight o'clock."

"Fine," she said.

Catherine went back to her apartment and did some washing and ironing. Each time she passed the telephone, she half-expected it to ring, but it remained silent. She thought of Larry Douglas trying to pump Annie for information about her and found that she was gritting her teeth. Maybe she would speak to Fraser about turning Douglas' name in to his draft board. *No, I won't bother,* she thought. *They'd prob-*

ably turn him down. He'd be tried and found wanton. She washed her hair, took a long luxurious bath and was drying herself when the phone rang. She went over to it and picked it up. "Yes?" she said coldly.

It was Fraser. "Hi," he said. "Anything wrong?"

"Of course not, Bill," she said quickly. "I—I was just in the bath."

"I'm sorry." His voice took on a teasing tone. "I mean I'm sorry I'm not there with you."

"So am I," she replied.

"I called to tell you I miss you. Don't be late."

Catherine smiled. "I won't."

She hung up, slowly, thinking about Bill. For the first time she felt that he was ready to propose. He was going to ask her to become Mrs. William Fraser. She said the name aloud. "Mrs. William Fraser." It had a nice dignified sound to it. *My God,* she thought. *I'm becoming blasé. Six months ago, I would have been jumping out of my skin, and now all I can say is it has a nice dignified sound to it.* Had she really changed that much? It was not a comforting thought. She looked at the clock and hurriedly began to dress.

The Jefferson Club was on "F" Street, a discreet brick building set back from the street and surrounded by a wrought-iron fence. It was one of the most exclusive clubs in a city full of exclusive clubs. The easiest way to become a member was to have a father who belonged. If one lacked that foresight, then it was necessary to be recommended by three members. Membership proposals were brought up once a year and one black ball was sufficient to keep a person out of the Jefferson Club for the rest of his life, since it was a firm rule that no candidate could ever be proposed twice.

William Fraser's father had been a founding member of the club, and Fraser and Catherine had dinner there at least once a week. The chef had been with the French branch of the Rothschilds for twenty years, the cuisine was superb, and the wine cellar ranked as the third best in America. The club had been decorated by one of the world's leading decorators and careful attention had been paid to the colors and the lighting, so the women were bathed in candlelight glow that enhanced their beauty. On any given night, diners would brush elbows with the Vice-President, members of the Cabinet or Supreme Court, senators and the powerful industrialists who controlled world-wide empires.

Fraser was in the foyer waiting for Catherine when she arrived.

"Am I late?" she asked.

"It wouldn't matter if you were," Fraser said, looking at her with open admiration. "Do you know you're fantastically beautiful?"

"Of course," she replied. "Everybody knows I'm the fantastically beautiful Catherine Alexander."

"I mean it, Cathy." His tone was so serious that she was embarrassed.

"Thank you, Bill," she said awkwardly. "And stop staring at me like that."

"I can't help it," he said. He took her arm.

Louis, the maître d', led them to a corner booth. "There you are, Miss Alexander, Mr. Fraser, enjoy your dinner."

Catherine liked being known by name by the maître d' of the Jefferson Club. She knew that it was childish and naïve of her, but it gave her a feeling of being somebody, of belonging. Now she sat back, relaxed and contented, surveying the room.

"Will you have a drink?" Fraser asked.

"No, thank you," Catherine said.

He shook his head. "I've got to teach you some bad habits."

"You already have," Catherine murmured.

He grinned at her and ordered a scotch and soda.

She studied him, thinking what a dear, sweet man he was. She was sure that she could make him very happy.

And she would be happy married to him. *Very happy,* she told herself fiercely. Ask anybody. Ask *Time* magazine. She hated herself for the way her mind was working. What in God's name was wrong with her? "Bill," she began—and froze.

Larry Douglas was walking toward them, a smile of recognition on his lips as he saw Catherine. He was wearing his Army Air Corps uniform from Central Casting. She watched unbelievingly as he came over to their table, grinning happily. "Hello there," he said. But he was not speaking to Catherine. He was speaking to Bill, who was getting up and shaking his hand.

"It's great to see you, Larry."

"It's good to see you, Bill."

Catherine stared at the two of them, her mind paralyzed, refusing to function.

Fraser was saying, "Cathy, this is Captain Lawrence Douglas. Larry, this is Miss Alexander—Catherine."

Larry Douglas was looking down at her, his dark eyes mocking her. "I can't tell you what a pleasure this is, Miss Alexander," he said solemnly.

Catherine opened her mouth to speak, but she suddenly realized there was nothing that she could say. Fraser was watching her, waiting for her to speak. All she could manage was a nod. She did not trust her voice.

"Will you join us, Larry?" Fraser asked.

Larry looked at Catherine and said modestly, "If you're sure I'm not intruding—"

"Certainly not. Sit down."

Larry took a seat next to Catherine.

"What would you like to drink?" Fraser asked.

"Scotch and soda," Larry replied.

"I'll have the same," Catherine said recklessly. "Make it a double."

Fraser looked at her in surprise. "I can't believe it."

"You said you wanted to teach me some bad habits," Catherine said. "I think I'd like to start now."

When Fraser had ordered the drinks, he turned to

Larry and said, "I've been hearing about some of your exploits from General Terry—both in the air and on the ground."

Catherine was staring at Larry, her mind spinning, trying to adjust. "Those medals . . ." she said.

He was looking at her innocently.

"Yes?"

She swallowed. "Er—where did you get them?"

"I won them in a carnival," he said gravely.

"Some carnival," Fraser laughed. "Larry's been flying with the RAF. He was the leader of the American Squadron over there. They talked him into heading up a fighter base in Washington to get some of our boys ready for combat."

Catherine turned to stare at Larry. He was smiling at her benevolently, his eyes dancing. Like the rerun of an old movie, Catherine remembered every word of their first meeting. She had ordered him to take off his captain's bars and his medals, and he had cheerfully obliged. She had been smug, overbearing—and she had called him a coward! She wanted to crawl under the table.

"I wish you had let me know you were coming into town," Fraser was saying. "I would have trotted out a fatted calf for you. We should have had a big party to celebrate your return."

"I like this better," Larry said. He looked over at Catherine, and she turned away, unable to meet his eyes. "As a matter of fact," Larry continued innocently, "I looked for you when I was in Hollywood, Bill. I heard you were producing an Air Corps training film."

He stopped to light a cigarette and carefully blew out the match. "I went over to the set, but you weren't there."

"I had to fly to London," Fraser replied. "Catherine was there. I'm surprised you didn't run into each other."

Catherine looked up at Larry, and he was watching

her, his eyes amused. Now was the time to mention
what had happened. She would tell Fraser, and they
would all laugh it off as an amusing anecdote. But
somehow the words stuck in her throat.

Larry gave her a moment, then said, "It was a pretty
crowded set. I guess we missed each other."

She hated him for helping her out, for making them
fellow conspirators against Fraser.

When the drinks arrived, Catherine downed hers
quickly and asked for another. This was going to be the
most terrible evening of her life. She could not wait to
get out of there, to get away from Larry Douglas.

Fraser asked him about his war experiences, and
Larry made them sound easy and amusing. He obviously didn't take anything seriously. He was a lightweight. And yet in all fairness, Catherine reluctantly
admitted to herself that a lightweight did not volunteer
for the RAF and become a hero fighting against the
Luftwaffe. Irrationally, she hated him even more because he was a hero. Her attitude didn't make sense to
her, and she brooded about it over her third double
scotch. What difference did it make whether he was a
hero or a bum? And then she realized that as long as
he was a bum, he fitted neatly into a pigeonhole that
she could deal with. Through the haze of the liquor she
sat back and listened to the two men talk. There was
an eager enthusiasm about Larry when he spoke, a vitality that was so palpable it reached across and
touched her. He seemed to her now like the most alive
man she had ever met. Catherine had a feeling that he
held nothing back from life, that he gave himself to everything wholeheartedly and that he mocked those who
were afraid to give. Who were afraid, period. Like herself.

She hardly touched her food, she had no idea what
she was eating. She met Larry's eyes, and it was as
though he were already her lover, as if they had already been together, belonged together, and she knew

it was insane. He was like a cyclone, a force of nature, and any woman who got sucked up in the vortex was going to be destroyed.

Larry was smiling at her. "I'm afraid we've been excluding Miss Alexander from the conversation," he said politely. "I'm sure she's more interesting than the both of us put together.

"You're wrong," Catherine said thickly. "I live a very dull life. I work with Bill." The moment she said it she heard how it sounded and turned red. "I didn't mean it like that," she said. "I meant—"

"I know what you meant," Larry said. And she hated him. He turned to Bill. "Where did you find her?"

"I got lucky," Fraser said warmly. "Very lucky. You're still not married?"

Larry shrugged. "Who'd have me?"

You bastard, Catherine thought. She looked around the room. Half a dozen women were staring at Larry, some covertly, some openly. He was like a sexual magnet. "How were the English girls?" Catherine said recklessly.

"They were fine," he said, politely. "Of course, I didn't have much time for that sort of thing. I was busy flying."

Like hell you didn't, Catherine thought. *I'll bet there wasn't a virgin left standing within a hundred miles of you.* Aloud, she said, "I feel sorry for those poor girls. Look at all they missed." Her tone was more biting than she had intended.

Fraser was looking at her, puzzled by her rudeness. "Cathy," he said.

"Let's have another drink," Larry cut in quickly.

"I think perhaps Catherine's had enough," Fraser replied.

"Thash not so," Catherine began, and to her horror she realized she was slurring her words. "I think I want to go home," she said.

"All right"—Fraser turned to Larry—"Catherine

doesn't drink as a rule," he said apologetically.

"I imagine she's excited about seeing you again," Larry said.

Catherine wanted to pick up a glass of water and throw it at him. She had hated him less when he was a bum. Now she hated him more. And she did not know why.

The next morning Catherine woke up with a hangover that she was convinced would make medical history. She had at least three heads on her shoulders, all of them pounding to the beat of different drummers. Lying still in bed was agony but trying to move was worse. As she lay there fighting nausea, the whole evening flooded back in her memory, and the pain increased. Unreasonably she blamed Larry Douglas for her hangover, for if it had not been for him, she would not have had anything to drink. Painfully Catherine turned her head and looked at the clock beside her bed. She had overslept. She debated whether to stay in bed or call a pulmotor squad. Carefully she pulled herself out of her deathbed and dragged herself into the bathroom. She stumbled into the shower, turned the water on cold and let the icy jets stream against her body. She screamed out loud as the water hit her, but when she came out of the shower, she was feeling better. *Not good,* she thought carefully. *Just better.*

Forty-five minutes later she was at her desk. Her secretary, Annie, came in full of excitement. "Guess what," she said.

"Not this morning," Catherine whispered. "Just be a good girl and speak softly."

"Look!" Annie thrust the morning paper at her. "It's *him.*"

On the front page was a picture of Larry Douglas in uniform, grinning at her insolently. The caption read: "AMERICAN RAF HERO RETURNS TO WASHINGTON TO HEAD UP NEW FIGHTER UNIT." A two-column story followed.

"Isn't that exciting?" Annie cried.

"Terribly," Catherine said. She slammed the paper into the wastebasket. "Can we get on with our work?"

Annie looked at her, surprised. "I'm sorry," she said. "I—I thought since he was a friend of yours, you'd be interested."

"He's not a friend," Catherine corrected her. "He's more of an enemy." She saw the look on Annie's face. "Could we just forget about Mr. Douglas?"

"Certainly," Annie said in a puzzled voice. "I told him I thought you'd be pleased."

Catherine stared at her. "When?"

"When he called this morning. He's called three times."

Catherine steeled herself to make her voice casual. "Why didn't you tell me?"

"You asked me not to tell you when he called." She was watching Catherine, her face filled with confusion.

"Did he leave a number?"

"No."

"Good." Catherine thought of his face, of those large, dark teasing eyes. "Good," she said again, more firmly. She finished dictating some letters and when Annie had left the room, Catherine went over to the wastebasket and retrieved the newspaper. She read the story about Larry word for word. He was an ace with eight German planes to his credit. He had been shot down twice over the Channel. She buzzed Annie. "If Mr. Douglas calls again, I'll talk to him."

There was only a fractional pause. "Yes, Miss Alexander."

After all, there was no point in being rude to the man. Catherine would simply apologize for her behavior at the studio and ask him to stop calling her. She was going to marry William Fraser.

She waited for another call from him all afternoon. He had not called by six o'clock. *Why should he?* Catherine asked herself. *He's out laying six other girls.*

You're lucky. Being involved with him would be like going to a butcher shop. You take your number and wait your turn.

On the way out she said to Annie, "If Mr. Douglas calls tomorrow, tell him I'm not in."

Annie did not even blink. "Yes, Miss Alexander. Good night."

"Good night."

Catherine rode down in the elevator, lost in thought. She was sure that Bill Fraser wanted to marry her. The best thing to do would be to tell him that she wanted to get married right away. She would tell him tonight. They would go away for a honeymoon. By the time they got back, Larry Douglas would have left town. Or something.

The elevator door opened at the lobby, and Larry Douglas was standing there, leaning against the wall. He had taken off his medals and ribbons and was wearing the bars of a second lieutenant. He smiled and walked up to her.

"Is this better?" he asked brightly.

Catherine stared at him, her heart pounding. "Isn't—isn't wearing the wrong insignia against regulations?"

"I don't know," he said earnestly. "I thought you were in charge of all that."

He stood there looking down at her, and she said in a small voice, "Don't do this to me. I want you to leave me alone. I belong to Bill."

"Where's your wedding ring?"

Catherine brushed past him and started toward the street door. When she reached it, he was there ahead of her, holding it open for her.

Outside he took her arm. She felt a shock go through her whole body. There was an electricity that came from him that burned her. "Cathy—" he began.

"For God's sake," she said desperately. "What do you want from me?"

"Everything," he said quietly. "I want you."

"Well, you can't have me," she wailed. "Go torture somebody else." She turned to walk away, and he pulled her back.

"What is that supposed to mean?"

"I don't know," Catherine said, her eyes filling with tears. "I don't know what I'm saying. I—I have a hangover. I want to die."

He grinned sympathetically. "I have a marvelous cure for hangovers." He guided her into the garage of the building.

"Where are we going?" she asked in a panic.

"We're getting my car."

Catherine looked up at him, searching his face for a sign of triumph, but all she saw was his strong, incredibly handsome face filled with warmth and compassion.

The attendant brought up a tan sports convertible with the top down. Larry helped Catherine into the car and slid in behind the wheel. She sat there looking straight ahead, knowing that she was throwing her whole life away and totally unable to stop herself. It was as though all this were happening to someone else. She wanted to tell the silly, lost girl in the car to flee.

"Your place or mine?" Larry asked gently.

She shook her head. "It doesn't matter," she said hopelessly.

"We'll go to my place."

So he was not totally insensitive. Or else he was afraid to compete with the shadow of William Fraser.

She watched him as he deftly tooled the car through the early evening traffic. No, he was not afraid of anything. That was part of his goddamn attraction.

She tried to tell herself that she was free to say no to him, free to walk away. How could she love William Fraser and feel this way about Larry?

"If it helps any," Larry said quietly, "I'm as nervous as you are."

Catherine looked over at him. "Thanks," she said. He was lying, of course. He probably said that to all his victims as he took them up to his bed to seduce them. But at least he wasn't gloating about it. What bothered her most was that she was betraying Bill Fraser. He was too dear a man to hurt, and this was going to hurt him very much. Catherine knew that and knew that what she was doing was wrong and senseless, but it was as though she had no will of her own anymore.

They had reached a pleasant residential area with large, shady trees lining the street. Larry pulled the car up in front of an apartment building. "We're home," he said quietly.

Catherine knew that this was her final chance to say no, to tell him to keep away from her. She watched silently as Larry came around and opened the door. She got out of the car and walked into his apartment building.

Larry's apartment had been decorated for a man. It had strong solid colors, and masculine-looking furniture.

As they walked in, Larry took off Catherine's coat and she shivered.

"Are you cold?" he asked.

"No."

"Would you like a drink?"

"No."

Gently he took her in his arms, and they kissed. It was as though her body were being set aflame. Without a word Larry led her into the bedroom. There was a growing urgency as they both silently undressed. She lay on the bed naked, and he moved beside her.

"Larry—" but his lips were on hers, and his hands began to move down her body, gently exploring, and she forgot everything except the pleasure that was happening to her, and her hands began to grope for him. And she felt him hot and hard and pulsating and his fingers were inside her, opening her up gently and lovingly and he was on top of her and in her, and there was an exquisite joy that she had never dreamed possible and then they were together, moving faster and faster in a fantastic rhythm that rocked the room and the world and the universe until there was an explosion that became a delirious ecstasy an unbelievable shattering journey an arriving and departure an ending and a beginning and Catherine lay there spent and numb holding him tightly never wanting to let him go never wanting this feeling to stop. Nothing she had ever read or heard could have prepared her for this. It was unbelievable that another person's body could bring such joy. She lay there at peace: a woman. And she knew that if she never saw him again, she would be grateful to him for the rest of her life.

"Cathy?"

She turned to look at him, slowly and lazily. "Yes?" Even her voice seemed deeper to her, more mature.

"Could you get your nails out of my back?"

She suddenly realized that she had been digging into his flesh. "Oh, I'm sorry!" she exclaimed. She started to examine his back, but he caught her hands and pulled her close to him.

"It doesn't matter. Are you happy?"

"Happy?" Her lip trembled and to her horror she began to cry. Great sobs that wrenched her body. He held her in his arms, stroking her soothingly, letting the storm spend itself.

"I'm sorry," she said. "I don't know what made me do that."

"Disappointment?"

Catherine looked at him quickly to protest, then saw that he was teasing her. He took her into his arms and made love to her again. It was even more incredible than before. Afterward they lay in bed and he talked, but she didn't listen. All she wanted to hear was the sound of his voice, and it didn't matter to her what he said. She knew there would never be anyone for her but this man. And she knew that this man could never belong to any one woman and that she would probably never see him again, that she was just another conquest to him. She was aware that his voice had stopped and that he was watching her.

"You haven't heard a word I said."

"Sorry," she said. "I was daydreaming."

"I should be hurt," he said reproachfully. "You're only interested in me for my body."

She ran her hands over his lean tanned chest and stomach. "I'm no expert," she said, "but I think this one will do nicely." She smiled. "It *did* nicely." She wanted to ask him whether he had enjoyed her, but she was afraid to.

"You're beautiful, Cathy."

She thrilled to his saying it and at the same time resented it. Anything he said to her he had said a thousand times to other women. She wondered how he was going to say good-bye. *Call me sometime?* Or, *I'll call you sometime?* Perhaps he would even want to see her again once or twice before he went on to someone else. Well, she had no one to blame but herself. She had known what she was getting into. *I walked into this with my eyes and my legs wide open. No matter what happens, I must never blame him.*

He slid his arms around her and held her close.

"Do you know you're a very special girl, Cathy?"

Do you know you're a very special girl—Alice, Susan, Margaret, Peggy, Lana.

"I felt it from the first time I saw you. I've never felt this way about anyone before."

—Janet, Evelyn, Ruth, Georgia, ad infinitum. She buried her head in his chest, not trusting herself to speak, and held him tightly, silently saying good-bye.

"I'm hungry," Larry said. "Do you know what I feel like?"

Catherine smiled. "Yes, I certainly do."

Larry grinned down at her. "You know something?" he asked. "You're a sex maniac."

She looked up. "Thank you."

He led her into the shower and turned it on. He took

a shower cap from a hook on the wall and put it on Catherine's head, tucking in her hair. "Come on," he said, and pulled her into the piercing jet water. He took a bar of soap and began to wash her body, starting with her neck and working down to her arms and slowly circling her breasts and moving down to her stomach and her thighs. She began to feel an excitement in her groin and she took the soap from him and began to wash him, lathering his chest and stomach and moving down between his legs. His organ began to grow hard in her hand.

He spread her legs and put his male hardness inside her and Catherine was transported again, drowning in a torrent of water that beat against her body, while inside she was filled with the same unbearable joy, until she screamed aloud in sheer happiness.

Afterward they dressed, got into his car and drove to Maryland, where they found a little restaurant that was still open and they had lobster and champagne.

At five o'clock in the morning, Catherine dialed William Fraser's number at home and stood there listening to the long rings eighty miles away until finally Fraser's sleepy voice came on the phone, and said, "Hello. . . ."

"Hello, Bill. It's Catherine."

"Catherine! I've been trying to call you all evening. Where are you? Are you all right?"

"I'm fine. I'm in Maryland with Larry Douglas. We just got married."

NOELLE
Paris: 1941

8

Christian Barbet was an unhappy man. The bald little detective sat at his desk, a cigarette between his stained, broken teeth, and gloomily contemplated the folder in front of him. The information it contained was going to cost him a client. He had been charging Noelle Page outrageous fees for his services, but it was not only the loss of the income that saddened him: He would miss the client herself. He hated Noelle Page and yet she was the most exciting woman he had ever met. Barbet built lurid fantasies around Noelle in which she always ended up in his power. Now the assignment was about to come to an end, and he would never see her again. He had kept her waiting in the reception office while he tried to figure out a way to handle things so that he could squeeze some additional money out of her to prolong the case. But he reluctantly concluded that there was no way. Barbet sighed, snuffed out his cigarette, walked over to the door and opened it. Noelle was sitting on the black imitation leather couch, and as he studied her, his heart caught in his throat for a moment. It was unfair for any woman to be so beautiful. "Good afternoon, Mademoiselle," he said. "Come in."

She entered his office moving with the grace of a model. It was good for Barbet to have a name client like Noelle Page, and he was not above dropping her name frequently. It attracted other clients, and Christian Barbet was not a man to lose any sleep over ethics. "Please sit down," he said, indicating a chair. "Can

I get you a brandy, an aperitif?"

Part of his fantasy was getting Noelle drunk so that she would beg him to seduce her.

"No," she replied. "I came for your report."

The bitch could have had a last drink with him! "Yes," Barbet said. "As a matter of fact I have several pieces of news." He reached over to the desk and pretended to study the dossier, which he had already memorized.

"First," he informed her, "your friend was promoted to Captain and transferred to the one hundred thirty-third squadron, where he was put in command. The field is at Coltisall, Duxtford, in Cambridgeshire. They flew"—he spoke slowly and deliberately, knowing that she was not interested in the technical part—"Hurricanes and Spitfire II's and then switched to Mark V's. They then flew—"

"Never mind," Noelle interrupted impatiently. "Where is he now?"

Barbet had been waiting for the question. "In the United States." He saw the reaction before she could control it, and he took savage satisfaction in it. "In Washington, D.C.," he continued.

"On leave?"

Barbet shook his head. "No. He's been discharged from the RAF. He's a Captain in the United States Army Air Corps."

He watched Noelle digesting the information, her expression giving no clue to what she was feeling. But Barbet was not finished with her yet. He picked up a newspaper clipping between his stained sausage fingers and handed it to her.

"I think this will interest you," he said.

He saw Noelle stiffen, and it was almost as though she knew what she was going to see. The clipping was from the New York *Daily News*. The caption read "War Ace Weds" and above it was a photograph of Larry Douglas and his bride. Noelle looked at it for a long moment, then held out her hand for the rest of the file. Christian Barbet shrugged, and slid all the papers into a manila envelope and handed it to her. As he opened his mouth to make his farewell speech, Noelle Page said, "If you don't have a correspondent in Washington, get one. I shall expect weekly reports." And she was gone, leaving Christian Barbet staring after her in a state of complete confusion.

When she returned to her apartment, Noelle went into the bedroom, locked the door and took the newspaper clippings out of the envelope. She laid them out on the bed before her and studied them. The photograph of Larry was exactly as she remembered him. If anything the image in her mind was clearer than the image in the newspaper, for Larry was more alive in her mind than he was in reality.

There was not a day that went by that Noelle did not relive the past with him. It was as though they had costarred in a play together long ago, and she was able to recapture scenes at will, playing some on certain days and saving others for other days, so that each memory was always alive and fresh.

Noelle turned her attention to Larry's bride. What she saw was a pretty, young, intelligent face with a smile on its lips.

The face of the enemy. A face that would have to be destroyed as Larry was going to be destroyed.

Noelle remained locked up with the photograph the whole afternoon.

Hours later when Armand Gautier pounded on her bedroom door, Noelle told him to go away. He waited outside in the drawing room, apprehensive about what her mood would be, but when Noelle finally emerged, she seemed unusually bright and gay, as though she had had a piece of good news. She offered no explanation to Gautier, and he knew her well enough not to ask for one.

After the theater that evening she made love to him with a wild passion that reminded him of their early days together. Later Gautier lay in bed trying to understand the beautiful girl who rested beside him but he did not have a clue.

During the night Noelle Page had a dream about Colonel Mueller. The hairless albino Gestapo officer was torturing her with a branding iron, making burning swastikas in her flesh. He kept asking her questions, but his voice was so soft that Noelle could not hear him, and he kept pressing the hot metal into her, and suddenly it was Larry on the table, screaming with pain. Noelle awoke in a cold sweat, her heart pounding, and turned on the bedside lamp. She lit a cigarette with trembling fingers and tried to calm her nerves. She thought about Israel Katz. His leg had been amputated with an ax, and though she had not seen him since that afternoon at the bakery, she had received word from the concierge that he was alive but weak. It was becoming more and more difficult to hide him, and he was helpless on his own. The search for him had intensified. If he was going to be transported out of Paris, it would have to be done quickly. Noelle had really done nothing for which the Gestapo could arrest her: yet. Was the dream a premonition, a warning not to help Israel Katz? She lay in bed remembering. He had aided her when she had the abortion. He had helped her kill Larry's baby. He had given her money and helped her find a job. Dozens of men had done more important things for her than he had, yet Noelle felt no debt to them. Each of them, including her father, had wanted something from her, and she had paid in full for everything she had ever received. Israel Katz had never asked her for anything. She had to help him.

Noelle did not underestimate the problem. Colonel Mueller was already suspicious of her. She remembered her dream and shuddered. She must see to it that Mueller was never able to prove anything against her. Israel Katz had to be smuggled out of Paris, but how? Noelle was sure that all exits were closely watched. They would be watching the roads and the river. The Nazis might be *cochons,* but they were efficient *cochons.* It was a challenge and it could be a deadly one, but she was determined to try it. The problem was that there was no one she could turn to for help. The Nazis had reduced Armand Gautier to a quivering gelatin. No, she would have to do this alone. She thought of Colonel Mueller and General Scheider, and she wondered if a clash ever came, which one would emerge victorious.

The evening following Noelle's dream she and Armand Gautier attended a supper party. The host was Leslie Rocas, a wealthy patron of the arts. It was an eclectic collection of guests—bankers, artists, political leaders and a gathering of beautiful women whom Noelle felt were there mainly for the benefit of the Germans who were present. Gautier had noticed Noelle's preoccupation, but when he asked her what was wrong, she told him that everything was fine.

Fifteen minutes before supper was announced, a new arrival lumbered through the door and the moment that Noelle saw him she knew that her problem was going to be solved. She walked over to the hostess and said, "Darling, be an angel and put me next to Albert Heller."

Albert Heller was France's leading playwright. He was a large, shambling bear of a man in his sixties with a shock of white hair and broad, sloped shoulders. He was unusually tall for a Frenchman, but he would have stood out in a crowd in any case, for he had a remarkably ugly face and piercing green eyes that missed nothing. Heller had a vividly inventive imagination and had written more than a score of hit plays and motion pictures. He had been after Noelle to star in a new play of his and had sent her a copy of the manuscript. Now as she sat next to him at dinner, Noelle said, "I just finished reading your new play, Albert. I adored it."

His face lit up. "Will you do it?"

Noelle put a hand on his. "I wish I could, darling. Armand has committed me to another play."

He frowned, then sighed resignedly. *"Merde!* Ah, well, one day we will work together."

"I would enjoy that," Noelle said. "I love the way you write. It fascinates me the way writers create plots. I don't know how you do it."

He shrugged. "The same way you act. It is our trade, the way we make our living."

"No," she replied. "The ability to use your imagination in that way is a miracle to me." She gave an embarrassed laugh. "I know. I've been trying to write."

"Oh?" he said politely.

"Yes, but I'm stuck." Noelle took a deep breath and then looked around the table. All the other guests were engrossed in their own conversations. She leaned toward Albert Heller and lowered her voice. "I have a situation where my heroine is trying to smuggle her lover out of Paris. The Nazis are searching for him."

"Ah." The big man sat there, toying with a salad fork, drumming it against a plate. Then he said, "Easy. Have him put on a German uniform and walk right through them."

Noelle sighed and said, "There is a complication. He's been wounded. He can't walk. He lost a leg."

The drumming suddenly stopped. There was a long pause, then Heller said, "A barge on the Seine?"

"Watched."

"And all transportation out of Paris is being searched?"

"Yes."

"Then you must have the Nazis do the work for you."

"How?"

"Your heroine," he said, without looking at Noelle, "is she attractive?"

"Yes."

"Supposing," he said, "your heroine befriended a German officer. Someone of high rank. Is that possible?" Noelle turned to look at him, but he avoided her eyes.

"Yes."

"All right, then. Have her make a rendezvous with the officer. They drive off to spend a weekend somewhere outside Paris. Friends could arrange for your hero to be hidden in the trunk of the car. The officer must be important enough so that his car would not be searched."

"If the trunk is locked," Noelle asked, "would he not smother?"

Albert Heller took a sip of wine, quietly lost in thought. Finally he said, "Not necessarily." He spoke to Noelle for five minutes, keeping his voice low, and when he had finished, he said, "Good luck." And he still did not look at her.

Early the next morning Noelle telephoned General Scheider. An operator answered the switchboard, and a few moments later Noelle was put through to an aide and finally to the General's secretary.

"Who is calling General Scheider, please?"

"Noelle Page," she said, for the third time.

"I am sorry, but the General is in conference. He cannot be disturbed."

She hesitated. "Could I call him back later?"

"He will be in conference all day. I suggest you write the General a letter stating your business."

Noelle sat there a moment contemplating the idea and an ironic smile touched her lips.

"Never mind," she said. "Just tell him I called."

One hour later her phone rang, and it was General Hans Scheider. "Forgive me," he apologized. "That idiot didn't give me your message until just now. I would have left word for them to put you through, but it never occurred to me that you would telephone."

"I'm the one who should apologize," Noelle said. "I know how busy you are."

"Please. What can I do for you?"

Noelle hesitated, choosing her words. "Do you remember what you said about us at dinner?"

There was a short pause, then "Yes."

"I've been thinking about you a great deal, Hans. I would like very much to see you."

"Will you have supper with me tonight?" There was a sudden eagerness in his voice.

"Not in Paris," Noelle replied. "If we're going to be together, I would like us to be away from here."

"Where?" General Scheider asked.

"I want it to be some place special. Do you know Etratat?"

"No."

"It's a lovely little village about a hundred and fifty kilometers from Paris, near Le Havre. There's a quiet old inn there."

"It sounds wonderful, Noelle. It's not easy for me to get away right now," he added apologetically. "I am in the middle of—"

"I understand," Noelle interrupted icily, "perhaps some other time."

"Wait!" There was a long pause. "When could you get away?"

"Saturday night after the show."

"I will make arrangements," he said. "We can fly down—"

"Why don't we drive?" Noelle asked. "It's so pleasant."

"Whatever you like. I'll pick you up at the theater."

Noelle thought quickly. "I have to come home and change first. Pick me up at my apartment, would you?"

"As you wish, my *liebchen*. Until Saturday night."

Fifteen minutes later Noelle was speaking to the concierge. He listened as she talked, shaking his head in vigorous protest.

"No, no, no! I will tell our friend, Mademoiselle, but he will not do it. He would be a fool to! You might as well ask him to go down and apply for a job at Gestapo headquarters."

"It can't fail," Noelle assured him. "The best brain in France figured it out."

When she walked out of the entrance of her apartment building that afternoon, she saw a man lounging against the wall pretending to be engrossed in a newspaper. As Noelle stepped into the crisp, winter air, the man straightened up and began to follow her at a discreet distance. Noelle strolled the streets slowly and leisurely, stopping to look into all the shop windows.

Five minutes after Noelle left the building, the concierge came out, glanced around to make sure he was not observed, then hailed a taxi and gave the address of a sporting goods shop in Montmartre.

Two hours later the concierge reported to Noelle. "He will be delivered to you Saturday night."

Saturday night when Noelle finished her performance, Colonel Kurt Mueller of the Gestapo was waiting for her backstage. A *frisson* of apprehension went through Noelle. The escape plan had been worked out to a split-second timing, and there was no room for any delays.

"I saw your performance from out front, Fräulein Page," Colonel Mueller said. "You improve each time."

The sound of his soft, high-pitched voice brought her dream back vividly.

"Thank you, Colonel. If you'll excuse me, I have to change."

Noelle started toward her dressing room, and he fell into step beside her.

"I will go with you," Colonel Mueller said.

She walked into her dressing room, the hairless albino Colonel close behind her. He made himself comfortable in an armchair. Noelle hesitated a moment and then began to undress as he watched indifferently. She knew that he was a homosexual, which deprived her of a valuable weapon—her sexuality.

"A little sparrow whispered something in my ear," Colonel Mueller said. "He is going to try to escape tonight."

Noelle's heart skipped a beat, but her face showed nothing. She began removing her makeup, fighting for time as she asked, "Who is going to try to escape tonight?"

"Your friend, Israel Katz."

Noelle swung around, and the movement made her suddenly conscious of the fact that she had removed her brassiere. "I don't know any—" She caught the quick triumphant gleam in his pink eyes and saw the trap just in time. "Wait," she said. "Are you talking about a young intern?"

"Ah, so you *do* remember him!"

"Barely. He treated me for pneumonia some time ago."

"And a self-induced abortion," Colonel Mueller said in that soft, high-pitched voice. The fear flooded back into her. The Gestapo would not have gone to this much trouble if they were not sure that she was involved. She was a fool to have gotten herself into this; but even as Noelle thought it, she knew that it was too late to back out. The wheels had already been set in motion and in a few hours Israel Katz would be either free . . . or dead. And she?

Colonel Mueller was saying, "You said that the last time you saw Katz was at the café a few weeks ago."

Noelle shook her head. "I said no such thing, Colonel."

Colonel Mueller looked steadily into her eyes, then let his gaze drop insolently to her naked breasts and down her belly to her sheer pants. Then he looked up into Noelle's eyes again and sighed. "I love beautiful things," he said softly. "It would be a shame to see beauty like yours destroyed. And all for a man who means nothing to you. How is your friend planning to get away, Fräulein?"

There was a quietness in his voice that sent shivers down her spine. She became Annette, the innocent, helpless character in her play.

"I really don't know what you're talking about,

Colonel. I'd like to help you, but I don't know how."

Colonel Mueller looked at Noelle a long time, then stiffly rose to his feet. "I will teach you how, Fräulein," he promised softly, "and I will enjoy it."

He turned at the door to deliver a parting shot. "By the way, I have advised General Scheider not to go away with you for the weekend."

Noelle felt her heart plummet. It was too late to reach Israel Katz. "Do Colonels always interfere in the private lives of Generals?"

"In this case, no," Colonel Mueller said regretfully. "General Scheider intends to keep his rendezvous." He turned and walked out.

Noelle stared after him, her heart racing. She looked at the gold clock on the dressing table and quickly began to dress.

At eleven forty-five the concierge telephoned Noelle to announce that General Scheider was on his way up to her apartment. His voice was trembling.

"Is his chauffeur in the car?" Noelle asked.

"No, Mademoiselle," the concierge replied carefully. "He's on his way up with the General."

"Thank you."

Noelle replaced the receiver and hurried into the bedroom to check her luggage once more. There must be no mistake. The front doorbell rang, and Noelle went into the living room and opened the door.

General Scheider stood in the corridor, his chauffeur, a young captain, behind him. General Scheider was out of uniform and looked very distinguished in a flawlessly cut charcoal-gray suit and a soft blue shirt and black tie. "Good evening," he said formally. He stepped inside, then nodded to his chauffeur.

"My bags are in the bedroom," Noelle said. She indicated the door.

"Thank you, Fräulein." The captain walked into the bedroom. General Scheider came over to Noelle and took her hands. "Do you know what I have been thinking about all day?" he asked. "I was thinking you might not be here, that you might change your mind. Every time the phone rang, I was afraid."

"I keep my promises," Noelle said. She watched as the captain came out of the bedroom carrying her makeup case and overnight bag. "Is there anything else?" he asked.

"No," Noelle said. "That's all."

The captain carried the suitcases out of the apartment.

"Ready?" General Scheider asked.

"Let's have a drink before we go," Noelle replied quickly. She walked over to a bottle of champagne on the bar, resting in a bucket of ice.

"Let me." He moved over to the ice bucket and opened the champagne.

"What shall we drink to?" he asked.

"Etratat."

He studied her a moment and then said, "Etratat."

They touched glasses in a toast and drank. As Noelle set her glass down, she surreptitiously glanced at her wristwatch. General Scheider was talking to her, but Noelle only half-heard the words. Her mind was visualizing what was happening downstairs. She must be very careful. If she moved too quickly or too slowly it would be fatal. For everyone.

"What are you thinking about?" General Scheider asked.

Noelle turned quickly. "Nothing."

"You were not listening."

"I'm sorry. I suppose I was thinking about us." She turned to him and gave him a quick smile.

"You puzzle me," he said.

"Aren't all women a puzzle?"

"Not like you. I would never believe that you are capricious and yet"—he made a gesture—"first you will not see me at all and now we are suddenly spending a weekend in the country."

"Are you sorry, Hans?"

"Of course not. But still I ask myself—why the country?"

"I told you."

"Ah yes," General Scheider said. "It is romantic. That is something else that puzzles me. I believe you are a realist, not a romanticist."

"What are you trying to say?" Noelle asked.

"Nothing," the General replied easily. "I am just thinking aloud. I enjoy solving problems, Noelle. In time I will solve you."

She shrugged. "Once you have the solution, the problem might not be interesting."

"We shall see." He set his glass down. "Shall we go?"

Noelle picked up the empty champagne glasses.

"I'll just put these in the sink," she said.

General Scheider watched as she walked into the kitchen. Noelle was one of the most beautiful and desirable women he had ever seen, and he meant to possess her. That did not mean, however, that he was either stupid or blind. She wanted something from him. He intended to find out what it was. Colonel Mueller had alerted him that she was in all probability giving aid to a dangerous enemy of the Reich, and Colonel Mueller made very few mistakes. If he was correct, Noelle Page was probably counting on General Scheider to protect her in some way. If so she knew nothing at all about the German military mind and still less about him. He would turn her over to the Gestapo without a qualm, but first he would have his pleasure. He was looking forward to the weekend.

Noelle came out of the kitchen. There was a worried expression on her face. "How many bags did your chauffeur take down?" she asked.

"Two," he replied. "An overnight bag and a makeup case."

She made a face. "Oh dear, I'm sorry, Hans. He forgot the other case. Do you mind?"

He watched as Noelle walked over to the telephone, picked it up and spoke into it. "Would you please ask the General's driver to come up again?" she said. "There's another bag to go down." She replaced the receiver. "I know we're only going to be there for the weekend," she smiled, "but I want to please you."

"If you want to please me," General Scheider said, "you will not need a lot of clothes." He glanced at a picture of Armand Gautier on the piano. "Does Herr Gautier know that you are going away with me?" he asked.

"Yes," Noelle lied. Armand was in Nice meeting with a producer about a motion picture, and she had seen no reason to alarm him by telling him of her plans. The doorbell rang, and Noelle walked over to the door and opened it. The captain stood there. "I understand there is another bag?" he asked.

"Yes," Noelle apologized. "It's in the bedroom."

The captain nodded and went into the bedroom.

"When must you return to Paris?" General Scheider asked her.

Noelle turned and looked at him. "I'd like to stay as long as I can. We'll come back late Monday afternoon. That will give us two days."

The captain came out of the bedroom. "Excuse me, Fräulein. What does the suitcase look like?"

"It is a large round blue case," Noelle said. She turned to the General. "It has a new gown in it that I haven't worn yet. I saved it for you."

She was babbling now, trying to cover up her nervousness.

The captain had gone back into the bedroom. A few moments later, he came out again. "I am sorry," he said. "I cannot find it."

"Let me," Noelle said. She went into the bedroom and began to search the closets. "That idiot of a maid must have hidden it away somewhere," she said. The three of them looked through every closet in the apartment. It was the General who finally found the bag in the hall closet. He lifted it and said, "It seems to be empty."

Noelle quickly opened the bag and looked inside. There was nothing in it. "Oh, that fool," she said. "She must have crammed that beautiful new dress in the suitcase with my other clothes. I hope she hasn't ruined it." She sighed in exasperation. "Do you have that much trouble with maids in Germany?"

"I think it is the same everywhere," General Scheider replied. He was watching Noelle closely. She was acting strangely, talking too much. She noticed his look.

"You make me feel like a schoolgirl," Noelle said. "I can't remember when I've been so nervous."

General Scheider smiled. So that was it. Or was she playing some kind of game with him? If she was, he would soon find it out. He glanced at his watch. "If we do not leave now, we will get there very late."

"I'm ready," Noelle said.

She prayed the others were.

When they reached the lobby, the concierge was standing there, his face chalk white. Noelle wondered if something had gone wrong. She looked at him for some signal, a sign, but before he could respond, the General had taken Noelle's arm and was leading her out the door.

General Scheider's limousine was parked directly in front of the door. The trunk of the car was closed. The street was deserted. The chauffeur sprang to open the rear door of the car. Noelle turned to look inside the lobby to see the concierge but the General moved in front of her and blocked her view. Deliberately? Noelle glanced at the closed trunk but it told her nothing. It would be hours before she knew whether her plan had succeeded, and the suspense was going to be unbearable.

"Are you all right?" General Scheider was staring at her. She felt that something had gone terribly wrong.

She had to find an excuse to go back into the lobby, to be alone with the concierge for a few seconds. She forced a smile to her lips.

"I just remembered," Noelle said. "A friend is going to call me. I must leave a message—"

General Scheider gripped her arm.

"Too late," he smiled. "From this moment on you must think only of me." And he guided her into the car. A moment later they were on their way.

Five minutes after General Scheider's limousine drove away from the apartment building, a black Mercedes screeched to a stop in front of the building and Colonel Mueller and two other Gestapo men spilled out of the car. Colonel Mueller looked hurriedly up and down the street. "They've gone," he said. The men sprinted into the lobby of Noelle's apartment building and rang the concierge's doorbell. The door opened and the concierge stood in the doorway, a startled expression on his face. "What—?" Colonel Mueller shoved him inside his small apartment.

"Fräulein Page!" he snapped. "Where is she?"

The concierge stared at him, panicky.

"She—she left," he said.

"I know that, you stupid fool! I asked you where she went!"

The concierge shook his head helplessly. "I have no idea, Monsieur. I only know she left with an army officer."

"Didn't she tell you where she could be reached?"

"N—No, Monsieur. Mademoiselle Page does not confide in me."

Colonel Mueller glared at the old man a moment and then turned on his heel.

"They can't have gotten far," he said to his men. "Contact all the roadblocks as fast as you can. Tell them that when General Scheider's car arrives I want them to hold it and call me at once!"

Because of the hour military traffic was light, which

meant that there was virtually no traffic at all. General Scheider's car swung onto the West Road that led out of Paris, passing Versailles. They drove through Mantes, Vernon, and Gaillon and in twenty-five minutes they were approaching the major arterial intersection that branched out into Vichy, Le Havre and the Côte d'Azur.

It seemed to Noelle that a miracle had happened. They were going to get out of Paris without being stopped. She should have known that even the Germans with all their efficiency would not be able to check every single road out of the city. And even as she thought it, out of the darkness ahead of them loomed a roadblock. Flashing red lights blinked from the center of the road, and in back of the lights a German Army lorry blocked the highway. On the side of the road were half a dozen German soldiers and two French police cars. A German Army lieutenant waved down the limousine and, as it came to a stop, he walked over to the driver.

"Get out and show your identification!"

General Scheider opened the rear window, leaned his head out and said, raspingly: "General Scheider. What the hell's going on here?"

The lieutenant snapped to attention.

"Excuse me, General. I did not know it was your car."

The General's eyes flicked over the roadblock. "What's this all about?"

"We have orders to inspect every vehicle leaving Paris, Herr General. Every exit from the city is blocked."

The General turned to Noelle. "The damned Gestapo. I'm sorry, *liebchen*."

Noelle could feel the color drain from her face, and she was grateful for the darkness of the car. When she spoke, her voice was steady.

"It's not important," she said.

She thought of the cargo in the trunk. If her plan

had worked, Israel Katz was in there, and in a moment he would be caught. And so would she.

The German lieutenant turned to the chauffeur.

"Open the luggage compartment, please."

"There's nothing in there but luggage," the captain protested. "I put it in myself."

"I'm sorry, Captain. My orders are clear. Every vehicle out of Paris is to be inspected. Open it."

Muttering under his breath, the driver opened his door and started to get out. Noelle's mind was racing furiously. She had to find a way to stop them, without arousing their suspicions. The driver was out of the car. Time had run out. Noelle stole a quick look at General Scheider's face. His eyes were narrowed and his lips were tight with anger. She turned to him and said guilelessly, "Shall we get out, Hans? Will they be searching us?" She could feel his body tense with fury.

"Wait!" The General's voice was like the crack of a whip. "Get back in the car," he ordered his driver. He turned to the lieutenant and his voice was filled with rage. "You tell whoever gave you your orders that they do not apply to generals of the German Army. I do not take orders from lieutenants. Get that roadblock out of my way."

The hapless lieutenant stared at the General's furious face, clicked his heels to attention and said, "Yes, General Scheider." He signaled the driver of the truck blocking the road and the truck lumbered off to the side.

"Drive on," General Scheider commanded.

And the car sped away into the night.

Slowly Noelle let her body relax into the seat, feeling the tension draining out of her. The crisis was past. She wished that she knew whether Israel Katz was in the trunk of the car. And if he was alive.

General Scheider turned to Noelle and she could feel the anger that was still seething in him.

"I apologize," he said, wearily. "This is a strange war. Sometimes it is necessary to remind the Gestapo that wars are run by armies."

Noelle smiled up at him and put her arm through his. "And armies are run by generals."

"Exactly," he agreed. "Armies are run by generals. I am going to have to teach Colonel Mueller a lesson."

Ten minutes after General Scheider's car had left the roadblock, a phone call came in from Gestapo Headquarters, alerting them to be on the lookout for the car.

"It has already passed through," the lieutenant reported, a feeling of foreboding flooding through him. A moment later he was speaking with Colonel Mueller.

"How long ago?" the Gestapo officer asked softly.

"Ten minutes."

"Did you search his car?"

The lieutenant felt his bowels turn to water. "No, sir. The General would not permit—"

"*Scheiss!* Which way was he headed?"

The lieutenant swallowed. When he spoke again, it was in the hopeless voice of a man who knew that his future was finished.

"I am not certain," he replied. "This is a large crossroad here. He could have been going inland to Rouen or to the sea, to Le Havre."

"I want you to present yourself to Gestapo Headquarters at nine A.M. tomorrow. My office."

"Yes, sir," the lieutenant responded.

Savagely Colonel Mueller rang off. He turned to the two men at his side and said, "Le Havre. Get my car. We're going cockroach-hunting!"

The road to Le Havre winds along the Seine, through the beautiful Seine Valley with its rich hills and fertile farms. It was a clear, starlit night and the farmhouses in the distance were pools of light, like oases in the darkness.

In the comfortable back seat of the limousine Noelle and General Scheider talked. He told her about his wife and his children and how difficult marriage was for an army officer. Noelle listened sympathetically and told him how difficult a romantic life was for an actress. Each was aware that the conversation was a game, both of them keeping the talk on a superficial level that would give away no insights. Noelle did not for a moment underestimate the intelligence of the man sitting beside her, and she fully understood how dangerous was the adventure in which she was engaged. She knew that General Scheider was too clever to believe that she had suddenly found him irresistible, that he must suspect that she was after something. What Noelle was counting on was that she would be able to outmaneuver him in the game they were playing. The General touched only briefly on the war, but he said something that she remembered long afterward.

"The British are a strange race," he said. "In peacetime, they are impossible to manage, but in a crisis they are magnificent. The only time a British sailor is truly happy is when his ship is sinking."

They reached Le Havre in the small hours of the morning on their way to the village of Etratat.

"May we stop for a bite to eat?" Noelle asked. "I'm starved."

General Scheider nodded. "Of course, if you wish." He raised his voice. "Look for an all-night restaurant."

"I'm sure there's one by the pier," Noelle suggested. The captain obediently swung the car toward the waterfront. He stopped the car at the water's edge, where several cargo ships were tied to the pier. A block away a sign said, "Bistro."

The captain opened the door and Noelle got out, followed by General Scheider.

"It's probably open all night for the dock workers," Noelle said. She heard the sound of a motor and turned around. A cargo-loading forklift had driven up and stopped near the limousine. Two men wearing coveralls and long, visored caps that concealed their faces got out of the machine. One of the men looked hard at Noelle, then took out a tool kit and began to tighten the forklift. Noelle felt the muscles in her stomach constrict. She took General Scheider's arm and they started toward the restaurant. Noelle looked back at the chauffeur sitting behind the wheel.

"Wouldn't he like some coffee?" Noelle asked.

"He will stay with the car," the General said.

Noelle stared at him. The chauffeur must *not* stay with the car or everything would be ruined. Yet Noelle dared not insist.

They walked on toward the café over the rough, uneven cobblestones. Suddenly, as she took a step, her ankle turned and Noelle fell, letting out a sharp cry of pain. General Scheider reached out and vainly tried to grab her before her body hit the cobblestones.

"Are you all right?" he asked.

The chauffeur, seeing what had happened, moved from behind the wheel of the car and started hurrying toward them.

"I'm so sorry," Noelle said. "I—I turned my ankle. It feels like it's broken."

General Scheider ran his hand expertly over her ankle. "There is no swelling. It is probably just a sprain. Can you stand on it?"

"I—I don't know," Noelle said.

The chauffeur reached her side and the two men lifted her to her feet. Noelle took a step and the ankle gave way under her.

"I'm sorry," she moaned. "If I could just sit down."

"Help me get her in there," General Scheider said, indicating the café.

With the two men supporting her on either side, they walked into the restaurant. As she walked through the door, Noelle risked a quick look back at the car. The two dock workers were at the trunk of the limousine.

"Are you sure you wouldn't rather go straight on to the Etratat?" the General was asking.

"No, believe me, I'll be fine," Noelle replied.

The proprietor led them to a corner table, and the two men eased Noelle into a chair.

"Are you in much pain?" General Scheider asked.

"A bit," Noelle replied. She put her hand on his. "Don't worry. I won't let this spoil anything for you, Hans."

At the moment Noelle and General Hans Scheider were sitting in the café, Colonel Mueller and two of his men were speeding into the city limits of Le Havre. The local captain of police had been roused from his sleep and was waiting for the Gestapo men in front of the police station. "A gendarme has located the General's car," he said. "It is parked down by the waterfront."

A gleam of satisfaction came into Colonel Mueller's face. "Take me there," he commanded.

Five minutes later, the Gestapo automobile with Colonel Mueller, his two men and the police captain raced up beside General Scheider's automobile on the pier. The men got out and surrounded the car. At that moment General Scheider, Noelle and the chauffeur were starting to leave the bistro. The chauffeur was the first to notice the men at the car. He started hurrying toward them.

"What's happening?" Noelle asked, and even as she spoke she recognized the figure of Colonel Mueller in the distance and felt a cold chill go through her.

"I don't know," General Scheider said. He started toward the limousine with long strides, Noelle limping after him.

"What are you doing here?" General Scheider asked Colonel Mueller as he reached the car.

"I am sorry to disturb your holiday," Colonel Mueller replied curtly. "I would like to inspect the trunk of your car, General."

"There is nothing but luggage in there."

Noelle reached the group. She noticed that the forklift had gone. The General and the Gestapo men were glaring at each other.

"I must insist, General. I have reason to believe that

a wanted enemy of the Third Reich is hiding in there and that your guest is his accomplice."

General Scheider stared at him for a long moment, then turned to study Noelle.

"I don't know what he's talking about," she said firmly.

The General's eyes traveled down to her ankle, then he made a decision and turned to his chauffeur. "Open it."

"Yes, General."

All eyes were riveted on the trunk as the chauffeur reached for the handle and turned it. Noelle felt suddenly faint. Slowly the lid opened.

The trunk was empty.

"Someone has stolen our luggage!" exclaimed the chauffeur.

Colonel Mueller's face was mottled with fury. "He got away!"

"Who got away?" demanded the General.

"Le Cafard," raged Colonel Mueller. "A Jew named Israel Katz. He was smuggled out of Paris in the trunk of this car."

"That's impossible," General Scheider retorted. "That trunk was tightly closed. He would have suffocated."

Colonel Mueller studied the trunk for a moment, then turned to one of his men. "Get inside."

"Yes, Colonel."

Obediently the man crawled into the trunk. Colonel Mueller slammed the lid tightly shut and looked at his watch. For the next four minutes, they stood there in silence, each engrossed in his own thoughts. Finally after what seemed an eternity to Noelle, Colonel Mueller opened the lid of the trunk. The man inside was unconscious. General Scheider turned to Colonel Mueller, a contemptuous expression on his face. "If anyone was riding in that trunk," the General declared, "they removed his corpse. Is there anything else I can do for you, Colonel?"

The Gestapo officer shook his head, seething with rage and frustration. General Scheider turned to his chauffeur. "Let's go." He helped Noelle into the car, and they drove toward Etratat, leaving the knot of men fading away into the distance.

Colonel Kurt Mueller instituted an immediate search of the waterfront, but it was not until late the following afternoon that an empty oxygen tank was found in a barrel in a corner of an unused warehouse. An African freighter had set sail for Capetown out of Le Havre the night before but it was now somewhere on the high seas. The missing luggage turned up a few days later in the lost-and-found department of the Gare du Nord in Paris.

As for Noelle and General Scheider, they spent the weekend in Etratat and returned to Paris late Monday afternoon in time for Noelle to do her evening performance.

CATHERINE
Washington: 1941-1944

9

Catherine had quit her job with William Fraser the morning after she had married Larry. Fraser asked her to have lunch with him the day she returned to Washington. He looked drawn and haggard and suddenly older. Catherine had felt a pang of compassion for him, but that was all. She was sitting opposite a tall, nice-looking stranger for whom she felt affection, but it was impossible now to imagine that she had ever contemplated marrying him. Fraser gave her a wan smile.

"So you're a married lady," he said.

"The most married lady in the world."

"It must have happened rather suddenly. I—I wish I'd had a chance to compete."

"*I* didn't even have a chance," Catherine said honestly. "It just—happened."

"Larry's quite a fellow."

"Yes."

"Catherine"—Fraser hesitated—"you don't really know much about Larry, do you?"

Catherine felt her back stiffening.

"I know I love him, Bill," she said evenly, "and I know that he loves me. That's a pretty good beginning, isn't it?"

He sat there frowning, silent, debating with himself. "Catherine—"

"Yes?"

"Be careful."

"Of what?" she asked.

Fraser spoke slowly, feeling his way carefully over a

minefield of words. "Larry's—different."

"How?" she asked, refusing to help him.

"I mean, he's not like most men." He saw the look on her face. "Oh, hell," he said. "Don't pay any attention to me." He managed a faint grin. "You've probably read the biography Aesop did on me. The fox and the sour grapes."

Catherine took his hand affectionately. "I'll never forget you, Bill. I hope we can remain friends."

"I hope so too," Fraser said. "Are you sure you won't stay on at the office?"

"Larry wants me to quit. He's old-fashioned. He believes that husbands should support their wives."

"If you ever change your mind," Fraser said, "let me know." The rest of the luncheon was concerned with office affairs and a discussion of who would take Catherine's place. She knew she would miss Bill Fraser very much. She supposed that the first man to seduce a girl would always hold a special place in that girl's life, but Bill had meant something to her beyond that. He was a dear man and a good friend. Catherine was disturbed by his attitude toward Larry. It was as though Bill had started to warn her about something and then stopped because he was afraid of spoiling her happiness. Or was it as he had said, just a case of sour grapes? Bill Fraser was not a small man or a jealous man. He would surely want her to be happy. And yet Catherine was sure he had tried to tell her something. Somewhere in the back of her mind was a vague foreboding. But an hour later when she met Larry and he smiled at her, everything went out of her head but the ecstasy of being married to this incredible, joyful, human being.

Larry was more fun to be with than anyone Catherine had ever known. Each day was an adventure, a holiday. They drove out to the country every weekend and stayed at small inns and explored county fairs. They went to Lake Placid and rode the huge toboggan slide and to Montauk where they went boating and fishing. Catherine was terrified of the water because she had never learned to swim, but Larry told her not to worry about it, and with him she felt safe.

Larry was loving and attentive and appeared to be remarkably unaware of the attraction he held for other women. Catherine seemed to be all that he wanted. On their honeymoon Larry had come across a little silver bird in an antique shop and Catherine had liked it so much that he had found a crystal bird for her and it had become the start of a collection. On a Saturday night they drove to Maryland to celebrate their third-month anniversary and had dinner at the same little restaurant.

The next day, Sunday, December 7, Pearl Harbor was attacked by the Japanese.

America's declaration of war against Japan came the following day at 1:32 P.M., less than twenty-four hours after the Japanese attack. On Monday while Larry was at Andrews Air Base, Catherine, unable to bear being alone in the apartment, took a taxi to the Capitol Building to see what was happening. Knots of people pressed around a dozen portable radio sets scattered through the crowd that lined the sidewalks of the Capitol Plaza. Catherine watched as the Presidential caravan raced up the drive and stopped at the south entrance to the Capitol. She was close enough to see the limousine door open and President Roosevelt disembark, assisted by two aides. Dozens of policemen stood at every corner, alert for trouble. The mood of the crowd seemed to Catherine to be mainly outrage, like a lynch mob eager to get into action.

Five minutes after President Roosevelt entered the Capitol, his voice came over the radio, as he addressed the Joint Session of Congress. His voice was strong and firm, filled with angry determination.

"America will remember this onslaught . . . Righteous might will win . . . We will gain the inevitable triumph, so help us, God."

Fifteen minutes after Roosevelt had entered the Capitol, House Joint Resolution 254 was passed, declaring war on Japan. It was passed unanimously except for Representative Jeannette Rankin of Montana, who voted against the declaration of war, so the final vote was 388 to 1. President Roosevelt's speech had taken exactly ten minutes—the shortest war message ever delivered to an American Congress.

The crowd outside cheered, a full-throated roar of approval, anger and a promise of vengeance. America was finally on the move.

Catherine studied the men and women standing near her. The faces of the men were filled with the same look of exhilaration that she had seen on Larry's face the day before, as though they all belonged to the same secret club whose members felt that war was an exciting sport. Even the women seemed caught up by the spontaneous enthusiasm that swept through the crowd. But Catherine wondered how they would feel when their men were gone and the women stood alone waiting for news of their husbands and sons. Slowly Catherine turned and walked back toward the apartment. On the corner she saw soldiers with fixed bayonets.

Soon, she thought, the whole country would be in uniform.

It happened even faster than Catherine had anticipated. Almost overnight Washington was transformed into a world of a citizen army in khaki.

The air was filled with an electric, contagious excitement. It was as though peace were a lethargy, a miasma that filled mankind with a sense of ennui, and it was only war that could stimulate man to the full exhilaration of life.

Larry was spending sixteen to eighteen hours at the Air Base, and he often remained there overnight. He told Catherine that the situation at Pearl Harbor and Hickam Field was much worse than the people had been led to believe. The sneak attack had been devastatingly successful. For all practical purposes America's Navy and a good part of its Air Corps had been destroyed.

"Are you saying that we could lose this war?" Catherine asked, shocked.

Larry looked at her thoughtfully. "It depends on how fast we can get ready," he replied. "Everyone thinks of the Japanese as funny little men with weak eyes. That's horseshit. They're tough, and they're not afraid to die. We're soft."

In the months that followed it seemed that nothing could stop the Japanese. The daily headlines screamed out their successes: They were attacking Wake . . . softening up the Philippine Islands for invasion . . . landing in Guam . . . in Borneo . . . in Hong Kong. General MacArthur declared Manila an open city, and the trapped American troops in the Philippines surrendered.

One day in April, Larry telephoned Catherine from the Base and asked her to meet him downtown for dinner at the Willard Hotel to celebrate.

"Celebrate what?" Catherine asked.

"I'll tell you tonight," Larry replied. There was a note of high excitement in his voice.

When Catherine hung up, she was filled with a dread premonition. She tried to think of all the possible reasons that Larry would have to celebrate, but it always came back to the same thing and she did not think she would have the strength to face it.

At five o'clock that afternoon Catherine was fully dressed, sitting on her bed staring into the dressing-room mirror.

I must be wrong, she thought. *Maybe he's been promoted. That's what we're celebrating. Or he's had some good news about the war.* Catherine told herself this but she did not believe it. She studied herself in the mirror, trying to be objective. While she would not give Ingrid Bergman any sleepless nights, she was, she decided dispassionately, attractive. Her figure was good, full of provocative curves. *You're intelligent, cheerful, courteous, kind and a sex pot,* she told herself. *Why would any normal red-blooded male be dying to leave you so that he could go off to war and try to get himself killed?*

At seven o'clock Catherine walked into the dining room of the Willard Hotel. Larry had not arrived yet, and the maître d' escorted her to a table. She said no she would not have a drink, then nervously changed her mind and ordered a martini.

When the waiter brought it and Catherine started to pick it up, she found that her hands were shaking. She looked up and saw Larry moving toward her. He threaded his way between the tables, acknowledging greetings along the way. He carried with him that incredible vitality, that aura that made every eye turn in his direction. Catherine watched him, remembering the day he had come to her table at the MGM commissary in Hollywood. She realized how little she had known him then, and she wondered how well she knew him now. He reached the table and gave her a quick kiss on the cheek.

"Sorry I'm late, Cathy," he apologized. "The Base has been a madhouse all day." He sat down, greeted the captain by name and ordered a martini. If he noticed that Catherine was drinking, he made no comment.

Catherine's mind was screaming out: *Tell me your surprise. Tell me what we're celebrating.* But she said nothing. There was an old Hungarian proverb: "Only a fool rushes bad news." She took another sip of her martini. Well maybe it wasn't an old Hungarian proverb. Maybe it was a new Catherine Douglas proverb designed to be worn over thin skins for protection. Maybe the martini was making her a little drunk. If her premonition was right, before this night was over she was going to get very drunk. But looking at Larry now, his face filled with love, Catherine knew that she had to be wrong. Larry could not bear to leave her any more than she could bear to leave him. She had been building up a nightmare out of whole cloth. From the happy expression on his face she knew that he had some really good news to tell her.

Larry was leaning toward her, smiling his boyish smile, taking her hand in his.

"You'll never guess what's happened, Cathy. I'm going overseas."

It was as though a filmy curtain descended, giving everything an unreal, hazy look. Larry was sitting next to her, his lips moving, but his face was going in and out of focus and Catherine could not hear any words. She looked over his shoulder and the walls of the restaurant were moving together and receding. She watched, fascinated.

"Catherine!" Larry was shaking her arm and slowly her eyes focused on him and everything came back to normal. "Are you all right?"

Catherine nodded, swallowed and said, shakily, "Great. Good news always does that to me."

"You understand that I have to do this, don't you?"

"Yes, I understand." *The truth is, I wouldn't understand if I lived to be a million years old, my darling. But if I told you that, you'd hate me, wouldn't you? Who needs a nagging wife? Heroes' wives should send their men off smiling.*

Larry was watching, concerned. "You're crying."

"I am not," Catherine said indignantly and found to her horror that she was. "I—I just have to get used to the idea."

"They're giving me my own squadron," Larry said.

"Are they really?" Catherine tried to pump pride

into her voice. His own squadron. When he was a small boy, he probably had had his own set of trains to play with. And now that he was a tall boy, they had given him his own squadron to play with. And these were real toys, guaranteed to get shot down and bleed and die. "I'd like another drink," she said.

"Of course."

"When—when will you have to leave?"

"Not until next month."

He made it sound as though he were eager to get away. It was terrifying, feeling the whole fabric of her marriage being torn apart. On the bandstand a singer was crooning, "A trip to the moon on gossamer wings . . ." *Gossamer,* she thought. *That's what my marriage is made of: gossamer.* That Cole Porter knew everything.

"We'll have plenty of time before I leave," Larry was saying.

Plenty of time for what? Catherine wondered bitterly. *Plenty of time to raise a family, to take our children skiing in Vermont, to grow old together?*

"What would you like to do tonight?" Larry asked.

I'd like to go down to the County Hospital and have one of your toes removed. Or have one of your ear drums pierced. Aloud, Catherine said, "Let's go home and make love." And there was a fierce, desperate urgency in her.

The next four weeks melted away. The clocks raced forward in a Kafka-ish nightmare that turned days into hours and hours into minutes, and then incredibly it was Larry's last day. Catherine drove him to the airport. He was talkative and happy and gay and she was somber and quiet and miserable. The last few minutes became a kaleidoscope of reporting in . . . a hurried good-bye kiss . . . Larry entering the plane that was to take him away from her . . . a last farewell wave. Catherine stood on the field watching his plane dwindle to a small speck in the sky and finally disappear. She stood there for an hour, and finally when it got dark she turned and drove back into town to her empty apartment.

In the first year following the attack on Pearl Harbor, ten great sea and air battles were fought against the Japanese. The Allies won only three, but two of them were decisive: Midway and the Battle of Guadalcanal.

Catherine read word for word the newspaper reports of every battle and then asked William Fraser to get her further details. She wrote to Larry daily, but it was eight weeks before she received his first letter. It was optimistic and full of excitement. The letter had been heavily censored so Catherine had no idea where he had been or what he was doing. Whatever it was she had a feeling that he seemed to be enjoying it, and in the long lonely hours of the night Catherine lay in bed puzzling over that, trying to figure out what it was in Larry that made him respond to the challenge of war and death. It was not that he had a death wish, for Catherine had never known anyone more alive and vital; but perhaps that was simply the other side of the coin, that what made the life-sense so keen was constantly honing it against death.

She had lunch with William Fraser. Catherine knew that he had tried to enlist and had been told by the White House that he could do more good by staying at his post. He had been bitterly disappointed. He had never mentioned it to Catherine, however. Now as Fraser sat across from Catherine at the luncheon table, he asked:

"Have you heard from Larry?"

"I got a letter last week."

"What did he say?"

"Well, according to the letter, the war is a kind of football game. We lost the first scrimmage, but now they've sent the first team in, and we're gaining ground."

He nodded. "That's Larry."

"But that's not the war," Catherine said quietly. "It's not a football game, Bill. Millions of people are going to be killed before this is over."

"If you're in it, Catherine," he said gently, "I imagine it's easier to think of it as a football game."

Catherine had decided that she wanted to go to work. The Army had created a branch for women called the WACs, and Catherine had thought of joining but had felt she might be more useful doing something more than driving cars and answering telephones. Although from what she had heard, the WACs were pretty colorful. There was so much pregnancy among them that there was a rumor that when volunteers went in for their physical examination, the doctors pressed their stomachs with a tiny rubber stamp. The girls tried to read the words but were unable to do so. Finally one of them hit upon the idea of getting a magnifying glass. The words read: "When you can read this with the naked eye, report to me."

Now as she sat lunching with Bill Fraser, she said, "I want to work. I want to do something to help."

He studied her a moment, then nodded. "I may know just the thing for you, Catherine. The Government's trying to sell War Bonds. I think you could help coordinate it."

Two weeks later Catherine went to work organizing the sale of War Bonds by celebrities. It had sounded ridiculously easy in concept, but the execution of it was something else again. She found the stars to be like children, eager and excited about helping the war effort, but difficult to pin down about specific dates. Their schedules had to be constantly juggled. Often it was not their fault, because pictures were delayed or schedules ran over. Catherine found herself commuting from Washington to Hollywood and New York. She got used to leaving on an hour's notice, packing enough clothes to last the length of each trip. She met dozens of celebrities.

"Did you really meet Cary Grant?" her secretary asked her when she returned from a trip to Hollywood.

"We had lunch together."

"Is he as charming as they say?"

"If he could package it," Catherine declared, "he'd be the richest man in the world."

It happened so gradually that Catherine was almost unaware of it. It had been six months earlier, when Bill Fraser told her about a problem that Wallace Turner was having with one of the advertising accounts that Catherine used to handle. Catherine had laid out a new campaign using a humorous approach, and the client had been very pleased. A few weeks later Bill had asked Catherine to help on another account, and before she realized it she was spending more than half her time with the advertising agency. She was in charge of half a dozen accounts, all of them doing well. Fraser had given her a large salary and a percentage. At noon on the day before Christmas Fraser came into her office. The rest of the staff had gone home, and Catherine was finishing up some last minute work.

"Having fun?" he asked.

"It's a living," she smiled and added warmly, "and a generous one. Thanks, Bill."

"Don't thank me. You've earned every penny of it—and then some. It's the 'then some' I want to talk to you about. I'm offering you a partnership."

She looked at him in surprise. "A partnership?"

"Half the new accounts we got in the last six months are because of you." He sat there looking at her thoughtfully, saying nothing more. And she understood how much it meant to him.

"You have a partner," she said.

His face lit up. "I can't tell you how pleased I am." Awkwardly, he held out his hand. She shook her head, walked past his outstretched arm, hugged him and gave him a kiss on the cheek.

"Now that we're partners," she teased, "I can kiss you." She felt him suddenly hold her tighter.

"Cathy," he said, "I . . ."

Catherine put her finger to his lips. "Don't say anything, Bill. Let's leave it the way it is."

"You know I'm in love with you."

"And I love you," she said warmly. *Semantics,* she thought. The difference between "I love you" and "I'm in love with you" was a bridgeless chasm.

Fraser smiled. "I won't bother you, I promise. I respect the way you feel about Larry."

"Thank you, Bill." She hesitated. "I don't know whether this helps any, but if there ever were anyone else, it would be you."

"That's a great help," he grinned. "It's going to keep me awake all night."

NOELLE
Paris: 1944

10

During the past year Armand Gautier had ceased
broaching the subject of marriage. In the beginning he
had felt himself in a superior position to Noelle. Now,
however, the situation was almost reversed. When they
gave newspaper interviews, it was Noelle to whom the
questions were directed, and wherever they went together, Noelle was the attraction, he was the after-
thought.

Noelle was the perfect mistress. She continued to
make Gautier comfortable, act as his hostess and in effect make him one of the most envied men in France;
but in truth he never had a moment's peace, for he
knew that he did not possess Noelle, nor ever could,
that there would come a day when she would walk out
of his life as capriciously as she had wandered into it
and when he remembered what had happened to him
the one time that Noelle had left him, Gautier felt sick
to his stomach. Against every instinct of his intellect,
his experience and his knowledge of women he was
wildly, madly in love with Noelle. She was the single
most important fact of his life. He would lie awake
nights devising elaborate surprises to make her happy
and when they succeeded, he was rewarded with a
smile or a kiss or an unsolicited night of love-making.
Whenever she looked at another man, Gautier was
filled with jealousy, but he knew better than to speak
of it to Noelle. Once after a party when she had spent
the entire evening talking to a renowned doctor, Gautier had been furious with her. Noelle had listened to

his tirade and then had answered quietly, "If my speaking to other men bothers you, Armand, I will move my things out tonight."

He had never brought up the subject again.

At the beginning of February, Noelle began her salon. It had started as a simple Sunday brunch with a few of their friends from the theater, but as word about it got around, it quickly expanded and began to include politicians, scientists, writers—anyone whom the group thought might be interesting or amusing. Noelle was the mistress of the salon and one of the chief attractions. Everyone found himself eager to talk to her, for Noelle asked incisive questions and remembered the answers. She learned about politics from politicians and about finance from bankers. A leading art expert taught her about art, and she soon knew all the great French artists who were living in France. She learned about wine from the chief vintner of Baron Rothschild and about architecture from Corbusier. Noelle had the best tutors in the world and they in turn had a beautiful and fascinating student. She had a quick probing mind and was an intelligent listener. Armand Gautier had the feeling that he was watching a Princess consorting with her ministers, and had he only been aware of it, it was the closest he would ever come to understanding Noelle's character.

As the months went by Gautier began to feel a little more secure. It seemed to him that Noelle had met everyone who might matter to her and she had shown no interest in any of them.

She had not yet met Constantin Demiris.

Constantin Demiris was the ruler of an empire larger and more powerful than most countries. He had no title or official position, but he regularly bought and sold prime ministers, cardinals, ambassadors and kings. Demiris was one of the two or three wealthiest men in the world and his power was legendary. He owned the largest fleet of cargo ships afloat, an airline, newspapers, banks, steel mills, gold mines—his tentacles were everywhere, inextricably woven throughout the woof and warp of the economic fabric of dozens of countries.

He had one of the most important art collections in the world, a fleet of private planes and a dozen apartments and villas scattered around the globe.

Constantin Demiris was above medium height, with a barrel chest and broad shoulders. His features were swarthy, and he had a broad Greek nose and olive black eyes that blazed with intelligence. He was not interested in clothes, yet he was always on the list of best-dressed men and it was rumored that he owned over five hundred suits. He had his clothes made wherever he happened to be. His suits were tailored by Hawes and Curtis in London, his shirts by Brioni in Rome, shoes by Daliet Grande in Paris and ties from a dozen countries.

Demiris had about him a presence that was magnetic. When he walked into a room, people who did not know who he was would turn to stare. Newspapers and magazines all over the world had written an incessant spate of stories about Constantin Demiris and his activities, both business and social.

The Press found him highly quotable. When asked by a reporter if friends had helped him achieve his success, he had replied, "To be successful, you need friends. To be *very* successful, you need enemies."

When he was asked how many employees he had, Demiris had said, "None. Only acolytes. When this much power and money is involved, business turns into religion and offices become temples."

He had been reared in the Greek Orthodox Church, but he said of organized religion: "A thousand times more crimes have been committed in the name of love than in the name of hate."

The world knew that he was married to the daughter of an old Greek banking family, that his wife was an attractive, gracious lady and that when Demiris entertained on his yacht or on his private island, his wife seldom went with him. Instead, he would be accompanied by a beautiful actress or ballerina or whoever else struck his current fancy. His romantic escapades were as legendary and as colorful as his financial adventures. He had bedded dozens of motion picture stars, the wives of his best friends, a fifteen-year-old novelist, freshly bereaved widows, and it was even rumored that he had once been propositioned by a group of nuns who needed a new convent.

Half a dozen books had been written about Demiris, but none of them had ever touched on the essence of the man or managed to reveal the wellspring of his success. One of the most public figures in the world, Constantin Demiris was a very private person, and he manipulated his public image as a facade that concealed his real self. He had dozens of intimate friends in every walk of life and yet no one really knew him. The facts were a matter of public record. He had started life in Piraeus as the son of a stevedore, in a family of fourteen brothers and sisters where there was never enough food on the table and if anyone wanted anything extra, he had to fight for it. There was something in Demiris that constantly demanded more, and he fought for it.

Even as a small boy Demiris' mind automatically converted everything into mathematics. He knew the number of steps on the Parthenon, how many minutes it took to walk to school, the number of boats in the harbor on a given day. Time was a number divided into segments, and Demiris learned not to waste it. The result was that without any real effort, he was able to accomplish a tremendous amount. His sense of organization was instinctive, a talent that operated automatically in even the smallest things he did. Everything became a game of matching his wits against those around him.

While Demiris was aware that he was cleverer than

most men, he had no excess vanity. When a beautiful woman wanted to go to bed with him, he did not for an instant flatter himself that it was because of his looks or personality, but he never permitted that to bother him. The world was a market-place, and people were either buyers or sellers. Some women, he knew, were attracted by his money, some by his power and a few—a rare few—by his mind and imagination.

Nearly every person he met wanted something from him: a donation to a charity, financing for a business project or simply the power that his friendship could bestow. Demiris enjoyed the challenge of figuring out exactly what it was that people were really after, for it was seldom what it appeared to be. His analytical mind was skeptical of surface truth, and as a consequence he believed nothing he heard and trusted no one.

The reporters who chronicled his life were permitted to see only his geniality and charm, the sophisticated urbane man of the world. They never suspected that beneath the surface, Demiris was a killer, a gutter-fighter whose instinct was to go for the jugular vein.

To the ancient Greeks the word *thekaeossini,* justice, was often synonymous with *ekthekissis,* vengeance, and Demiris was obsessed with both. He remembered every slight he had ever suffered, and those who were unlucky enough to incur his enmity were paid back a hundredfold. They were never even aware of it, for Demiris' mathematical mind made a game of exacting retribution, patiently working out elaborate traps, spinning complex webs that finally caught and destroyed its victims.

When Demiris was sixteen years old, he had gone into his first business enterprise with an older man named Spyros Nicholas. Demiris had conceived the idea of opening a small stand on the docks to serve hot food to the stevedores on the night shift. He had scraped together half the money for the enterprise, but when it had become successful Nicholas had forced him out of the business and had taken it over himself. Demiris had accepted his fate without protest and had gone ahead to other enterprises.

Over the next twenty years Spyros Nicholas had gone into the meat-packing business and had become rich and successful. He had married, had three children and was one of the most prominent men in Greece. During those years, Demiris patiently sat back and let Nicholas build his little empire. When he decided that Nicholas was as successful and as happy as he was ever going to be, Demiris struck.

Because his business was booming, Nicholas was contemplating buying farms to raise his own meat and opening a chain of retail stores. An enormous amount of money was required. Constantin Demiris owned the bank with which Nicholas did business, and the bank encouraged Nicholas to borrow money for expansion at interest rates that Nicholas could not resist. Nicholas plunged heavily, and in the midst of the expansion his notes were suddenly called in by the bank. When the bewildered man protested that he could not make the payments, the bank immediately began foreclosure proceedings. The newspapers owned by Demiris prominently played up the story on the front pages, and other creditors began foreclosing on Nicholas. He went to other banks and lending institutions, but for reasons he could not fathom, they refused to come to his assistance. The day after he was forced into bankruptcy Nicholas committed suicide.

Demiris' sense of *thekaeossini* was a two-edged sword. Just as he never forgave an injury, neither did he ever forget a favor. A landlady who had fed and clothed the young man when he was too poor to pay her suddenly found herself the owner of an apartment building, without any idea who her benefactor was. A young girl who had taken the penniless young Demiris in to live with her had been given a villa and a lifetime pension anonymously. The people who had had dealings with the ambitious young Greek lad forty years earlier had no idea how the casual relationship with him would affect their lives. The dynamic young Demiris had needed help from bankers and lawyers, ship captains and unions, politicians and financiers. Some had encouraged and helped him, others had snubbed and cheated him. In his head and in his heart the proud Greek had kept an indelible record of every transaction. His wife Melina had once accused him of playing God.

"Every man plays God," Demiris had told her. "Some of us are better equipped for the role than others."

"But it is wrong to destroy the lives of men, Costa."

"It is not wrong. It is justice."

"Vengeance."

"Sometimes it is the same. Most men get away with the evil they do. I am in a position to make them pay for it. That is justice."

He enjoyed the hours he spent devising traps for his adversaries. He would study his victims carefully, analyzing their personalities, assessing their strengths and their weaknesses.

When Demiris had had three small freighters and needed a loan to expand his fleet, he had gone to a Swiss banker in Basel. The banker had not only turned him down but had telephoned other banker friends of his to advise them not to give the young Greek any money. Demiris had finally managed to borrow the money in Turkey.

Demiris had bided his time. He decided that the banker's Achilles' heel lay in his greed. Demiris was in negotiation with Ibn Saud of Arabia to take over leases on a newly discovered oil development there. The leases would be worth several hundred million dollars to Demiris' company.

He instructed one of his agents to leak the news to the Swiss banker about the deal that was about to take place. The banker was offered a 25-percent participation in the new company if he put up five million dollars in cash to buy shares of the stock. When the deal went through, the five million dollars would be worth more than fifty million. The banker quickly checked the deal and confirmed its authenticity. Not having that kind of money available personally, he quietly borrowed it from the bank without notifying anyone, for he had no wish to share his windfall. The transaction was to take place the following week, at which time he would be able to replace the money he had taken.

When Demiris had the banker's check in his hand, he announced to the newspapers that the arrangement with Arabia had been canceled. The stock plummeted. There was no way for the banker to cover his losses, and his embezzlement was discovered. Demiris picked up the banker's shares of stock at a few cents on the dollar and then went ahead with the oil deal. The stock soared. The banker was convicted of embezzlement and given a prison sentence of twenty years.

There were a few players in Demiris' game with whom he had not yet evened the score, but he was in no hurry. He enjoyed the anticipation, the planning and the execution. It was like a chess game, and Demiris was a chess master. These days he made no enemies, for no man could afford to be his enemy, so his quarry was limited to those who had crossed his path in the past.

This, then, was the man who appeared one afternoon at Noelle Page's Sunday salon. He was spending a few hours in Paris on his way to Cairo, and a young sculptress he was seeing suggested that they stop in at the salon. From the moment Demiris saw Noelle, he knew that he wanted her.

Aside from royalty itself which was unavailable to the daughter of a Marseille fishmonger, Constantin Demiris was probably the closest thing there was to a king. Three days after she had met him Noelle quit her play without notice, packed her clothes and joined Constantin Demiris in Greece.

Because of the prominence of their respective positions it was inevitable that the relationship between Noelle Page and Constantin Demiris become an international *cause célèbre*. Photographers and reporters were constantly trying to interview Demiris' wife, but if her composure was ruffled, she never betrayed it. Melina Demiris' only comment to the press was that her husband had many good friends around the world and that she saw nothing wrong with that. Privately she told her outraged parents that Costa had had affairs before and that this would soon wear itself out like all the others. Her husband would leave on extended business trips, and she would see newspaper photographs of him with Noelle in Constantinople or Tokyo or Rome. Melina Demiris was a proud woman, but she was determined to endure the humiliation because she truly loved her husband. She accepted the fact, though she could never fathom the reason, that some men needed more than one woman and that even a man in love with his wife could sleep with another woman. She would have died before she let another man touch her. She never reproached Constantin, because she knew that it would serve no purpose except to alienate him. They had on balance a good marriage. She was aware that she was not a passionate woman, but she let her husband use her in bed whenever he wished, and she tried to give him what pleasure she could. If she had known of the ways that Noelle made love to her husband, she would have been shocked, and if she had known how much her husband enjoyed it, she would have been miserable.

Noelle's chief attraction for Demiris, for whom women no longer held any surprises, was that she was a constant surprise. To him who had a passion for puzzles, she was an enigma, defying solution. He had never met anyone like her. She accepted the beautiful things he gave her, but she was just as happy when he gave her nothing. He bought her a lavish villa at Portofino overlooking the exquisite blue, horseshoe bay, but he knew that it would have made no difference if it had been a tiny apartment in the old Plaka section of Athens.

Demiris had met many women in his life who had tried to use their sex to manipulate him in one way or another. Noelle never asked anything of him. Some women had come to him to bask in his reflected glory, but in Noelle's case *she* was the one who attracted the newspapermen and photographers. She was a star in her own right. For a while Demiris toyed with the idea that perhaps she was in love with him for himself, but he was too honest to maintain the delusion.

In the beginning it was a challenge to try to reach the deep core inside Noelle, to subjugate it and make it his. At first Demiris had tried to do it sexually, but for the first time in his life, he had met a woman who was more than a match for him. Her sensual appetites exceeded his. Anything he could do, she could do better and more often and with more skill, until finally he learned to relax in bed and enjoy her as he had never enjoyed another woman in his life. She was a phenomenon, constantly revealing new facets for him to enjoy. Noelle could cook as well as any of the chefs to whom he paid a king's ransom and knew as much about art as the curators he kept on yearly retainers to seek out paintings and sculpture for him. He enjoyed listening to them discussing art with Noelle and their amazement at the depth of her knowledge.

Demiris had recently purchased a Rembrandt, and Noelle happened to be at his summer island when the painting arrived. There was a young curator there who had found the painting for him.

"It's one of the Master's greatest," the curator had said as he unveiled it.

It was an exquisite painting of a mother and daughter. Noelle was seated in a chair, sipping an ouzo, quietly watching.

"It's a beauty," Demiris agreed. He turned to Noelle. "How do you like it?"

"It's lovely," she said. She turned to the curator. "Where did you find it?"

"I traced it to a private dealer in Brussels," he replied proudly, "and persuaded him to sell it to me."

"How much did you pay for it?" Noelle asked.

"Two hundred and fifty thousand pounds."

"It's a bargain," Demiris declared.

Noelle picked up a cigarette, and the young man rushed to light it for her. "Thank you," she said. She looked at Demiris. "It would have been more of a bargain, Costa, if he had bought it from the man who owned it."

"I don't understand," Demiris said.

The curator was looking at her oddly.

"If this is genuine," Noelle explained, "then it came from the estate of the Duke of Toledo in Spain." She turned to the curator. "Is that not so?" she asked.

His face had turned white. "I—I have no idea," he stammered. "The dealer didn't tell me."

"Oh, come now," Noelle chided him. "You mean you bought a painting for this amount of money without establishing its provenance? That's difficult to believe. The estate priced the painting at one hundred and seventy-five thousand pounds. Someone's been cheated out of seventy-five thousand pounds."

And it had proven to be true. The curator and the art dealer were convicted of collusion and sent to prison. Demiris returned the painting. In thinking it over later he decided that he was less impressed by Noelle's knowledge than by her honesty. If she had wished to, she could simply have called the curator aside, threatened to blackmail him and split the money with him. Instead she had challenged him openly in front of Demiris with no ulterior motive. He had bought her a very expensive emerald necklace in appreciation, and she had accepted it with the same casual appreciation with which she would have accepted a cigarette lighter. Demiris insisted on taking Noelle with him everywhere. He trusted no one in business and therefore was forced to make all his decisions by himself. He found it helpful to discuss business deals with Noelle. She was amazingly knowledgeable about business, and the mere fact of being able to talk with someone sometimes made it easier for Demiris to make a decision. In time Noelle knew more about his business affairs than anyone with the possible exception of his lawyers and accountants. In the past Demiris had always had several mistresses at a time, but now Noelle gave him everything he needed, and one by one he dropped them. They accepted the *congé* without bitterness, for Demiris was a generous man.

He owned a yacht that was a hundred and thirty-five feet long, with four G.M. diesels. It carried a seaplane, a crew of twenty-four, two speed boats and had a freshwater swimming pool. There were twelve beautifully appointed guest suites and a large apartment for himself, crammed with paintings and antiques.

When Demiris entertained on his yacht, it was Noelle who was his hostess. When Demiris flew or sailed to his private island, it was Noelle he took with him while Melina remained at home. He was careful never to bring his wife and Noelle together, but he knew of course that his wife was aware of her.

Noelle was treated like royalty wherever she went. But then it was only her due. The little girl who had looked out at her fleet of ships through the dirty apartment window in Marseille had moved on to the largest fleet in the world. Noelle was not impressed by Demiris' wealth or his reputation: She was impressed by his intelligence and strength. He had the mind and will of a giant and he made other men seem pusillanimous in comparison. She sensed the implacable cruelty in him, but somehow this made him even more exciting, for it was in her also.

Noelle constantly received offers to star in plays and in motion pictures, but she was indifferent. She was playing the lead in her own life story, and it was more fascinating than anything any scriptwriter could concoct. She dined with kings and prime ministers and ambassadors, and they all catered to her because they knew that she had the ear of Demiris. They would drop subtle hints about what their needs were and they promised her the world if she would help them.

But Noelle already had the world. She would lie in bed with Demiris and tell him what each man had asked for, and out of this information Demiris would gauge their needs and their strengths and their weaknesses. Then he would put on appropriate pressures, and from this more money would pour into his already overflowing coffers.

Demiris' private island was one of his great joys. He had purchased an island that was raw land and had transformed it into a paradise. It had a spectacular hilltop villa in which he lived, a dozen charming guest cottages, a hunting preserve, an artificial freshwater lake, a harbor where his yacht could anchor and a landing field for his planes. The island was staffed by eighty servants, and armed guards kept out intruders. Noelle liked the solitude of the island, and she enjoyed it most when there were no other guests there. Constantin Demiris was flattered, assuming that it was because Noelle preferred to be alone with him. He would have been astonished if he had known how preoccupied she was with a man of whose existence he was not even aware.

Larry Douglas was half a world away from Noelle, fighting secret battles on secret islands, and yet she knew more about him than his wife, with whom he corresponded fairly regularly. Noelle traveled to Paris to see Christian Barbet at least once a month and the bald, myopic little detective always had an up-to-date report ready for her.

The first time Noelle had returned to France to see Barbet and had tried to leave there had been trouble about her exit visa. She had been kept waiting in a Customs office for five hours and had finally been allowed to place a call to Constantin Demiris. Ten minutes after she had spoken to Demiris, a German officer had rushed in to offer the profuse apologies of his government. Noelle had been issued a special visa, and she had never been stopped again.

The little detective looked forward to Noelle's visits. He was charging her a fortune, but his trained nose smelled even bigger money. He was very pleased with her new liaison with Constantin Demiris. He had a feeling that in one way or another it was going to be of great financial benefit to him. First he had to make sure that Demiris knew nothing of his mistress' interest in Larry Douglas, then he had to find out how much the information would be worth to Demiris. Or to Noelle Page for him to keep quiet. He was on the verge of an enormous coup, but he had to play his cards carefully. The information Barbet was able to gather on Larry was surprisingly substantial, for Barbet could afford to pay his sources well.

While Larry's wife was reading a letter postmarked from an anonymous APO, Christian Barbet was reporting to Noelle, "He's flying with the Fourteenth Fighter Group, Forty-eighth Fighter Squadron."

Catherine's letter read ". . . all I can tell you is that I'm somewhere in the Pacific, baby . . ."

And Christian Barbet was telling Noelle, "They're on Tarawa. Guam's next."

". . . I really miss you, Cathy. Things are picking up here. I can't give you any details, but we finally have planes that are better than the Jap Zeros . . ."

"Your friend is flying P-Thirty-eights, P-Forties and P-Fifty-ones."

". . . I'm glad you've been keeping busy in Washington. Just stay true to me, baby. Everything's fine here. I'll have a little news for you when I see you . . ."

"Your friend has been awarded the D.F.C. and has been promoted to Lieutenant-Colonel."

While Catherine thought about her husband and prayed for him to come home safely, Noelle followed Larry's every move and she too prayed for Larry's safe return. The war would be over soon and Larry Douglas would be coming home. To both of them.

CATHERINE
Washington: 1945-1946

11

On the morning of May 7, 1945, at Rheims, France, Germany surrendered unconditionally to the Allies. The thousand-year reign of the Third Reich had come to an end. Those insiders who knew of the crippling devastation at Pearl Harbor, those who had watched Dunkirk narrowly miss going into history as England's Waterloo, those who had commanded the RAF and knew how helpless London's defenses would have been against an all-out attack by the Luftwaffe: All these people were aware of the series of miracles that had brought victory to the Allies—and knew by what a narrow margin it had missed going the other way. The powers of evil had almost emerged triumphant, and the idea was so preposterous, so contrary to the Christian ethic of Right triumphing and Evil succumbing, that they turned away from it in horror, thanking God and burying their blunders from the eyes of posterity in mountains of files marked *TOP SECRET*.

The attention of the free world turned now to the Far East. The Japanese, those short, nearsighted comic figures, were bloodily defending every inch of land they held, and it looked as though it was going to be a long and costly war.

And then on August 6, an atomic bomb was dropped on Hiroshima. The destruction was beyond belief. In a few short minutes, most of the population of a major city lay dead, victims of a pestilence greater than the combined wars and plagues of all the Middle Ages.

On August 9, three days later, a second atomic

bomb was dropped, this time on Nagasaki. The results were even more devastating. Civilization had finally reached it finest hour; it was able to achieve genocide that could be calculated at the rate of x number of millions of persons per second. It was too much for the Japanese, and on September 2, 1945, on the battleship *Missouri,* General Douglas MacArthur received the unconditional surrender of the Japanese Government. World War II was ended.

For one long moment when the news was flashed, the world held its breath and then let out a grateful heartfelt cheer. Cities and hamlets around the globe were filled with hysterical parades of people celebrating the end of the war to end all wars to end all wars to end all wars . . .

The following day, through some magic that he would never explain to Catherine, Bill Fraser was able to get a telephone call through to Larry Douglas on an island somewhere in the South Pacific. It was to be a surprise for Catherine. Fraser asked her to wait in her office for him so that they could go to lunch together. At 2:30 in the afternoon, she buzzed Bill on the intercom system.

"When are you going to feed me?" she demanded. "It'll be time for dinner soon."

"Sit tight," Fraser replied. "I'll be with you in a minute."

Five minutes later, he buzzed her and said, "There's a call for you on line one."

Catherine picked up the phone. "Hello?" She heard a crackling and a swell of sound like the waves of a distant ocean. "Hello," she repeated.

A male voice said, "Mrs. Larry Douglas?"

"Yes," Catherine said, puzzled. "Who's this?"

"Just a moment, please."

Through the receiver, she heard a high-pitched whine. Another crackling sound and then a voice saying "Cathy?"

She sat there, her heart pounding, unable to speak. "Larry? Larry?"

"Yes, baby."

"Oh, Larry!" She began to cry and unexpectedly her whole body was trembling.

"How are you, honey?"

She dug her fingernails into her arm, trying to hurt herself enough so that she could stop the hysteria that had suddenly swept over her. "I'm f—fine," she said. "W—where are you?"

"If I tell you, we'll be cut off," he said. "I'm somewhere in the Pacific."

"That's close enough!" She began to get control of her voice. "Are you all right, darling?"

"I'm fine."

"When will you be coming home?"

"Any second," he promised.

Catherine's eyes flooded with tears again. "OK, let's sy—synchronize our watches."

"Are you crying?"

"Of course I'm crying, you idiot! I'm just glad you can't see the mascara running down my face. Oh Larry . . . Larry . . ."

"I've missed you, baby," he said.

Catherine thought of the long, lonely nights that had stretched into weeks and months and years without him, without his arms around her, without his strong, wonderful body next to her, without his comfort and protection and love. And she said, "I've missed you, too."

A man's voice came on the line. "I'm sorry, Colonel, but we're going to have to disconnect."

Colonel!

"You didn't tell me you were promoted."

"I was afraid it would go to your head."

"Oh, darling, I—"

The roar of the ocean grew louder, and suddenly there was a silence and the line was dead. Catherine sat at her desk staring at the telephone. And then she buried her head in her arms and began to cry.

Ten minutes later, Fraser's voice came over the intercom. "I'm ready for lunch when you are, Cathy," he said.

"I'm ready for anything now," she said joyfully. "Give me five minutes." She smiled warmly as she thought of what Fraser had done and how much trouble it must have cost him. He was the dearest man she had ever known. Next to Larry, of course.

Catherine had visualized Larry's arrival so often that the arrival itself was almost an anticlimax. Bill Fraser had explained to her that Larry was probably coming home in an Air Transport Command plane or a MATS plane and they didn't run at fixed times like commercial scheduled airlines. You conned a ride on the first flight you could get on—and it didn't matter too much where the plane was headed—just so it was flying in the right general direction.

Catherine stayed home all day waiting for Larry. She tried to read, but she was too nervous. She sat and listened to the news and thought about Larry returning home to her, this time forever. By midnight, he had still not arrived. She decided he probably would not be home until the next day. At two in the morning, when Catherine could keep her eyes open no longer, she went to bed.

She was awakened by a hand on her arm and she opened her eyes and he was standing over her, her Larry was standing there, looking down at her, a grin on his lean, tanned face, and in a flash Catherine was in his arms and all the worry and loneliness and pain of the past four years were washed away in a cleansing flood of joy that seemed to fill every fiber of her being. She hugged him until she was afraid that she was going to break his bones. She wanted to stay like this forever, never letting him go.

"Easy, honey," Larry said finally. He pulled away from her, a smile on his face. "It's going to look funny in the newspapers. 'Flyer comes home safely from the war and gets hugged to death by his wife.' "

Catherine turned on the lights, every one of them, flooding the room so that she could see him, study him, devour him. His face had a new maturity. There were lines around his eyes and mouth that had not been there before. The overall effect was to make him handsomer than ever.

"I wanted to meet you," Catherine babbled, "But I didn't know where. I called the Air Corps and they couldn't give me any information at all, so I just waited here and . . ."

Larry moved toward her and shut her up with a kiss. His kiss was hard and demanding. Catherine had expected to feel the same physical eagerness for him and she was surprised to find that this was not so. She loved him very much and yet she would have been content to just sit with him and talk, instead of making love as he so urgently wanted to do. She had sublimated her sexual feelings for so long that they were deeply buried, and it would take time before they could be aroused and brought to the surface again.

But Larry was giving her no time. He was throwing off his clothes and saying, "God, Cathy, you don't know how I've dreamed about this moment. I was going crazy out there. And look at you. You're even more beautiful than I remembered."

He ripped off his shorts and was standing there naked. And somehow it was a stranger pushing her down on the bed, and she wished that Larry would give her time to get used to his being home, to get used to his nakedness again. But he was getting on top of her without any preliminaries, forcing himself into her and she knew that she was not ready for him. He was tearing into her, hurting her and she bit her hand to keep from crying out as he lay on top of her, making love like a wild animal.

Her husband was home.

* * *

For the next month with Fraser's blessing Catherine stayed away from the office and she and Larry spent almost every moment together. She cooked for him all of his favorite dishes, and they listened to records and talked and talked and talked, trying to fill in the gaps of the lost years between them. At night they went to parties or to the theater and when they returned home, they made love. Her body was ready for him now and she found him as exciting a lover as always. Almost.

She did not want to admit it even to herself, but there was something indefinably changed about Larry. He was more demanding, less giving. There was still foreplay before they made love, but he did it mechanically, as though it were a duty to be disposed of before he went on to the sexual attack. And it was an attack, a savage and fierce taking, as though his body were seeking vengeance for something, meting out punishment. Each time they finished making love, Catherine felt bruised and battered, as though she had taken a beating. Perhaps, she defended him, it's just because he's been so long without a woman.

As the days passed, his lovemaking remained the same and it was that fact that finally led Catherine to look for other changes in Larry. She tried to study him dispassionately, tried to forget that this was the husband whom she adored. She saw a tall, well-built, black-haired man with deep dark eyes and a devastatingly beautiful face. Or perhaps "beautiful" no longer applied. The lines around his mouth had added a harshness to his features. Looking at this stranger, Catherine would have thought, *Here is a man who could be selfish and ruthless and cold.* And yet she told herself that she was being ridiculous. This was her Larry, loving and kind and thoughtful.

She proudly introduced him to all her friends and the people she worked with, but they seemed to bore him. At parties he would wander off into a corner and spend the evening drinking. It seemed to Catherine that he made no effort to be sociable. "Why should I?"

he snapped at her one evening when she tried to discuss it with him. "Where the fuck were all those fat cats when I was up there getting my ass shot at?"

A few times Catherine broached the subject of what Larry was going to do with his future. She had thought that he would want to remain in the Air Corps, but almost the first thing Larry did when he returned home was to resign his commission.

"The Service is for suckers. There's nowhere to go but down," he had said.

It was almost like a parody of the first conversation Catherine had had with him in Hollywood. Only then, he had been joking.

Catherine had to discuss the problem with someone and she finally decided to talk to Bill Fraser. She told him what was troubling her, leaving out the more personal things.

"If it's any consolation to you," Fraser said sympathetically, "there are millions of women all over the world going through what you're going through now. It's really very simple, Catherine. You're married to a stranger."

Catherine looked at him, saying nothing.

Fraser stopped to fill his pipe and light it. "You can't really expect to pick up where you left off when Larry went away four years ago, can you? That place in time doesn't exist any more. You've moved past it, and so has Larry. Part of what makes a marriage work is that a husband and wife have common experiences. They grow together and their marriage grows. You're going to have to find a common meeting ground again."

"I feel disloyal even discussing it, Bill."

Fraser smiled. "I knew you first," he reminded her. "Remember?"

"I remember."

"I'm sure that Larry's feeling his way, too," Fraser continued. "He's been living with a thousand men for four years and now he has to get used to living with a girl."

She smiled. "You're right about everything you said. I suppose I just had to hear someone say it."

"Everyone's full of helpful advice about how to handle the wounded," Fraser remarked, "but there are some wounds that don't show. Sometimes they go deep." He saw the look on Catherine's face. "I don't mean anything serious," he added quickly. "I'm just talking about the horrors that any combat soldier sees. Unless a man is a complete fool, it's bound to have an enormous effect on his outlook. You see what I mean?"

Catherine nodded. "Yes." The question was: What effect had it had?

When Catherine finally went back to work, the men at the agency were overjoyed to see her. For the first three days she did almost nothing but go over campaigns and layouts for new accounts and catch up on old accounts. She worked from early in the morning until late in the evening, trying to make up for the time she had lost, badgering copywriters and sketch artists and reassuring nervous clients. She was very good at her job and she loved it.

Larry would be waiting for Catherine when she returned to the apartment at night. In the beginning she had asked what he did while she was gone, but his answers were always vague and she finally stopped asking him. He had put up a wall, and she did not know how to breach it. He took offense at almost everything Catherine said, and there were constant quarrels over nothing. Occasionally they would dine with Fraser and she went out of her way to make those evenings pleasant and gay so that Fraser would not think there was anything wrong.

But Catherine had to face the fact that something was very wrong. She felt that it was partly her failure. She still loved Larry. She loved the look of him and the feel of him and the memory of him, but she knew that if he went on this way, it would destroy them both.

She was having lunch with William Fraser.

"How's Larry?" he asked.

The automatic Pavlovian response of "fine" started to come to her lips and she stopped. "He needs a job," Catherine said bluntly.

Fraser leaned back and nodded. "Is he getting restless about not working?"

She hesitated, not wanting to lie. "He doesn't want to do just anything," she said carefully. "It would have to be the right thing."

Fraser studied her, trying to assess the meaning that lay behind her words.

"How would he like to be a pilot?"

"He doesn't want to go back into the Service again."

"I was thinking about one of the airlines. I have a friend who runs Pan Am. They'd be lucky to get someone with Larry's experience."

Catherine sat there thinking about it, trying to put herself in Larry's mind. He loved flying more than anything in the world. It would be a good job, doing what he loved to do. "It—it sounds wonderful," she said cautiously. "Do you really think you could get it for him, Bill?"

"I'll give it a try," he said. "Why don't you sound Larry out first and see how he feels about it?"

"I will." Catherine took his hand in hers gratefully. "Thanks so much."

"For what?" Fraser asked lightly.

"For always being there when I need you."

He put his hand over hers. "It goes with the territory."

When Catherine told Larry about Bill Fraser's suggestion that night, he said, "That's the best idea I've heard since I came home," and two days later, he had an appointment to see Carl Eastman at Pan Am headquarters in Manhattan. Catherine pressed Larry's suit for him, selected a shirt and tie and shined his shoes until she could see her image in them. "I'll call you as soon as I can and let you know how it went." He kissed her, smiled that quick boyish grin of his and left.

In many ways Larry *was* like a small boy, Catherine thought. He could be petulant and quick-tempered and surly, but he was also loving and generous.

"My luck," sighed Catherine. "I have to be the only perfect person in the whole universe."

She had a busy schedule ahead of her, but she was unable to think of anything but Larry and his meeting. It was more than just a job. She had a feeling that her whole marriage hinged on what was going to happen.

It was going to be the longest day of her life.

Pan American headquarters was in a modern building at Fifth Avenue and Fifty-third Street. Carl Eastman's office was large and comfortably furnished, and he obviously held a position of importance.

"Come in and sit down," he greeted Larry as Larry entered the office.

Eastman was about thirty-five, a trim, lantern-jawed man with piercing hazel eyes that missed nothing. He motioned Larry to a couch, then sat on a chair across from him.

"Coffee?"

"No thanks," Larry said.

"I understand you'd like to work for us."

"If there's an opening."

"There's an opening," Eastman said, "only a thousand stick jockeys have applied for it." He shook his head ruefully. "It's incredible. The Air Corps trains thousands of bright young men to fly the most complicated pieces of machinery ever made. Then when they do their job and do it damn well, the Air Corps tells 'em to get lost. They have nothing for them." He sighed. "You wouldn't believe the people who come in here all day long. Top pilots, aces like yourself. There's only one job open for every thousand applicants—and all the other airlines are in exactly the same position."

A feeling of disappointment swept over Larry. "Why did you see me?" he asked stiffly.

"Two reasons. Number One, because the man upstairs told me to."

Larry felt an anger rising in him.

"I don't need—"

Eastman leaned forward. "Number Two, you have a damn good flying record."

"Thanks," Larry said, tightly.

Eastman studied him. "You'd have to go through a training program here, you know. It would be like going back to school."

Larry hesitated, not certain where the conversation was leading.

"That sounds all right," he said, cautiously.

"You'll have to take your training in New York out of LaGuardia."

Larry nodded, waiting.

"There are four weeks of ground school and then a month of flight training."

"You flying DC-Fours?" asked Larry.

"Right. When you finish your training, we'll put you on as a navigator. Your training base pay will be three fifty a month."

He had the job! The son-of-a-bitch had needled him about all the thousands of pilots who were after it. But he had the job! What had he been worried about? No one in the whole damned Air Corps had a better record than he did.

Larry grinned. "I don't mind starting as a navigator, Eastman, but I'm a pilot. When does *that* happen?"

Eastman sighed. "The airlines are unionized. The only way anyone moves up is through seniority. There are a lot of men ahead of you. Do you want to give it a try?"

Larry nodded. "What have I got to lose?"

"Right," Eastman said. "I'll arrange all the formalities. You'll have to take a physical, of course. Any problems there?"

Larry grinned. "The Japanese didn't find anything wrong with me."

"How soon can you go to work?"

"Is this afternoon too early?"

"Let's make it Monday." Eastman scribbled a name on a card and handed it to Larry. "Here. They'll be expecting you at nine o'clock Monday morning."

When Larry phoned Catherine to tell her the news, there was an excitement in his voice that Catherine had not heard for a long time. She knew then that everything was going to be all right.

NOELLE
Athens: 1946

12

Constantin Demiris owned a fleet of airplanes for his personal use, but his pride was a converted Hawker Siddeley that transported sixteen passengers in luxurious comfort, had a speed of three hundred miles per hour and carried a crew of four. It was a flying palace. The interior had been decorated by Frederick Sawrin and Chagall had done the murals on the walls. Instead of airplane seats, easy chairs and comfortable couches were sprinkled throughout the cabin. The aft compartment had been converted into a luxurious bedroom. Forward behind the cockpit was a modern kitchen. Whenever Demiris or Noelle flew on the plane, there was a chef aboard.

Demiris had chosen as his personal pilots a Greek flyer named Paul Metaxas and an English ex-RAF fighter pilot named Ian Whitestone. Metaxas was a stocky, amiable man with a perpetual smile on his face and a hearty, contagious laugh. He had been a mechanic, had taught himself how to fly and had served with the RAF in the Battle of Britain, where he had met Ian Whitestone. Whitestone was tall, red-haired and painfully thin, with the diffident manner of a schoolmaster on his first day of the term at a second-rate school for incorrigible boys. In the air Whitestone was something else again. He had the rare, natural skill of a born pilot, a feel that can never be taught or learned. Whitestone and Metaxas had flown together for three years against the Luftwaffe and each had a high regard for the other.

Noelle made frequent trips in the large plane, sometimes on business with Demiris, sometimes for pleasure. She had gotten to know the pilots but had paid no particular attention to them.

And then one day she overheard them reminiscing about an experience they had had in the RAF.

From that moment on Noelle either spent some part of each flight in the cockpit talking to the two men or invited one of them to join her back in the cabin. She encouraged them to talk about their war experiences and, without ever asking a direct question, eventually learned that Whitestone had been a liaison officer in Larry Douglas' squadron before Douglas had left the RAF and that Metaxas had joined the squadron too late to meet Larry. Noelle began to concentrate on the English pilot. Encouraged and flattered by the interest of his boss' mistress, Whitestone talked freely about his past life and his future ambitions. He told Noelle he had always been interested in electronics. His brother-in-law in Australia had opened a small electronics firm and wanted Whitestone to go in with him, but Whitestone lacked the capital.

"The way I live," he said to Noelle, grinning, "I'll never make it."

Noelle continued to visit Paris once a month to see Christian Barbet. Barbet had established a liaison with a private detective agency in Washington, and there was a constant stream of reports on Larry Douglas. Cautiously testing Noelle, the little detective had offered to send the reports to her in Athens, but she told him that she preferred picking them up in person. Barbet had nodded his head slyly and said in a conspiratorial tone, "I understand, Miss Page." So she did *not* want Constantin Demiris to know about her interest in Larry Douglas. The possibilities for blackmail staggered Barbet's mind.

"You have been most helpful, Monsieur Barbet," Noelle said, "and most discreet."

He smiled unctuously. "Thank you, Miss Page. My

business depends on discretion."

"Exactly," Noelle replied, "I know you are discreet because Constantin Demiris has never mentioned your name to me. The day he does, I will ask him to destroy you." Her tone was pleasant and conversational, but the effect was like a bombshell.

Monsieur Barbet stared at Noelle for a long, shocked moment, licking his lips. He scratched his crotch nervously and stammered, "I—I assure you, Mademoiselle, that I would n—never . . ."

"I'm sure you won't," Noelle said and departed.

On the commercial plane taking her back to Greece, Noelle read the confidential report in the sealed manila envelope.

ACME SECURITY AGENCY
1402 "D" Street
Washington, D.C.

Reference: #2-179-210   February 2, 1946
Dear Monsieur Barbet:

One of our operatives spoke to a contact in the personnel office at Pan Am: Subject is regarded as a skilled combat pilot, but they question whether he is disciplined enough to work out satisfactorily within a large, structured organization.

Subject's personal life-style follows the same pattern as in our previous reports. We have followed him to the apartments of various women whom he had picked up, where he remained for periods of from one hour to as long as five hours, and we presume that he is having a series of casual sexual relations with these women. (Names and addresses are on file if you wish them.)

In view of the Subject's new employment, it is possible that this pattern may change. We will follow up on this per your request.

Please find our bill enclosed.

Very truly yours,
R. Ruttenberg,
Managing Supervisor

Noelle returned the report to the folder and leaned back in her seat and closed her eyes. She visualized Larry, restless and tormented, married to a woman he did not love, caught in a trap baited with his own weaknesses.

His new job with the airline might slow Noelle's plan down a bit, but she had patience. In time she would bring Larry to her. Meanwhile there were certain steps she could take to move things along.

Ian Whitestone was delighted to be invited to lunch with Noelle Page. In the beginning he had flattered himself that she was attracted to him, but all of their encounters had been on a pleasant but formal basis that let him know that he was an employee, and she was an untouchable. He had often puzzled over what Noelle wanted of him, for Whitestone was an intelligent man, and he had the odd feeling that their random conversations meant something more to her than they meant to him.

On this particular day Whitestone and Noelle drove to a small seaside town near Cape Sunion, where they were having lunch. Noelle was dressed in a white summer frock and sandals, with her soft blond hair blowing free, and she had never looked more beautiful. Ian Whitestone was engaged to a model in London and while she was pretty, she could not compare to Noelle. Whitestone had never met anyone who could, and he would have envied Constantin Demiris except that Noelle always seemed more desirable to him in retrospect. When Whitestone was actually with her, he found himself slightly intimidated. Now Noelle had turned the conversation to his plans for the future, and he wondered, not for the first time, whether she was probing on Demiris' orders to find out whether he was loyal to his employer.

"I love my job," the pilot assured Noelle earnestly. "I'd like to keep it until I'm too old to see where I'm flying."

Noelle studied him a moment, aware of his suspicions. "I'm disappointed," she said ruefully. "I was hoping that you had more ambition than that."

Whitestone stared at her. "I don't understand."

"Didn't you tell me that you'd like to have your own electronics company one day?"

He recalled mentioning it to her casually, and it surprised him that she had remembered.

"That was just a pipe dream," he replied. "It would take a lot of money."

"A man with your ability," Noelle said, "shouldn't be stopped by a lack of money."

Whitestone sat there uneasily, not knowing what Noelle Page expected him to say. He did like his job. He was making more money than he had ever made in his life, the hours were good and the work interesting. On the other hand he was at the beck and call of an eccentric billionaire who expected him to be available at any hour of the day or night. It had raised hell with his personal life, and his fiancée was not happy about what he was doing, good salary or no.

"I've been talking to a friend of mine about you," Noelle said. "He likes to invest in new companies."

Her voice had controlled enthusiasm, as though she were excited about what she was saying and yet was being careful not to push him too hard. Whitestone raised his eyes and met hers.

"He's very interested in you," she said.

Whitestone swallowed. "I—I don't know what to say, Miss Page."

"I don't expect you to say anything now," Noelle assured him. "I just want you to think about it."

He sat there a moment, thinking about it. "Does Mr. Demiris know about this?" he asked finally.

Noelle smiled conspiratorially. "I'm afraid Mr. Demiris would never approve. He doesn't like to lose employees, especially good ones. However—" she paused fractionally, "I think someone like you is entitled to get everything out of life that he can. Unless of course," she added, "you want to go on working for someone else the rest of your life."

"I don't," Whitestone said quickly and suddenly realized that he had committed himself. He studied Noelle's face to see if there was any suggestion that this could be some kind of a trap, but all he saw was a sympathetic understanding. "Any man worth his salt would like to have his own business," he said defensively.

"Of course," Noelle agreed. "Give it some thought, and we'll talk about it again." And then she added warningly, "It will be just between us."

"Fair enough," Whitestone said, "and thank you. If it works out, it will really be exciting."

Noelle nodded. "I have a feeling that it's going to work out."

CATHERINE
Washington-Paris: 1946

13

At nine o'clock on Monday morning Larry Douglas reported to the chief pilot, Captain Hal Sakowitz, at the Pan American office at LaGuardia Airport in New York. As Larry walked in the door, Sakowitz picked up the transcript of Larry's service record that he had been studying and shoved it into a desk drawer.

Captain Sakowitz was a compact, rugged-looking man with a seamed, weather-beaten face and the largest hands that Larry had ever seen. Sakowitz was one of the real veterans of aviation. He had started out in the days of traveling air circuses, had flown single-engine airmail planes for the Government and had been an airline pilot for twenty years and Pan American's chief pilot for the past five years.

"Glad to have you with us, Douglas," he said.

"Glad to be here," Larry replied.

"Eager to get into a plane again?"

"Who needs a plane?" grinned Larry. "Just point me into the wind, and I'll take off."

Sakowitz indicated a chair. "Sit down. I like to get acquainted with you boys who come in here to take over my job."

Larry laughed. "You noticed."

"Oh, I don't blame any of you. You're all hotshot pilots, you have great combat records, you come in here and think 'if that schmuck Sakowitz can be Chief Pilot, they oughta make me Chairman of the Board.' None of you guys plan to stay navigators very long. It's just a stepping stone to pilot. Well, that's fine. That's the way it should be."

"I'm glad you feel that way," Larry said.

"But there's one thing you have to know out front. We all belong to a union, Douglas, and promotions are strictly by seniority."

"I understand."

"The only thing you might *not* understand is that these are damn good jobs and there are more people coming in than there are leaving. That slows up the rate of promotion."

"I'll take my chances," Larry replied.

Sakowitz's secretary brought in coffee and Danish pastries and the two men spent the next hour talking and getting acquainted. Sakowitz's manner was friendly and affable, and many of his questions were seemingly irrelevant and trivial, but when Larry left to go to his first class, Sakowitz knew a great deal about Larry Douglas. A few minutes after Larry had departed, Carl Eastman came into the office.

"How did it go?" Eastman asked.

"OK."

Eastman gave him a hard look. "What do you think, Sak?"

"We'll try him."

"I asked you what you thought."

Sakowitz shrugged. "OK. I'll tell you. My hunch is he's a goddamn good pilot. He has to be, with his war record. Put him in a plane with a bunch of enemy fighters shooting at him, and I don't think you'll find anyone better." He hesitated.

"Go on," Eastman said.

"The thing is, there aren't a hell of a lot of enemy fighters around Manhattan. I've known guys like Douglas. For some reason I've never figured out, their lives are geared for danger. They do crazy things like climbing impossible mountains or diving to the bottom of the ocean, or whatever the hell else danger they can find. When a war breaks out, they rise to the top like cream in a cup of scalding coffee." He swerved his chair around and looked out the window. Eastman stood there, saying nothing, waiting.

"I have a hunch about Douglas, Carl. There's something wrong with him. Maybe if he were captain of one of our ships, flying it himself, he could make it. But I don't think he's psychologically geared to take orders from an engineer, a first officer and a pilot, especially when he thinks he could outfly them all." He swung back to face Eastman. "And the funny part is, he probably could."

"You're making me nervous," Eastman said.

"Me, too," Sakowitz confessed. "I don't think he's—" He stopped, searching for the right word, "stable. Talking to him, you get a feeling he has a stick of dynamite up his ass, ready to explode."

"What do you want to do?"

"We're doing it. He'll go to school and we'll keep a close eye on him."

"Maybe he'll wash out," Eastman said.

"You don't know that breed of cat. He'll come out number one man in his class."

Sakowitz's prediction was accurate.

The training course consisted of four weeks of ground school followed by an additional month of flight training. Since the trainees were already experienced pilots with many years of flying behind them, the course was devised to serve two purposes: the first was to run through such subjects as navigation, radio, communication, map reading and instrument flying to refresh the memories of the men and pinpoint their potential weaknesses, and the second was to familiarize them with the new equipment they would be using.

The instrument flying was done in a Link Trainer, a small mock-up of an airplane cockpit that rested on a movable base, enabling the pilot in the cockpit to put the plane through any maneuver, including stalls, loops, spins and rolls. A black hood was put over the top of the cockpit so that the pilot was flying blind, using only the instruments in front of him. The instructor outside the Trainer fed orders to the pilot, giving him directions for takeoffs and landings in the face of strong wind velocity, storms, mountain ranges and every other simulated hazard conceivable. Most inexperienced pilots went into the Link Trainer with a feeling of confidence, but they soon learned that the little Trainers were much more difficult to operate than they appeared to be. It was an eerie sensation to be alone in the tiny cockpit, all senses cut off from the outside world.

Larry was a gifted pupil. He was attentive in class and absorbed everything he was taught. He did all his homework and did it well and carefully. He showed no sign of impatience, restlessness or boredom. On the contrary, he was the most eager pupil in the course and certainly the most outstanding. The only area that was new to Larry was the equipment, the DC-4. The Douglas planes were long, sleek aircraft with some equipment that had not been in existence when the war began. Larry spent hours going over every inch of the plane, studying the way it had been put together and the way it functioned. Evenings he pored over the dozens of service manuals of the plane.

Late one night after all the other trainees had left the hangar Sakowitz had come upon Larry in one of the DC-4s, lying on his back under the cockpit, examining the wiring.

"I tell you, the son-of-a-bitch is gunning for my job," Sakowitz told Carl Eastman the next morning.

"The way he's going, he may get it," Eastman grinned.

At the end of the eight weeks there was a little graduation ceremony. Catherine proudly flew to New York to be there when they presented Larry with his navigator's wings.

He tried to make light of it. "Cathy, it's just a stupid little piece of cloth they give you so you'll remember what your job is when you get into the cockpit."

"Oh, no, you don't," she said. "I talked to Captain Sakowitz and he told me how good you are."

"What does a dumb Polack know?" Larry said. "Let's go celebrate."

That night Catherine and Larry and four of Larry's classmates and their wives went to the Twenty-one Club on West Fifty-second Street for dinner. The foyer was crowded, and the maître d' told them that without reservations there were no tables available.

"To hell with this place," Larry said. "Let's go next door to Toots Shor's."

"Wait a minute," Catherine said. She went over to the captain and asked to see Jerry Berns.

A few moments later a short, thin man with inquisitive gray eyes bustled up.

"I'm Jerry Berns," he said. "May I help you?"

"My husband and I are with some friends," Catherine explained. "There are ten of us."

He started to shake his head. "Unless you have a reservation . . ."

"I'm William Fraser's partner," Catherine said.

Jerry Berns looked at Catherine reproachfully. "Why didn't you tell me? Can you give me fifteen minutes?"

"Thank you," Catherine said gratefully.

She went back to where the group was standing.

"Surprise!" Catherine said. "We have a table."

"How did you manage that?" Larry asked.

"It was easy," Catherine said. "I mentioned Bill Fraser's name." She saw the look that came into Larry's eyes. "He comes in here often," Catherine went on quickly. "And he told me if I ever came in and needed a table, to mention his name."

Larry turned to the others. "Let's get the hell out of here. This is for the birds."

The group started toward the door. Larry turned to Catherine. "Coming?"

"Of course," Catherine said hesitantly, "I just wanted to tell them that we're not . . ."

"Fuck 'em," said Larry loudly. "Are you coming or aren't you?"

People were turning to stare. Catherine felt her face redden.

"Yes," she said. She turned and followed Larry out the door.

They went to an Italian restaurant on Sixth Avenue and had a bad dinner. Outwardly Catherine acted as though nothing had happened, but inwardly she was fuming. She was furious with Larry for his childish behavior and for humiliating her in public.

When they got home, she walked into the bedroom without saying a word, undressed, turned out the light and got into bed. She heard Larry in the living room, mixing a drink.

Ten minutes later he came into the bedroom and turned on the light and walked over to the bed. "You planning to become a martyr?" he asked.

She sat up, furious. "Don't try to put me on the defensive," she said. "Your behavior tonight was inexcusable. What got into you?"

"The same guy that got into you."

She stared at him. "What?"

"I'm talking about Mr. Perfection. Bill Fraser."

She looked at him, not understanding. "Bill's never done anything but help us."

"You bet your ass," he said. "You owe him your business. I owe him my job. Now we can't even sit down in a restaurant without Fraser's permission. Well, I'm sick of having him shoved down my throat every day." It was Larry's tone that shook Catherine even more than what he was saying. It was so filled with frustration and impotence that she realized for the first time how tormented he must be. And why not? He had come back from four years of fighting to find his wife in partnership with her former lover. And to make it worse, he himself had not even been able to get a job without the help of Fraser.

As she looked at Larry, Catherine knew that this

was a turning point in their marriage. If she stayed
with him, he would have to come first. Before her job,
before everything. For the first time Catherine felt that
she really understood Larry.

As though reading her mind Larry said contritely,
"I'm sorry I acted like a shit-heel this evening. But
when we couldn't get a table until you mentioned
Fraser's magic name, I—I'd suddenly had it up to
here."

"I'm sorry, Larry," Catherine said, "I'll never do
that to you again."

And they were in each other's arms, and Larry said,
"Please don't ever leave me, Cathy," and Catherine
thought of how close she had come to it, and she held
him tighter and said, "I won't leave you, darling, ever."

Larry's first assignment as a navigator was on Flight
147 from Washington to Paris. He stayed over in Paris
for forty-eight hours after each flight, then returned
home for three days before he flew out again.

One morning Larry called Catherine at her office,
his voice excited. "Hey, I've got a great restaurant for
us. Can you get away for lunch?"

Catherine looked at the pile of layouts that had to
be finished and approved before noon. "Sure," she
said, recklessly.

"I'll pick you up in fifteen minutes."

"You're not leaving me!" Lucia, her assistant,
wailed. "Stuyvesant will have kittens if we don't get
this campaign to him today."

"It will have to wait," Catherine said. "I'm going to
have lunch with my husband."

Lucia shrugged. "I don't blame you. If you ever get
tired of him, will you let me know?"

Catherine grinned. "You'll be too old."

Larry picked Catherine up in front of the office, and
she got into the car.

"Did I screw up your day for you?" he asked mis-
chievously.

"Of course not."

He laughed. "All those executive types are going to have a stroke."

Larry headed the car toward the airport.

"How far is the restaurant?" Catherine asked. She had five appointments in the afternoon, beginning at two o'clock.

"Not far . . . Do you have a busy afternoon?"

"No," she lied. "Nothing special."

"Good."

When they reached the airport turnoff, Larry swung the car into the entrance.

"Is the restaurant at the airport?"

"At the other end," Larry replied. He parked the car, took Catherine's arm and led her inside to the Pan-Am gate. The attractive girl behind the desk greeted Larry by name.

"This is my wife," Larry said proudly. "This is Amy Winston."

They exchanged hellos.

"Come on." Larry took Catherine's arm and they moved toward the departure ramp.

"Larry—" Catherine began. "Where . . . ?"

"Hey, you're the nosiest girl I've ever taken to lunch."

They had reached Gate 37. Two men behind the ticket counter were processing the tickets of emplaning passengers. A sign on the information board read: "Flight 147 to Paris—Departing 1:00 P.M."

Larry walked up to one of the men behind the desk. "Here she is, Tony." He handed the man a plane ticket. "Cathy, this is Tony Lombardi. This is Catherine."

"I've sure heard a lot about you," the man grinned. "Your ticket's all in order." He handed the ticket to Catherine.

Catherine stared at it, dazed. "What's this for?"

"I lied to you," Larry smiled. "I'm not taking you to lunch. I'm taking you to Paris. Maxim's."

Catherine's voice broke. "M—Maxim's? In Paris? *Now?*"

"That's right."

"I can't," Catherine wailed. "I can't go to Paris now."

"Sure you can," he grinned. "I've got your passport in my pocket."

"Larry," she said, "you're mad! I have no clothes. I have a million appointments. I—"

"I'll buy you some clothes in Paris. Cancel your appointments. Fraser can get along without you for a few days."

Catherine stared at him, not knowing what to say. She remembered the resolutions she had made to herself. Larry was her husband. He had to come first. Catherine realized that it wasn't just taking her to Paris that was important to Larry. He was showing off for her, asking her to fly in the plane he was navigating. And she had almost spoiled it. She put her hand in his and smiled up at him.

"What are we waiting for?" Catherine asked. "I'm starved!"

Paris was a whirlwind of fun. Larry had arranged to take a full week off, and it seemed to Catherine that every hour of the day and night was crammed with things to do. They stayed at a charming little hotel on the Left Bank.

Their first morning in Paris Larry took Catherine to a salon on the Champs Élysées where he tried to buy out the entire store for her. She bought only the things she needed and was shocked at how expensive everything was.

"You know your problem?" Larry said. "You worry too much about money. You're on your honeymoon."

"Yes, sir," she said. But she refused to buy an evening dress that she did not need. When she tried to ask Larry where all the money was coming from, he did not want to discuss it, but she finally insisted on knowing.

"I got an advance on my salary," Larry told her. "What's the big deal?"

And Catherine had not the heart to tell him. He was like a child about money, generous and carefree, and that was part of his charm.

Just as it had been part of her father's charm.

Larry took her on the visitor's tour of Paris: to the Louvre, the Tuileries and Les Invalides to see Napoleon's Tomb. He took her to a colorful little restaurant near the Sorbonne. They went to Les Halles, the storied marketplace of Paris, and watched the fresh fruit and meat and vegetables brought in from the farms of France, and spent their last Sunday afternoon at Versailles, and then had dinner in the breathtaking garden at the Coq Hardi outside of Paris. It was a perfect second honeymoon.

Hal Sakowitz sat in his office looking over the weekly personnel reports. In front of him was the report on Larry Douglas. Sakowitz was leaning back in his chair, studying it, pulling thoughtfully at his lower lip. Finally he leaned forward and pressed an intercom switch. "Send him in," he said.

A moment later, Larry walked in, wearing his Pan-Am uniform and carrying his flight bag. He flashed Sakowitz a smile. "Morning, Chief," he said.

"Sit down."

Larry slouched into a chair opposite the desk and lit a cigarette.

Sakowitz said, "I have a report here that last Monday in Paris you checked in for your flight briefing forty-five minutes late."

Larry's expression changed. "I was caught in a parade on the Champs Élysées. The plane took off on time. I didn't know we were running a boy's camp here."

"We're running an airline," Sakowitz said, quietly. "And we're running it by the book."

"OK," Larry said angrily. "I'll keep away from the

Champs Élysées. Anything else?"

"Yes. Captain Swift thinks you'd had a drink or two before takeoff on the last couple of flights."

"He's a goddamned liar!" Larry snapped.

"Why would he lie?"

"Because he's afraid I'll take his job away." There was a sharp anger in Larry's voice. "The son-of-a-bitch is a timid old maid who should have been retired ten years ago."

"You've flown with four different captains," Sakowitz said. "Which ones did you like?"

"None of them," retorted Larry. He saw the trap too late. Quickly, he added, "I mean—they're all right. I have nothing against them."

"They don't like flying with you either," Sakowitz said evenly. "You make them nervous."

"What the hell does that mean?"

"It means that if ever there's an emergency, you want to be damn sure about the man in the seat next to you. They're not sure about you."

"For Christ's sake!" Larry exploded. "I lived through four years of emergencies over Germany and in the South Pacific, risking my fucking neck every day, while they were back here sitting on their fat asses, collecting big salaries, and they don't have confidence in *me?* You must be joking!"

"No one says you're not great in a fighter plane," Sakowitz replied quietly. "But we're flying passengers. It's a different ball game."

Larry sat there clenching his fists, trying to control his anger. "OK," he said sullenly. "I get the message. If you're through, I have a flight leaving in a few minutes."

"Someone else is taking it over," Sakowitz said. "You're fired."

Larry stared at him unbelievingly. "I'm *what?*"

"In a way, I suppose it's my fault, Douglas. I shouldn't have hired you in the first place."

Larry got to his feet, his eyes blazing with fury.

"Then why the hell did you?" he demanded.

"Because your wife had a friend named Bill Fraser
. . ." Sakowitz began.

Larry moved across the desk, his fist crashing into
Sakowitz's face. The blow propelled Sakowitz against
the wall. He used the momentum to bounce up. He hit
Larry twice, then stepped back, fighting for control.
"Get out of here," he said. "Now!"

Larry stared at him, his face twisted with hatred.
"You son-of-a-bitch," he said. "I wouldn't come near
this airline again if you begged me!" He turned and
stormed out of the office.

Sakowitz stood there looking after him. His secretary came hurrying in. She saw the overturned chair
and Sakowitz's bloody lip.

"Are you all right?" she asked.

"Terrific," he said. "Ask Mr. Eastman if he can see
me."

Ten minutes later Sakowitz had finished relating the
incident to Carl Eastman.

"What do you think's wrong with Douglas?" Eastman asked.

"Honestly? I think he's a psycho."

Eastman regarded him with his piercing hazel eyes.
"That's pretty strong, Sak. He wasn't drunk when he
was flying. No one could even prove that he'd had a
drink on the ground. And anyone can be late once in a
while."

"If that's all it was, I wouldn't have fired him, Carl.
Douglas has a low boiling point. To tell you the truth I
was trying to provoke him today, and it wasn't hard. If
he had stood up under the pressure, I might have taken
a chance and kept him on. You know what worries
me?"

"What?"

Sakowitz said, "A few days ago I ran into an old
buddy who flew with Douglas in the RAF. He told me
a crazy story. It seems that when Douglas was in the
Eagle Squadron he fell for a little English girl who was

engaged to a boy named Clark in Douglas' Squadron. Douglas did everything he could to move in, but the girl wasn't having any. A week before she and Clark were to get married, the Squadron went up to cover some B-Seventeens in a raid over Dieppe. Douglas was flying at the rear of the Squadron. The fortresses dropped their bombs and everyone headed for home. Coming back over the Channel, they were hit by some Messerschmidts, and Clark was shot down." He stopped, lost in some reverie of his own. Eastman waited for him to go on and finally Sakowitz looked up at him. "According to my friend there were no Messerschmidts anywhere near Clark when he got it."

Eastman stared at him unbelievingly. "Jesus! Are you saying that Larry Douglas . . . ?"

"I'm not saying anything. I'm just telling you an interesting story I heard." He put his handkerchief to his lip again. The bleeding had stopped. "It's hard to tell what's happening in the middle of a dogfight. Maybe Clark just ran out of gas. One thing is certain. He sure as hell ran out of luck."

"What happened to his girl?"

"Douglas moved in with her until he came back to the States, then he dumped her." He looked at Eastman thoughtfully. "I'll tell you one thing, for sure. I feel sorry for Douglas' wife."

Catherine was in the conference room having a staff meeting when the door opened and Larry walked in.

His eye was bruised and swollen, his cheek was cut. She hurried over to him. "Larry, what happened?"

"I quit my job," he mumbled.

Catherine took him into her office, away from the curious gazes of the others, and put a cold cloth to his eye and his cheek. "Tell me about it," she said, holding in her anger at what they had done to him.

"They've been riding me for a long time, Cathy. I think they were jealous because I was in the war and they weren't. Anyway, today was the topper. Sakowitz called me in and told me the only reason they hired me in the first place was because you were Bill Fraser's sweetheart."

Catherine looked at him, speechless.

"I hit him," Larry said. "I couldn't help it."

"Oh, darling!" Catherine said. "I'm so sorry."

"Sakowitz is sorrier," Larry replied. "I really clobbered him. Job or no job, I wasn't going to let anyone talk about you that way."

She held him close to her, reassuringly. "Don't worry. You can go to work for any airline in the country."

Catherine proved to be a poor prophet. Larry applied to all the airlines and several of them gave him interviews but nothing came of any of them. Bill Fraser had lunch with Catherine and she told him what had happened. Fraser said nothing, but he was very thoughtful all through lunch. Several times she felt he was on the verge of telling her something, but each time he stopped. Finally he said, "I know a lot of people, Cathy. Would you like me to see what I can do for Larry somewhere else?"

"Thanks," Catherine said gratefully. "But I don't think so. We'll work it out ourselves."

Fraser regarded her a moment, then nodded. "Let me know if you change your mind."

"I will," she said appreciatively. "It seems I'm always coming to you with my problems."

ACME SECURITY AGENCY
1402 "D" Street
Washington, D.C.

Reference #2-179-210   April 1, 1946
Dear Monsieur Barbet:

Thank you for your letter of March 15, 1946, and your bank draft.

Since my last report, Subject has secured employment as a pilot with The Flying Wheels Transport Company, a small independent freight company operating out of Long Island. A Dun and Bradstreet check shows that they are capitalized under $750,000. Their equipment consists of a converted B-26 and a converted DC-3. They have bank loans in excess of $400,000. The Vice-President of the Banque de Paris in New York where they have their major account assures me that the company has an excellent growth potential and future. The bank is considering loaning them sufficient money to buy additional airplanes based on their current income of $80,000 per year with projected increases of 30% per year, over the next five years.

If you wish further details on the financial aspects of the company, please let me know.

Subject began work on March 19, 1946. The personnel manager (who is also one of the owners) informed my operative that he felt very fortunate to have Subject flying for him. More details to follow.

Sincerely,
R. Ruttenberg
Managing Supervisor

Banque de Paris
New York City, New York

Philippe Chardon
President of the Board
Chèr Nelle,

Tu es vraiment mauvaise! Je ne sais pas ce que cet homme t'a fait, mais quoique ce soit, il a payé. Il a été mis à la porte aux Flying Wheels cie, et mon ami me dit qu'il en a piqué une crise.

Je pense être à Athenes, et je compte te voir.

Mes amitiés à Costa—et ne tien fais pas la petite faveur que je t'ai faite restera notre secret.

Affectuesement à toi,
Philippe

ACME SECURITY AGENCY
1402 "D" Street
Washington, D.C.

Reference #2-179-210   May 22, 1946
Dear Monsieur Barbet:

This is a follow-up to my report of May 1, 1946.

On May 14, 1946, Subject was fired by The Flying Wheels Transport Company. I have tried to make discreet inquiries as to the reason, but each time have run up against a brick wall. No one there will discuss it, I can only assume that the Subject did something to disgrace himself, and they don't want to talk about it.

Subject is looking for another flying job, but apparently has no immediate prospects.

I will continue to try to get more information about why he was discharged.

> Sincerely,
> R. Ruttenberg
> Managing Supervisor

C A B L E G R A M   May 29, 1946
Christian Barbet
Cable Chrisbar
Paris, France

CABLE ACKNOWLEDGED STOP WILL IMMEDIATELY DROP INVESTIGATION OF REASON FOR SUBJECT BEING FIRED STOP WILL CONTINUE EVERYTHING ELSE AS BEFORE

> REGARDS,
> R. RUTTENBERG
> ACME SECURITY AGENCY

ACME SECURITY AGENCY
1402 "D" Street
Washington, D.C.

Reference #2-179-210   June 16, 1946
Dear Monsieur Barbet:

Thank you for your letter of June 10th and your bank draft.

On June 15th, Subject obtained employment as a co-pilot with Global Airways, a regional feeder airline operating between Washington, Boston and Philadelphia.

Global Airways is a small new airline with a fleet of three converted war planes, and as far as I have been able to ascertain, they are undercapitalized and in debt. A Vice-President of the firm informed me that they have been promised a loan from the Dallas First National Bank within the next sixty days which will give them enough capital to consolidate their bills and to expand.

Subject is held in high esteem and appears to have a good future there.

Please let me know whether you require any further information about Global Airways.

> Sincerely,
> R. Ruttenberg,
> Managing Supervisor

ACME SECURITY AGENCY
1402 "D" Street
Washington, D.C.

Reference #2-179-210   July 20, 1946
Dear Monsieur Barbet:

Global Airways has unexpectedly filed for bankruptcy and is going out of operation. As far as I can learn, this move was forced by the refusal of the Dallas First National Bank to grant the loan that was promised. Subject is now unemployed again and back to earlier patterns of behavior, as outlined in previous reports.

I will not pursue any investigation into the rea-

son for the bank's refusal of the loan or Global
Airways' financial difficulties unless you specifi-
cally advise me to do so.

Sincerely,
R. Ruttenberg
Managing Supervisor

Noelle kept all the reports and the clippings in a special leather bag to which she had the only key. The bag
was kept inside a locked suitcase and stored at the
back of her bedroom closet, not because she thought
Demiris would pry into her things, but because she
knew how much he loved intrigue. This was Noelle's
personal vendetta, and she wanted to be sure that Demiris remained unaware of it.

Constantin Demiris was going to play a part in her
plan of vengeance, but he would never know about it.
Noelle took a last look at the memorandum and locked
it away, satisfied.

She was ready to begin.

It started with a phone call.

Catherine and Larry were having an uneasy silence-
filled dinner at home. Larry had been home very little
lately, and when he was home he was surly and rude.
Catherine understood his unhappiness.

"It's as though some demon is on my back," he had
told her when Global Airways had gone bankrupt. And
it was true. He had had an incredible run of bad luck.
Catherine tried to reassure Larry, to keep reminding
him of what a wonderful pilot he was and how lucky
anyone would be to have him. But it was like living
with a wounded lion. Catherine never knew when he
would lash out at her, and because she was afraid of
letting him down, she tried to understand his wild rages
and overlook them. The phone rang as she was serving
dessert. She picked up the receiver.

"Hello."

There was an Englishman's voice on the other end

of the line and it said, "Is Larry Douglas in, please? Ian Whitestone here."

"Just a moment." She held the receiver out to Larry. "It's for you. Ian Whitestone."

He frowned, puzzled. "Who?" Then his face cleared. "For Christ's sake!" He walked over and took the receiver from Catherine. "Ian?" He gave a short laugh. "My God, it's been almost seven years. How the hell did you ever track me down?"

Catherine watched Larry nodding and smiling as he listened. At the end of what seemed like five minutes, he said, "Well, that sounds interesting, old buddy. Sure I can. Where?" He listened. "Right. Half an hour. I'll see you then." Thoughtfully, he replaced the receiver.

"Is he a friend of yours?" Catherine asked.

Larry turned to face her. "No, not really. That's what's so funny. He's a guy I flew with in the RAF. We never really got along all that well. But he says he has a proposition for me."

"What kind of proposition?" Catherine asked.

Larry shrugged. "I'll let you know when I get home."

It was almost three o'clock in the morning when Larry returned to the apartment. Catherine was sitting up in bed reading. Larry appeared at the bedroom door.

"Hi."

Something had happened to him. He radiated an excitement that Catherine had not seen in him for a long time. He walked over to the bed.

"How did your meeting go?"

"I think it went great," Larry said, carefully. "In fact it went so great I still can't believe it. I think I may have a job."

"Working for Ian Whitestone?"

"No. Ian's a pilot—like me. I told you we flew together."

"Yes."

"Well—after the war, a Greek buddy of his got him a job as a private pilot for Demiris."

"The shipping tycoon?"

"Shipping, oil, gold—Demiris owns half the world. Whitestone had a beautiful setup over there."

"What happened?"

Larry looked at her and grinned. "Whitestone's quit his job. He's going to Australia. Someone's setting him up in his own business over there."

"I still don't understand," said Catherine. "What does all this have to do with you?"

"Whitestone spoke to Demiris about my taking his place. He just quit, and Demiris hasn't had a chance to look around for a replacement. Whitestone thinks I'm a cinch for the job." He hesitated. "You don't know what this could mean, Cathy."

Catherine thought of the other times, the other jobs, and she remembered her father and his empty dreams, and she kept her voice noncommittal, not wishing to encourage any false hopes in Larry, and yet not wanting to dampen his enthusiasm.

"Didn't you say you and Whitestone weren't particularly good friends?"

He hesitated. "Yeah." A small frown creased his forehead. The truth of the matter was that he and Ian Whitestone had never liked each other at all. The telephone call tonight had been a big surprise. At the meeting, Whitestone had seemed oddly ill at ease. When he had explained the situation and Larry had said, "I'm surprised that you thought of me," there had been an awkward pause, and then Whitestone had said, "Demiris wants a great pilot, and that's what you are." It was almost as though Whitestone were pressing the job on him and that Larry would be doing him a favor. He had appeared very relieved when Larry said he was interested and then seemed anxious to leave. All in all it had been a strange meeting.

"This could be the chance of a lifetime," Larry told Cathy. "Demiris was paying Whitestone fifteen thousand drachmas a month. That's five hundred dollars and he lived like a king over there."

"But wouldn't that mean you'd be living in Greece?"

"*We'd* be living in Greece," Larry corrected her. "With that kind of money, we could save enough to be independent in a year. I've got to take a shot at it."

Catherine was hesitant, choosing her words carefully. "Larry, it's so far away and you don't even know Constantin Demiris. There must be a flying job here that . . ."

"No!" His tone was savage. "Nobody gives a shit here how good a pilot you are. All they care about is how long you've paid your goddam union dues. Over there, I'd be independent. It's the kind of thing I've been dreaming of, Cathy. Demiris has a fleet of planes you wouldn't believe, and I'll be flying again, baby. The only one I'd have to please would be Demiris, and Whitestone says he'll love me."

She thought again of Larry's job at Pan Am and the hopes he had had for it and his failures with the small airlines. *My God,* she thought. *What am I getting myself into?* It would mean giving up the business she had built, going to live in a strange place with strangers, with a husband who was almost a stranger.

He was watching her. "Are you with me?"

She looked up at his eager face. This was her husband and if she wanted to keep her marriage, she would have to live where he lived. And how lovely it would be if it did work out. He would be the old Larry again. The charming, amusing, wonderful man she had married. She had to give it a chance.

"Of course I'm with you," Catherine said. "Why don't you fly over and see Demiris? If the job works out, then I'll come over and join you."

He smiled, that charming, boyish grin. "I knew I could count on you, baby." He put his arms around her and held her close. "You'd better take off that nightgown," Larry said, "or I'm going to poke holes in it."

But as Catherine slowly took it off, she was thinking

about how she was going to tell Bill Fraser.

Early the next morning Larry flew to Athens to meet Constantin Demiris.

During the next few days Catherine heard nothing from her husband. As the week dragged by, she found herself hoping that things had not worked out in Greece and that Larry would be coming home. Even if he got the position with Demiris, there was no way of telling how long it would last. Surely he could find a job in the United States.

Six days after Larry had left, Catherine received an overseas phone call.

"Catherine?"

"Hello, darling."

"Get packed. You're talking to Constantin Demiris' new personal pilot."

Ten days later, Catherine was on her way to Greece.

Book Two

NOELLE AND CATHERINE

Athens: 1946

14

Men mold some cities, some cities mold men. Athens is an anvil that has withstood the hammer of centuries. It has been captured and despoiled by the Saracens, the Anglos, the Turks, but each time it patiently survived. Athens lies toward the southern end of the great central plain of Attica, which slopes gently toward the Saronic Gulf on the southwest and is overlooked on the east by the majestic Mount Hymettus. Underneath the shiny patina of the city one still found a village filled with ancient ghosts and steeped in rich tradition of timeless glories, where its citizens lived as much in their past as in the present, a city of constant surprise, full of discovery, and in the end unknowable.

Larry was at the Hellenikon Airport to meet Catherine's plane. She saw him hurrying toward the ramp, his face eager and excited as he ran toward her. He looked tanner and leaner than when she had last seen him, and he seemed to be free of strain.

"I've missed you, Cathy," he said as he scooped her up in his arms.

"I've missed you too." And as she said it, she realized how much she meant it. She kept forgetting the strong physical impact that Larry had on her until they met after an absence and each time it hit her anew.

"How did Bill Fraser take the news?" Larry asked as he helped her through Customs.

"He was very good about it."

"He had no choice, had he?" Larry said, sardonically.

Catherine remembered her meeting with Bill Fraser. He had looked at her, shocked. "You're going to go off to Greece to *live?* Why, for God's sakes?"

"It's in the fine print of my marriage contract," she had replied lightly.

"I mean, why can't Larry get a job here, Catherine?"

"I don't know why, Bill. Something always seems to go wrong. But he has a job in Greece and he seems to feel that it's going to work out."

After his first impulsive protest Fraser had been wonderful. He had made everything easy for her and insisted that she keep her interest in the firm. "You're not going to stay away forever," he kept saying.

Catherine was thinking of his words now as she watched Larry arrange for a porter to carry her luggage to a limousine.

He spoke to the porter in Greek and Catherine marveled at Larry's facility for language.

"Wait'll you meet Constantin Demiris," Larry said. "He's like a goddamn king. All the moguls in Europe seem to spend their time figuring out what they can do to please him."

"I'm glad you like him."

"And he likes me."

She had never heard him sound so happy and enthusiastic. It was a good omen.

On the way to the hotel Larry described his first meeting with Demiris. Larry had been met at the airport by a liveried chauffeur. Larry had asked to take a look at Demiris' fleet of planes, and the chauffeur had driven him to an enormous hangar at the far end of the field. There were three planes, and Larry inspected each one with a critical eye. The Hawker Siddeley was a beauty, and he longed to get behind the wheel and fly it. The next ship was a six-place Piper in topnotch condition. He estimated that it could easily do three hundred miles per hour. The third plane was a two-seater converted L-5, with a Lycoming engine, a wonderful plane for shorter flights. It was an impressive private fleet. When Larry had finished his inspection, he rejoined the watching chauffeur.

"They'll do," Larry said. "Let's go."

The chauffeur had driven him to a villa in Varkiza, the exclusive suburb twenty-five kilometers from Athens.

"You wouldn't believe Demiris' place," Larry told Catherine.

"What did it look like?" Catherine asked, eagerly.

"It's impossible to describe. It's about ten acres with electric gates, guards, watchdogs, and the whole bit. The outside of the villa is a palace, and the inside is a museum. It has an indoor swimming pool, a full stage and a projection room. You'll see it one day."

"Was he nice?" Catherine asked.

"You bet he was," Larry smiled. "I got the red-carpet treatment. I guess my reputation preceded me."

In fact Larry had sat in a small anteroom for three hours waiting to see Constantin Demiris. In ordinary circumstances Larry would have been furious at the slight, but he knew how much depended on this meeting and he was too nervous to be angry. He had told Catherine how important this job was to him. But he had not told her how desperately he needed it. His one superb skill was flying and without it he felt lost. It was as though his life had sunk to some unexplored emotional depth and the pressures on him were too great to be borne. *Everything* depended on this job.

At the end of three hours a butler had come in and announced that Mr. Demiris was ready to see him. He had led Larry through a large reception hall that looked like it belonged at Versailles. The walls were delicate shades of gold, green and blue, and Beauvais tapestries hung on the walls, framed by panels of rosewood. A magnificent oval Savonnerie rug was on the floor, and above it an enormous chandelier of crystal

De Roche and bronze Doré.

At the entry to the library were a pair of green onyx columns with capitals of gold bronze. The library itself was exquisite, designed by a master artisan, and the walls were carved, paneled fruitwoods. In the center of one wall stood a white marble mantelpiece with gold gilt ornamentations. On it rested two beautiful bronze Chénets of Philippe Caffieri.

From mantel top to ceiling rose a heavily carved trumeau mirror with a painting by Jean Honoré Fragonard. Through an open French window Larry caught a glimpse of an enormous patio overlooking a private park filled with statues and fountains.

At the far end of the library was a great Bureau Plat desk and behind it a magnificent tall back chair covered in Aubusson tapestry. In front of the desk were two bergères with Gobelin upholstery.

Demiris was standing near the desk, studying a large Mercator map on the wall, dotted with dozens of colored pins. He turned as Larry entered and held out his hand.

"Constantin Demiris," he said, with the faintest trace of an accent. Larry had seen photographs of him in news magazines throughout the years, but nothing had prepared him for the vital force of the man.

"I know," Larry said, shaking his hand. "I'm Larry Douglas."

Demiris saw Larry's eyes go to the map on the wall. "My empire," he said. "Sit down."

Larry took a chair opposite the desk.

"I understand that you and Ian Whitestone flew together in the RAF?"

"Yes."

Demiris leaned back in his chair and studied Larry. "Ian thinks very highly of you."

Larry smiled. "I think highly of him. He's a hell of a pilot."

"That's what he said about you, except he used the word 'great.'"

Larry felt again that sense of surprise he had had when Whitestone had first spelled out the offer. He had obviously given Demiris a big buildup about him, far out of proportion to the relationship that he and Whitestone had had. "I'm good," Larry said. "That's my business."

Demiris nodded. "I like men who are good at their business. Did you know that most of the people in the world are not?"

"I hadn't given it much thought one way or the other," Larry confessed.

"I have." He gave Larry a wintry smile. "That's *my* business—people. The great majority of people hate what they're doing, Mr. Douglas. Instead of devising ways to get into something they like, they remain trapped all their lives, like brainless insects. It's rare to find a man who loves his work. Almost invariably when you find such a man, he is a success."

"I suppose that's true," Larry said modestly.

"You are *not* a success."

Larry looked up at Demiris, suddenly wary. "That depends on what you mean by success, Mr. Demiris," he said carefully.

"What I mean is," Demiris said bluntly, "you did brilliantly in the war, but you are not doing very well in the peace."

Larry felt the muscles of his jaw begin to tighten. He felt that he was being baited, and he tried to hold back his anger. His mind raced frantically, trying to figure out what he could say to salvage this job he needed so desperately. Demiris was watching him, his olive black eyes quietly studying him, missing nothing.

"What happened to your job with Pan American, Mr. Douglas?"

Larry found a grin he didn't feel like. "I didn't like the idea of sitting around for fifteen years waiting to become a co-pilot."

"So you hit the man you worked for."

Larry showed his surprise. "Who told you that?"

"Oh, come, Mr. Douglas," Demiris said impatiently, "if you went to work for me, I would be putting my life in your hands every time I flew with you. My life happens to be worth a great deal to me. Did you really think I would hire you without knowing *everything* about you?"

"You were fired from two flying jobs after you were fired from Pan Am," Demiris went on. "That's a poor record."

"It had nothing to do with my ability," Larry retorted, anger beginning to rise in him again. "Business was slow with one company, and the other couldn't get a bank loan and went bankrupt. I'm a damned good pilot."

Demiris studied him a moment, then smiled. "I know you are," he said. "You don't respond well to discipline, do you?"

"I don't like being given orders by idiots who know less than I do."

"I trust I will not fall into that category," Demiris said dryly.

"Not unless you're planning to tell me how to fly your planes, Mr. Demiris."

"No, that would be your job. It would also be your job to see that I got where I was going efficiently, comfortably and safely."

Larry nodded. "I'd do my best, Mr. Demiris."

"I believe that," Demiris said. "You've been out to look at my planes."

Larry tried to keep the surprise out of his face. "Yes, sir."

"How did you like them?"

Larry could not conceal his enthusiasm. "They're beauties."

Demiris responded to the look on Larry's face. "Have you ever flown a Hawker Siddeley?"

Larry hesitated a moment, tempted to lie. "No, sir."

Demiris nodded. "Think you could learn?"

Larry grinned. "If you've got someone who can spare ten minutes."

Demiris leaned forward in his chair and pressed his long, slender fingers together. "I could choose a pilot who is familiar with all my planes."

"But you won't," Larry said, "because you'll keep getting new planes, and you want someone who can adapt to anything you buy."

Demiris nodded his head. "You are correct," he said. "What I am looking for is a pilot—a pure pilot— a man who is at his happiest when he is flying."

That was the moment when Larry knew the job was his.

Larry was never aware of how close he had come to not being hired. A great deal of Constantin Demiris' success was due to a highly developed instinct for trouble, and it had served him often enough so that he seldom disregarded it. When Ian Whitestone had come to inform him that he was quitting, a silent alarm went off in Demiris' mind. It was partly because of Whitestone's manner. He was acting unnaturally and seemed uneasy. It wasn't a question of money, he assured Demiris. He had a chance to go into business for himself with his brother-in-law in Sydney and he had to try it. Then he had recommended another pilot.

"He's an American, but we flew together in the RAF. He's not just good, he's great, Mr. Demiris. I don't know a better flyer."

Demiris quietly listened as Ian Whitestone went on extolling the virtue of his friend, trying to find the false note that jarred him. He finally recognized it. Whitestone was overselling, but possibly that was because of his embarrassment at quitting his job so abruptly.

Because Demiris was a man who left not even the smallest detail to chance, he made several phone calls to various countries after Whitestone left. Before the afternoon was over Demiris had ascertained that someone had indeed put up money to finance Whitestone in a small electronics business in Australia, with his brother-in-law. He had spoken to a friend in the British Air Ministry and two hours later had been given a verbal report on Larry Douglas. "He was a bit erratic on the ground," his friend had said, "but he was a superb flyer." Demiris had then made telephone calls to Washington and New York and had been quickly brought up-to-date on Larry Douglas' current status.

Everything on the surface appeared to be just as it ought to be. And yet Constantin Demiris still felt that vague sense of unease, a presentiment of trouble. He had discussed the matter with Noelle, suggesting that perhaps he might offer Ian Whitestone more money to stay on. Noelle had listened attentively and then said, "No. Let him go, Costa. And if he recommends this American flyer so highly, then I would certainly try him."

And that finally had decided him.

From the moment Noelle knew that Larry Douglas was on his way to Athens she was able to think of nothing else. She thought of all the years it had taken, the careful, patient laying of plans, the slow, inexorable tightening of the web, and she was sure that Constantin Demiris would have been proud of her if he had known. It was ironic, Noelle reflected. If she had never met Larry, she could have been happy with Demiris. They complemented each other perfectly. They both loved power and knew how to use it. They were above ordinary people. They were gods, meant to rule. In the end they could never lose, because they had a deep, almost mystic patience. They could wait forever. And now, for Noelle, the waiting was over.

Noelle spent the day in the garden lying in a hammock, going over her plan; and by the time the sun began to sink toward the western sky, she was satisfied.

In a way, she thought, it was a pity that so much of the last six years had been filled with her plans for vengeance. It had motivated almost every waking moment, given her life a vitality and drive and excitement, and now in a few short weeks the quest would have come to an end.

At that moment, lying under the dying Grecian sun with the late afternoon breezes beginning to cool the quiet green garden, Noelle had no idea that it was just beginning.

The night before Larry was to arrive, Noelle was unable to sleep. She lay awake all night, remembering Paris and the man who had given her the gift of laughter and taken it away from her again . . . feeling Larry's baby in her womb, possessing her body as its father had possessed her mind. She remembered that afternoon in the dreary Paris flat and the agony of the pointed metal coat hanger ripping into her flesh deeper and deeper until it tore into the baby with the sweet, unbearable pain driving her into a frenzy of hysteria and the endless river of blood pouring from her. She remembered all these things and relived them again . . . the pain, the agony and the hatred . . .

At five A.M., Noelle was up and dressed, sitting in her room looking out at the huge fireball rising over the Aegean. It reminded her of another morning in Paris when she had arisen early and dressed and waited for Larry—only this time he would be here. Because she had seen to it that he had to be. As Noelle needed him before, so Larry needed her now, even though he was still unaware of it.

Demiris sent a message up to Noelle's suite that he would like her to have breakfast with him, but she was too excited, and she was afraid that her mood might arouse his curiosity. She had long ago learned that Demiris had the sensitivity of a cat: He missed nothing. Again, Noelle reminded herself that she must be careful. She wanted to take care of Larry herself in her own way. She had thought long and hard about the fact that she was using Constantin Demiris as an un-witting tool. If he ever found out, he would not like it.

Noelle had a demitasse of thick Greek coffee and half a freshly baked roll. She had no appetite. Her mind was feverishly dwelling on the meeting that would take place in a few short hours. She had taken unusual care with her makeup and the selection of a dress, and she knew that she looked beautiful.

Shortly after eleven o'clock, Noelle heard the lim-ousine pull up in front of the house. She took a deep breath to control her nervousness, then slowly walked over to the window. Larry Douglas was getting out of the car. Noelle watched as he moved toward the front door and it was as though the march of years had rolled away, and the two of them were back in Paris. Larry was a little more mature, and the fighting and the living had added new lines to his face, but they only served to make him handsomer than he had been. Looking at him through the window ten yards away Noelle could still feel the animal magnetism, still feel the old desire and it welled up in her, mixing with the hatred until she was filled with a sense of exhilaration that was almost like a climax. She took one last quick look at herself in the mirror and then went downstairs to meet the man she was about to destroy.

As she walked down the stairs, Noelle wondered what Larry's reaction would be when he saw her. Had he bragged to his friends and perhaps even his wife that Noelle Page had once been in love with him? She wondered, as she had wondered a hundred times be-fore, whether he ever relived the magic of those days and nights they had together in Paris and whether he regretted what he had done to her. How it must have eaten at his soul that Noelle had become internation-ally famous and that his own life consisted of a series of small failures! Noelle wanted to see some of that in Larry's eyes now when they came face to face for the first time in almost seven years.

Noelle had reached the reception hall when the front door opened and the butler ushered him in. Larry was staring at the enormous foyer in awe when he turned and saw Noelle. He looked at her for a long moment, his face lighting up in appreciation at the sight of a beautiful woman. "Hello," he said, politely. "I'm Larry Douglas. I have an appointment to see Mr. Demiris."

And there was no sign of recognition on his face.

None at all.

Driving through the streets of Athens toward their hotel, Catherine was dazed by the succession of ruins and monuments that appeared all around them.

Ahead she saw the breathtaking spectacle of the white-marbled Parthenon rising high atop the Acropolis. Hotels and office buildings were everywhere, yet in an odd way it seemed to Catherine that the newer buildings appeared temporary and impermanent while the Parthenon loomed immortal and timeless in the chiseled clarity of the air.

"Impressive, isn't it?" Larry grinned. "The whole city is like that. One big beautiful ruin."

They passed a large park in the center of the city with dancing fountains in the middle. Hundreds of tables with green and orange poles lined the park, and the air above them was carpeted with blue awnings.

"That's Constipation Square," Larry said.

"What?"

"Its real name is Constitution Square. People sit at those tables all day drinking Greek coffee and watching the world go by."

On almost every block there were outdoor cafés, and on the corners men were selling freshly caught sponges. Everywhere flowers were sold by vendors, and their booths were a rage of violently colored blossoms.

"The city is so white," Catherine said. "It's dazzling."

The hotel suite was large and charming, overlooking

Syntagma Square, the large square in the center of the city. In the room were beautiful flowers and an enormous bowl of fresh fruit.

"I love it, darling," Catherine said, going around the suite.

The bellboy had put her suitcases down and Larry tipped him. *"Parapolee,"* the boy said.

"Parakalo," Larry replied.

The bellboy left, closing the door behind him.

Larry walked over and put his arms around Catherine. "Welcome to Greece." He kissed her hungrily, and she felt the hardness of his body pressing into the softness of hers and she knew how much he had missed her and she was glad. He led her into the bedroom.

On the dressing table was a small package. "Open it," Larry told her.

Her fingers tore the wrapping apart and in a small box inside was a tiny bird carved in jade. As busy as he was, Larry had remembered, and Catherine was touched. Somehow the bird was a talisman, an omen that everything was going to be all right, that the problems of the past were finished.

As they made love, Catherine said a little prayer of gratitude, thankful to be in the arms of the husband whom she loved so much, in one of the most exciting cities in the world, starting out on a new life. This was the old Larry, and all their problems had only made their marriage stronger.

Nothing could hurt them now.

The next morning Larry arranged for a real-estate agent to show Catherine some apartments. The agent turned out to be a short, dark, heavily moustached man named Dimitropolous who spoke in a rapid tongue that he sincerely believed was perfect English but which consisted of Greek words interlaced with an occasional undecipherable English phrase.

By throwing herself on his mercy—a trick that Catherine was to use often in the months to come—she persuaded him to speak very slowly so that she was able to sift out some of the English words and try to make a wild stab at what he was trying to say.

The fourth place he showed her was a bright and sunny four-room apartment in what she later learned was the Kolonaki section, the fashionable suburb of Athens, lined with beautiful residential buildings and smart shops.

When Larry returned to the hotel that evening, Catherine told him about the apartment, and two days later they moved in.

Larry was away during the day but he tried to be home to have dinner with Catherine. Dinner in Athens was any time between nine and twelve o'clock. Between two and five in the afternoon, everyone had a siesta, and the shops opened again until late evening. Catherine found herself completely absorbed in the city. On her third night in Athens Larry brought home a friend, Count George Pappas, an attractive Greek about forty-five, tall and slim with dark hair with a touch of gray at the temples. There was a curious old-fashioned dignity about him that Catherine liked. He took them to dinner at a small taverna in the Plaka, the ancient section of the city. The Plaka comprised a few steep acres carelessly flung together in the heart of downtown Athens, with twisting alleys and crumbling, worn-down staircases that led to tiny houses built under Turkish rule when Athens was a mere village. The Plaka was a place of whitewashed, rambling structures, fresh fruit and flower stalls, the marvelous aroma of coffee roasting in the open, howling cats and vociferous street fights. The effect was enchanting. In any other city, Catherine thought, a section like this would be the slums. Here, it's a monument.

The taverna that Count Pappas took them to was outdoors on top of a roof overlooking the city; the waiters were dressed in colorful costumes.

"What would you like to eat?" the Count asked Catherine.

She studied the alien menu helplessly. "Would you mind ordering for me? I'm afraid I might order the proprietor."

Count Pappas ordered a sumptuous banquet, choosing a variety of dishes so Catherine would get a chance to taste everything. They had *dolmades,* meatballs wrapped in vine leaves; *mousaka,* a succulent meat and eggplant pie; *stiffado,* stewed hare with onions— Catherine wasn't told what it was until she had eaten half of it, and she was unable to eat another bite of it—and *taramosalata,* the Greek salad of caviar with olive oil and lemon. The Count ordered a bottle of retsina.

"This is our national wine," he explained. He watched Catherine with amusement as she tasted it. It had a piney, resonated taste, and Catherine struggled gamely to down it.

"Whatever I had," she gasped, "I think this just cured it."

As they ate, three musicians began to play Bozoukia music. It was lively and gay and infectious and, as the group watched, customers began to get to their feet and move out onto the dance floor to dance to the music. What amazed Catherine was that the dancers were all male, and they were magnificent. She was enjoying herself tremendously.

They did not leave the café until after three A.M. The Count drove them back to their new apartment. "Have you done any sightseeing yet?" he asked Catherine.

"Not really," she confessed. "I'm waiting for Larry to get some time off."

The Count turned to Larry. "Perhaps I could show Catherine some of the sights until you are able to join us."

"That would be great," Larry said. "If you're sure it wouldn't be too much trouble."

"It would be my pleasure," the Count replied. He turned to Catherine. "Would you mind having me as your guide?"

She looked at him and thought of Dimitropolous, the little real-estate man who spoke fluent gibberish.

"I'd love it," she replied sincerely.

The next few weeks were fascinating. Catherine would spend mornings fixing up the apartment, and in the afternoon, if Larry was away, the Count would pick her up and take her sightseeing.

They drove out to Olympia. "This is the site of the first Olympic Games," the Count told her. "They were held here every year for a thousand years in spite of wars, plagues and famines."

Catherine stood looking in awe at the ruins of the great arena, thinking of the grandeur of the contests that had been held there through the centuries, the triumphs, the defeats.

"Talk about the playing fields of Eton," Catherine said. *"This* is where the spirit of sportsmanship really started, isn't it?"

The Count laughed. "I'm afraid not," he said. "The truth is a little embarrassing."

Catherine looked up, interested. "Why?"

"The first chariot race ever held here was fixed."

"Fixed?"

"I'm afraid so," Count Pappas confessed. "You see, there was a rich prince named Pelops who was feuding with a rival. They decided to hold a chariot race here to see who was the better man. The night before the race Pelops tampered with the wheel of his rival's chariot. When the race began, the whole countryside was here to cheer on their favorite. At the first turn the wheel of the rival's chariot flew off, and his chariot overturned. Pelop's rival was entangled in the reins and dragged to his death. Pelops drove on to victory."

"That's terrible," Catherine said. "What did they do to him?"

"That's really the disgraceful part of the story," the Count replied. "By now the whole populace was aware of what Pelops had done. It made him such a big hero that a huge pediment was raised in his honor at Olympia's Temple of Zeus. It is still there." He smiled wryly. "I'm afraid that our villain prospered and lived happily ever after. As a matter of fact," he added, "the whole region south of Corinth is called the Peloponnesus after him."

"Who said crime doesn't pay?" marveled Catherine.

Whenever Larry was free, he and Catherine would explore the city together. They found wonderful shops where they would spend hours haggling over prices, and out-of-the-way little restaurants that they made their own. Larry was a gay and charming companion, and Catherine was grateful that she had given up her job in the States to be with her husband.

Larry Douglas had never been happier in his life. The job with Demiris was the dream of a lifetime.

The money was good, but Larry was not interested in that. He was interested only in the magnificent machines he flew. It took him exactly one hour to learn to fly the Hawker Siddeley and five more flights to master it. Most of the time Larry flew with Paul Metaxas, Demiris' happy-go-lucky little Greek copilot. Metaxas had been surprised by the sudden departure of Ian Whitestone, and he had been apprehensive about Whitestone's replacement. He had heard stories about Larry Douglas, and he was not sure he liked what he heard. Douglas, however, seemed genuinely enthusiastic about his new job and the first time Metaxas flew with him, he knew that Douglas was a superb pilot.

Little by little Metaxas relaxed his guard and the two men became friends.

Whenever he was not flying, Larry spent time learning every idiosyncrasy of Demiris' fleet of planes. Before he was through, he was able to fly them all better than anyone had ever flown them before.

The variety in his job fascinated Larry. He would fly members of Demiris' staff on business trips to Brindisi and Corfu and Rome, or pick up guests and fly them to Demiris' island for a party or to his chalet in Switzerland for skiing. He became used to flying people whose photographs he was constantly seeing on the front pages of newspapers and magazines, and he would regale Catherine with stories about them. He flew the president of a Balkan country, a British prime minister, an Arabian oil chieftain and his entire harem. He flew opera singers and a ballet company and the cast of a Broadway play that was staging a single performance in London for Demiris' birthday. He piloted Justices of the Supreme Court, a congressman and a former President of the United States. During the flights Larry spent most of the time in the cockpit, but from time to time he would wander back to the cabin to make sure the passengers were comfortable. Sometimes he would hear bits of discussion between tycoons about impending mergers or stock deals. Larry could have made a fortune from the information he gleaned but he was simply not interested. What concerned him was the airplane he flew, powerful and alive and in his control.

It was two months before Larry piloted Demiris himself.

They were in the Piper and Larry was flying his employer from Athens to Dubrovnik. It was a cloudy day and there was a report of wind storms and squalls along the route. Larry had carefully plotted out the least stormy course, but the air was so full of turbulence that it was impossible to avoid it.

An hour out of Athens he flashed on the "seat belt" sign and said to Metaxas, "Hold on, Paul. This may cost us both our jobs."

To Larry's surprise Demiris appeared in the cockpit. "May I join you?" he said.

"Help yourself," Larry said. "It's going to be rough."

Metaxas gave up his seat to Demiris and Demiris

strapped himself in. Larry would have preferred to have the copilot sitting next to him, ready to act if anything went wrong, but it was Demiris' airplane.

The storm lasted almost two hours. Larry circled the large mountains of clouds that puffed up ahead of them, lovely white and deadly.

"Beautiful," Demiris commented.

"They're killers," Larry said. "Cumulus. The reason they're so nice and fluffy is that there's wind inside of them puffing them up. The inside of that cloud can tear a plane apart in ten seconds. You can rise and fall thirty thousand feet in less than a minute with no control of your plane."

"I'm sure you won't let that happen," Demiris said calmly.

The winds caught at the plane and tried to fling it across the sky, but Larry fought to keep it under control. He forgot that Demiris was there, focusing his entire attention on the craft he was flying, using every skill he had ever learned. Finally they were out of the storm. Larry turned, drained, and found that Demiris had left the cockpit. Metaxas was in the seat.

"That was a lousy first trip for him, Paul," Larry said. "I may be in trouble."

He was taxiing down the small, mountain-ringed tabletop airport at Dubrovnik when Demiris appeared in the doorway of the cockpit.

"You were right," Demiris said to Larry. "You're very good at what you do. I'm pleased."

And Demiris was gone.

One morning as Larry was getting ready to leave on a flight to Morocco, Count Pappas telephoned to suggest that he take Catherine driving through the countryside. Larry insisted that she go.

"Aren't you jealous?" she asked.

"Of the Count?" Larry laughed.

And Catherine suddenly understood. During the time she and the Count had spent together, he had never made an improper advance toward her or even given her a suggestive look. "He's a homosexual?" she asked.

Larry nodded. "That's why I've left you in his tender care."

The Count picked Catherine up early, and they started driving south toward the broad plain of Thessaly. Peasant women dressed in black walked along the road bent over with heavy loads of wood strapped to their backs.

"Why don't the men do the heavy work?" Catherine asked.

The Count shot her an amused glance.

"The women don't want them to," he replied. "They want their men fresh at night for other things."

There's a lesson there for all of us, Catherine thought wryly.

In the late afternoon they approached the forbidding-looking Pindus Mountains, their rocky crags towering high in the sky. The road was blocked by a flock of sheep being herded by a shepherd and a scrawny sheep dog. Count Pappas stopped the car as they waited for the sheep to clear the road. Catherine watched in wonder as the dog nipped at the heels of the stray sheep, keeping them in line and forcing them in the direction he wanted them to go.

"That dog is almost human," Catherine exclaimed admiringly.

The Count gave her a brief look. There was something in it that she did not understand.

"What's the matter?" she asked.

The Count hesitated. "It's a rather unpleasant story."

"I'm a big girl."

The Count said, "This is a wild area. The land is rocky and inhospitable. At best the crops are meager, and when the weather turns bad, there are no crops at all and a good deal of hunger." His voice trailed off.

"Go on," Catherine prompted.

"A few years ago there was a bad storm here and

the crops were ruined. There was little food for anyone. All the sheep dogs in this area revolted. They
deserted the farms they worked on and gathered together in a large band." As he continued, he tried to
keep the horror out of his voice. "They began attacking the farms."

"And killed the sheep!" Catherine said.

There was a silence before he answered. "No. They
killed their masters. And ate them."

Catherine stared at him, shocked.

"They had to send in federal troops from Athens to
restore human government here. It took almost a
month."

"How horrible."

"Hunger does terrible things," Count Pappas said
quietly.

The sheep had crossed the road now. Catherine
looked at the sheep dog again and shuddered.

As the weeks went by, the things that had seemed so
foreign and strange to Catherine began to become
familiar to her. She found the people open and
friendly. She learned where to do her marketing and
where to shop for clothes on Voukourestiou Street.
Greece was a marvel of organized inefficiency, and one
had to relax and enjoy it. No one was in a hurry, and if
you asked someone for directions he was likely to
take you where you wanted to go. Or he might say,
when you asked how far it was: *"Enos cigarou dro-
mos,"* which Catherine learned meant "one cigarette
away." She walked the streets and explored the city
and drank the warm dark wine of the Greek summer.

Catherine and Larry visited Mykonos with its colorful windmills and Melos, where the Venus de Milo was
discovered. But Catherine's favorite place was Paros, a
graceful, verdant island capped by a flower-covered
mountain. When their boat docked, a guide stood on
the quay. He asked if they would like him to guide
them to the top of the mountain on mule-back, and

they clambered aboard two bony mules.

Catherine was wearing a broad-brimmed straw hat to protect her from the hot sun. As she and Larry rode up the steep path leading toward the mountain top, black-clad women called out, *"Ke-lee meh-ra,"* and handed Catherine gifts of fresh herbs, oregano and basil to put in her hat band. After a two-hour ride, they reached a plateau, a beautiful tree-filled plain with millions of flowers in spectacular bloom. The guide stopped the mules and they gazed in wonder at the incredible profusion of colors.

"This named Valley of the Butterflies," the guide said in halting English.

Catherine looked around for a butterfly but saw none. "Why do they call it that?" she asked.

The guide grinned as though he had been waiting for her question. "I show you," he said. He dismounted from his mule and picked up a large fallen limb. He walked over to a tree and hit the limb against it with all his might. In a split second the "flowers" on hundreds of trees suddenly took to the air in a wild rainbow of flight, leaving the trees bare. The air was filled with hundreds of thousands of gaily colored butterflies dancing in the sunlight.

Catherine and Larry gazed in awe. The guide stood watching them, his face filled with a deep pride, as though he felt responsible for the beautiful miracle they were seeing. It was one of the loveliest days of Catherine's life, and she thought that if she could choose one perfect day to relive, it would be the day she spent with Larry on Paros.

"Hey, we got a VIP this morning," Paul Metaxas grinned cheerfully. "Wait till you see her."

"Who is it?"

"Noelle Page, the boss's lady. You can look, but you mustn't touch."

Larry Douglas remembered the brief glimpse he had

had of the woman in Demiris' home the morning
Douglas had arrived in Athens. She was a beauty and
looked familiar, but that of course was because he had
seen her on the screen, in a French picture that Catherine had once dragged him to. No one had to tell Larry
the rules of self-preservation. Even if the world were
not filled with eager females, he would not have gone
anywhere near Constantin Demiris' girl friend. Larry
liked his job too much to jeopardize it by doing anything so stupid. Well, maybe he would get her auto-
graph for Catherine.

The limousine taking Noelle to the airport was
slowed down several times by work gangs repairing the
roads, but Noelle welcomed the delays. She was going
to see Larry Douglas for the first time since the meeting at Demiris' house. Noelle had been deeply shaken
by what had happened. Or, more accurately, what had
not happened.

Over the past six years Noelle had imagined their
encounter in a hundred different ways. She had played
the scene over and over in her mind. The one thing
that had never even occurred to her was that Larry
would not remember her. The most important event in
her life had meant nothing more to him than another
little cheap affair, one of hundreds. Well, before she
was through with him, he would remember her.

Larry was crossing the airfield, flight plan in hand,
when a limousine pulled up in front of the big plane,
and Noelle Page emerged. Larry walked over to the car
and said pleasantly, "Good morning, Miss Page, I'm
Larry Douglas. I'll be flying you and your guests to
Cannes."

Noelle turned and walked past him as though he had
not spoken, as though he did not exist. Larry stood
there, looking after her, bewildered.

Thirty minutes later the other passengers, a dozen of
them, had boarded the plane, and Larry and Paul

Metaxas took off. They were flying the group to the Côte d'Azur where they would be picked up and taken aboard Demiris' yacht. It was an easy flight except for the normal turbulence off the southern coast of France in summer, and Larry landed the plane smoothly and taxied over to where some limousines were waiting for his passengers. As Larry left the plane with his stubby little copilot, Noelle walked up to Metaxas, ignoring Larry, and said in a voice filled with contempt, "The new pilot is an amateur, Paul. You should give him flying lessons." And Noelle got into a car and was driven away, leaving Larry standing there, filled with a stunned, helpless anger.

He told himself that she was a bitch and he had probably happened to catch her on a bad day. But the next incident a week later convinced him that he was facing a serious problem.

On Demiris' orders Larry picked Noelle up in Oslo and flew her to London. Because of what had happened Larry had gone over the flight plan with particular care. There was a high pressure area to the north and some possible thunderheads building up to the east. Larry worked out a route that skirted these areas, and the flight proved to be perfectly smooth. He brought the ship down in a flawless three-point landing, and he and Paul Metaxas strolled back to the cabin. Noelle Page was putting on some lipstick. "I hope you enjoyed your flight, Miss Page," Larry said politely.

Noelle glanced up at him a moment, her face expressionless, then turned to Paul Metaxas. "I'm always nervous when I'm flown by an incompetent."

Larry felt his face redden. He started to speak, and Noelle said to Metaxas, "Please ask him not to address me in the future unless I speak to him first."

Metaxas swallowed and mumbled, "Yes, ma'am."

Larry stared at Noelle, his eyes filled with fury, as she rose and left the plane. His impulse had been to slap her, but he knew that would have been the end of him. He loved this job more than anything he had ever done, and he did not intend to let anything happen to it. He knew that if he were fired, it could be the last flying job he would ever get. No, he would have to be very careful in the future.

When Larry got home, he talked to Catherine about what had happened.

"She's out to get me," Larry said.

"She sounds horrible," Catherine replied. "Could you have offended her in some way, Larry?"

"I haven't spoken a dozen words to her."

Catherine took his hand. "Don't worry," she said, consolingly. "Before you're through, you'll charm her. Wait and see."

The next day when Larry flew Constantin Demiris on a brief business trip to Turkey, Demiris came into the cockpit and took Metaxas' seat. He dismissed the copilot with a wave of his hand, and Larry and Demiris were alone. They sat there in silence, watching the small stratus clouds slicing the plane into fluffy geometric patterns.

"Miss Page has taken a dislike to you," Demiris said, finally.

Larry felt his hands tighten on the controls and deliberately forced them to relax. He fought to keep his voice calm. "Did—did she say why?"

"She said you were rude to her."

Larry opened his mouth to protest, then thought better of it. He would have to work this out in his own way.

"I'm sorry. I'll try to be more careful, Mr. Demiris," he said evenly.

Demiris got to his feet. "Do that. I would suggest that you not offend Miss Page any further." He left the cockpit.

Any further! Larry racked his brain, trying to think of what he might have done to offend her. Perhaps she just did not like his type. Or she could have been jealous of the fact that Demiris liked and trusted him, but that didn't make sense. Nothing Larry could think of made any sense. And yet Noelle Page was trying to get him fired.

Larry thought about what it was like being out of a job, the indignity of filling out applications like a damned schoolboy, the interviews, the waiting, the endless hours of trying to kill time with cheap bars and amateur whores. He remembered Catherine's patience and tolerance and how he had hated her for it. No, he could not go through all that again. He could not stand another failure.

On a layover in Beirut a few days later Larry passed a movie theater and noticed that the picture playing there starred Noelle Page. On an impulse he went to see it, prepared to hate the picture and its star, but Noelle was so brilliant in it that he found himself completely carried away by her performance. Again he had the curious feeling of familiarity. The following Monday, Larry flew Noelle Page and some business associates of Demiris' to Zurich. Larry waited until Noelle Page was alone and then approached her. He had hesitated about talking to her, remembering her last warning to him, but he had decided that the only way he could break through her antagonism was to go out of his way to be pleasant to her. All actresses were egotistical and liked to be told they were good, and so now he came up to her and said, with careful courtesy, "Excuse me, Miss Page, I just wanted to tell you that I saw you in a movie the other night. *The Third Face.* I think you're one of the greatest actresses I've ever seen."

Noelle stared at him a moment and then replied, "I would like to believe that you are a better critic than you are a pilot, but I doubt very much that you have either the intelligence or the taste." And she walked away.

Larry stood rooted there, feeling as though he had been struck. The goddamned cunt! For an instant he was tempted to follow her and tell her what he thought

of her, but he knew it would be playing into her hands.
No. From now on he would simply do his job and keep
as far away from her as possible.

During the next few weeks Noelle was his passenger
on several flights. Larry did not speak to her at all, and
he tried desperately hard to arrange it so that she did
not see him. He kept out of the cabin and had Metaxas
handle any necessary communications with the passengers. There were no further comments from Noelle
Page, and Larry congratulated himself on having
solved the problem.

As it turned out, he congratulated himself too soon.

One morning Demiris sent for Larry at the villa.
"Miss Page is flying to Paris for me on some confidential business. I want you to stay at her side."

"Yes, Mr. Demiris."

Demiris studied him for a moment, started to add
something else, then changed his mind. "That's all."

Noelle was the only passenger on the flight to Paris
and Larry decided to fly the Piper. He arranged for
Paul Metaxas to make Noelle comfortable and stayed
in the cockpit, out of sight during the entire flight.
When they landed, Larry walked back to her seat and
said, "Excuse me, Miss Page. Mr. Demiris asked me to
stay with you while you're in Paris."

She looked up at him with contempt and said, "Very
well. Just don't let me know that you're around."

He nodded in icy silence.

They rode into the city from Orly in a private limousine. Larry sat up front with the driver and Noelle
Page sat in back. She did not speak to him during the
journey into the city. Their first stop was Paribas, the
Banque de Paris et des Bas. Larry went into the lobby
with Noelle and waited while she was ushered into the
office of the president and then down to the basement
where the safe-deposit boxes were kept. Noelle was
gone about thirty minutes, and when she returned, she
swept straight past Larry without a word. He stared after her a moment, then turned and followed her.

Their next stop was the rue du Faubourg-St.-Honoré. Noelle dismissed the car. Larry followed her into a department store and stood nearby while she selected the items she wanted, then handed him the packages to carry. She shopped in half a dozen stores: Hermes for some purses and belts, Guerlain for perfume, Celine for shoes, until Larry was burdened down with packages. If she was aware of his discomfiture, Noelle gave no sign. Larry might have been some pet animal that she was leading around.

As they walked out of Celine's, it began to rain. Pedestrians were scurrying to take shelter. "Wait here for me," Noelle commanded.

Larry stood there and watched her disappear into a restaurant across the street. He waited in the driving rain for two hours, his arms full of packages, cursing her and cursing himself for putting up with her behavior. He was trapped and he did not know how to get out of it.

And he had a terrible foreboding that it was going to get worse.

The first time Catherine met Constantin Demiris was at his villa. Larry had gone there to deliver a package he had flown in from Copenhagen, and Catherine had gone to the house with him. She was standing in the huge reception hall admiring a painting, when a door opened and Demiris came out. He watched her a moment, then said "Do you like Manet, Mrs. Douglas?"

Catherine swung around and found herself face to face with the legend she had heard so much about. She had two immediate impressions: Constantin Demiris was taller than she had imagined, and there was an overpowering energy in him that was almost frightening. Catherine was amazed that he knew her name and who she was. He seemed to go out of his way to put her at ease. He asked Catherine how she liked Greece, whether her apartment was comfortable, and to let him know if he could do anything to help make her stay

pleasant. He even knew—though God alone knew
how!—that she collected miniature birds. "I saw a
lovely one," he told her. "I will send it to you."

Larry appeared, and he and Catherine left.

"How did you like Demiris?" Larry asked.

"He's a charmer," she said. "No wonder you enjoy
working for him."

"And I'm going to keep working for him." There
was a grimness in his voice that Catherine did not understand.

The following day a beautiful porcelain bird was delivered to Catherine.

Catherine saw Constantin Demiris twice after that,
once when she went to the races with Larry and once
at a Christmas party Demiris gave at his villa. Each
time he went out of his way to be charming to her. All
in all, Catherine thought, Constantin Demiris was quite
a remarkable person.

In August the Athens Festival began. For two
months the city presented plays, ballets, operas, concerts—all given in the Herodes Atticus, the ancient
open-air theater at the foot of the Acropolis. Catherine
saw several of the plays with Larry, and when he was
away she went with Count Pappas. It was fascinating
to watch ancient plays staged in their original settings
by the race that had created them.

One night after Catherine and Count Pappas had
gone to see a production of *Medea,* they were talking
about Larry.

"He's an interesting man," Count Pappas said. *"Polymechanos."*

"What does that mean?"

"It is difficult to translate." The Count thought for a
moment. "It means 'fertile in devices.' "

"You mean 'resourceful'?"

"Yes, but more than that. Someone who is always
very ready with a new idea, a new plan."

"Polymechanos," Catherine said. "That's my boy."

Above them there was a beautiful, waxing gibbous moon. The night was balmy and warm. They walked through the Plaka toward Omonia Square. As they started to cross the street, a car raced around the corner, headed straight toward them and the Count pulled Catherine to safety.

"Idiot!" he yelled after the disappearing driver.

"Everyone here seems to drive like that," Catherine said.

Count Pappas smiled ruefully. "Do you know the reason? The Greeks haven't made the transition to automobiles. In their hearts they're still driving donkeys."

"You're joking."

"Unfortunately no. If you want insight into the Greeks, Catherine, don't read the guidebooks; read the old Greek tragedies. The truth is, we still belong to other centuries. Emotionally we're very primitive. We're filled with grand passions, deep joys and great sorrows, and we haven't learned how to cover them up with a civilized veneer."

"I'm not sure that's a bad thing," Catherine replied.

"Perhaps not. But it distorts reality. When outsiders look at us, they are not seeing what they think they see. It is like looking at a distant star. You are not really seeing the star, you are looking at a reflection of the past."

They had reached the square. They passed a row of little stores with signs in the windows that said "Fortune-Telling."

"There are a lot of fortune-tellers here, aren't there?" Catherine asked.

"We are a very superstitious people."

Catherine shook her head. "I'm afraid I don't believe in it."

They had reached a small taverna. A hand-lettered sign in the window read: "MADAME PIRIS, FORTUNE-TELLING."

"Do you believe in witches?" Count Pappas asked.

Catherine looked at him to see if he was teasing. His

face was serious. "Only on Halloween."

"By a witch I do not mean broomsticks and black cats and boiling kettles."

"What do you mean?"

He nodded toward the sign. "Madame Piris is a witch. She can read the past and the future."

He saw the skepticism on Catherine's face. "I will tell you a story," Count Pappas said. "Many years ago, the Chief of Police in Athens was a man named Sophocles Vasilly. He was a friend of mine and I used my influence to help him get into office. Vasilly was a very honest man. There were people who wished to corrupt him and since he would not be corrupted, they decided that he would have to be eliminated." He took Catherine's arm and they crossed the street toward the park.

"One day, Vasilly came to tell me of a threat that had been made on his life. He was a brave man, but this threat disturbed him because it came from a powerful and ruthless racketeer. Detectives were assigned to watch the racketeer and to protect Vasilly, but still he had an uneasy feeling that he did not have long to live. That was when he came to me."

Catherine was listening, fascinated. "What did you do?" she asked.

"I advised him to get a reading from Madame Piris." He was silent, his thoughts prowling restlessly in some dark arena of the past.

"Did he go?" Catherine finally asked.

"What? Oh, yes. She told Vasilly that death was going to come to him unexpectedly and quickly and warned him to beware of a lion at noon. There are no lions in Greece, except for a few old mangy ones at the zoo and the stone ones you have seen on Delos."

Catherine could feel the tension in Pappas' voice as he continued.

"Vasilly went to the zoo personally to check the cages to make sure that the animals were secure, and he made inquiries as to any wild animals that might have recently been brought into Athens. There were none.

"A week went by and nothing happened, and Vasilly decided that the old witch had been wrong and that he had been a superstitious fool for paying any attention to her. On a Saturday morning I dropped by the police station to pick him up. It was his son's fourth birthday, and we were going to take a boat trip to Kyron to celebrate.

"I drove up in front of the station just as the clock in the Town Hall was striking twelve. As I reached the entrance, there was a tremendous explosion from inside the building. I hurried inside to Vasilly's office." His voice sounded stiff and awkward. "There was nothing left of the office—or of Vasilly."

"How horrible," Catherine murmured.

They walked on for a moment in silence. "But the witch was wrong, wasn't she?" Catherine asked. "He wasn't killed by a lion."

"Ah, but he was, you see. The police reconstructed what had happened. As I told you, it was the boy's birthday. Vasilly's desk was piled with gifts that he was going to bring to his son. Someone had brought in a birthday gift, a toy, and laid it on Vasilly's desk."

Catherine felt the blood leaving her face. "A toy lion."

Count Pappas nodded. "Yes. 'Beware of a lion at noon.'"

Catherine shuddered. "That gives me the creeps."

He looked down at her sympathetically. "Madame Piris is not a 'fun' fortune-teller to go to."

They had crossed through the park and reached Piraios Street. An empty taxi was passing by. The Count hailed it, and ten minutes later Catherine was back at her apartment.

As she prepared for bed, she told Larry the story, and as she told it, her flesh began to crawl again. Larry held her tightly and made love to her, but it was a long time before Catherine was able to fall asleep.

NOELLE AND CATHERINE

Athens: 1946

15

If it had not been for Noelle Page, Larry Douglas would have had no worries. He was where he wanted to be, doing what he wanted to do. He enjoyed his job, the people he met, and the man for whom he worked. On the ground his life was equally satisfactory. When he was not flying, he spent a good part of his time with Catherine; but because Larry's job was so mobile, Catherine was not always aware of where he was, and Larry found innumerable opportunities to go out on his own. He went to parties with Count Pappas and Paul Metaxas, his copilot, and a satisfying number of them turned into orgies. Greek women were filled with passion and fire. He had found a new one, Helena, a stewardess who worked for Demiris, and when they had a stopover away from Athens, she and Larry shared a hotel room. Helena was a beautiful, slim, dark-eyed girl, and insatiable. Yes, everything considered, Larry Douglas decided that his life was perfect.

Except for Demiris' blond bitch mistress.

Larry had not the slightest clue as to what made Noelle Page despise him, but whatever it was, it was endangering his way of life. Larry had tried being polite, aloof, friendly, and each time Noelle Page succeeded in making him look like a fool. Larry knew that he could go to Demiris, but he had no illusions about what would happen if it came to a choice between him and Noelle. Twice, he had arranged for Paul Metaxas to take over Noelle's flight but shortly before each flight Demiris' secretary had telephoned to tell him that Mr.

Demiris would like to have Larry pilot her himself.

On an early morning in late November Larry received a call that he was to fly Noelle Page to Amsterdam that afternoon. Larry checked with the airport and received a negative report on the weather in Amsterdam. A fog was beginning to roll in and by afternoon they expected zero visibility. Larry phoned Demiris' secretary to tell her that it would be impossible to fly to Amsterdam that day. The secretary said she would get back to him. Fifteen minutes later she phoned to say that Miss Page would be at the airport at two o'clock, ready to take off. Larry checked with the airport again, thinking that perhaps there had been a break in the weather, but the report was the same.

"Jesus Christ," Paul Metaxas exclaimed. "She must be in one hell of a hurry to get to Amsterdam."

But Larry had the feeling that Amsterdam was not the issue. This was a contest of wills between the two of them. For all he cared Noelle Page could crash into a mountain peak and good riddance, but Larry was damned if he was going to risk his own neck for the stupid bitch. He tried to phone Demiris to discuss it with him, but he was in a meeting and unavailable. Larry slammed down the phone, seething. He had no choice now but to go to the airport and try to talk his passenger out of making the flight. He arrived at the airport at 1:30. By three o'clock Noelle Page had not appeared. "She probably changed her mind," Metaxas said.

But Larry knew better. As the time wore on, he became more and more furious, until he realized that that was her intention. She was trying to drive him into a rash action that would cost him his job. Larry was in the terminal building talking to the airport manager when Demiris' familiar gray Rolls drove up and Noelle Page emerged. Larry walked outside to meet her.

"I'm afraid the flight's off, Miss Page," he said, making his voice flat. "The airport at Amsterdam is fogged in."

Noelle looked past Larry as though he did not exist and said to Paul Metaxas, "The plane carries automatic landing equipment, does it not?"

"Yes, it does," Metaxas said, awkwardly.

"I'm really surprised," she replied, "that Mr. Demiris would hire a pilot who's a coward. I'll speak to him about it."

Noelle turned and walked toward the plane. Metaxas looked after her and said, "Jesus Christ! I don't know what's gotten into her. She never used to act like this. I'm sorry, Larry."

Larry watched Noelle walk across the field, her blond hair blowing in the wind. He had never hated anyone so much in his life.

Metaxas was watching him. "Are we going?" he asked.

"We're going."

The copilot gave a deep, expressive sigh, and the two men slowly walked toward the plane.

Noelle Page was sitting in the cabin, leisurely thumbing through a fashion magazine when they entered the plane. Larry stared at her a moment, so filled with anger that he was afraid to speak. He went up into the cockpit and began his preflight check.

Ten minutes later he had received clearance from the tower and they were airborne for Amsterdam.

The first half of the flight was uneventful. Switzerland lay below in a mantle of snow. By the time they were over Germany, it was dusk. Larry radioed ahead to Amsterdam for a weather check. They reported that fog was blowing in from the North Sea and getting thicker. He cursed his bad luck. If the winds had changed and the fog had cleared, his problem would have been solved, but now he had to decide whether to risk an instrument landing at Amsterdam or fly to an alternate airport. He was tempted to go back and discuss it with his passenger, but he could visualize the contemptuous look on her face.

"Special Flight one-oh-nine, would you give us your flight plan, please?" It was the tower at Munich. Larry had to make a decision swiftly. He could still land at Brussels, Cologne or Luxembourg.

Or Amsterdam.

The voice crackled over the speaker again. "Special Flight one-oh-nine, would you give us your flight plan, please?"

Larry snapped down the transmitting key. "Special Flight one-oh-nine to Munich Tower. We're going to Amsterdam." He flicked the switch up and was aware of Metaxas watching him.

"Jesus, maybe I should have doubled my life insurance," Metaxas said. "You really think we're going to make it?"

"Do you want to know the truth?" Larry said, bitterly. "I don't give a shit."

"Fantastic! I'm up in a plane with two fucking maniacs!" Metaxas moaned.

For the next hour Larry was wholly absorbed in flying the aircraft, listening to the frequent weather reports without comment. He was still hoping for a wind change, but thirty minutes out of Amsterdam the report was still the same. Heavy fog. The field was closed to all air traffic except for emergencies. Larry made contact with the control tower at Amsterdam. "Special Flight one-oh-nine to Amsterdam Tower. Approaching airport from 75 miles east of Cologne, ETA nineteen hundred hours."

Almost instantly a voice on the radio crackled back, "Amsterdam Tower to Special Flight one-oh-nine. Our field is closed down. We suggest you return to Cologne or land at Brussels."

Larry spoke into the handmike. "Special Flight one-oh-nine to Amsterdam Tower. Negative. We have an emergency."

Metaxas turned to stare at him in surprise.

A new voice came over the speaker. "Special Flight

one-oh-nine, this is Chief of Operations at Amsterdam Airport. We are completely fogged in here. Visibility zero. Repeat: visibility zero. What is the nature of your emergency?"

"We're running out of fuel," Larry said. "I have barely enough to reach you."

Metaxas' eyes went to the fuel gauges, which registered half full. "For Christ's sakes," Metaxas exploded. "We could fly to China!"

The radio was silent. Suddenly it exploded into life again.

"Amsterdam Tower to Special Flight one-oh-nine. You have an emergency clearance. We'll bring you in."

"Roger." Larry flicked off the switch and turned to Metaxas. "Jettison the fuel," he ordered.

Metaxas swallowed and said in a choked voice, *"J—jettison the fuel?"*

"You heard me, Paul. Leave just enough to bring us in."

"But, Larry . . ."

"Damn it, don't argue. If we roll in there with a tank half full of gas, they'll jerk our licenses away so fast you won't know what hit you."

Metaxas nodded glumly and reached for the fuel-ejection handle. He began to pump, keeping a close eye on the gauge. Five minutes later they were in the fog, wrapped in a soft white cotton that wiped out everything but the dimly lit cockpit they sat in. It was an eerie sensation, cut off from time and space and the rest of the world. The last time Larry had been through this was in the Link Trainer. But that was a game where there were no risks. Here the stakes were life and death. He wondered what it was doing to his passenger. He hoped it gave her a heart attack. The Amsterdam control tower came on again.

"Amsterdam control tower to Special Flight one-oh-nine. I am going to bring you in on A.L.S. You will please follow my instructions exactly. We have you on our radar. Turn three degrees west and maintain present altitude until further instructions. At your present airspeed, you should be landing in eighteen minutes."

The voice coming over the radio sounded tense. With good reason, thought Larry grimly. One slight mistake and the plane would plough into the sea. Larry made the correction and shut out everything from his mind but the disembodied voice that was his sole link to survival. He flew the plane as though it were a part of himself, flying it with his heart, his soul and his mind. He was dimly aware of Paul Metaxas sweating beside him, calling out a constant instrument check in a low, strained voice, but if they came out of this alive, it would be Larry Douglas who did it. Larry had never seen fog like this. It was a ghostly enemy, charging at him from every side, blinding him, seducing him, trying to lure him into making one fatal mistake. He was hurtling through the sky at two hundred and fifty miles an hour, unable to see beyond the windshield of the cockpit. Pilots hated fog, and the first rule was: Climb over it or dive under it, but get out of it! Now there was no way, because he was locked into an impossible destination by the whim of a spoiled tart. He was helpless, at the mercy of instruments that could go wrong and men on the ground who could make mistakes. The disembodied voice came over the speaker again, and it seemed to Larry that it had a new, nervous quality.

"Amsterdam Tower to Special Flight one-oh-nine. You are coming into the first leg of your landing pattern: Lower your flaps and begin your descent. Descend to two thousand feet . . . fifteen hundred feet . . . one thousand feet . . ."

Still no sign of the airport below. They could have been in the middle of nowhere. He could feel the ground rushing up to meet the plane.

"Decrease your airspeed to one hundred twenty . . . lower your wheels . . . you're at six hundred feet . . . airspeed one hundred . . . you're at four hundred feet . . ." And still no sign of the goddamn airport! The blanket of smothering cotton seemed thicker now.

Metaxas' forehead gleamed with perspiration. "Where in the hell is it?" he whispered.

Larry stole a swift glance at the altimeter. The needle was edging down toward three hundred feet. Then it was below three hundred feet. The ground was rushing up to meet them at one hundred miles per hour. The altimeter showed only one hundred fifty feet. Something was wrong. He should have been able to see the airport lights by now. He strained to see ahead of the plane, but there was only the treacherous, blinding fog whipping across the windshield.

Larry heard Metaxas' voice, tense and hoarse. "We're down to sixty feet." And still nothing.

"Forty feet."

And the ground racing up to meet them in the darkness.

"Twenty feet."

It was no good. In another two seconds, the margin of safety would be gone and they would crash. He had to make an instant decision.

"I'm going to take it back up," Larry said. His hand tightened on the wheel and started to pull back and at that instant, a row of electric arrows blazed out on the ground ahead of them, lighting up the runway below. Ten seconds later, they were on the ground, taxiing toward the Schiphol terminal.

When they had come to a stop, Larry switched off the engines with numb fingers and sat motionless for a long time. Finally he pushed himself to his feet and was surprised to find that his knees were trembling. He noticed a strange odor in the air and turned to Metaxas. Metaxas grinned sheepishly.

"Sorry," he said. "I shat."

Larry looked down at him and nodded. "For both of us," he said. He turned and walked back into the cabin. The bitch was in there, calmly thumbing through a magazine. Larry stood there studying her, aching to tell her off, wishing desperately that he could find the key to what made her tick. Noelle Page must have known how close she had come to death in the past few minutes, and yet she sat there looking serene and undisturbed, not a hair out of place.

"Amsterdam," Larry announced.

They drove into Amsterdam in a heavy silence, No-elle in the back seat of the Mercedes 300 and Larry in front with the chauffeur. Metaxas had stayed at the airport to have the plane serviced. The fog was still thick and they drove slowly until suddenly, when they reached the Lindenplatz, it began to lift.

They rode through the City Square, crossed the Eider Bridge over the Amstel River and stopped in front of the Amstel Hotel. When they reached the lobby, Noelle said to Larry, "You will pick me up at ten sharp tonight," then turned away and walked toward the elevator, the manager of the hotel bowing and scraping at her heels. A bellboy led Larry to a small, uncomfortable single room at the back of the hotel on the first floor. The room was next to the kitchen, and through the wall Larry could hear the clatter of dishes and smell the mixed aromas from the steaming kettles.

Larry took one look at the tiny room and snapped, "I wouldn't put my dog in here."

"I'm sorry," the bellboy said apologetically. "Miss Page requested the cheapest room we had for you."

Okay, Larry thought, *I'll find a way to beat her. Constantin Demiris isn't the only man in the world who uses a private pilot. I'll start checking tomorrow. I've met a lot of his rich friends. There are half a dozen of them who would be damned glad to hire me.* But then, he thought: *Not if Demiris fires me. If that happens, none of them will touch me. I have to hang in there.* The bathroom was down the hall, and Larry unpacked and took out a robe so that he could go take a bath, then thought: *To hell with it, why should I bathe for her? I hope I smell like a pig.* He went to the hotel bar to have a badly needed drink. He was on his third

martini when he looked up at the clock over the bar
and saw that it was 10:15. *Ten o'clock sharp,* she had
said. Larry was filled with a sudden panic. He hastily
slapped some bills on the bar and headed toward the
elevator. Noelle was in the Emperor Suite on the fifth
floor. He found himself running down the long corridor
and cursing himself for letting her do this to him. He
knocked at the door to her suite, his mind forming excuses for his tardiness. No one answered his knock and
when Larry turned the knob, it was off the latch. He
walked into the large, luxuriously furnished living
room and stood there a moment, uncertainly, then
called out, "Miss Page." There was no answer. So *that*
was her plan.

*I'm sorry, Costa darling, but I warned you that he
was unreliable. I asked him to pick me up at ten
o'clock, but he was down in the bar getting drunk. I
had to leave without him.*

Larry heard a sound from the bathroom and went
toward it. The bathroom door was open. He walked inside just as Noelle Page stepped out of the shower. She
wore nothing but a turkish towel turbanned around her
head.

Noelle turned and saw him standing there. An apol-
ogy sprang to Larry's lips, trying to head off her indignation, but before he could speak, Noelle said indifferently, "Hand me that towel," as though he were a
maid. Or a eunuch. Larry could have coped with her
indignation or anger, but her arrogant indifference
made something explode inside him.

He moved toward her and grabbed her, knowing as
he did it that he was throwing away everything he
wanted for the cheap satisfaction of a petty revenge,
but there was no way he could have stopped himself.
The rage inside him had been building up for months,
fed by the indignities he had received from her, the
gratuitous insults, the humiliation, the risking of his
life. All these things were burning in him as he reached
for her naked body. If Noelle had screamed, Larry

would have knocked her senseless. But she saw the wild look on his face and made no sound as he picked her up and carried her into the bedroom.

Somewhere in Larry's mind a voice was shouting to him to stop, to apologize, to say that he was drunk, to get out before it was too late to save himself, but he knew it was already too late. There was no going back. He threw her savagely down on the bed and moved toward her.

He concentrated on her body, refusing to let his mind think of what his punishment was going to be for what he was doing. He had no illusions as to what Demiris would do to him for this, for the Greek's honor would not be satisfied with merely firing him. Larry knew enough about the tycoon to know that his vengeance would be far more terrible, and yet knowing this Larry could not stop himself. She lay on the bed looking up at him, her eyes blazing. He moved down on top of her and was entering her, never realizing until that instant how much he had been wanting to do this all along, and somehow the need was all mixed up with the hate, and he felt her arms wrap around his neck, holding him close, as though she would never let him go, and she said, "Welcome back," and it flashed through Larry's mind that she was crazy or she was confusing him with someone else, but he didn't care because her body was twisting and writhing beneath him, and he forgot everything else in the sensation of what was happening to him, and the sudden blinding wonderful knowledge that now everything was going to be all right.

NOELLE AND CATHERINE
Athens: 1946

16

Inexplicably, Time had become Catherine's enemy. She was unaware of it at first, and looking back she could not have told the exact moment that Time began to work against her. She was not aware when Larry's love had gone or why or how, but one day it had simply disappeared somewhere down the endless corridor of time and all that was left was a cold hollow echo. She sat in the apartment alone day after day, trying to figure out what had happened, what had gone wrong. There was nothing specific Catherine could think of, no single moment of revelation that she could point to and say, *That was it, that was when Larry stopped loving me.* Possibly it had started when Larry came back after three weeks in Africa where he had flown Constantin Demiris on a safari. Catherine had missed Larry more than she had thought possible. *He's away all the time,* she thought. *It's like during the war, only this time there's no enemy.*

But she was wrong. There was an enemy.

"I haven't told you the good news," Larry said. "I got a raise. Seven hundred a month. How about that?"

"That's wonderful," she replied. "We can go back home that much sooner." She saw his face tighten. "What's the matter?"

"This is home," Larry said, curtly.

She stared at him uncomprehendingly. "Well, for now," she agreed weakly, "but I mean—you wouldn't want to live here forever."

"You've never had it so good," Larry retorted. "It's

like living at a vacation resort."

"But it's not like living in America, is it?"

"Fuck America," Larry said. "I risked my ass for it for four years and what did it get me? A handful of two-bit medals. They wouldn't even give me a job after the war."

"That's not true," she said. "You . . ."

"I what?"

Catherine did not want to provoke an argument, particularly on his first night back. "Nothing, darling," she said. "You're tired. Let's go to bed early."

"Let's not." He went to the bar to pour himself a drink. "A new act's opening at the Argentina Night Club. I told Paul Metaxas that we'd join him and a few friends."

Catherine looked at him. "Larry—" She had to fight to keep her voice steady. "Larry, we haven't seen each other for almost a month. We never get a chance to— to just sit and talk."

"I can't help it if my work takes me away," he replied. "Don't you think I'd like to be with you?"

She shook her head and said, "I don't know. I'll have to ask the Ouija board."

He put his arms around her then and grinned that innocent, boyish grin. "To hell with Metaxas and the whole crowd. We'll stay in tonight, just the two of us. Okay?"

Catherine looked into his face and knew that she was being unreasonable. Of course he couldn't help it if his job took him away from her. And when he got home, it was natural that he would want to see other people. "We'll go out if you like," she decided.

"Uhn-uhn." He held her close. "Just the two of us."

They did not leave the apartment all weekend. Catherine cooked and they made love and sat in front of the fire and talked and played gin rummy and read, and it was everything that Catherine could have asked.

Sunday night after a delicious dinner that Catherine prepared, they went to bed and made love again. She lay in bed watching Larry as he walked down toward the bathroom, naked, and she thought what a beautiful man he is and how lucky I am that he belongs to me, and the smile was still on her face when Larry turned at the bathroom door and said casually, "Make a lot of dates next week, will you, so we won't have to be stuck with each other like this again with nothing to do." And he went into the bathroom leaving Catherine with the smile still frozen on her face.

Or perhaps the trouble had started with Helena, the beautiful Greek stewardess. One hot summer afternoon, Catherine had been out shopping. Larry was out of town. She was expecting him home the following day and had decided to surprise him with his favorite dishes. As Catherine was leaving the market with her arms full of groceries, a taxi passed her. In the back seat was Larry, his arms around a girl in a stewardess' uniform. Catherine had one brief glimpse of their faces laughing together, and then the taxi turned a corner and was out of sight.

Catherine stood there numb, and it was not until some small boys came running up to her that she realized the grocery bags had slipped from her nerveless fingers. They had helped Catherine pick up everything and she had stumbled home, her mind refusing to think. She had tried to tell herself that it had not been Larry she had seen in the taxi, it had been someone who resembled him. But the truth was that no one in the world resembled Larry. He was unique, an original work of God, a priceless creation of nature. And he was all hers. Hers and the brunette's in the taxi, and how many others?

Catherine sat up all that night waiting for Larry to walk in, and when he did not come home, she knew that there was no excuse that he could give her that could hold their marriage together, and no excuse that she could give herself. He was a liar and a cheat, and she could not stay married to him any longer.

Larry did not return home until late the following afternoon.

"Hi," he said cheerfully, as he walked into the apartment. He put down his flight bag and saw her face. "What's wrong?"

"When did you get back to town?" Catherine asked stiffly.

Larry looked at her, puzzled. "About an hour ago. Why?"

"I saw you in a taxi yesterday with a girl." *It was as simple as that,* Catherine thought. *Those are the words that ended my marriage. He's going to deny it, and I'm going to call him a liar and leave him and never see him again.*

Larry was standing there staring at her.

"Go ahead," she said. "Tell me it wasn't you."

Larry looked at her, nodding. "Of course it was me." The sudden sharp pain Catherine felt at the pit of her stomach made her realize how much she had wanted him to deny it.

"Christ," he said, "what have you been thinking?"

She started to speak and her voice trembled with anger. "I—"

Larry held up a hand. "Don't say anything you'll be sorry for."

Catherine looked at him incredulously. *"I'll* be sorry for?"

"I flew back to Athens yesterday for fifteen minutes to pick up a girl named Helena Merelis to fly her to Crete for Demiris. Helena works for him as a stewardess."

"But . . ." It was possible. Larry could have been telling the truth; or was it *polymechanos,* fertile in devices? "Why didn't you telephone me?" Catherine asked.

"I did," Larry said curtly. "There was no answer. You were out, weren't you?"

Catherine swallowed. "I—I went out shopping for your dinner."

"I'm not hungry," Larry snapped. "Nagging always makes me lose my appetite." He turned and walked out the door, leaving Catherine standing there, her right hand still raised, as though it was silently beseeching him to come back.

It was shortly after that that Catherine began to drink. It started in a small, harmless way. She would be expecting Larry home for dinner at seven o'clock, and when nine o'clock came and he had not called, Catherine would have a brandy to help kill the time. By ten o'clock, she would have had several brandies, and by the time he came home, if he did, the dinner would have been long since ruined, and she would be a little tight. It made it much easier to face what was happening to her life.

Catherine could no longer hide from herself the fact that Larry was cheating on her and had probably been cheating from the time they were married. Going through his uniform trousers one day before sending them to the cleaners, she found a lace handkerchief with dried semen. There was lipstick on his shorts.

She thought of Larry in the arms of some other woman.

And she wanted to kill him.

NOELLE AND CATHERINE
Athens: 1946

17

As Time had become Catherine's enemy, so it had become Larry's friend. The night in Amsterdam had been nothing less than a miracle. Larry had courted disaster and in so doing had, incredibly, found the solution to all his problems. *It's the Douglas luck,* he thought with satisfaction.

But he knew that it was more than luck. It was some obscure, perverse instinct in him that needed to challenge the Fates, to brush against the parameters of death and destruction, a testing, a pitting of himself against Fortune for life-and-death stakes.

Larry remembered a morning over the Truk Islands when a squadron of Zeros had zoomed out of a cloud cover. He had been flying point, and they had concentrated their attack on him. Three Zeros had maneuvered him away from the rest of the squadron and opened fire on him. In a kind of supraclarity that came to him in moments of danger, he was blindingly aware of the island below, the dozens of ships bobbing on the rolling seas, the roaring planes slashing at each other in the bright blue sky. It was one of the happiest moments of Larry's life, the fulfillment of Life and the mocking of Death.

He had put the plane into a spin and had pulled out of it on the tail of one of the Zeros. He had watched it explode as he opened up with his machine guns. The other two planes had closed in on either side. Larry watched them as they raced down to him, and at the last instant he pulled the plane into an Immelmann, and the two Japanese planes collided in mid-air. It was a moment Larry savored in his mind often.

For some reason it had come back to him that night in Amsterdam. He had made wild, violent love to No- elle, and afterward she had lain in his arms, talking of the two of them in Paris together before the war, and it suddenly brought back a dim memory of an eager young girl, but good God, there had been hundreds of eager young girls since then, and Noelle was no more than an elusive, half-recalled wisp of memory in his past.

How lucky it was, Larry thought, that their paths had crossed again accidentally, after all these years.

"You belong to me," Noelle said. "You're mine now."

Something in her tone made Larry uneasy. *And yet,* he asked himself, *what do I have to lose?*

With Noelle under his control, he could stay on with Demiris forever, if he wanted to.

She was studying him as though reading his mind, and there was an odd expression in her eyes that Larry did not understand.

It was just as well.

On a return trip from Morocco Larry took Helena out to dinner and spent the night at her apartment.

In the morning he drove to the airport to check out his plane. He had lunch with Paul Metaxas.

"You look like you hit the jackpot," Metaxas said. "Can you spare a piece for me?"

"My boy," Larry grinned, "you couldn't handle them. It takes a master."

They had a pleasant lunch and then Larry drove back into town to pick up Helena, who was to be on his flight.

He knocked at the door of her apartment and after a long while, Helena slowly opened it. She was naked. Larry stared at her, not recognizing her. Her face and body were a mass of ugly bruises and puffy swellings.

Her eyes were slits of pain. She had been beaten up by a professional.

"Christ!" Larry exclaimed. "What happened?"

Helena opened her mouth and Larry saw that three of her upper front teeth had been knocked out. "T—two men," she chattered. "They came in as soon as you l—left."

"Didn't you call the police?" Larry demanded, horrified.

"Th—they said they would kill me if I told anyone. They meant it, L—Larry." She stood there in shock, holding onto the door for support.

"Did they rob you?"

"N—no. They f—forced their way in and raped me and then they—they beat me up."

"Get some clothes on," he ordered. "I'm taking you to the hospital."

"I can't g—go out with my face like this," she said.

And of course she was right. Larry telephoned a doctor who was a friend of his and arranged for him to come over.

"I'm sorry I can't stay," Larry told Helena. "I have to fly Demiris out in half an hour. I'll see you as soon as I return."

But he never saw her again. When Larry returned two days later, the apartment was empty, and the landlady told him that the young lady had moved and had left no forwarding address. Even then Larry had no suspicion of the truth. It was not until several nights later when he was making love to Noelle that he had an inkling of what had happened. "You're so goddamn fantastic," he said. "I've never known anybody like you."

"Do I give you everything you want?" she asked.

"Yes," he moaned, "Oh, Christ, yes."

Noelle stopped what she was doing. "Then don't ever sleep with another woman," she said softly. "Next time, I'll kill her."

Larry remembered her words: You belong to me.

And they suddenly took on a new and ominous meaning. For the first time he had the premonition that this was not some fly-by-night affair that he could get out of anytime he felt like it. He sensed the cold, deadly, untouchable center that was in Noelle Page, and he was chilled and a little frightened by it. Half a dozen times during the night he started to bring up the subject of Helena, and each time he stopped because he was afraid to know, afraid to have it put into words, as though the words had more power than the deed itself. If Noelle were capable of that . . .

At breakfast the next morning Larry studied Noelle when she was unaware of it, looking for signs of cruelty, of sadism, but all he saw was a loving, beautiful woman, telling him amusing anecdotes, anticipating and catering to his every want. *I have to be wrong about her,* he thought. But after that he was careful not to date any other girls, and in a few short weeks he had lost all desire to do so because Noelle had become a complete obsession with him.

From the beginning Noelle warned Larry that it was essential that they keep their affair from Constantin Demiris.

"There must never be the slightest whisper of suspicion about us," Noelle cautioned.

"Why don't I rent an apartment?" Larry suggested. "A place where we . . ."

Noelle shook her head. "Not in Athens. Someone would recognize me. Let me think about it."

Two days later Demiris sent for Larry. At first Larry was apprehensive, wondering whether the Greek tycoon could have heard about Noelle and him, but Demiris greeted him pleasantly and led him into a discussion of a new plane he was considering buying.

"It's a converted Mitchell Bomber," Demiris told him. "I want you to have a look at it."

Larry's face lit up. "It's a great plane," he said. "For its weight and size, it will give you the best ride you can buy."

"How many passengers will it carry?"

Larry thought a moment. "Nine in luxury, plus a pilot, navigator and flight engineer. It flies at four hundred eighty miles an hour."

"It sounds interesting. Will you check it out for me and give me a report?"

"I can't wait," Larry grinned.

Demiris rose to his feet. "By the way Douglas, Miss Page is going to Berlin in the morning. I want you to fly her there."

"Yes, sir," Larry said. And then added, innocently, "Did Miss Page tell you that we're getting along better?"

Demiris looked up at him. "No," he said, puzzled. "As a matter of fact this morning she complained to me about your insolence."

Larry stared at him in surprise, and then as realization flooded through him, he quickly tried to cover up his blunder. "I'm trying, Mr. Demiris," he said earnestly. "I'll try harder."

Demiris nodded. "Do that. You're the best pilot I've ever had, Douglas. It would be a shame to . . ." He let his voice trail off, but the message was clear.

On the drive home Larry cursed himself for a fool. He had better remember he was playing in the big leagues now. Noelle had been bright enough to realize that any sudden change in her attitude toward Larry would make Demiris suspicious. The old relationship between them was a perfect cover for what they were doing. Demiris was trying to bring them together. The thought made Larry laugh aloud. It was a good feeling to know that he had something that one of the most powerful men in the world thought belonged to him.

On the flight to Berlin Larry turned the wheel over to Paul Metaxas and told him that he was going back to talk to Noelle Page.

"Aren't you afraid of getting your head bitten off?" Metaxas asked.

Larry hesitated, tempted to brag. But he conquered the impulse. "She's a bitch on wheels," Larry shrugged, "but if I don't find some way to soften her up, I could find myself out on my ass."

"Good luck," Metaxas said soberly.

"Thanks."

Larry carefully closed the cockpit door and went back to the lounge where Noelle was seated. The two stewardesses were at the rear of the plane. Larry started to sit down across from Noelle.

"Be careful," she warned softly. "Everyone who works for Constantin reports back to him."

Larry glanced toward the stewardesses and thought of Helena.

"I've found a place for us," Noelle said. There was pleasure and excitement in her voice.

"An apartment?"

"A house. Do you know where Rafina is?"

Larry shook his head. "No."

"It's a little village on the sea, a hundred kilometers north of Athens. We have a secluded villa there."

He nodded. "Whose name did you rent it in?"

"I bought it," Noelle said, "in someone else's name."

Larry wondered what it must feel like to be able to afford to buy a villa just to get in the hay with someone once in a while. "Great," he said. "I can't wait to see it."

She studied him a moment. "Will you have any trouble getting away from Catherine?"

Larry looked at Noelle in surprise. It was the first time she had ever mentioned his wife. He had certainly made no secret of his marriage, but it was a strange feeling to hear Noelle use Catherine's name. Obviously she had done some checking, and knowing her as well as he was beginning to, it was probably very thorough. She was waiting for an answer. "No," Larry replied. "I come and go as I please."

Noelle nodded, satisfied. "Good. Constantin is going

on a business cruise to Dubrovnik. I've told him I can't
go with him. We'll have ten lovely days together.
You'd better go now."

Larry turned and walked back to the cockpit.

"How did it go?" Metaxas asked. "Loosen her up
any?"

"Not much," Larry replied, carefully. "It's going to
take time."

Larry owned a car, a Citroen convertible, but at Noelle's insistence, he went to a small rent-a-car agency in
Athens and hired an automobile. Noelle had driven up
to Rafina alone and Larry was to join her there. The
drive was a pleasant one on a winding ribbon of dusty
road high above the sea. Two and a half hours out of
Athens Larry came to a tiny, charming village nestled
along the coastline. Noelle had given him careful directions so that he would not have to stop and inquire at
the village. As he reached the outskirts of the village,
he turned to the left and drove down a small dirt road
that led to the sea. There were several villas, each one
secluded behind high stone walls. At the end of the
road built on an outcropping of rock on a promontory
that jutted out over the water was a large, luxurious-
looking villa.

Larry drove up to the gate and rang the bell. A moment later the electric gate swung open. He drove inside and the gate closed behind him. He found himself
in a large courtyard with a fountain in the center. The
sides of the courtyard were filled with a profusion of
flowers. The house itself was a typical Mediterranean
villa, as impregnable as a fortress. The front door
opened and Noelle appeared, wearing a white cotton
dress. They stood there smiling at each other, and then
she was in his arms.

"Come and see your new house," she said eagerly,
and she took him inside.

The interior of the house was cavernous, large
spacious rooms with high domed ceilings. There was an

enormous living room downstairs, a library, a formal dining room and an old-fashioned kitchen with a circular cooking range in the center. The bedrooms were upstairs.

"What about the servants?" Larry asked.

"You're looking at them."

Larry regarded her in surprise. *"You're* going to do the cooking and cleaning?"

She nodded. "There will be a couple coming in to clean after we leave here, but they will never see us. I arranged it through an agency."

Larry grinned sardonically.

There was a warning note in Noelle's voice. "Don't ever make the mistake of underestimating Constantin Demiris. If he finds out about us, he will kill both of us."

Larry smiled. "You're exaggerating," he said. "The old man may not like it, but . . ."

Her violet eyes locked on his. "He will kill us both." There was something in her voice that sent a feeling of apprehension through him.

"You're serious, aren't you?"

"I was never more serious in my life. He's ruthless."

"But when you say he'll *kill* us," Larry protested, "he wouldn't . . ."

"He won't use bullets," Noelle said flatly. "He'll find a complicated, ingenious way to do it, and he'll never be punished for it." Her tone lightened. "But he won't find out, darling. Come, let me show you our bedroom." She took his hand and they went up the sweeping stairway. "We have four guest bedrooms," she said and added with a smile, "we can try them all." She took him into the master bedroom, a huge corner suite that overlooked the sea. From the window Larry could see a large terrace and the short path that wound down to the water. There was a dock with a large sailboat and a motor boat moored to it.

"Who do the boats belong to?"

"You," she said. "It's your welcome-home present."

He turned to her and found that she had slipped out of her cotton dress. She was naked. They spent the rest of the afternoon in bed.

The next ten days flew by. Noelle was quicksilver, a nymph, a genie, a dozen beautiful servants catering to Larry's every wish before he even knew what he wanted. He found the library in the villa stocked with his favorite books and records. Noelle cooked all his favorite dishes to perfection, sailed with him, swam in the warm blue sea with him, made love to him, gave him massages at night until he fell asleep. In a sense they were prisoners there together, for they dared not see anyone else. Every day Larry found new facets in Noelle. She entertained him with fascinating anecdotes about famous people she knew. She tried to discuss business and politics with him until she found that he was interested in neither.

They played poker and gin rummy, and Larry was furious because he could never win. Noelle taught him chess and backgammon and he could never beat her at either. On their first Sunday at the villa she fixed a delicious picnic lunch, and they sat on the beach in the sun and enjoyed it. While they were eating, Noelle looked up and saw two men in the distance. They were strolling toward them along the beach.

"Let's go inside," Noelle said.

Larry looked up and saw the men. "Jesus, don't be so jumpy. They're just a couple of villagers out for a walk."

"Now," she commanded.

"OK," he said ungraciously, irritated by the incident and by her tone.

"Help me pack up the things."

"Why don't we just leave them?" he asked.

"Because it would look suspicious."

Quickly they stuffed everything into the picnic hamper and started toward the house. Larry was silent for the rest of the afternoon. He sat in the library, his mind preoccupied, while Noelle worked in the kitchen.

Late in the afternoon she came into the library and sat at his feet. With her uncanny knack of reading his mind, she said. "Stop thinking about them."

"They were just a couple of goddamn villagers," Larry snapped. "I hate sneaking around like some kind of criminal." He looked at her and his voice changed. "I don't want to have to hide from anybody. I love you."

And Noelle knew that this time it was true. She thought of the years during which she had planned to destroy Larry and of the fierce pleasure she had taken in imagining his destruction: And yet the moment Noelle had seen Larry again she had known instantly that there was something deeper than hate still alive in her. When she had pushed him to the brink of death, forcing him to risk both their lives on that terrible flight to Amsterdam, it was as though she were testing his love for her in a wild defiance of fate. She had been with Larry in that cockpit, flying the plane with him, suffering with him, knowing that if he died they would die together, and he had saved them both. And when he had come to her room in Amsterdam and made love to her, her hatred and her love had become intermingled with their two bodies, and somehow time had expanded and contracted and they were back in their little hotel room in Paris and Larry was saying to her, "Let's get married; we'll find some little *maire* in the country," and the present and the past had exploded dazzlingly into one and Noelle knew then that they were timeless, had always been timeless, that nothing had really changed and that the depths of her hatred for Larry had come from the heights of her love. If she destroyed him she would be destroying herself, for she had given herself completely to him long ago and nothing could ever change that.

It seemed to Noelle that everything she had achieved in her life had been through her hatred. Her father's betrayal had molded and shaped her, annealed and hardened her, filled her with a hunger for vengeance that could be satisfied with nothing less than a kingdom of her own in which she was all-powerful, in which she could never be betrayed again, never be hurt. She had finally achieved that. And now she was ready to give it up for this man. Because she knew now that what she had always wanted was for Larry to need her, to love her. And, at last, he did. And that, finally, was her real kingdom.

NOELLE AND CATHERINE

Athens: 1946

18

For Larry and Noelle the next three months was one of those rare, idyllic periods when everything went right, a magic time of floating from one wonderful day to the next, with not the faintest cloud on the horizon. Larry spent his working hours doing what he loved to do, flying, and whenever he had time off he went to the villa in Rafina and spent a day or a weekend or a week with Noelle. In the beginning Larry had been afraid that the arrangement would become a millstone that would drag him down into the kind of domesticity that he loathed; but each time he saw Noelle, he became more enchanted and he began to look eagerly forward to the hours he would spend with her. When she had to cancel one weekend because of an unexpected trip with Demiris, Larry stayed alone at the villa, and he found himself angry and jealous, thinking about Noelle and Demiris together. When he saw Noelle the following week, she was surprised and pleased by his eagerness.

"You missed me," she said.

He nodded. "A lot."

"Good."

"How's Demiris?"

She hesitated a moment. "All right."

Larry noticed her hesitation. "What is it?"

"I was thinking of something you said."

"What?"

"You said you hated the feeling of sneaking around like a criminal. I hate it too. Every moment I was with Constantin, I wanted to be with you. I once told you,

Larry, I want all of you. I meant it. I don't want to share you with anyone. I want you to marry me."

He stared at her in surprise, caught off guard.

Noelle was watching him. "Do you want to marry me?"

"You know I do. But how? You keep telling me what Demiris will do if he finds out about us."

She shook her head. "He won't find out. Not if we're clever and plan it properly. He doesn't own me, Larry. I'll leave him. There's nothing he can do about that. He has too much pride to try to stop me. A month or two later, you'll quit your job. We'll go away somewhere, separately, perhaps to the United States. We can be married there. I have more money than we'll ever need. I'll buy you a charter airline, or a flying school or whatever you like."

He stood there listening to what she was saying, weighing what he would be giving up against what he would be gaining. And what would he be giving up? A lousy job as a pilot. The thought of owning his own planes sent a small thrill coursing through him. He'd have his own converted Mitchell. Or maybe the new DC-6 that had just come out. Four radial engines, eighty-five passengers. And Noelle, yes, he wanted Noelle. Jesus, what was he even hesitating about?

"What about my wife?" he asked.

"Tell her you want a divorce."

"I don't know if she'll give me one."

"Don't ask her," Noelle replied. "Tell her." There was a final implacable note in her voice.

Larry nodded. "All right."

"You won't be sorry, darling. I promise," Noelle said.

For Catherine time had lost its circadian rhythm; she had fallen into a tesseract of time, and day and night blended into one. Larry was almost never home, and she had long since stopped seeing any of their friends, because she did not have the energy to make any more excuses or to face people. Count Pappas had made half a dozen attempts to see her, and had finally given up. She found herself only able to cope with people secondhand: by telephone or letter or cable. But face to face, she turned to stone, and conversations flinted off her in hopeless, futile sparks. Time brought pain and people brought pain, and the only surcease Catherine found was in the wonderful forgetfulness of liquor. Oh how it eased the suffering, softened the sharp edge of rebuffs and gentled down the pitiless sun of reality that beat down on everyone else.

When Catherine had first come to Athens, she and William Fraser had written to each other frequently, swapping news and keeping each other up-to-date on the activities of their mutual friends and foes. Since Catherine's problems with Larry had begun, however, she had not had the heart to write to Fraser. His last three letters had gone unanswered, and his last letter had gone unopened. She simply did not have the energy to cope with anything outside the microcosm of self-pity in which she was trapped.

One day a cable arrived for Catherine, and it was still lying on the table unopened a week later, when the doorbell rang and William Fraser appeared. Catherine stared at him, unbelievingly. "Bill!" she said, thickly. "Bill Fraser!"

He started to speak and she saw the excited look in his eyes turn to something else, something startled and shocked.

"Bill, darling," she said. "What are you doing here?"

"I had to come to Athens on business," Fraser explained. "Didn't you get my cable?"

Catherine looked at him, trying to remember. "I don't know," she said finally. She led him into the living room, strewn with old newspapers, filled ashtrays and plates of half-eaten food. "Sorry the place is such a mess," she said, waving a vague hand. "I've been busy."

Fraser was studying her worriedly. "Are you all right, Catherine?"

"Me? Fantastic. How about a little drink?"

"It's only eleven o'clock in the morning."

She nodded. "You're right. You're absolutely right, Bill. It's too early to have a drink, and to tell you the truth I wouldn't have one except to celebrate your coming here. You're the only one in the whole world who could make me have a drink at eleven o'clock in the morning."

Fraser watched with dismay as Catherine staggered to the liquor cabinet and poured a large drink for herself and a smaller one for him.

"Do you like Greek brandy?" she asked as she carried his drink to him. "I used to hate it, but you get used to it."

Fraser took his drink and set it down. "Where's Larry?" he asked quietly.

"Larry? Oh, good old Larry's flying around somewhere. He works for the richest man in the world, you know. Demiris owns everything, even Larry."

He studied her for a moment. "Does Larry know you drink?"

Catherine slammed down her glass and stood swaying in front of him. "What do you mean, does Larry know I drink?" she demanded indignantly. "Who says I drink? Just because I want to celebrate seeing an old friend, don't you start attacking me!"

"Catherine," he began, "I'm . . ."

"You think you can come in here and accuse me of being some kind of a drunk?"

"I'm sorry, Catherine," Fraser said painfully, "I think you need help."

"Well you're wrong," she retorted. "I don't need any help. Do you know why? Because I'm—I'm self—I'm self . . ." she groped for the word and finally gave it up. "I don't need any help."

Fraser watched her for a moment. "I have to go to a

conference now," he said. "Have dinner with me tonight."

"OK." She nodded.

"Good, I'll pick you up at eight."

Catherine watched Bill Fraser as he walked out the door. Then with unsteady steps, she walked into her bedroom and slowly opened the closet door, staring into the mirror hanging on the back of the door. She stood there frozen, unable to believe what she was seeing, sure that the mirror was playing some dreadful trick on her. Inside she was still the pretty little girl adored by her father, still the young college girl standing in a motel room with Ron Peterson and hearing him say, "My God, Cathy, you're the most beautiful thing I've ever seen," and Bill Fraser holding her in his arms and saying, "You're so beautiful, Catherine," and Larry saying, "Stay this beautiful, Cathy, you're gorgeous," and she looked at the figure in the mirror and croaked aloud, "Who are you?" and the sad, shapeless woman in the mirror began to cry, hopeless, empty tears that coursed down the obscene bloated face. Hours later the doorbell rang. She heard Bill Fraser's voice calling, "Catherine! Catherine, are you there?" And then the bell rang some more, and finally the voice stopped and the ringing stopped and Catherine was left alone with the stranger in the mirror.

At nine o'clock the following morning, Catherine took a taxi to Patission Street. The doctor's name was Nikodes and he was a large, burly man with a white shaggy mane, a wise face with kind eyes, and an easy, informal manner.

A nurse ushered Catherine in to his private office and Doctor Nikodes indicated a chair. "Sit down, Mrs. Douglas."

Catherine took a seat, nervous and tense, trying to stop her body from trembling.

"What seems to be your problem?"

She started to answer and then stopped helplessly.

Oh, God, she thought, *where can I begin?* "I need help," she said, finally. Her voice was dry and scratchy, and she ached for a drink.

The doctor was leaning back in his chair watching her. "How old are you?"

"Twenty-eight." She watched his face as she said it. He tried to conceal the look of shock, but she caught it and in some perverse way was pleased by it.

"You're an American?"

"Yes."

"Are you living in Athens?"

She nodded.

"How long have you lived here?"

"A thousand years. We moved here before the Peloponnesian War."

The doctor smiled. "I feel that way sometimes too." He offered Catherine a cigarette. She reached for it, trying to control the trembling of her fingers. If Doctor Nikodes noticed, he said nothing. He lit it for her. "What kind of help do you need, Mrs. Douglas?"

Catherine looked at him helplessly. "I don't know," she whispered. "I don't know."

"Do you feel ill?"

"I am ill. I think I must be very ill. I've become so ugly." She knew she was not crying and yet she felt tears running down her cheeks.

"Do you drink, Mrs. Douglas?" the doctor asked gently.

Catherine stared at him in panic, feeling cornered, attacked. "Sometimes."

"How much?"

She took a deep breath. "Not much. It—it depends."

"Have you had a drink today?" he asked.

"No."

He sat there studying her. "You're not really ugly, you know," he said gently. "You're overweight, your body is bloated and you haven't been taking care of your skin or your hair. Underneath that facade there's a very attractive young woman."

She burst into tears, and he sat there letting her cry herself out. Dimly over her racking sobs Catherine heard the buzzer on his desk ring several times, but the doctor ignored it. The spasm of sobbing finally subsided. Catherine pulled out a handkerchief and blew her nose. "I'm sorry," she apologized. "C—can you help me?"

"That depends entirely on you," Doctor Nikodes replied. "We don't really know what your problem is yet."

"Take a look at me," Catherine responded.

He shook his head. "That's not a problem, Mrs. Douglas, that's a symptom. Forgive me for being blunt, but if I am to help you, we must be totally honest with each other. When an attractive young woman lets herself go as you have, there must be a very strong reason. Is your husband alive?"

"Holidays and weekends."

He studied her. "Do you live with him?"

"When he's home."

"What is his work?"

"He's Constantin Demiris' personal pilot." She saw the reaction on the doctor's face, but whether he was reacting to the name of Demiris or whether he knew something about Larry, she could not tell. "Have you heard of my husband?" she asked.

"No." But he could have been lying. "Do you love your husband, Mrs. Douglas?"

Catherine opened her mouth to answer and then stopped. She knew that what she was going to say was very important, not only to the doctor, but to herself. Yes, she loved her husband and yes, she hated him, and yes, at times she felt such a rage toward him that she knew she was capable of killing him, and yes, at times she was so overwhelmed by a tenderness for him that she knew she would gladly die for him and what was the word that could say all that? Perhaps it was love. "Yes," she said.

"Does he love you?"

Catherine thought of the other women in Larry's life and his unfaithfulness and she thought of the awful stranger in the mirror last night and she could not blame Larry for not wanting her. But who was to say which came first? Did the woman in the mirror create his infidelity, or did his infidelity create the woman in the mirror? She became aware that her cheeks were wet with tears again.

Catherine shook her head helplessly. "I—I don't know."

"Have you ever had a nervous breakdown?"

She was watching him now, her eyes wary. "No. Do you think I need one?"

He did not smile. He spoke slowly, choosing his words with care. "The human psyche is a delicate thing, Mrs. Douglas. It can take only so much pain and when the pain becomes unbearable, it escapes into hidden recesses of the mind that we are just beginning to explore. Your emotions are stretched very tight." He looked at her a moment. "I think it is a good thing you came to someone for help."

"I know I'm a little nervous," Catherine said defensively. "That's why I drink. To relax me."

"No," he said bluntly. "You drink to escape." Nikodes got up and walked over to her. "I think there's probably a good deal we can do for you. By 'we,' I mean you and I. It will not be simple."

"Tell me what to do."

"To begin with I am going to send you to a clinic for a thorough physical examination. My feeling is that they will find nothing basically wrong with you. Next, you are going to stop drinking. Then I am going to put you on a diet. All right so far?"

Catherine hesitated, then nodded.

"You are going to enroll in a gymnasium, where you will work out regularly to get your body back in shape. I have an excellent physiotherapist who will give you massages. You will go to a beauty parlor once a week.

All this will take time, Mrs. Douglas. You did not get in this condition overnight, and it will not be changed overnight." He smiled at her reassuringly. "But I can promise you that in a few months—even a few weeks—you will begin to look and feel like a different woman. When you look in your mirror, you will feel proud—and when your husband looks at you, he will find you attractive."

Catherine stared at him, her heart lifting. It was as though some unbearable burden had been removed from deep inside her, as though she had suddenly been given a new chance to live.

"You must clearly understand that I can only suggest this program for you," the doctor was saying. "It is you who must do it."

"I will," Catherine said fervently. "I promise."

"To stop drinking will be the most difficult part."

"No, it won't," Catherine said. And as she said it, she knew it was true. The doctor had been right: She had been drinking in order to escape. Now she had a goal, she knew where she was going. She was going to win back Larry. "I won't touch another drop," she said firmly.

The doctor saw the look on her face and nodded, satisfied. "I believe you, Mrs. Douglas."

Catherine rose to her feet. It amazed her how clumsy and awkward her body was, but all that would change now. "I'd better go out and start buying some skinny clothes," she smiled.

The doctor wrote something on a card. "This is the address of the clinic. They will be expecting you. I will see you again after you have had your examination."

On the street Catherine looked for a taxi, then she thought, *to hell with that. I might as well start getting used to exercise.* She began to walk. She passed a shop window and stopped to stare at her reflection.

She had been so quick to blame Larry for the disintegration of their marriage without ever questioning what share of the blame was hers. Why would he want to come home to someone who looked like she did? How slowly and subtly this stranger had crept in without her being aware of it. She wondered how many marriages had died in this same way, not with a bang—*and there certainly hasn't been much of that lately,* Catherine thought, wryly—but with a whimper, just like good old T.S. Eliot said. Well, that was all in the past. From now on she would not look back, she would only look ahead to the wonderful future.

Catherine had reached the fashionable Salonika district. She was walking past a beauty parlor and on a sudden impulse she turned and went inside. The reception room was white marble, large and elegant. A haughty receptionist looked at Catherine disapprovingly and said, "Yes, may I help you?"

"I want to make an appointment for tomorrow morning," Catherine said. "I want everything. The works." The name of their top hair stylist suddenly popped into her head. "I want Aleko."

The woman shook her head. "I can give you an appointment, Madame, but you will have to take someone else."

"Listen," Catherine said firmly, "you tell Aleko that he either takes me or I'll go around Athens telling everyone I'm one of his regular customers."

The woman's eyes opened wide in shocked surprise. "I—I will see what I can do," she said hastily. "Come in at ten in the morning."

"Thanks," Catherine grinned. "I'll be here." And she walked out.

Ahead of her she saw a small taverna with a sign in the window that read "MADAME PIRIS—FORTUNE-TELLING." It seemed vaguely familiar and she suddenly remembered the day that Count Pappas had told her a story about Madame Piris. It was something about a policeman and a lion—but she could not remember the details. Catherine did not believe in fortune-tellers and yet the impulse to go in was irresistible. She needed reassurance, someone to confirm her feeling about her wonderful new future, to tell her that life was going to be beautiful again, worth living again. She opened the door and walked inside.

After the bright sunshine it took Catherine several moments to get used to the cavernous darkness of the room. She made out a bar in the corner and a dozen tables and chairs. A tired-looking waiter walked up to her and addressed her in Greek.

"Nothing to drink, thank you," Catherine said. She enjoyed hearing herself say the words and she repeated them. "Nothing to drink. I want to see Madame Piris. Is she here?"

The waiter gestured toward an empty table in the corner of the room and Catherine walked over and sat down. A few minutes later, she felt someone standing at her side, and looked up.

The woman was incredibly old and thin, dressed in black, with a face that had been washed by time into desiccated angles and planes.

"You asked to see me?" Her English was halting.

"Yes," Catherine said. "I would like a reading, please."

The woman sat down and raised a hand, and the waiter came over to the table bearing a cup of thick black coffee on a small tray. He set it down in front of Catherine.

"Not for me," Catherine said. "I . . ."

"Drink it," Madame Piris said.

Catherine looked at her in surprise, then picked up the cup and took a sip of the coffee. It was strong and bitter. She put down the cup.

"More," the woman said.

Catherine started to protest, then thought, *What the hell. What they lose on the fortune-telling, they make up on the coffee.* She swallowed another mouthful. It was vile.

"Once more," Madame Piris said.

Catherine shrugged and took a final sip. In the bottom of the cup were thick, viscous dregs. Madame Piris nodded, reached over and took the cup from Catherine. She stared into it for a long time, saying nothing. Catherine sat there feeling foolish. *What's a nice, intelligent girl like me doing in a place like this, watching an old Greek nut staring into an empty coffee cup?*

"You come from a faraway place," the woman said suddenly.

"Bull's eye," Catherine said flippantly.

Madame Piris looked up into her eyes and there was something in the look of the old woman that chilled Catherine.

"Go home."

Catherine swallowed. "I—I am home."

"Go back where you came from."

"You mean—America?"

"Anywhere. Get away from this place—quickly!"

"Why?" Catherine said, a sense of horror slowly filling her. "What's wrong?"

The old woman shook her head. Her voice was harsh and she was finding it difficult to get the words out. "It is all around you."

"What is?"

"Get out!" There was an urgency in the woman's voice, a high, shrill keening sound like an animal in pain. Catherine could feel the hair on her scalp begin to rise.

"You're frightening me," she moaned. "Please tell me what's wrong."

The old woman shook her head from side to side, her eyes wild. "Go away before it gets you."

Catherine felt a panic rising in her. It was difficult for her to breathe. "Before *what* gets me?"

The old woman's face was contorted with pain and terror. "Death. It is coming for you." And the woman rose and disappeared into the back room.

Catherine sat there, her heart pounding, her hands trembling, and she clasped them tightly together to stop them. She caught the waiter's eye and started to order a drink, but stopped herself. She was not going to let a crazy woman spoil her bright future. She sat there breathing deeply until she had gotten control of herself, and after a long time she rose, picked up her purse and gloves and walked out of the taverna.

Out in the dazzlingly bright sunlight Catherine felt better again. She had been foolish to let an old woman frighten her. A horror like that should be arrested instead of being allowed to terrify people. *From now on*, Catherine told herself, *you'll stick to fortune cookies*.

She stepped into her apartment and looked at the living room, and it was as though she were seeing it for the first time. It was a dismaying sight. Dust was thick everywhere, and articles of clothing were strewn around the room. It was incredible to Catherine that in her drunken haze she had not even been aware of it. Well, the first exercise she was going to get was making this place look spic and span. She was starting toward the kitchen when she heard a drawer close in the bedroom. Her heart leaped in sudden alarm, and she moved cautiously toward the bedroom door.

Larry was in the bedroom. A closed suitcase lay on his bed, and he was finishing packing a second suitcase. Catherine stood there a moment, watching him. "If those are for the Red Cross," she said, "I already gave."

Larry glanced up. "I'm leaving."

"Another trip for Demiris?"

"No," he said without stopping, "this one's for me. I'm getting out of here."

"Larry . . ."

"There's nothing to discuss."

She moved into the bedroom fighting for self-control. "But—but there is. There's a lot to discuss. I went to see a doctor today and he told me I'm going to be fine." The words were coming out in a torrent. "I'm going to stop drinking and . . ."

"Cathy, it's over. I want a divorce."

The words hit her like a series of blows to the stomach. She stood there, clamping her jaw tight so that she would not retch, trying to fight down the bile that rose in her throat. "Larry," she said, speaking slowly to keep her voice from trembling, "I don't blame you for the way you feel. A lot of it is my fault—maybe most of it—but it's going to be different. I'm going to change—I mean *really* change." She held out her hand pleadingly. "All I ask is a chance."

Larry turned to face her and his dark eyes were cold and contemptuous. "I'm in love with someone else. All I want from you is a divorce."

Catherine stood there a long moment, then turned and walked back into the living room and sat on the couch, looking at a Greek fashion magazine while he finished packing. She heard Larry's voice saying, "My attorney will be in touch with you" and then the slam of a door. Catherine sat there carefully turning the pages of the magazine, and when she had come to the end she set it down neatly in the center of the table, went into the bathroom, opened the medicine chest, took out a razor blade and slashed her wrists.

NOELLE AND CATHERINE

Athens: 1946

19

There were ghosts in white and they floated around her and then drifted away into space with soft whispers in a language that Catherine could not understand, but she understood that this was Hell and that she had to pay for her sins. They kept her strapped down on the bed, and she supposed that was part of her punishment, and she was glad of the straps because she could feel the earth spinning around through space and she was afraid she was going to fall off the planet. The most diabolical thing they had done was to put all her nerves on the outside of her body so that she felt everything a thousandfold, and it was unbearable. Her body was alive with terrifying and unfamiliar noises. She could hear the blood as it ran through her veins, and it was like a roaring red river moving through her. She heard the strokes of her heart, and it sounded like an enormous drum being pounded by giants. She had no eyelids and the white light poured into her brain, dazzling her with its brightness. All the muscles of her body were alive, in constant, restless motion like a nest of snakes under her skin ready to strike.

Five days after Catherine had been admitted to Evangelismos Hospital, she opened her eyes and found herself in a small, white hospital room. A nurse in a starched white uniform was adjusting her bed, and Dr. Nikodes had a stethoscope to her chest.

"Hey, that's cold," she protested weakly.

He looked at her and said, "Well, well, look who's awake."

Catherine moved her eyes slowly around the room. The light seemed normal and she could no longer hear the roaring of her blood or the pounding of her heart or the dying of her body.

"I thought I was in Hell." Her voice was a whisper.

"You have been."

She looked at her wrists. For some reason, they were bandaged. "How long have I been here?"

"Five days."

She suddenly remembered the reason for the bandages. "I guess I did a dumb thing," she said.

"Yes."

She squeezed her eyes shut and said, "I'm sorry," and opened them and it was night and Bill Fraser was sitting in a chair beside her bed, watching her. Flowers and candy were on her bedside table.

"Hi there," he said cheerfully. "You're looking much better."

"Better than what?" she asked weakly.

He put his hand over hers. "You really gave me a scare, Catherine."

"I'm so sorry, Bill." Her voice started to choke up, and she was afraid that she was going to cry.

"I brought you some flowers and candy. When you're feeling stronger, I'll bring you some books."

She looked at him, at his kind strong face, and she thought: *Why don't I love him? Why am I in love with the man I hate? Why did God have to turn out to be Groucho Marx?* "How did I get here?" Catherine asked.

"In an ambulance."

"I mean—who found me?"

Fraser paused. "I did. I tried phoning you several times and when you didn't answer I got worried and broke in."

"I suppose I should say thanks," she said, "but to tell you the truth, I'm not sure yet."

"Do you want to talk about it?"

Catherine shook her head and the movement caused her head to begin throbbing. "No," she said in a small voice.

Fraser nodded. "I have to fly home in the morning. I'll keep in touch."

She felt a gentle kiss on her forehead and closed her eyes to shut out the world and when she opened them again, she was alone and it was the middle of the night.

Early the next morning Larry came to visit her. Catherine watched him as he walked into the room and sat down in a chair next to her bed. She had expected him to be drawn-looking and unhappy, but the truth was that he looked wonderful, lean and tan and relaxed. Catherine wished desperately that she had had a chance to comb her hair and put on some lipstick.

"How do you feel, Cathy?" he asked.

"Terrific. Suicide always stimulates me."

"They didn't expect you to pull through."

"I'm sorry to have disappointed you."

"That's not a very nice thing to say."

"It's true though, isn't it, Larry? You'd have been rid of me."

"For Christ's sake, I don't want to be rid of you that way, Catherine. All I want is a divorce."

She looked at him, this bronzed, handsome man she had married, his face a little more dissipated now, his mouth a little harder, his boyish charm worn a bit thin. What was she hanging onto? Seven years of dreams? She had given herself to him with such love and high hopes and she could not bear to let them go, could not bear to admit that she had made a mistake that had turned her life into a barren wasteland. She remembered Bill Fraser and their friends in Washington and the fun they had known. She could not remember the last time she had laughed aloud, or even smiled. But none of that really mattered. In the end the reason that she would not let Larry go was that she still loved him. He was standing there waiting for an answer. "No," Catherine said. "I'll never give you a divorce."

* * *

Larry met Noelle that night at the deserted monastery of Kaissariani in the mountains and reported his conversation with Catherine.

Noelle listened intently and asked, "Do you think she will change her mind?"

Larry shook his head. "Catherine can be as stubborn as hell."

"You must speak to her again."

And Larry did. For the next three weeks he exhausted every argument he could think of. He pleaded, cajoled, raged, at her, offered her money, but nothing moved Catherine. She still loved him, and she was sure that if he gave himself a chance he could love her again.

"You're my husband," she said stubbornly. "You're going to be my husband until I die."

He repeated what she had said to Noelle.

Noelle nodded. "Yes," she said.

Larry looked at her, puzzled. "Yes, what?"

They were lying on the beach at the villa, fluffy white towels spread out beneath them, shielding their bodies from the hot sand. The sky was a deep, blazing blue, dotted with white patches of cirrus clouds.

"You must get rid of her." She rose to her feet and strode back to the villa, her long graceful legs moving smoothly across the sand. Larry lay there, bewildered, thinking that he must have misunderstood her. Surely she had not meant that she wanted him to *kill* Catherine.

And then he remembered Helena.

They were having supper on the terrace. "Don't you see? She doesn't deserve to live," Noelle said. "She's holding onto you to be vengeful. She's trying to ruin your life, our lives, darling."

They lay in bed smoking, the glowing embers of the

cigarette ends winking into the infinity of the mirrors covering the ceiling.

"You would be doing her a favor. She's already tried to kill herself. She wants to die."

"I could never do it, Noelle."

"Couldn't you?"

She stroked his naked leg, gently moving up toward his belly, making small circles with the tips of her fingernails.

"I'll help you."

He started to open his mouth to protest, but Noelle's two hands had found him, and they began working on him, moving in opposite directions, one softly and slowly, the other one hard and quickly. And Larry moaned and reached for her and put Catherine out of his mind.

Sometime during the night Larry awakened in a cold sweat. He had dreamed that Noelle had run away and left him. She was lying in bed next to him, and he took her in his arms and held her close. He lay awake the rest of the night, thinking what it would do to him if he lost her. He was not aware that he had made any decision, but in the morning while Noelle was preparing breakfast, Larry said suddenly, "What if we're caught?"

"If we're clever, we won't be." If she was pleased by his capitulation, she gave no sign of it.

"Noelle," he said earnestly, "every busybody in Athens knows that Catherine and I don't get along. If anything happened to her, the police would be damned suspicious."

"Of course they would be," Noelle agreed calmly. "That is why everything will be planned very carefully."

She served them both and then sat down and began to eat. Larry pushed his plate away from him, his food untasted.

"Isn't it good?" Noelle asked, concerned.

He stared at her, wondering what kind of person she was, able to enjoy a meal while she was planning the murder of another woman.

Later, sailing on the boat, they talked about it further, and the more they talked about it, the more of a reality it became, so that what had begun as a casual idea had been fleshed out with words until it had become a fact.

"It must look like an accident," Noelle said, "so that there will be no police investigation. The police in Athens are very clever."

"What if they *should* investigate?"

"They won't. The accident will not happen here."

"Where, then?"

"Ioannina." She leaned forward and began to talk. He listened to her as she elaborated on her plan, meeting every objection that he raised, improvising brilliantly. At the end when Noelle finished, Larry had to admit that the plan was flawless. They could really get away with it.

Paul Metaxas was nervous. The Greek pilot's usually jovial face was drawn and tense and he could feel a nervous tic pulling at the corner of his mouth. He had had no appointment with Constantin Demiris, and one did not simply barge in on the great man, but Metaxas had told the butler it was urgent, and now Paul Metaxas found himself standing in the enormous hallway of Demiris' villa, staring at him and stammering clumsily, "I—I am terribly sorry to bother you, Mr. Demiris." Metaxas surreptitiously wiped the sweaty palm of his hand against the leg of his flight uniform.

"Has something happened to one of the planes?"

"Oh, no, sir. I—It's—it's a personal matter."

Demiris studied him without interest. He made it a policy never to get involved in the affairs of his underlings. He had secretaries to handle that kind of thing for him. He waited for Metaxas to go on.

Paul Metaxas was becoming more nervous by the

second. He had spent a lot of sleepless nights before making the decision that had brought him here. What he was doing now was alien to his character and therefore distasteful, but he was a man of fierce loyalty, and his first allegiance was to Constantin Demiris.

"It's about Miss Page," he said, finally.

There was a moment of silence.

"Come in here," Demiris said. He led the pilot into the paneled library and closed the doors. Demiris took a flat Egyptian cigarette out of a platinum case and lit it. He looked at the perspiring Metaxas. "What about Miss Page?" he asked, almost absently.

Metaxas swallowed, wondering if he had made a mistake. If he had estimated the situation correctly, his information would be appreciated, but if he was mistaken . . .

He cursed himself for his rashness in having come here, but he had no choice now but to plunge ahead.

"It's—it's about her and Larry Douglas." He watched Demiris' face, trying to read his expression. There was not even the faintest flicker of interest. Christ! Metaxas forced himself to stumble on. "They—they're living in a beach house together in Rafina."

Demiris flicked the ash of the cigarette into a gold, dome-shaped ashtray. Metaxas had the feeling that he was about to be dismissed, that he had made a terrible blunder and that it was going to cost him his job. He had to convince Demiris that he was telling the truth. The words began spilling out of him. "My—my sister is a housekeeper in one of the villas there. She sees the two of them on the beach together all the time. She recognized Miss Page from her pictures in the paper, but she didn't think anything about it until a couple of nights ago when she came down to the airport to have dinner with me. I introduced her to Larry Douglas and—well, she told me he was the man Miss Page is living with."

Demiris' olive black eyes stared at him, completely devoid of expression.

"I—I just thought you would want to know," Metaxas finished lamely.

When Demiris spoke, his voice was toneless. "What Miss Page does with her private life is her own affair. I am sure she would not appreciate anyone's spying on her."

Metaxas' forehead was beaded with sweat. Jesus Christ, he had gotten the whole situation wrong. And he had only wanted to be loyal. "Believe me, Mr. Demiris, I was only trying to . . ."

"I am sure you thought you were serving my best interests. You were mistaken. Is there anything else?"

"No—no, sir." Metaxas turned and fled.

Constantin Demiris leaned back in his chair, his black eyes fixed on the ceiling, staring at nothing.

At nine o'clock the following morning Paul Metaxas received a call to report to Demiris' mining company in the Congo, where Metaxas was to spend ten days ferrying equipment from Brazzaville to the mine. On a Wednesday morning on the third flight his plane crashed into the dense, green jungle. No traces of Metaxas' body or the wreckage were ever found.

Two weeks after Catherine was released from the hospital, Larry came to visit her. It was a Saturday evening, and Catherine was in the kitchen preparing an omelet. The sounds of cooking had prevented her from hearing the front door open, and she was not aware of Larry's presence until she turned and saw him standing in the doorway. She jumped involuntarily, and he said, "Sorry if I scared you. I just dropped in to see how you were getting along."

Catherine felt her heart beating faster and despised herself because he could still affect her that way.

"I'm just fine," she said. She turned and took the omelet out of the pan.

"Smells good," Larry said. "I haven't had time for dinner. If it isn't too much trouble, would you mind fixing me one of those?"

She looked at him a long moment, then shrugged.

She made him dinner but she was so unnerved by his presence that Catherine could not eat a bite. He talked to her, telling her about a flight he had just made and an amusing anecdote about one of Demiris' friends. He was the old Larry, warm and charming and irresistible as though nothing had gone wrong between them, as though he had not smashed their lives together.

When dinner was over, Larry helped Catherine wash and dry the dishes. He stood next to her at the sink, and his nearness gave her a physical ache. How long had it been? It did not bear thinking about.

"I've really enjoyed it," Larry was saying, with that easy, boyish grin of his. "Thanks, Cathy."

And that, Catherine thought, was the end of that.

Three days later, the phone rang and it was Larry phoning from Madrid to say that he was on his way home and to ask whether she would go out to dinner with him that evening. Catherine clutched the phone, listening to his friendly, easy voice, determined not to go. "I'm free for dinner tonight," she said.

They dined at Tourkolimano at the harbor at Piraeus. Catherine was barely able to touch her food. Being with Larry was far too painful a reminder of other restaurants they had dined in, of too many exciting evenings together in the long-dead past, of the love that was going to last them both a lifetime.

"You're not eating, Cathy. Would you like me to order something else for you?" he asked, concerned.

"I had a late lunch," she lied. *He probably won't ever ask me out again,* Catherine thought, *but if he does I will say no.*

A few days later Larry called and they had lunch at a lovely restaurant in a hidden maze off Syntagma

Square. It was called Gerofinikas, the Old Palm Tree, and was reached through a long, cool passageway with a palm tree in front of it. They had an excellent meal, with Hymettus, the light, dry Greek wine. Larry was at his most entertaining.

The following Sunday he asked Catherine to fly to Vienna with him. They had dinner at the Sacher Hotel and flew back the same night. It had been a wonderful evening, filled with wine and music and candlelight, but Catherine had the eerie feeling that somehow it didn't belong to her. It belonged to that other Catherine Douglas who was long since dead and buried. When they got back to the apartment, she said, "Thank you, Larry, it was a lovely day."

He moved toward her and took her in his arms and started to kiss her. Catherine pulled away, her body rigid, her mind filled with a sudden, unexpected panic.

"No," she said.

"Cathy . . ."

"No!"

He nodded. "All right. I understand."

Her body was trembling. "Do you?" she asked.

"I know how badly I've behaved," Larry said softly. "If you'll give me a chance, I'd like to make it up to you, Cathy."

Good God, she thought. She pressed her lips together, willing herself not to cry and shook her head, her eyes bright with unshed tears. "It's too late," she whispered.

And she stood there watching him walk out the door.

Catherine heard from Larry again within the week. He sent flowers with a little note and, after that, miniature birds from the various countries to which he flew. He had obviously gone to a great deal of trouble, for there was an astonishing variety, one in porcelain, one in jade, one in teak, and she was touched that he had remembered.

When the phone rang one day and Catherine heard

Larry's voice on the other end saying, "Hey, I found a wonderful Greek restaurant that serves the best Chinese food this side of Peking," she laughed and said, "I can't wait."

And that was when it really began again. Slowly, tentatively, hesitantly, but it was a beginning. Larry did not attempt to kiss her again, nor would she have let him, because Catherine knew that if she let go of her emotions, if she gave herself wholeheartedly to this man she loved, and he betrayed her again, it would destroy her. Finally and forever. And so she dined with him and laughed with him, but all the time the deep secret personal part of her lay back in reserve, carefully aloof, untouched and untouchable.

They were together almost every night. Some evenings Catherine cooked dinner at home, other nights Larry took her out. Once she mentioned the woman that he had said he was in love with, and he replied tersely, "It's over," and Catherine never brought it up again. She watched closely for signs that Larry was seeing other women, but there were none. He was totally attentive to her, never pressing, never demanding. It was as though he were doing a penance for the past.

And yet Catherine admitted to herself that it was something more than that. He really seemed interested in her as a woman. At night she would stand in front of the mirror, naked, and examine her reflection and try to figure out why. Her face was not bad, the face of a once-pretty girl who had gone through pain, a sadness in the solemn gray eyes that stared back at her. Her skin was a little puffy and her chin was heavier than it should be, but there was really nothing wrong with the rest of her body that diet and massage could not take care of. She remembered the last time she had thought about this and had wound up with her wrists slashed. A shudder went through her. To hell with Larry, she thought defiantly. If he really wants me, he'll take me as I am.

* * *

They had been to a party and Larry had brought her home at four A.M. It had been a marvelous evening, and Catherine had worn a new dress and looked rather attractive and made people laugh and Larry had been proud of her. When they walked into the apartment, Catherine reached for the light switch and Larry put his hand over hers and said, "Wait. I can say this easier in the dark." His body was close to hers, not even touching her, yet she could feel the physical waves that pulled at her.

"I love you, Cathy," he said. "I've never really loved anyone else. I want another chance."

He switched on the light then to look at her. She was standing there, rigid and frightened, on the brink of panic. "I know you may not be ready yet, but we could start slowly." He grinned. That darling, boyish grin. "We could start out by holding hands."

He reached out and took her hand. And she pulled him to her and they were kissing and his lips were gentle and tender and careful, and hers were demanding and wild with all the pent-up longing that had been stored in her body these long, lonely months. And they were in bed together, making love and it was as though no time had passed, and they were on their honeymoon. But it was more than that. The passion was still there, fresh and wonderful, but with it an appreciation for what they had together, the knowledge that this time it would be all right, this time they would not hurt each other.

"How would you like to go away on a second honeymoon?" Larry was asking.

"Oh, yes, darling. Can we?"

"Sure, I have a vacation coming. We'll leave on Saturday. I know a wonderful little place we can go. It's called Ioannina."

NOELLE AND CATHERINE

Athens: 1946

20

The drive to Ioannina took nine hours. To Catherine, the scenery seemed almost Biblical, something out of another age. They drove along the Aegean Sea, past small whitewashed cottages with crosses on the roofs and endless fields of fruit trees, lemon and cherry and apple and orange. Every inch of the land was terraced and farmed and the windows and roofs of the farmhouses were painted with gay blue colors as though in defiance of the hard life being carved out of the rocky soil. Stands of tall, graceful cypress trees grew in wild profusion on the steep mountainsides.

"Look, Larry," Catherine exclaimed, "aren't they beautiful?"

"Not to the Greeks," Larry said.

Catherine looked at him. "What do you mean?"

"They consider them a bad omen. They use them to decorate cemeteries."

They passed field after field of primitive scarecrows, with a scrap of cloth tied to each fence.

"They certainly must have gullible crows around here," Catherine laughed.

They drove through a series of small villages with impossible names: Mesologian and Agelkastron and Etolikon and Amfilhoia.

Late in the afternoon they reached the village of Rion, sloping gently down to the Rio River, where they were to catch the ferryboat to Ioannina. Five minutes later they were sailing toward the island of Epirus where Ioannina lay.

Catherine and Larry sat on a bench outside on the ferry's upper deck where in the distance ahead of them they saw a large island begin to loom out of the afternoon mist. It seemed wild to Catherine and somehow a little ominous. It had a primitive look to it as though it had been created for the Greek gods, and mere mortals were unwelcome intruders. As the boat steamed closer, Catherine could see that the bottom of the island was ringed with sheer rock that dropped off to the sea below. The foreboding mountain had a scarred, gashed look where men had gouged a road out of it. Twenty-five minutes later the ferry was docking at the little harbor of Epirus, and a few moments later Catherine and Larry were driving up the mountain toward Ioannina.

Catherine was reading to Larry from the guidebook.

"Nestled high in the Pindus Mountains, in a steep bowl surrounded by towering Alps, from a distance Ioannina takes on the shape of a double-headed eagle, and at the claw of the eagle is the bottomless Lake Pamvotis, where excursion boats carry passengers across its dark green water to the island in the center of the lake and then on to the distant shores across the lake."

"It sounds perfect," Larry said.

They arrived in the late afternoon and drove directly to their hotel, an old beautifully kept one-story building on a hill high above the town, with a series of guest bungalows scattered about the grounds. An old man in a uniform came out to greet them. He looked at their happy faces.

"Honeymooners," he said.

Catherine glanced at Larry and smiled. "How did you know?"

"You can always tell," the old man declared. He led them into the lobby where they registered and then showed them to their bungalow. It consisted of a living room and bedroom, a bathroom and kitchen and a large terrazzo terrace. Over the tops of the cypresses they had a magnificent view of the village and the lake below, dark and brooding. It had the unreal beauty of a picture postcard.

"It's not much"—Larry smiled—"but it's all yours."

"I'll take it," Catherine exclaimed.

"Happy?"

She nodded. "I don't remember when I've been so happy." She walked over to him and held him tightly. "Don't ever let me go," she whispered.

His strong arms were around her, holding her close. "I won't," he promised.

While Catherine was unpacking, Larry strolled back to the lobby to talk to the room clerk.

"What do people do around here?" Larry asked.

"Everything," the clerk said proudly. "In the hotel we have a health spa. Around the village there is hiking, fishing, swimming, boating."

"How deep is the lake?" Larry inquired casually.

The clerk shrugged. "No one knows, sir. It is a volcanic lake. It is bottomless."

Larry nodded thoughtfully. "What about the caves near here?" he asked.

"Ah! The Caves of Perama. They are only a few miles from here."

"Have they been explored?"

"A few of them. Some are still closed."

"I see," said Larry.

The clerk continued. "If you like mountain climbing, I suggest Mount Tzoumerka. If Mrs. Douglas is not afraid of heights."

"No," smiled Larry. "She's quite an expert climber."

"Then she will enjoy it. You're lucky with the weather. We've been expecting the *meltemi,* but it hasn't come. Now it probably won't."

"What's the *meltemi?*" Larry asked.

"It's a terrible wind that blows down from the north. I suppose it is like your hurricane. When it comes, everyone stays indoors. In Athens, even ocean liners are forbidden to leave the harbor."

"I'm glad we missed it," Larry said.

When Larry returned to the bungalow, he suggested to Catherine that they go down to the village for dinner. They took the steep, rocky footpath that led down the slope to the edge of the village. Ioannina consisted of a main street, King George Avenue, with two or three smaller streets on both sides of it. Off of those streets, a warren of tiny dirt roads radiated out to homes and apartments. The buildings were old and weatherbeaten, made of stone carried down by cart from the mountains.

The middle of King George Avenue was sectioned off by ropes, so that cars drove on the left side of the street and pedestrians were free to walk on the right side.

"They should try that on Pennsylvania Avenue," Catherine said.

At the town square was a charming little park with a high tower with a large, lighted clock in it. A street lined with huge Platanus trees ran down to the lake. It appeared to Catherine that all the streets in the village led to the water. It seemed to her that there was something frightening about the lake. It had a strange, brooding quality. All along the shores grew clumps of tall reeds that reached out like greedy fingers, as though waiting for someone.

Catherine and Larry walked down the colorful little shopping center, with shops crowded together on each side. There was a jewelry store and next to it a bakery shop, an open air butcher shop, a tavern, a shoe store. Children stood outside a barber shop, silently watching a customer getting shaved. Catherine thought they were the most beautiful children she had ever seen.

In the past, Catherine had talked to Larry about having a baby, but he had always dismissed the idea, saying that he was not ready to settle down. Now, however, he might feel differently. Catherine glanced at him as he walked at her side, taller than the other men, looking like a Greek god, and she resolved that she would discuss it with him before they left. After all, it was their honeymoon.

They passed a movie theater, the Palladian. Two very old American pictures were playing. They stopped to look at the display posters.

"We're in luck," Catherine joked. *"South of Panama* with Roger Pryor and Virginia Vale, and *Mr. D.A. in The Carter Case."*

"Never even heard of them," Larry snorted. "This theater must be older than it looks."

They ate *mousaka* in the square, seated outdoors under an unbelievable full moon and then went back to the hotel and made love. It had been a perfect day.

In the morning Catherine and Larry drove around the lovely countryside, exploring the narrow road that wound along the lake, running along the rocky coast for a few miles, then drunkenly weaving its way back up again into the hills. Stone houses were perched on the edge of the steep mountainsides. High above the shore set back in the woods they caught a glimpse of a huge whitewashed building that looked like an ancient castle.

"What's that?" Catherine asked.

"I have no idea," Larry said.

"Let's find out."

"All right."

Larry swung the car onto the dirt track that led to the building, through a meadow, past grazing goats and a shepherd who stared at them as they drove by. They pulled up in front of the deserted entrance to the building. Up close it looked like an old ruined fortress.

"It must be a leftover ogre's castle," Catherine said. "Probably out of the Brothers Grimm."

"Do you really want to find out?" Larry asked.

"Sure. We may be just in time to rescue a maiden in distress."

Larry gave Catherine a quick, strange look.

They got out of the car and walked up to the massive wooden door with a huge iron knocker fastened to the center. Larry hit it several times and they waited. There were no sounds except the buzz of summer insects in the meadow and the whisper of the breeze through the grass.

"I guess no one's home," Larry said.

"They're probably getting rid of bodies," Catherine whispered.

Suddenly the huge door began to creak open slowly. A nun dressed in black stood facing them.

It caught Catherine off guard. "I—I'm sorry," she said. "We didn't know what this place was. There's no sign or anything."

The nun regarded the two of them for a moment, then gestured for them to enter. They stepped through the doorway and found themselves in a large courtyard that was the center of a compound. There was a strangely still atmosphere, and Catherine suddenly realized what was missing: the sound of human voices.

She turned to the Sister and said, "What place is this?"

The Sister silently shook her head and motioned for them to wait there. They watched as she turned and walked toward an old stone building at the end of the compound.

"She's gone to get Bela Lugosi," Catherine whispered.

Beyond the building toward a promontory that rose above the sea, they could see a cemetery framed by rows of tall cypress trees.

"This place gives me the creeps," Larry said.

"It's as though we've stumbled into another century," Catherine replied. Unconsciously they were whispering, as though afraid to disturb the heavy silence. Through the window of the main building they could see inquisitive faces staring out at them, all women, all of them dressed in black.

"It's some kind of religious nuthouse," Larry decided.

A tall, thin woman emerged from the building and started walking briskly toward them. She wore a nun's habit and had a pleasant, friendly face.

"I am Sister Theresa," she said. "May I help you?"

"We were just passing by," Catherine said, "and we were curious about this place." She looked at the faces peering from the windows. "We didn't mean to disturb you."

"We are not honored with many visitors," Sister Theresa said. "We have almost no contact with the outside world. We are an Order of Carmelite nuns. We have taken a vow of silence."

"For how long?" Larry asked.

"*Gia panta*—for the rest of our lives. I am the only one here permitted to speak and then only when necessary."

Catherine gazed around at the large, silent courtyard and repressed a shudder. "Does no one ever leave here?"

Sister Theresa smiled. "No. There is no reason to. Our life is within these walls."

"Forgive us for troubling you," Catherine said.

The Sister nodded. "Not at all. Go with God."

As Catherine and Larry walked out, the huge gate slowly swung closed behind them. Catherine turned to look back at it. It was like a prison. But somehow this seemed worse. Perhaps because it was a voluntary penance, a waste, and Catherine thought of the young women she had seen from the window, walled up here, shut away from the world for the rest of their lives, living in the deep permanent silence of the grave. She knew she would never forget this place.

NOELLE AND CATHERINE

Athens: 1946

21

Early the following morning Larry went down to the village. He asked Catherine to join him, but she demurred, telling him that she was going to sleep late. The moment he left, Catherine got out of bed, hurriedly dressed and went over to the hotel gymnasium which she had investigated the day before. The instructress, a Greek Amazon, told her to strip, then examined her body critically.

"You have been lazy, lazy," she scolded Catherine. "That was a good body. If you are willing to work hard, *Theou thellondos*—God willing—it can be good again."

"I'm willing," said Catherine. "Let's see how God shapes up."

Under the tutelage of the Amazon Catherine worked out every day, going through the agonies of body-contouring massage, a Spartan diet and grueling exercises. She kept all this from Larry, but by the end of the fourth day the change in her was noticeable enough for him to comment on it.

"This place really agrees with you," he said. "You look like a different girl."

"I am a different girl," Catherine replied, suddenly shy.

On Sunday morning Catherine went to church. She had never seen a Greek Orthodox mass. In a village as small as Ioannina she had expected to find a little country church, but to her surprise she walked into a large, richly decorated church with beautiful elaborate carvings on the walls and ceiling and a marble floor. In front of the altar were a dozen enormous silver candelabras, and around the room were frescoes of Biblical paintings. The priest was thin and swarthy with a black beard. He wore an elaborate gold and red robe and a tall black hat, and he stood on what looked to Catherine like a sedan chair on a raised platform.

Along the wall were individual wooden benches and next to them a row of wooden chairs. The men sat in the front of the church and the women in the rear. *I guess the men get to Heaven first,* Catherine thought.

A chanting began in Greek, and the priest stepped down from the platform and moved to the altar. A red curtain parted and behind it was a lavishly robed, white-bearded patriarch. On a table in front of him stood a symbolical jeweled hat and a gold cross. The old man lit three candles tied together, representing, Catherine supposed, the Holy Trinity, and handed them to the priest.

The mass lasted for one hour, and Catherine sat there savoring the sights and sounds and thinking about how lucky she was and she bowed her head and gave a prayer of gratitude.

The next morning Catherine and Larry were having breakfast on their bungalow terrace that overlooked the lake. It was a perfect day. The sun was shining down, and a lazy breeze was coming off the water. A pleasant young waiter had brought the food. Catherine was wearing a negligee and when the waiter came in, Larry had put his arms around Catherine and kissed her on the neck. "What a great night," Larry murmured.

The waiter had stifled a smile and discreetly retreated. Catherine had been a little embarrassed. It was unlike Larry to be affectionate in front of strangers. He really has changed, Catherine thought. It seemed that every time a maid or bellboy came into the room, Larry would put his arm around Catherine and show his affection, as though he wanted the whole world to know how much he loved her. Catherine found it very touching.

"I have a great morning planned for us," Larry said. He pointed to the east, where they could see a giant peak towering into the sky. "We're going to climb Mount Tzoumerka."

"I have a rule," Catherine declared. "I never climb anything I can't spell."

"Come on, they say there's a fantastic view from up there."

Catherine saw that Larry was serious. She looked up at the mountain again. It looked as though it went straight up. "Climbing's not what I do best, darling," she said.

"It's an easy hike. Paths all the way up." He hesitated. "If you don't want to go with me, I can go alone." There was sharp disappointment in his voice.

It would be so simple to say no, so simple to just sit here and enjoy the day. The temptation was almost overpowering. But Larry wanted her with him. That was enough for Catherine.

"OK. I'll see if I can find an alpine hat," she said.

A look of such relief came over Larry's face that Catherine was glad she had decided to go. Besides it might be interesting.

She had never climbed a mountain before.

They drove to a meadow at the edge of the village where the mountain trail began and parked the car. There was a small food stand at the side of the road, and Larry bought some sandwiches, fruit, candy bars and a large thermos of coffee.

"If it's nice up there," he told the proprietor, "my bride and I may want to spend the night." He gave Catherine a hug, and the proprietor grinned.

Catherine and Larry walked up to the beginning of the trail. There were really two trails, branching off in opposite directions. Catherine admitted to herself that it looked like an easy climb. The paths seemed wide and not too steep. When she turned her head to gaze at the top of the mountain, it seemed grim and forbidding, but then they would not be going that high. They would climb a little way up and have a picnic.

"This way," Larry said, and he led Catherine toward the path going to the left. As they started to climb, the Greek proprietor watched them with concern. Should he run after them and tell them they had taken the wrong path? The one they were on was dangerous, for expert climbers only. At that moment some customers came up to the stand and the proprietor put the two Americans out of his mind.

The sun was hot, but as they climbed higher, the breezes grew cooler, and Catherine thought that the combination of the two was delicious. It was a beautiful day and she was with the man she loved. From time to time Catherine glanced down and was amazed at how high they had already climbed. The air seemed to be getting thinner, and breathing was becoming more difficult. She had been walking behind Larry, for the path was now too narrow to permit them to walk side by side. She wondered when they were going to stop and have their picnic.

Larry became aware that Catherine was straggling behind and he stopped to wait for her.

"Sorry," Catherine gasped. "The altitude is beginning to get to me a little." She looked down. "It's going to take a long time to get down."

"No, it won't," Larry replied. He turned and started up the narrow path again. Catherine looked after him, sighed and doggedly started up the trail.

"I should have married a chess player," she called after him. Larry made no response.

He had come to a sudden, sharp turn in the path, and in front of him was a small wooden bridge with a single rope for a handhold that had been built across a deep gorge. The bridge was swaying in the wind and did not look secure enough to carry the weight of a man. Larry put one foot on a rotting wooden plank of the bridge and it started to sink with his weight, then held. He looked down. The gorge was about one thousand feet below. Larry started across, carefully testing each step, and heard Catherine's voice, "Larry!"

He turned. She had reached the foot of the bridge.

"We're not going to cross on *that*, are we?" Catherine asked. "That wouldn't hold a *cat!*"

"We are unless you can fly."

"But it doesn't look safe."

"People cross it every day." Larry turned and started moving across it again, leaving Catherine standing at the foot of the bridge.

Catherine stepped on the bridge, and it began to vibrate. She looked down at the deep gorge, and fear began to fill her. This was no longer fun; it was dangerous. Catherine looked ahead and saw that Larry had almost reached the other side. She gritted her teeth, grabbed the rope and started walking across, the bridge swaying with every step. On the other side Larry had turned to watch her. Catherine was moving slowly, keeping one hand tightly on the rope, trying not to look down at the abyss below. Larry could see the fear written on her face. When Catherine reached Larry's side, she was shivering, either from terror or from the chill wind that was beginning to sweep across the snow-capped mountain tops.

Catherine said, "I don't think I'm cut out to be a mountain climber. Could we go back now, darling?"

Larry looked at her in surprise. "We haven't even seen the view yet, Cathy."

"I've seen enough to last me a lifetime."

He put his arms on hers. "Tell you what," he smiled, "up ahead is a nice quiet place for our picnic. We'll stop there. How's that?"

Catherine nodded reluctantly. "All right."

"That's my girl."

Larry gave her a brief smile, then turned and started up the path again, Catherine following behind him.

Catherine had to admit that the view of the village and the valley far below was breathtaking, a peaceful idyllic scene out of a Currier & Ives postcard. She was really glad that she had come. It had been a long time since she had seen Larry so exuberant. He seemed to be possessed by a sense of excitement that kept growing as they climbed higher. His face was flushed, and he chattered on about trivia as though he had to keep talking to release some of his nervous energy. Everything seemed to excite him: the climb, the view, the flowers along the path. Each thing seemed to take on an extraordinary importance as though his senses had somehow been stimulated beyond normal. He was climbing effortlessly, not even out of breath, while the increasingly rarefied air was making Catherine pant.

Her legs were beginning to feel like lead. Her breath was coming in labored gasps now. She had no idea how long they had been climbing, but when she looked down, the village was a tiny miniature far below. It seemed to Catherine that the path was getting steeper and narrower. It wound along the edge of a precipice and Catherine hugged the side of the mountain as closely as she could. Larry had said that it was an easy climb. *For a mountain goat,* Catherine thought. The trail was almost nonexistent, and there was no sign that anyone else had used it. The flowers had thinned out and the only vegetation was moss and a strange-looking, brownish weed that seemed to be growing out of the stones. Catherine was not sure how much longer she could keep climbing. As they rounded a sharp turn, the path suddenly dropped away and a dizzying abyss appeared below her feet.

"Larry!" It was a scream.

He was at Catherine's side instantly. He grabbed her arm and pulled her back, guiding her over the rocks to where the path resumed. Catherine's heart was pounding wildly. *I must be crazy,* she thought. *I'm too old to go on safari.* The altitude and the exertion had made her dizzy and her head was swimming. She turned to speak to Larry, and above him around the next turn, she saw the top of the mountain. They had arrived.

Catherine lay there on the flat ground getting her strength back, feeling the cool breeze teasing at her hair. The terror had subsided. There was nothing more to fear now. Larry had said the way down was easy. Larry sat down beside her.

"Feeling better?" he asked.

She nodded. "Yes." Her heart had stopped pounding and she was beginning to breathe normally again. She took a deep breath and smiled up at him.

"The hard part's finished, isn't it?" Catherine asked.

Larry looked at her a long moment. Then he said, "Yes. It's finished, Cathy."

Catherine raised herself up on one elbow. A wooden observation platform had been set up on the small plateau. There was an old railing around the edge, from which there was a spectacular view of the dizzying panorama below. A dozen feet away Catherine could see the path leading down the other side of the mountain.

"Oh, Larry, it *is* beautiful," Catherine said. "I feel like Magellan." She smiled at him, but Larry was looking away and Catherine realized that he wasn't listening to her. He seemed preoccupied—*tense,* as though he were worried about something. Catherine glanced up and said, "Look!" A fluffy white cloud was drifting toward them, pushed along by the brisk mountain breezes. "It's coming this way. I've never stood in the clouds before. It must be like being in Heaven."

Larry watched as Catherine scrambled to her feet and moved toward the edge of the cliff to the rickety wooden railing. Larry leaned forward on his elbows, suddenly thoughtful, watching the cloud as it moved toward Catherine. It had almost reached her, was starting to envelop her.

"I'm going to stand in it," she called, "and let it go right through me!"

An instant later Catherine was lost in the swirling gray mist.

Quietly, Larry rose to his feet. He stood there a moment, stock still, then began to move silently toward her. In seconds he was immersed in the fog. He stopped, not sure exactly where she was. Then ahead of him he heard her voice calling, "Oh, Larry, this is wonderful! Come and join me." He started moving slowly forward toward the sound of her voice, muffled by the cloud. "It's like a soft rain," she cried. "Can you feel it?" Her voice was closer now, only a few feet ahead of him. He took another step forward, his hands outstretched, groping for her.

"Larry! Where are you?"

He could make out her figure now, wraithlike in the mist, just in front of him at the very edge of the cliff. His hands reached out toward her and at that moment the cloud blew past them, and she turned and they were facing each other, no more than three feet apart.

She took a step back in surprise, so that her right foot was at the very edge of the cliff. "Oh! You startled me," she exclaimed.

Larry took another step toward her, smiling reassuringly, and he reached out for her with his two hands, and at that moment a loud voice said, "For Chrissakes, we got bigger mountains than this in Denver!"

Larry swung around in shock, his face white. A group of tourists led by a Greek guide emerged from the far path around the other face of the mountain. The guide stopped as he saw Catherine and Larry.

"Good morning," he said in surprise. "You must have climbed the east slope."

"Yes," Larry said tightly.

The guide shook his head. "They're crazy. They should have told you that that is the dangerous way. The other slope is much easier."

"I'll remember that next time," Larry said. His voice was hoarse.

The excitement that Catherine had noticed seemed

to have gone out of him, as though a switch had been suddenly turned off.

"Let's get the hell out of here," Larry said.

"But—we just got here. Is anything wrong?"

"No," he snapped. "I just hate mob scenes."

They took the easy path back, and on the way down Larry did not speak at all. It was as though he was filled with an icy rage and Catherine could not imagine why. She was sure she had not said or done anything to offend him. It had been when the other people appeared that his manner had changed so abruptly. Suddenly Catherine thought she guessed the reason for his mood, and smiled. He had wanted to make love to her in the cloud! That was why he had started moving toward her with his arms outstretched. And his plans had been spoiled by the group of tourists. She almost laughed aloud with joy. She watched Larry as he strode down the trail ahead of her, and she was infused with a feeling of warmth. *I'll make it up to him when we get back to the hotel,* she promised herself.

But when they returned to their bungalow, and Catherine put her arms around him and started to kiss him, Larry told her that he was tired.

At three o'clock in the morning Catherine lay in bed, too excited to sleep. It had been a long day and a frightening one. She thought of the mountain path and the shaky bridge and the climb up the face of the rock. And finally she fell asleep.

The following morning Larry went to talk to the reception clerk.

"Those caves you mentioned the other day," Larry began.

"Ah, yes," the clerk replied. "The Caves of Perama. Very colorful. Very interesting. You must not miss them."

"I guess I'll have to see them," Larry said lightly. "I don't care for caves much, but my wife heard about them and she's been after me to take her there. She loves that kind of thing."

"I am certain you will both enjoy it, Mr. Douglas. Just be sure to hire a guide."

"Do I need one?" Larry asked.

The clerk nodded. "It is advisable. There have been several tragedies there, people getting lost." He lowered his voice. "One young couple has not been found to this day."

"If it's so dangerous," Larry asked, "why do they allow people in?"

"It is only the new section that is dangerous," the clerk explained. "It has not been explored yet and there are no lights. But with a guide you will not have to worry."

"What time do they close the caves?"

"At six o'clock."

Larry found Catherine outside, reclining under a giant oxya tree, the beautiful Greek oak, reading.

"How's the book?" he asked.

"Put-downable."

He hunched beside her. "The hotel clerk told me about some caves near here."

Catherine looked up, faintly apprehensive. "Caves?"

"He said it's a must. All the honeymooners go there. You make a wish inside, and it comes true." His voice was boyish and eager. "How about it?"

Catherine hesitated a moment, thinking how like a little boy Larry really was. "If you would like it," she said.

He smiled. "Great. We'll go after lunch. You go ahead and read. I have to drive into town and pick up a few things."

"Would you like me to come with you?"

"No," he said easily, "I'll be right back. You take it easy."

She nodded. "All right."

He turned and left.

In town Larry found a small general store that was able to supply him with a pocket flashlight, some fresh batteries and a ball of twine.

"Are you staying up at the hotel?" the shopkeeper asked as he counted out Larry's change.

"No," Larry said. "Just passing through on my way to Athens."

"I'd be careful if I was you," the man advised.

Larry looked up at him sharply. "Of what?"

"There's a storm coming up. You can hear the sheep crying."

Larry returned to the hotel at three o'clock. At four o'clock, Larry and Catherine left for the caves. A troubled wind had sprung up, and to the north large thunderheads were starting to form, erasing the sun from the sky.

The Caves of Perama lie thirty kilometers east of Io-annina. Over the centuries tremendous stalagmites and stalactites have formed into the shapes of animals and palaces and jewels, and the caves have become an important tourist attraction.

When Catherine and Larry arrived at the caves, it was five o'clock, one hour before closing. Larry bought two tickets and a pamphlet at the ticket booth. A shabbily dressed guide came up and offered his services.

"Only fifty drachmas," he intoned, "and I will give you the best guided tour."

"We don't need a guide," Larry said, curtly.

Catherine looked at him, surprised by his sharp tone.

He took Catherine's arm. "Come on."

"Are you sure we shouldn't have a guide?"

"What for? It's a racket. All we do is go inside and look at the cave. The pamphlet will tell us anything we need to know."

"All right," Catherine said agreeably.

The entrance to the cave was larger than she had expected, brightly lit with flood lamps and filled with milling tourists. The walls and roof of the cave seemed to be crammed with heroic figures sculpted out of the

396   *The Other Side of Midnight*

rocks: birds and giants and flowers and crowns.

"It's fantastic," Catherine exclaimed. She studied the pamphlet. "No one knows how old it is."

Her voice sounded hollow, reverberating against the rock ceiling. Over their heads, stalactites hung down. A tunnel carved into the rock led to a second smaller room that was lit by naked bulbs wired near the ceiling of the cave. There were more fanciful figures in here, a wild profligate display of nature's art. At the far end of the cave was a printed sign that read: *Danger: Keep Away.*

Beyond the sign was the entrance to a yawning black cavern. Casually Larry walked over to it and looked around. Catherine was studying a carving near the entrance. Larry took the sign and tossed it to one side. He walked back to Catherine.

"It's damp in here," she said. "Shall we leave?"

"No." Larry's tone was firm.

She looked at him in surprise.

"There's more to see," Larry explained. "The hotel clerk told me that the most interesting part is the new section. He said we mustn't miss it."

"Where is it?" Catherine asked.

"Over there." Larry took her arm and they walked toward the rear of the cave and stood in front of the gaping black chasm.

"We can't go in there," Catherine said. "It's dark."

Larry patted her arm. "Not to worry. He told me to bring a flashlight." He produced it from his pocket. "And—*voilà*—see?" He turned it on, and its narrow beam lit up a long dark corridor of ancient rock.

Catherine stood there, staring at the tunnel. "It looks so big," she said uncertainly. "Are you sure it's safe?"

"Of course," Larry replied. "They bring schoolchildren here."

Catherine still hesitated, wishing they could stay with the other tourists. Somehow this seemed dangerous to her.

"All right," she said.

They started into the passage. They had traveled only a few feet when the circle of light from the main cave behind them was swallowed up in the blackness. The passage made an abrupt turn to the left and then curved to the right. They were alone in a cold, timeless primeval world. In the beam of Larry's flashlight Catherine caught a glimpse of his face in the reflection of light and she saw that look of animation again. It was the same way he had looked on the mountain. Catherine tightened her grip on his arm.

Ahead of them the tunnel forked. Catherine could see the rough stone on the low ceiling as it split off in separate directions. She thought of Theseus and the Minotaur in the cave, and she wondered whether they were going to bump into them. She opened her mouth to suggest that they turn back, but before she could speak, Larry said, "We go to the left."

She looked at him and said in what she hoped was a casual voice, "Darling, don't you think we should start back? It's getting late. The caves will be closing."

"They're open until nine," Larry replied. "There's one particular cave I want to find. They just excavated it. It's supposed to be really fantastic." He started to move forward.

Catherine hesitated, casting about for an excuse not to go farther. After all why *shouldn't* they go exploring? Larry was enjoying it. If that was what it took to make him happy, she would become the world's greatest—what was the word?—spelunker.

Larry had stopped and was waiting for her. "Coming?" he asked impatiently.

She tried to sound enthusiastic. "Yes. Just don't lose me," she said.

Larry did not reply. They took the fork that branched to the left and began walking, careful of the small stones that slipped under their feet. Larry reached into his pocket, and a moment later Catherine heard something fall to the ground. Larry kept walking.

"Did you drop something?" Catherine asked. "I thought I heard—"

"I kicked a stone," he said. "Let's walk faster." And they moved ahead, Catherine unaware that behind them a ball of twine was unwinding.

The ceiling of the cave seemed to be lower here and the walls damper and—Catherine laughed at herself for thinking it—ominous. It was as though the tunnel was beginning to close in on them, threatening and maleficent. "I don't think this place likes us," Catherine said.

"Don't be ridiculous, Cathy; it's just a cave."

"Why do you suppose we're the only ones here?"

Larry hesitated. "Not many people know about this section."

They walked on and on until Catherine began to lose all sense of time and place.

The passage was narrowing again, and the rocks on the sides tore at them with sharp, unexpected protuberances.

"How much farther do you think it is?" Catherine asked. "We must be getting near China."

"It's not far now."

When they spoke, their voices sounded muffled and hollow, like a series of continuous dying echoes.

It was getting cold now, but it was a damp, clammy cold. Catherine shivered. Ahead the beam of the flashlight caught another bifurcation of the passage. They walked up to it and stopped. The tunnel running to the right seemed smaller than the one to the left.

"They should put up neon road signs," Catherine said. "We've probably gone too far."

"No," Larry said. "I'm sure it's the one on the right."

"I'm really getting chilly, darling," she said. "Let's go back now."

He turned to look at her. "We're almost there, Cathy." He squeezed her arm. "I'll warm you up when we get back to our bungalow." He saw the reluctance on her face. "I'll tell you what—if we haven't found the place in the next two minutes, we'll turn around and go home. OK?"

Catherine felt her heart lighten. "OK," she said thankfully.

"Come on."

They turned down the tunnel to the right, the beam of the flashlight making an eerie, wavering pattern on the gray rock ahead. Catherine glanced back over her shoulder and behind her was complete blackness. It was as though the little flashlight was carving brightness out of the Stygian gloom, moving it forward a few feet at a time, encapsulating them in its tiny womb of light. Larry stopped suddenly.

"Damn!" he said.

"What's the matter?"

"I think we took the wrong turn back there."

Catherine nodded. "All right. Let's go back."

"Let me make sure. You stay here."

She looked at him in surprise. "Where are you going?"

"Just a few feet. Back to that entrance." His voice sounded strained and unnatural.

"I'll come with you."

"I can do it faster alone, Catherine. I just want to check the fork where we made the last turn." He sounded impatient. "I'll be back in ten seconds."

"All right," she said, uneasily.

Catherine stood there watching as Larry turned away from her and walked back into the dark from which they had come, enclosed in a halo of light like a moving angel in the bowels of the earth. A moment later the light disappeared, and she was plunged into the deepest blackness she had ever known. She stood there, shivering, counting off the seconds in her mind. And then the minutes.

Larry did not return.

Catherine waited, feeling the blackness lapping

around her like malicious invisible waves. She called
out, "Larry?" and her voice was hoarse and uncertain,
and she cleared her throat and tried again louder.
"Larry?" She could hear the sound dying a few feet
away from her, murdered by the darkness. It was as
though nothing could live in this place, and Catherine
began to feel the first tendrils of terror. *Of course
Larry will be right back,* she told herself. *All I have to
do is stay where I am and remain calm.*

The black minutes dragged by, and she began to
face the fact that something had gone terribly wrong.
Larry could have had an accident, he could have
slipped on the loose stones and hit his head on the sharp
sides of the cave. Perhaps at this moment he was lying
just a few feet away from her, bleeding to death. Or
perhaps he was lost. His flashlight could have gone out
and he might be somewhere in the bowels of this cave
trapped, as she was trapped.

A feeling of suffocation began to close in on Catherine, choking her, filling her with a mindless panic. She
turned and began to walk slowly in the direction from
which she had come. The tunnel was narrow, and if
Larry was lying on the ground, helpless and hurt, she
had a good chance of finding him. Soon she would
come to the place where the passage had divided. She
moved cautiously, the loose stones rolling beneath her
feet. She thought she heard a distant sound and
stopped to listen. Larry? It was gone, and she began to
move again, and then she heard it once more. It was a
whirring sound, as though someone were running a
tape recorder. There *was* someone down here!

Catherine yelled aloud and then listened as the
sound of her voice drowned in the silence. There it was
again! The whirring noise. It was coming this way. It
grew louder, racing toward her in a great screaming
rush of wind. It was getting closer and closer. Suddenly
it leaped on her in the dark; cold and clammy skin
brushed against her cheeks and kissed her lips and she
felt something crawling on her head and sharp claws in

her hair and her face was smothered by the mad beating of wings of some nameless horror attacking her in the blackness.

She fainted.

She was lying on a sharp spike of stone and the discomfort of it brought her back to consciousness. Her cheek was warm and sticky, and it was a minute before Catherine realized that it was her blood. She remembered the wings and the claws that had attacked her in the dark and she began to shiver.

There were bats in the cave.

She tried to recall what she knew about bats. She had read somewhere that they were flying rats and that they congregated by the thousands. The only other information she could conjure up from her memory was that there were vampire bats, and she quickly dropped that thought. Reluctantly Catherine sat up, the palms of her hands stinging from being scraped on the sharp stones.

You can't just sit here, she told herself. *You've got to get up and do something.* Painfully she dragged herself to her feet. She had lost a shoe somehow and her dress was torn, but Larry would buy her a new one tomorrow. She pictured the two of them going into a little shop in the village, laughing and happy and buying a white summer dress for her, but somehow the dress became a shroud and her mind began to fill with panic again. She must keep thinking about tomorrow, not the nightmare she was engulfed in now. She must keep walking. But which way? She was turned around. If she walked the wrong way, she would be going deeper into the cave, and yet she knew she could not stay here. Catherine tried to estimate how much time had elapsed since they had entered the cave. It must have been an hour, possibly two. There was no way of knowing how long she had been unconscious. Surely they would be looking for Larry and her. But what if no one missed them? There was no check on who went in or out of the caves. She could be down here forever.

She took off her other shoe and began to walk, taking slow, careful steps, holding her burning hands out to avoid bumping into the rough sides of the tunnel. *The longest journey begins with but a single step,* Catherine told herself. *The Chinese said that and look how smart they are. They invented firecrackers and chop suey, and they were too clever to get caught in some dark hole in the ground where no one could find them. If I keep walking, I'm going to bump into Larry or some tourists and we'll go back to the hotel and have a drink and laugh about all this. All I have to do is keep walking.*

She stopped suddenly. In the distance she could hear the whirring sound again, moving toward her like some ghostly, phantom express train, and her body began to tremble uncontrollably, and she began to scream. An instant later, they were on her, hundreds of them, swarming over her, beating at her with their cold, clammy wings and smothering her with their furry rodent bodies in a nightmare of unspeakable horror.

The last thing she remembered before losing consciousness was calling Larry's name.

She was lying on the cold, damp floor of the cave. Her eyes were closed, but her mind had suddenly awakened, and she thought, *Larry wants to kill me.* It was as though her subconscious had put the idea there intact. In a series of kaleidoscopic flashes she heard Larry saying, *I'm in love with someone else . . . I want a divorce . . .* and Larry moving toward her through the cloud on the mountaintop, his hands reaching for her . . . She remembered looking down the steep mountain and saying, *It will take a long time to get down,* and Larry saying, *No, it won't . . .* and Larry saying, *We don't need a guide . . . I think we took the wrong turn. Wait here . . . I'll be back in ten seconds . . .* And then the terrifying blackness.

Larry had never intended to return for her. The reconciliation, the honeymoon . . . it was all pretense, part of a plan to murder her. All the time she had been smugly thanking God for giving her a second chance, Larry was plotting to kill her. And he had succeeded, for Catherine knew she would never get out of here. She was buried alive in a black tomb of horror. The bats had gone, but she could feel and smell the filthy slime they had left all over her face and body, and she knew that they would be back for her. She did not know if she could keep her sanity through another attack. The thought of them made her begin to tremble again, and she forced herself to take slow, deep breaths.

And then Catherine heard it again and knew she could not stand it another time. It started as a low humming, and then a louder wave of sound, moving toward her. There was a sudden, anguished scream, and it rang out into the darkness over and over, and the other sound kept coming louder and louder, and out of the black tunnel a light appeared, and she heard voices calling out and hands began to reach for her and lift her and she wanted to warn them about the bats, but she was unable to stop screaming.

NOELLE AND CATHERINE
Athens: 1946

22

She lay still and rigid so that the bats could not find her, and she listened for the whirr of their wings, her eyes tightly shut.

A man's voice said, "It is a miracle that we found her."

"Is she going to be all right?"

It was Larry's voice.

Terror suddenly flooded through Catherine again. It was as though her body were filled with screaming nerves that warned her to flee. Her killer had come for her. She moaned, "No . . ." and opened her eyes. She was in her bed in the bungalow. Larry stood at the foot of the bed, and next to him was a man she had never seen before. Larry moved toward her. "Catherine . . ."

She flinched as he started toward her. "Don't touch me!" Her voice was weak and hoarse.

"Catherine!" Larry's face was filled with distress.

"Get him away from me," Catherine begged.

"She is still in shock," the stranger said. "Perhaps it would be better if you waited in the other room."

Larry studied Catherine a moment, his face expressionless. "Of course. I want whatever is best for her." He turned and walked out.

The stranger came closer. He was a short, fat man with a pleasant face and a nice smile. He spoke English with a heavy accent. "I am Doctor Kazomides. You have had a most unpleasant time, Mrs. Douglas, but I

assure you you are going to be fine. A mild concussion
and a severe shock, but in a few days you will be good
as new." He sighed. "They should close those damned
caves. This is the third accident this year."

Catherine started to shake her head, then stopped,
as it began to throb violently. "It was no accident," she
said thickly. "He tried to kill me."

He looked down at her. "Who tried to kill you?"

Her mouth was dry and her tongue was thick. It was
difficult to get the words out. "M—my husband."

"No," he said.

He did not believe her. Catherine swallowed and
tried again. "He l—left me in the cave to die."

He shook his head. "It was an accident. I am going
to give you a sedative and when you wake up, you will
feel much better."

A surge of fear flowed through her. "No!" she
pleaded. "Don't you understand? I'll never wake up.
Take me out of here. Please!"

The doctor was smiling reassuringly. "I told you you
are going to be fine, Mrs. Douglas. All you need is a
nice, long sleep." He reached into a black medical bag
and began searching for a hypodermic.

Catherine tried to sit up, but a searing pain shot
through her head and she was instantly bathed in perspiration. She fell back on the bed, her head pounding
unbearably.

"You must not try to move yet," Dr. Kazomides
warned. "You have been through a terrible ordeal." He
took out the hypodermic, filled the needle from a vial
of amber fluid and turned to her. "Turn over, please.
When you waken, you will feel like a new person."

"I won't waken," Catherine whispered. "He'll murder me while I'm asleep."

There was a look of concern on the doctor's face.
He walked over to her. "Please turn over, Mrs. Douglas."

She stared at him, her eyes stubborn.

Gently he turned Catherine on her side, pulled up her nightgown and she felt a sharp sting in her hip. "There you are."

She rolled on her back and whispered. "You've just killed me." Her eyes filled with helpless tears.

"Mrs. Douglas," the doctor said, quietly, "do you know how we found you?"

She started to shake her head, then remembered the pain. His voice was gentle. "Your husband led us to you."

She stared at him, not comprehending what he was saying.

"He took the wrong turn and got lost in the cave," he explained. "When he could not find you, he became frantic. He summoned the police and we immediately organized a search party."

She looked at him, still not understanding. "Larry . . . sent for help?"

"He was in a terrible state. He blamed himself for what happened."

She lay there trying to take it in, trying to adjust to this new information. If Larry had tried to kill her, he would not have organized a search party to find her, he would not have been frantic about her safety. She was filled with a terrible confusion. The doctor was watching her sympathetically.

"You will sleep now," he told her. "I will come back to see you in the morning."

She had believed that the man she loved was a murderer. She knew she had to tell Larry and ask his forgiveness, but her head was getting heavy and her eyes kept closing. *I'll tell him later,* she thought, *when I wake up. He'll understand and he'll forgive me. And everything will be wonderful again, just the way it was. . . .*

She was awakened by a sudden, sharp cracking sound, and her eyes flew open, her pulse racing. A torrent of rain was savagely drumming against the bedroom window, and a flash of lightning lit everything in a pale blue light that made the room look like an over-exposed photograph. The wind was clawing at the house, trying to scream its way in and the rain beating on the roof and windows sounded like a thousand tiny drums. Every few seconds there was an ominous roll of thunder followed by a flash of lightning.

It was the sound of thunder that had awakened Catherine. She dragged herself up to a sitting position and looked at the small bedside clock. She was groggy from the sedative that the doctor had given her, and she had to squint to make out the figures on the dial. It was three A.M. She was alone. Larry must be in the other room keeping vigil, worried about her. She had to see him, to apologize. Carefully Catherine swung her feet off the edge of the bed and tried to stand up. A wave of dizziness swept over her. She started to fall and held herself against the bedpost until it passed. She walked unsteadily to the door, her muscles feeling stiff and unused, and the pounding in her head a painful, aching throb. She stood there a moment, clinging to the door knob for support, then opened the door and stepped into the living room.

Larry was not there. There was a light on in the kitchen, and she stumbled toward it. Larry was standing in the kitchen, his back to her, and she called out, "Larry!" but her voice was washed away by the loud clap of thunder. Before she could call again, a woman moved into view. Larry said, "It's dangerous for you to—" The screaming wind carried the rest of his words away.

"—had to come. I had to make sure you—"

"—see us together. No one will ever—"

"—I told you I'd take care of—"

"—went wrong. There's nothing they can—"

"—now, while she's asleep."

Catherine stood there paralyzed, unable to move. It was like listening to stroboscopic sounds, quick pulsating phrases of words. The rest of the sentences were lost in the howling wind and crack of thunder.

"—we have to move quickly before she—"

All the old terrors returned, shuddering through her body, engulfing her in a nameless, sickening panic. Her nightmare had been real. He was trying to kill her. She had to get out of here before they found her, before they murdered her. Slowly, her whole body trembling, she started backing away. She brushed against a lamp, and it started to fall, but she caught it before it could hit the floor. The pounding of her heart was so loud that she was afraid they would be able to hear it over the sound of the thunder and the rain. She reached the front door and opened it and the wind almost tore it out of her hands.

Catherine stepped outside into the night and quickly closed the door behind her. She was instantly drenched by the cold, driving rain, and for the first time she became aware that she was wearing nothing but a thin nightgown. It did not matter. All that mattered was that she escape. Through the torrents of rain she could see the lights of the hotel lobby in the distance. She could go there and ask for help. But would they believe her? She remembered the doctor's face when she had told him Larry was trying to kill her. No, they would think she was hysterical, they would turn her over to Larry. She must get away from this place. She headed for the steep rocky path that led down to the village.

The torrential storm had turned the path into a muddy, slippery mire that sucked at her bare feet and slowed her down so that she had the feeling that she was running in a nightmare, vainly trying to escape in slow motion while her pursuers raced after her. She kept slipping and falling to the ground and her feet were bleeding from the sharp stones on the path, but she was not even aware of it. She was in a state of shock, moving like an automaton, falling when a gust of wind hurled her down and picking herself up and moving down the path toward the village again, unaware of where she was running. She was no longer conscious of the rain.

The path suddenly opened out onto a dark, deserted street on the edge of the village. She kept stumbling ahead like a hunted animal, mindlessly putting one foot in front of the other, terrified by the awful sounds that rent the night and the flashes of lightning that turned the sky into an inferno.

She reached the lake and stood there staring at it, the wind whipping the thin nightgown around her body. The calm water had turned into a seething, churning ocean driven by demonic winds that built up high waves that brutally smashed against one another.

Catherine stood there, trying to remember what she was doing here. And suddenly it came to her. She was on her way to meet Bill Fraser. He was waiting for her at his beautiful mansion so they could be married. Across the water Catherine caught a glimpse of a yellow light through the driving rain. Bill was there, waiting. But how was she going to get to him? She looked down and below her she saw the rowboats tied to their moorings, spinning around in the turbulent water, straining to break free.

She knew then what she had to do. She scrambled down to a boat and jumped in. Fighting to keep her balance she untied the rope holding it to the dock. Instantly the boat leaped away from the dock, soaring in its sudden freedom. Catherine was knocked off her feet. She pulled herself onto a seat and picked up the oars, trying to remember how Larry had used them. But there was no Larry. It must have been Bill. Yes, she could remember Bill rowing with her. They were going to meet his mother and father. Now she tried to use the oars, but the giant waves kept pitching the boat from side to side and spinning it around, and the oars were pulled out of her hands and sucked into the water. She sat there watching them disappear from sight. The boat was hurtling toward the center of the lake. Catherine's teeth began to chatter from the cold, and she began to shiver in an uncontrollable spasm. She felt something lap at her feet and she looked down and saw that the boat was filling with water. She started to cry, because her wedding dress was going to get wet. Bill Fraser had bought it for her and now he was going to be angry with her.

She wore a wedding gown because she and Bill were in a church and the minister who looked like Bill's father said *if anyone objects to this marriage speak up now or* . . . and then a woman's voice said, *now, while she's asleep,* and the lights went out and Catherine was back in the cave and Larry was holding her down and the woman was throwing water on her, drowning her. She looked around for the yellow light in Bill's house, but it was gone. He did not want to marry her any more, and now she had no one.

The shore was very far away now, hidden somewhere beyond the beating, driving rain, and Catherine was alone in the stormy night, with the screaming, banshee wind of the *meltemi* in her ears. The boat began to rock treacherously as the huge waves smashed against it. But Catherine was no longer afraid. Her body was slowly filling with a delicious warmth, and the rain felt like soft velvet on her skin. She clasped her hands in front of her like a small child and began to recite the prayer that she had learned as a little girl.

"Now I lay me down to sleep . . . I pray the Lord my soul to keep . . . If I should die before I wake . . . I pray the Lord my soul to take." And she was filled with a wonderful happiness because she knew at last that everything was all right. She was on her way home.

At that moment a large wave caught the stern of the boat, and it slowly began to overturn in the black bottomless lake.

Book Three

THE TRIAL
Athens: 1947

23

Five hours before the murder trial of Noelle Page and
Larry Douglas was to begin, Room 33 in the Arsakion
Courthouse in Athens was overflowing with spectators.
The courthouse is an enormous gray building that
takes up an entire square block on University Street
and Stada. Of the thirty courtrooms in the building,
only three rooms are reserved for criminal trials:
Rooms 21, 30 and 33. Number 33 had been chosen
for this trial because it was the largest. The corridors
outside Room 33 were jammed and police in gray uniforms and gray shirts were stationed at the two en-
trances to control the crowd. The sandwich stand in
the corridor was sold out in the first five minutes, and
there was a long line in front of the telephone booth.

Georgios Skouri, the Chief of Police, was personally
supervising the security arrangements. Newspaper photographers were everywhere and Skouri managed to
have his photograph taken with pleasing frequency.
Passes to the courtroom were at a premium. For weeks
members of the Greek judiciary had been besieged
with requests from friends and relatives. Insiders who
were able to secure them bartered them in exchange
for other favors or sold them to the jackals who were
scalping them for as high as five hundred drachmas
apiece.

The actual setting of the murder trial was common-
place. Courtroom 33 on the second floor of the courthouse was musty and old, the arena of thousands of
legal battles that had taken place over the years. The

room was about forty feet wide and three hundred feet
long. The seats were divided into three rows, six feet
apart, with nine wooden benches to each row.

At the front of the courtroom was a raised dais behind a six-foot polished mahogany partition with high-
backed leather chairs for the three presiding judges.
The center chair was for the President of the Court
and above it hung a square, dirty mirror reflecting a
section of the courtroom.

In front of the dais was the witness stand, a small
raised platform on which was fixed a reading lectern
with a wooden tray to hold papers. On the lectern in
gold leaf was the crucifix, Jesus on the cross with two
of his disciples by his side. Against the far wall was the
jury box, filled now with its ten jurors. On the far left
was the box where the accused sat. In front of the defendants' box was the lawyers' table.

The walls of the room were of stucco, and there was
linoleum on the floor in contrast to the worn wooden
floors in the courtrooms on the first floor. A dozen
electric light bulbs hung from the ceiling, covered with
glass globes. In a far corner of the room, the airduct of
an old-fashioned heater ascended into the ceiling. A
section of the room had been reserved for the press,
and representatives were there from Reuters, United
Press, International News Service, Shsin Hau Agency,
French Press Agency and Tass, among others.

The circumstances of the murder trial itself would
have been sensational enough, but the personae were
so famous that the excited spectators did not know
where to look first. It was like a three-ring circus. In
the first row of benches was Philippe Sorel, the star,
who, it was rumored, was a former lover of Noelle
Page. Sorel had smashed a camera on the way into the
courtroom and had adamantly refused to speak to the
press. He sat in his seat now, withdrawn and silent, an
invisible wall around him. One row in back of Sorel sat
Armand Gautier. The tall, saturnine director was constantly scanning the courtroom as though mentally

making notes for his next picture. Near Gautier sat Israel Katz, the famous French surgeon and resistance hero.

Two seats away from him sat William Fraser, special assistant to the President of the United States. Next to Fraser a seat had been reserved and a rumor swept through the courtroom like wildfire that Constantin Demiris was going to appear.

Everywhere the spectators turned was a familiar face: a politician, a singer, a well-known sculptor, an internationally famous author. But though the audience in the judicial circus was filled with celebrities, the main focus of attention was in the center ring.

At one end of the defendant's box sat Noelle Page, exquisitely beautiful, her honey skin a bit paler than usual, and dressed as though she had just stepped out of Madame Chanel's. There was a regal quality about Noelle, a noble presence that heightened the drama of what was happening to her. It whetted the excitement of the spectators and sharpened their blood-lust.

As an American newsweekly expressed it: *The emotion that flowed toward Noelle Page from the crowd that had come to witness her trial was so strong that it became an almost physical presence in the courtroom. It was not a feeling of sympathy or of enmity, it was simply a feeling of expectation. The woman being tried for murder by the state was a superwoman, a goddess on a golden pedestal, who was high above them, and they were there to watch their idol being brought down to their level and destroyed. The feeling in the courtroom must have been the same feelings that were in the hearts of the peasants who watched Marie Antoinette riding to her doom in the tumbrel.*

Noelle Page was not the only act in the legal circus. At the other end of the defendant's box sat Larry Douglas, filled with a smoldering anger. His handsome face was pale, and he had lost weight, but those things only served to accentuate his sculptured features, and many of the women in the courtroom had an urge to take him in their arms and console him in one way or another. Since Larry had been arrested, he had received hundreds of letters from women all over the world, dozens of gifts and proposals of marriage.

The third star of the circus was Napoleon Chotas, a man who was as well known in Greece as Noelle Page. Napoleon Chotas was acknowledged to be one of the greatest criminal lawyers in the world. He had defended clients ranging from heads of government who had been found with their fingers in the public coffers, to murderers who had been caught red-handed by the police, and he had never lost a major case. Chotas was thin and emaciated-looking and he sat in the courtroom watching the spectators with large, sad bloodhound eyes in a ruined face. When Chotas addressed a jury, his speech was slow and hesitant, and he had great difficulty expressing himself. Sometimes he was in such an agony of embarrassment that a juror would helpfully blurt out the word that Napoleon Chotas was fumbling for, and when this happened the lawyer's face would fill with such relief and inexpressible gratitude that the entire panel of jurors would feel a wave of affection for the man. Outside the courtroom Chotas was a crisp, incisive speaker with a consummate mastery of language and syntax. He spoke seven languages fluently and when his busy schedule permitted, he gave lectures to jurists all over the world.

Seated on the lawyer's bench a few feet away from Chotas, was Frederick Stavros, the defense attorney for Larry Douglas. The experts agreed that while Stavros might be competent enough to handle routine cases, he was hopelessly out of his depth in this one.

Noelle Page and Larry Douglas had already been tried in the newspapers and in the minds of the populace and had been found guilty. No one doubted their guilt for a moment. Professional gamblers were offering thirty to one that the defendants would be convicted. To the trial, then, was lent the added excitement of watching the greatest criminal lawyer in Europe work his magic against enormous odds.

When it had been announced that Chotas was going to defend Noelle Page, the woman who had betrayed Constantin Demiris and held him up to public ridicule, the news had created a furor. As powerful as Chotas was, Constantin Demiris was a hundred times more powerful and no one could imagine what had possessed Chotas to go against Constantin Demiris. The truth was even more interesting than the bizarre rumors that were flying around.

The lawyer had taken on Noelle Page's defense at the personal request of Demiris.

Three months before the trial was scheduled to begin, the warden himself had come to Noelle's cell at the Saint Nikodemous Street Prison to tell her that Constantin Demiris had asked permission to visit her. Noelle had wondered when she would hear from Demiris. There had been no word from him since her arrest, only a deep, foreboding silence.

Noelle had lived with Demiris long enough to know how deep was his sense of *amour-propre* and to what lengths he would go to avenge even the smallest slight. Noelle had humiliated him as no other person ever had before, and he was powerful enough to exact a terrible retribution. The only question was: How would he go about it? Noelle was certain Demiris would disdain anything as simple as the bribing of a jury or judges. He would be satisfied with no less than some complex Machiavellian plot to exact his revenge, and Noelle had lain awake on her cell cot night after night putting herself in Demiris' mind, discarding strategy after strategy, just as he must have done, searching for a perfect plan. It was like playing mental chess with Demiris, except that she and Larry were the pawns, and the stakes were life and death.

It was probable that Demiris would want to destroy her and Larry, but Noelle knew better than anyone the

subtlety of Demiris' mind, so it was also possible that
he might plan to destroy only one of them and let the
other one live and suffer. If Demiris arranged for them
both to be executed, he would have his vengeance, but
it would be over with too quickly—there would be
nothing left for him to savor. Noelle had carefully examined every possibility, each possible variation of the
game, and it seemed to her that Constantin Demiris
might arrange to let Larry die and let her live, either in
prison or under Demiris' control, because that would
be the surest way to prolong his vengeance indefinitely.
First Noelle would suffer the pain of losing the man
she loved, and then she would have to endure whatever
exquisite agonies Demiris had planned for her future.
Part of the pleasure Demiris would derive from his
vengeance would be in telling Noelle in advance, so she
could taste the full measure of despair.

It had therefore come as no surprise to Noelle when
the warden had appeared at her cell to tell her that
Constantin Demiris wished to see her.

Noelle had been the first to arrive. She had been
ushered into the warden's private office where she had
been discreetly left alone with a makeup case brought
by her maid, to prepare herself for Demiris' visit.

Noelle ignored the cosmetics and the combs and
brushes that lay on the desk and walked over to the
window and looked out. It was the first sight she had
had of the outside world in three months, other than
the quick glimpses when she had been taken from the
Saint Nikodemous Street Prison to the Arsakion, the
courthouse, on the day of her arraignment. She had
been transported to the courthouse in a prison van with
bars and escorted to the basement, where a narrow
cage elevator had carried her and her warders to the
second-floor corridor. The hearing had been held there
and she had been remanded for trial and returned to
the prison.

Now Noelle stared out the window and watched the

traffic below on University Street, men and women and children hurrying home to be united with their families. For the first time in her life Noelle felt frightened. She had no illusions about her chances of acquittal. She had read the newspapers and she knew that this was going to be more than a trial. This was going to be a blood bath in which she and Larry were to be served up as victims to satisfy the conscience of an outraged society. The Greeks hated her because she had mocked the sanctity of marriage, envied her because she was young and beautiful and rich and despised her because they sensed that she was indifferent to their feelings.

In the past Noelle had been careless of life, recklessly squandering time as though it were eternal: but now something in her had changed. The imminent prospect of death had made Noelle realize for the first time how much she wanted to live. There was a fear in her that was like a growing cancer, and if she could, she was ready to make a deal for her life, even though she knew that Demiris would find ways to make it a hell on earth. She would face that when it happened. When the time came, she would find a way to outwit him.

Meanwhile she needed his help to stay alive. She had one advantage. She had always taken the idea of death lightly, so Demiris had no idea how much life meant to her now. If he had, he would surely let her die. Noelle wondered again what webs he had been weaving for her over the past few months, and even as she wondered, she heard the office door open and she turned around and saw Constantin Demiris standing in the doorway and after one shocked look at him, Noelle knew that she had nothing more to fear.

Constantin Demiris had aged ten years in the few months since Noelle had seen him. He looked gaunt and haggard, and his clothes hung loosely on his frame. But it was his eyes that held her attention. They were the eyes of a soul that had been through hell. The es-

sence of power that had been within Demiris, the dynamic, overpowering core of vitality was gone. It was
as though a light switch had been turned off, and all
that was left was the pale afterglow of a faded, once
remembered brilliance. He stood there, staring at her,
his eyes filled with pain.

For a split second Noelle wondered whether this
could be some kind of trick, part of a plan, but no man
on earth could be that good an actor. It was Noelle
who broke the long silence. "I'm sorry, Costa," she
said.

Demiris nodded slowly, as though the movement
cost him an effort.

"I wanted to kill you," he said wearily, and it was an
old man's voice. "I had everything worked out."

"Why didn't you?"

He replied quietly, "Because you killed me first. I've
never needed anyone before. I suppose I've never really been in pain before."

"Costa—"

"No. Let me finish. I'm not a forgiving man. If I
could do without you, believe me I would. But I can't.
I can't go through any more. I want you back, Noelle."

She fought to show nothing of what she was feeling
inside. "That's really not up to me anymore, is it?"

"If I could have you freed, would you come back to
me? To stay?"

To stay. A thousand images flashed through Noelle's
mind. She would never see Larry again, never touch
him, hold him. Noelle had no choice, but even if she
had, life was sweeter. And as long as she was alive,
there was always a chance. She looked up at Demiris.

"Yes, Costa."

Demiris stared at her, his face filling with emotion.
When he spoke, his voice was husky. "Thank you," he
said. "We're going to forget the past. It's gone and
nothing will change it." His voice brightened. "It's the
future I'm interested in. I'm going to engage an attorney for you."

"Who?"

"Napoleon Chotas."

And that was the moment that Noelle really knew she had won the chess match. Check. Checkmate.

Now Napoleon Chotas sat at the long wooden lawyer's table thinking about the battle that was about to take place. Chotas would have much preferred that the trial be held in Ioannina rather than in Athens, but that was impossible, since by Greek law a trial could not take place in the district where the crime had been committed. Chotas had not the slightest doubt about the guilt of Noelle Page, but that was unimportant to him, for like all criminal lawyers he felt that the guilt or innocence of a client was immaterial. Everyone was entitled to a fair trial.

The trial that was about to begin, however, was something different. For the first time in his professional life Napoleon Chotas had allowed himself to become emotionally involved with a client: He was in love with Noelle Page. He had gone to see her at Constantin Demiris' request and though Chotas had been familiar with the public image of Noelle Page, he had been totally unprepared for the reality. She had received him as though he were a guest paying a social call. Noelle had showed neither nervousness nor fear, and at first Chotas had attributed it to her lack of understanding of the desperateness of her situation. The opposite had proved to be true. Noelle was the most intelligent and fascinating woman he had ever encountered and certainly the most beautiful. Chotas, though his appearance belied it, was a connoisseur of women, and he recognized the special qualities that Noelle possessed. It was a joy for Chotas merely to sit and talk with her. They discussed law and art and crime and history, and she was a constant amazement to him. He could fully appreciate Noelle's liaison with a man like Constantin Demiris, but her involvement with Larry Douglas puzzled him. He felt that she was far above

Douglas, and yet Chotas supposed that there was some unexplainable chemistry that made people fall in love with the most unlikely partners. Brilliant scientists married empty-headed blondes, great writers married stupid actresses, intelligent statesmen married trollops.

Chotas remembered the meeting with Demiris. They had known each other socially over the years, but Chotas' law firm had never done any work for him. Demiris had asked Chotas to his home at Varkiza. Demiris had plunged into the conversation without preamble. "As you may know," he had said, "I have a deep interest in this trial. Miss Page is the only woman in my life I have ever truly loved." The two men had talked for six hours, discussing every aspect of the case, every possible strategy. It was decided that Noelle's plea would be Not Guilty. When Chotas rose to leave, a deal had been agreed upon. For undertaking Noelle's defense Napoleon Chotas would be given double his usual fee, and his firm would become the major legal counsel to Constantin Demiris' far-flung empire, a plum worth untold millions.

"I don't care how you do it," Demiris had concluded, fiercely. "Just see to it that nothing goes wrong."

Chotas had accepted the bargain. And then, ironically, he had fallen in love with Noelle Page. Chotas had remained a bachelor, though he kept a string of mistresses, and now when he had found the one woman he wanted to marry, she was out of his reach. He looked at Noelle now, sitting in the defendant's box, beautiful and serene. She wore a simple black wool suit with a plain, high-necked white blouse, and she looked like a Princess from a fairy tale.

Noelle turned and saw Chotas staring at her and gave him a warm smile. He smiled back, but his mind was already turning to the difficult task that lay ahead of him. The clerk was calling the Court to order.

The spectators rose as two judges in business suits entered and took their seats on the bench. The third judge, the President of the Court, followed and took the center seat. He intoned, *"I synethriassis archetai."*

The trial had begun.

Peter Demonides, Special Prosecutor for the State, nervously rose to make his opening address to the jury. Demonides was a skilled and able prosecutor, but he had been up against Napoleon Chotas before—many times, in fact—and the results were invariably the same. The old bastard was unbeatable. Almost all trial lawyers browbeat hostile witnesses, but Chotas coddled them. He nurtured them and loved them and before he was through, they were contradicting themselves all over the place, trying to be helpful to him. He had a knack of turning hard evidence into speculation and speculation into fantasy. Chotas had the most brilliant legal mind Demonides had ever encountered and the greatest knowledge of jurisprudence, but that was not his strength. His strength was his knowledge of people. A reporter had once asked Chotas how he had learned so much about human nature.

"I don't know a damned thing about human nature," Chotas had answered. "I only know about *people*," and the remark had been widely quoted.

In addition to everything else this was the kind of trial that was tailor-made for Chotas to take before a jury, filled as it was with glamour, passion and murder. Of one thing Demonides was certain: Napoleon Chotas would let nothing stop him from winning this case. But neither would Demonides. He knew that he had a strong evidential case against the defendants, and while Chotas might be able to spellbind the jury into overlooking the evidence, he would not be able to sway the three judges on the bench. So it was with a feeling of determination mixed with apprehension that the Special Prosecutor for the State began his opening address.

In skillful, broad strokes Demonides outlined the State's case against the two defendants. By law the foreman of the ten-man jury was an attorney, so

Demonides directed his legal points to him and his general points to the rest of the jury.

"Before this trial has ended," Demonides said, "the State will prove that these two people conspired together to cold-bloodedly murder Catherine Douglas because she stood in the way of their plans. Her only crime was in loving her husband, and for this she was killed. The two defendants have been placed at the scene of the murder. They are the only ones who had the motive and the opportunity. We shall prove beyond a shadow of a doubt . . ."

Demonides kept his address short and to the point, and it was the turn of the Attorney for the Defense.

The spectators in the courtroom watched Napoleon Chotas as he clumsily gathered his papers together and prepared to make his opening speech. Slowly he approached the jury box, his manner hesitant and difficult as though awed by his surroundings.

Watching him William Fraser could not but marvel at his skill. If he had not once spent an evening with Chotas at a party in the British Embassy, Fraser too would have been deceived by the man's manner. He could see the jurors helpfully straining forward to catch the words that fell softly from Napoleon Chotas' lips.

"This woman on trial," Chotas was saying to the jurors, "is not being tried for murder. There has been no murder. If there *had* been a murder, I am sure that my brilliant colleague for the State would have been good enough to have shown us the body of the victim. He has not done so, so we must assume that there is no body. And therefore no murder." He stopped to scratch the crown of his head and looked down at the floor as though trying to remember where he had left off. He nodded to himself, then looked up at the jury. "No, gentlemen, that is not what this trial is about. My client is being tried because she broke *another* law, an unwritten law that says you must not fornicate with another woman's husband. The press has already found her guilty of that charge, and the public has found her guilty, and now they are demanding that she be punished."

Chotas stopped to pull out a large white handkerchief, stared at it a moment as if wondering how it had gotten there, blew his nose and replaced the handkerchief in his pocket. "Very well. If she has broken a law, let us punish her. But not for murder, gentlemen. Not for a murder that was never committed. Noelle Page was guilty of being the mistress of—" he paused delicately "—a most important man. His name is a secret, but if you must know it, you can find it on the front page of any newspaper."

There was appreciative laughter from the spectators.

Auguste Lanchon swung around in his seat and glared at the spectators, his little piggy eyes blazing with rage. How dare they laugh at his Noelle! Demiris meant nothing to her, nothing. It was the man to whom a woman gave up her virginity that she always cherished. The fat little shopkeeper from Marseille had not been able to communicate with Noelle yet, but he had paid four hundred precious drachmas for a courtroom pass, and he would be able to watch his beloved Noelle every day. When she was acquitted, Lanchon would step forward and take over her life. He turned his attention to the lawyer.

"It has been said by the prosecution that the two defendants, Miss Page and Mr. Lawrence Douglas, murdered Mr. Douglas' wife so that the defendants could marry each other. Look at them."

Chotas turned to look at Noelle Page and Larry Douglas and every eye in the courtroom did the same.

"Are they in love with each other? Possibly. But does that make them plotters and schemers and murderers? No. If there are any victims in this trial, you are looking at them now. I have gone into all the evidence very carefully and I have convinced myself, as I will convince you, that these two people are innocent. Please let me make it clear to the jury that I am not representing Lawrence Douglas. He has his own coun-

sel and a very able fellow he is. But it has been alleged
by the state that the two people sitting there are fellow
conspirators, that they have plotted and committed
murder together. So if one is guilty, both are guilty. I
tell you now that both are innocent. And nothing less
than the corpus delicti will make me change my mind.
And there is none."

Chotas' voice was growing angrier. "It is a fiction.
My client has no more idea than you do whether
Catherine Douglas is dead or alive. How would she
know? She has never even met her, let alone harmed
her. Imagine the enormity of being accused of killing
someone you have never laid eyes on. There are many
theories as to what could have happened to Mrs.
Douglas. That she was murdered is one of them. But
only one. The most probable theory is that somehow
she discovered that her husband and Miss Page were in
love, and out of a feeling of hurt—not fear, gentlemen—*hurt,* she ran away. It is as simple as that, and
for that you do not execute an innocent woman and an
innocent man."

Frederick Stavros, Larry Douglas' attorney, gave a
surreptitious sigh of relief. His constant nightmare had
been that Noelle Page would be acquitted, while his
client would be convicted. If that happened he would
become the laughing-stock of the legal profession.
Stavros had been looking for a way to hitch onto
Napoleon Chotas' star and now Chotas had done it for
him. By linking the two defendants together as he had
just done, Noelle's defense had become his own client's
defense. Winning this trial was going to change Frederick Stavros' entire future, give him everything he had
ever wanted. He was filled with a feeling of warm gratitude for the old master.

Stavros noted with satisfaction that the jury was
hanging on Chotas' every word.

"This was not a woman who was interested in material things," Chotas was saying with admiration. "She

was willing to give everything up without hesitation for the man she loved. Surely, my good friends, that is not the character of a scheming, conniving murderess."

As Chotas went on, the emotions of the jurors shifted like a visible tide, reaching out toward Noelle Page with growing empathy and understanding. Slowly and skillfully the attorney built up a portrait of a beautiful woman who was the mistress of one of the most powerful and richest men in the world, who had every luxury and privilege lavished upon her, but who in the end had succumbed to her love for a penniless young pilot she had only known a short time.

Chotas played on the emotions of the jurors like a master musician, making them laugh, bringing tears to their eyes and always holding their rapt attention. When his opening address was over, Chotas clumsily shuffled back to the long table and awkwardly sat down, and it was all that the spectators could do to keep from applauding.

Larry Douglas sat in the witness box listening to Chotas' defense of him, and Larry was furious. He did not need anyone to defend him. He had done nothing wrong, this whole trial was a stupid mistake, and if there was any blame it was Noelle's. It had all been her idea. Larry looked at her now, beautiful and serene. But he felt no stirring of desire, only the memory of a passion, a faint emotional shadow, and he marveled that he had put his life in jeopardy for this woman. Larry's eyes swung toward the press box. An attractive girl reporter in her twenties was staring at him. He gave her a little smile and watched her face light up.

Peter Demonides was examining a witness.
"Would you please tell the Court your name?"
"Alexis Minos."
"And your occupation?"
"I am an attorney."

"Would you look at the two defendants seated in the defendant's box, Mr. Minos, and tell the Court if you have ever seen either of them before?"

"Yes, sir. One of them."

"Which one?"

"The man."

"Mr. Lawrence Douglas?"

"That's correct."

"Would you tell us, please, under what circumstances you saw Mr. Douglas?"

"He came to my office six months ago."

"Did he come to consult you in your professional capacity?"

"Yes."

"In other words he required some legal service of you?"

"Yes."

"And would you please tell us what it was that he wanted you to do for him?"

"He asked me to get him a divorce."

"And did he retain you for this purpose?"

"No. When he explained the circumstances to me, I told him it would be impossible for him to get a divorce in Greece."

"And what were the circumstances?"

"First of all he said there must not be any publicity, and secondly he said that his wife refused to give him a divorce."

"In other words he had asked his wife for a divorce and she had refused?"

"That is what he told me."

"And you explained to him that you couldn't help him? That unless his wife was willing to give him a divorce, it would be difficult or impossible for him to obtain one, and that there very well might be publicity?"

"That is correct."

"So, short of taking desperate measures, there was nothing the defendant could—"

"Objection!"

"Sustained."

"Your witness."

Napoleon Chotas lifted himself out of his chair with a sigh and slowly walked over to the witness. Peter Demonides was not worried. Minos was a lawyer and too experienced to be deceived by Chotas' forensic bag of tricks.

"You're an attorney, Mr. Minos."

"I am."

"And an excellent one, I'm sure. I'm surprised that our professional paths have not crossed sooner. The firm I'm with deals in many branches of law. Perhaps you've run across one of my partners in some corporate litigation?"

"No. I don't do corporate work."

"I beg your pardon. Perhaps in some tax case, then?"

"I am not a tax lawyer."

"Oh." Chotas was beginning to look puzzled and ill-at-ease, as though he was making a fool of himself. "Securities?"

"No." Minos was beginning to enjoy the lawyer's humiliation. His face took on a smug look and Peter Demonides began to worry. How many times had he seen that look on the faces of witnesses that Napoleon Chotas was preparing for the slaughter?

Chotas was scratching his head in bafflement. "I give up," he said ingenuously. "What kind of law do you specialize in?"

"Divorce cases." The answer was a barbed shaft, perfectly delivered.

A rueful look appeared on Chotas' face and he shook his head. "I should have known my good friend Mr. Demonides would have an expert up here."

"Thank you, sir." Alexis Minos made no attempt to conceal his smugness now. Not every witness got a chance to score off Chotas and in Minos' mind he was already embellishing the story to tell at the club that evening.

"I've never even handled a divorce case," Chotas was confiding in an embarrassed voice, "so I'll have to defer to your expertise."

The old lawyer was caving in completely. It would make an even better story than Minos had anticipated.

"I'll bet you keep very busy," Chotas said.

"I have as many cases as I can handle."

"As many as you can handle!" There was open admiration in Napoleon Chotas' voice.

"Sometimes more."

Peter Demonides looked down at the floor, unable to watch what was happening.

Chotas' voice took on an awed tone. "I don't want to pry into your personal business, Mr. Minos, but as a matter of professional curiosity, how many clients would you say walk through your door in a year?"

"Well, that's pretty difficult to say."

"Come on now, Mr. Minos. Don't be modest. Make a guess."

"Oh, I suppose two hundred. That's an approximation, you understand."

"Two hundred divorces a year! The paper work alone must be staggering."

"Well, there aren't actually two hundred divorces."

Chotas rubbed his chin, perplexed. "What?"

"They're not *all* divorces."

A puzzled look came over Chotas' face. "Didn't you say that you only handled divorce cases?"

"Yes, but—" Minos' voice wavered.

"But what?" Chotas asked in bewilderment.

"Well, what I mean is, they don't all get divorced."

"But isn't that why they come to see you?"

"Yes, but some of them—well—change their minds for one reason or another."

Chotas nodded in sudden understanding. "Ah! You mean there's a reconciliation or something of the sort?"

"Exactly," Minos said.

"So that what you're saying is that—what?—ten percent don't bother to go through with the divorce action?"

Minos shifted in his chair uneasily. "The percentage is a bit higher."

"How much higher? Fifteen percent? Twenty?"

"Closer to forty."

Napoleon Chotas stared at him in amazement. "Mr. Minos, are you telling us that almost half the people who come to see you decide not to get a divorce?"

"Yes."

Tiny beads of sweat were popping out on Minos' forehead. He turned to look at Peter Demonides, but Demonides was studiously concentrating on a crack in the floor.

"Well, I'm sure it's not a lack of confidence in your ability," said Chotas.

"Certainly not," Minos said defensively. "They very often come to me on a stupid impulse. A husband or wife will have a fight and feel they hate each other and think they want a divorce, but when you come right down to it, in most cases they change their minds."

He stopped abruptly as he realized the full import of his words.

"Thank you," Chotas said gently. "You've been most helpful."

Peter Demonides was examining the witness.

"Your name, please?"

"Kasta. Irene Kasta."

"Miss or Mrs.?"

"Mrs. I'm a widow."

"What is your occupation, Mrs. Kasta?"

"I'm a housekeeper."

"Where do you work?"

"For a rich family in Rafina."

"That's a village near the sea, is it not? A hundred kilometers north of Athens?"

"Yes."

"Would you please take a look at the two defendants seated at the table? Have you ever seen them before?"

"Sure. Lots of times."

"Would you tell us under what circumstances?"

"They live in the house next to the villa where I work. I seen them on the beach a lot. They was naked."

There was a gasp from the spectators and then a quick buzz of conversation. Peter Demonides glanced over at Chotas to see if he was going to object, but the old lawyer sat at the table, a dreamy smile on his face. The smile made Demonides more nervous than ever. He turned back to the witness.

"You are certain that these are the two people you saw? You are under oath, you know."

"Them's the two, all right."

"When they were together on the beach, did they seem friendly?"

"Well, they didn't act like brother and sister."

A laugh from the spectators.

"Thank you, Mrs. Kasta." Demonides turned to Chotas. "Your witness."

Napoleon Chotas nodded amiably and rose and ambled over to the formidable-looking woman in the witness box.

"How long have you worked at this villa, Mrs. Kasta?"

"Seven years."

"Seven years! You must be very good at your job."

"You bet I am."

"Perhaps you could recommend a good housekeeper for me. I've been thinking about buying a place on the beach at Rafina. My problem is, I need privacy so I can work. As I remember those villas, they're all bunched together."

"Oh, no, sir. Each villa is separated by a big wall."

"Oh, good. And they're not crowded next to one another?"

"No, sir, not at all. Those villas are at least a hundred yards away from each other. I know one that's up for sale. You'd have all the privacy you need and I can recommend my sister to do the housekeeping for you. She's good and she's tidy and she cooks a bit."

"Well, thank you, Mrs. Kasta, that sounds wonderful. Perhaps I could call her this afternoon."

"She does a bit of day work. She'll be home at six."

"What time is it now?"

"I don't carry a watch."

"Ah. There's a large clock on the wall over there. What does it say?"

"Well, it's hard to make out. It's clear across the room."

"How far away would you say that clock was?"

"About—er—fifty feet."

"Twenty-three feet, Mrs. Kasta. No more questions."

It was the fifth day of the trial. Doctor Israel Katz's missing leg was paining him again. While he was performing an operation, he could stand on his artificial leg for hours on end, and it never bothered him. But sitting here without the intense concentration to divert his attention, the nerve ends kept sending memory messages to a limb that was no longer there. Katz shifted restlessly in his seat, trying to ease the pressure on his hip. He had tried to see Noelle every day since he had arrived in Athens but with no success. He had spoken to Napoleon Chotas, and the lawyer had explained that Noelle was too upset to see old friends and that it would be best to wait until the trial was over. Israel Katz had asked him to tell Noelle that he was here to help her in every way he could, but he could not be certain that she ever received the message. He had sat in court day after day, hoping Noelle would look his way, but she never even glanced at the spectators.

Israel Katz owed his life to her, and he felt frustrated because there was no way he could help repay that debt. He had no idea how the trial was going or whether Noelle would be convicted or acquitted. Chotas was good. If any man in the world could free Noelle it was he. Yet somehow Israel Katz was filled with unease. The trial was far from over. There could still be some surprises ahead.

A witness for the prosecution was being sworn in.

"Your name?"

"Christian Barbet."

"You are a French national, Mr. Barbet?"

"Yes."

"And where is your residence?"

"In Paris."

"Would you tell the Court your occupation?"

"I am the owner of a private detective agency."

"And where is that agency located?"

"The main office is in Paris."

"What kind of cases do you handle?"

"Many kinds . . . commercial pilfering, missing persons, surveillance for jealous husbands or wives. . . ."

"Monsieur Barbet, would you be good enough to look around this courtroom and tell us whether anyone in this room has ever been a client of yours?"

A long, slow look around the room. "Yes, sir."

"Would you tell the Court who this person is, please?"

"The lady sitting over there. Miss Noelle Page."

A murmur of interest from the spectators.

"Are you telling us that Miss Page hired you to do some detective work for her?"

"I am, monsieur."

"And would you tell us exactly what that work consisted of?"

"Yes, sir. She was interested in a man named Larry Douglas. She wanted me to find out everything I could about him."

"That is the same Larry Douglas who is on trial in this courtroom?"

"Yes, sir."

"And Miss Page paid you for this?"

"Yes, sir."

"Would you please look at these exhibits in my hand. Are these the records of the payments that were made to you?"

"That is correct."

"Tell us, Monsieur Barbet, how did you go about obtaining this information on Mr. Douglas?"

"It was very difficult, monsieur. You see I was in France, and Mr. Douglas was in England and later the United States, and with France occupied by the Germans—"

"I beg your pardon?"

"I said, with France occupied—"

"Just a moment. I want to be sure that I understand what you are saying, Monsieur Barbet. We have been told by Miss Page's attorney that she and Larry Douglas met a few short months ago and fell madly in love. Now you are telling this Court that their love affair started—how long ago?"

"At least six years ago."

Pandemonium.

Demonides flashed Chotas a triumphant look. "Your witness."

Napoleon Chotas rubbed his eyes, rose from the long table at which he was sitting and walked over to the witness box.

"I won't detain you long, Mr. Barbet. I know you must be anxious to get back to your family in France."

"You may take your time, monsieur." Smugly.

"Thank you. Forgive me for being personal, but that's certainly a fine-looking suit you're wearing, Mr. Barbet."

"Thank you, monsieur."

"Made in Paris, was it?"

"Yes, sir."

"It fits beautifully. I don't seem to have any luck with my suits. Have you ever tried the English tailors? They're supposed to be excellent, also."

"No, monsieur."

"I'm sure you've been to England many times?"

"Well—no."

"Never?"

"No, sir."

"Have you ever been to the United States of America?"

"No."

"Never?"

"No, sir."

"Have you ever visited the South Pacific?"

"No, sir."

"Then you must truly be a fantastic detective, Mr. Barbet. My hat is off to you. These reports of yours cover the activities of Larry Douglas in England and the United States and the South Pacific—and yet you tell us that you have never even been to any of these places. I can only assume that you are psychic."

"Permit me to correct you, monsieur. It was not necessary for me to have been in any of those places. I employ what we call correspondent agencies in England and in America."

"Ah, forgive my stupidity. Of course! So it was actually *those* people who covered the activities of Mr. Douglas?"

"Exactement."

"And so the fact is that you yourself have no personal knowledge of Larry Douglas' movements."

"Well . . . no, sir."

"So in reality all your information is secondhand."

"I suppose . . . in a sense, yes."

Chotas turned to the judges. "I move to strike the entire testimony of this witness, Your Honors, on the grounds that it is hearsay."

Peter Demonides leaped to his feet. "Objection, Your Honors! Noelle Page hired Mr. Barbet to get information on Larry Douglas. That is not hearsay—"

"My learned colleague has submitted the records as

evidence," Chotas said gently. "I am perfectly willing to accept it—if he wishes to bring the men here who actually conducted the surveillance of Mr. Douglas. Otherwise I must ask the Court to assume that there was no such surveillance and ask that the testimony of this witness be held inadmissible."

The President of the Court turned to Demonides. "Are you prepared to bring your witnesses here?" he asked.

"That's impossible," Peter Demonides spluttered. "Mr. Chotas knows that it would take weeks to locate them!"

The President turned to Chotas. "Motion granted."

Peter Demonides was examining.

"Would you state your name, please?"

"George Mousson."

"What is your occupation?"

"I am a reception clerk at the Palace Hotel at Ioannina."

"Would you please take a look at the two defendants sitting at the table. Have you ever seen them before?"

"The man. He was a guest at the hotel last August."

"That would be Mr. Lawrence Douglas?"

"Yes, sir."

"Was he alone when he checked into the hotel?"

"No, sir."

"Would you tell us who he was with?"

"His wife."

"Catherine Douglas?"

"Yes, sir."

"They registered as Mr. and Mrs. Douglas?"

"Yes, sir."

"Did you and Mr. Douglas ever discuss the Caves of Perama?"

"Yes, sir, we did."

"Did you bring up the subject or did Mr. Douglas?"

"As I recall, he did. He asked me about them and

said his wife was anxious for him to take her there. That she loved caves. I thought that was unusual."

"Oh? Why was that?"

"Well, women aren't interested in exploring and things like that."

"You didn't happen to discuss the caves with Mrs. Douglas at any time, did you?"

"No, sir. Only with Mr. Douglas."

"And what did you tell him?"

"Well, I remember telling him that the caves could be dangerous."

"Was anything said about a guide?"

The clerk nodded. "Yes, I'm sure I suggested that he use a guide. I recommend one to all our guests."

"No more questions. Your witness, Mr. Chotas."

"How long have you been in the hotel business, Mr. Mousson?"

"Over twenty years."

"And before that you were a psychiatrist?"

"Me? No, sir."

"A psychologist perhaps?"

"No, sir."

"Oh. Then you're *not* an expert on the behavior of women?"

"Well, I may not be a psychiatrist, but in the hotel business you learn a lot about women."

"Do you know who Osa Johnson is?"

"Osa—? No."

"She's a world famous explorer. Have you ever heard of Amelia Earhart?"

"No, sir."

"Margaret Mead?"

"No, sir."

"Are you married, Mr. Mousson?"

"Not now. But I've been married three times, so I *am* something of an expert on women."

"On the contrary, Mr. Mousson. I suggest that if you

were really an expert on women, you would have been able to handle *one* marriage. No further questions."

"Your name, please?"

"Christopher Cocyannis."

"Would you tell us your occupation?"

"I am a guide at the Caves of Perama."

"How long have you been a guide there?"

"Ten years."

"Is business good?"

"Very good. Thousands of tourists come to see the caves every year."

"Would you please look at the man sitting over in that box. Have you ever seen Mr. Douglas before?"

"Yes, sir. He came to the caves in August."

"Are you sure?"

"Positive."

"Well now, I'm sure that puzzles all of us, Mr. Cocyannis. Out of all the thousands of people who come to the caves, you can remember one individual?"

"I'm not likely to forget him."

"Why is that, Mr. Cocyannis?"

"First of all he wouldn't take a guide."

"Do all of your visitors take guides?"

"The Germans and the French are too stingy, but all the Americans do."

Laughter.

"I see. Was there any other reason you remembered Mr. Douglas?"

"You bet there was. I wouldn't have noticed him especially except for the guide thing, and the woman with him seemed kind of embarrassed when he said no. Then about an hour later, I saw him hurry out of the entrance, and he was alone and he seemed awfully upset, and I thought maybe the woman had had an accident or something. I went up to him and asked if the lady was all right and he stared at me kind of funny and said, 'What lady?' and I said, 'The lady you took in the caves with you.' And he turned kind of white and I thought he was going to hit me. Then he started yelling, 'I've lost her. I need help,' and he began carrying on like a crazy man."

"But he didn't call for help until you asked where the missing woman was?"

"That's right."

"What happened next?"

"Well, I organized the other guides and we began a search. Some damned fool had moved the Danger sign from the new section. That's not open to the public. That's where we finally found her about three hours later. She was in pretty bad shape."

"One last question. And answer this very carefully. When Mr. Douglas first came out of the cave, was he looking around for someone to help him, or did you get the impression that he was leaving?"

"He was leaving."

"Your witness."

Napoleon Chotas' voice was very gentle.

"Mr. Cocyannis, are you a psychiatrist?"

"No, sir. I'm a guide."

"And you're not psychic?"

"No, sir."

"I ask this because over the past week, we've had hotel clerks who are experts on human psychology, eyewitnesses who are nearsighted, and now you tell us that you can look at a man who attracted your attention because he seemed agitated, and you can read his mind. How did you *know* he wasn't looking for help when you went up and spoke to him?"

"He didn't look like it."

"And you can remember his behavior that well?"

"That's right."

"You obviously have a remarkable memory. I want you to look around the courtroom. Have you ever seen anyone in this room before today?"

"The defendant."

"Yes. Aside from him? Take your time."

"No."

"If you had, you would have remembered?"

"Absolutely."

"Have you ever seen me before today?"

"No, sir."

"Would you look at this piece of paper, please. Can you tell me what it is?"

"It's a ticket."

"To what?"

"The Caves of Perama."

"And the date on it?"

"Monday. Three weeks ago."

"Yes. That ticket was purchased and used by me, Mr. Cocyannis. There were five others in my party. You were our guide. No further questions."

"What is your occupation?"

"I'm a bellboy at the Palace Hotel in Ioannina."

"Would you please look at the defendant seated in the defendant's box. Have you ever seen her before?"

"Yes, sir. In movies."

"Did you ever see her in person before today?"

"Yes, sir. She came into the hotel and asked me what room Mr. Douglas was staying in. I told her she'd have to inquire at the desk and she said she preferred not to bother them, so I gave her the number of his bungalow."

"And this was when?"

"The first day of August. The day of the *meltemi*."

"And are you sure that this is the same woman?"

"How could I forget her? She tipped me two hundred drachmas."

The trial was going into its fourth week. Everyone agreed that Napoleon Chotas was conducting the best defense they had ever witnessed. But in spite of this the web of guilt was being woven tighter and tighter.

Peter Demonides was building up a picture of two lovers, desperate to be together, to be married, with only Catherine Douglas standing in their way. Slowly day by day, Demonides elaborated on the plot to murder her.

Larry Douglas' attorney, Frederick Stavros, had gladly abdicated his position and relied on Napoleon Chotas. But now even Stavros began to feel that it would take a miracle to get an acquittal. Stavros stared at the empty chair in the packed courtroom and wondered if Constantin Demiris was really going to make an appearance. If Noelle Page was convicted, the Greek tycoon would probably not come, for it would mean that he had been defeated. On the other hand, if the tycoon knew there would be an acquittal, he would probably show up. The empty chair was becoming a symbol of which way the trial would go.

The seat remained empty.

It was on a Friday afternoon that the case finally exploded.

"Would you state your name, please?"

"Doctor Kazomides. John Kazomides."

"Did you ever meet Mr. or Mrs. Douglas, Doctor?"

"Yes, sir. Both of them."

"What was the occasion?"

"I got a call to come to the Caves of Perama. A woman had been lost in there, and when the search party finally found her, she was in a state of shock."

"Had she been hurt physically?"

"Yes. There were multiple contusions. Her hands and arms and cheeks had been badly scraped on the rocks. She had fallen down and hit her head, and I diagnosed a probable concussion. I immediately gave her a shot of morphine for the pain and ordered them to take her to the local hospital."

"And is that where she went?"

"No, sir."

"Would you tell the jury why not?"

"At her husband's insistence she was taken back to their bungalow at the Palace Hotel."

"Did that strike you as peculiar, Doctor?"

"He said he wanted to look after her himself."

"So Mrs. Douglas was taken back to her hotel. Did you accompany her there?"

"Yes. I insisted on going back to her bungalow with her. I wanted to be at her bedside when she awakened."

"And were you there when she awakened?"

"Yes, sir."

"Did Mrs. Douglas say anything to you?"

"She did."

"Would you tell the Court what she said."

"She told me that her husband had tried to murder her."

It was a full five minutes before they could quiet the uproar in the courtroom, and it was not until the President threatened to clear the room that the hubbub finally subsided. Napoleon Chotas had walked over to the defendant's box and was holding a hurried conference with Noelle Page. For the first time she seemed upset. Demonides was going on with the questioning.

"Doctor, you said in your testimony that Mrs. Douglas was in shock. In your professional opinion was she lucid when she told you that her husband tried to murder her?"

"Yes, sir. I had already given her one sedative at the caves, and she was relatively calm. However when I told her I was going to give her another sedative, she became extremely agitated and begged me not to."

The President of the Court leaned down and asked, "Did she explain why?"

"Yes, Your Honor. She said that her husband would kill her while she was asleep."

The President leaned back in his chair thoughtfully and said to Peter Demonides, "You may continue."

"Dr. Kazomides, did you in fact administer a second sedative to Mrs. Douglas?"

"Yes."

"While she was in her bed at the bungalow?"

"Yes."

"How did you administer it?"

"By hypodermic. In the hip."

"And she was asleep when you left?"

"Yes."

"Was there any chance Mrs. Douglas could have awakened any time in the next few hours, gotten out of bed without assistance, dressed herself and walked out of that house unaided?"

"In her condition? No. It would be most unlikely. She was very heavily sedated."

"That is all, thank you, Doctor."

The jurors were staring at Noelle Page and Larry Douglas and their faces had turned cold and unfriendly. A stranger could have walked into that courtroom and known instantly how the case was going.

Bill Fraser's eyes were bright with satisfaction. After Dr. Kazomides' testimony there could no longer be the slightest doubt that Catherine had been murdered by Larry Douglas and Noelle Page. There was nothing Napoleon Chotas would be able to do to eradicate from the minds of the jurors the image of a terrified woman, drugged and defenseless, begging not to be left in the hands of her murderer.

Frederick Stavros was in a panic. He had gladly let Napoleon Chotas run the show, following his lead in blind faith, confident that Chotas would be able to secure an acquittal for his client and therefore for Stavros' client. Now he felt betrayed. Everything was falling apart. The doctor's testimony had been irreparably damaging, both for its evidential and its emotional impact. Stavros looked around the room. Except for the one mysteriously reserved seat the room was filled. The world press was here, waiting to report what happened next.

Stavros had a momentary vision of himself leaping to his feet, confronting the doctor and brilliantly tearing his testimony to shreds. His client would be acquitted and he, Stavros, would be a hero. He knew this would be his last chance. The outcome of this case would mean the difference between fame and obscurity. Stavros could actually feel his thigh muscles bunching up, urging him to get to his feet. But he could not move. He sat there, paralyzed by the overpowering specter of failure. He turned to look at Chotas. The deep, sad eyes in the bloodhound face were studying the doctor on the witness stand, as though trying to come to some decision.

Slowly Napoleon Chotas rose to his feet. But instead of walking over to the witness, he moved toward the bench and quietly addressed the judges.

"Mr. President, Your Honors, I do not wish to cross-examine the witness. With the Court's permission, I would like to ask for a recess in order to confer *in camera* with the Court and the Prosecuting Attorney."

The President of the Court turned to the Prosecutor. "Mr. Demonides?"

"No objection," Demonides said, his voice wary.

The Court was recessed. Not one person moved from his chair.

Thirty minutes later Napoleon Chotas returned to the courtroom alone. The instant he walked through the chamber door, everyone in the courtroom sensed that something important had taken place. There was an air of secret self-satisfaction in the lawyer's face, his walk was faster and springier, as though some charade had ended and it was no longer necessary to play games. Chotas walked over to the defendant's box and stared down at Noelle. She looked up into his face, her violet eyes probing, anxious. And suddenly a smile touched the lawyer's lips, and from the light in his eyes Noelle knew that somehow he had done it, he had performed the miracle in spite of all the evidence, in spite of all the odds. Justice had triumphed, but it was the Justice of Constantin Demiris. Larry Douglas was staring at Chotas, too, filled with fear and with hope.

Whatever Chotas had done would have been for Noelle. But what about him?

Chotas addressed Noelle in a carefully neutral voice.
"The President of the Court has given me permission
to speak with you in his chambers." He turned to Frederick Stavros, who was sitting in an agony of uncer-
tainty, not knowing what was going on. "You and
your client have permission to join u₃ if you wish."

Stavros nodded. "Of course." He scrambled to his
feet, almost knocking over his chair in his eagerness.

Two bailiffs accompanied them to the empty chambers of the President. When the bailiffs had left and
they were alone, Chotas turned to Frederick Stavros.
"What I am about to say," he said quietly, "is for the
benefit of my client. However, because they are co-
defendants, I have been able to arrange for your
client to be accorded the same privilege as mine."

"Tell me!" Noelle demanded.

Chotas turned to her. He spoke slowly, choosing his
words with great care. "I have just had a conference
with the judges," he said. "They were impressed with
the case the prosecution has made against you. However—" he paused, delicately, "I was able to—er—
persuade them that the interests of justice would not
be served by punishing you."

"What's going to happen?" Stavros demanded in a fe-
ver of impatience.

There was a note of deep satisfaction in Chotas'
voice as he continued, "If the defendants are willing to
change their pleas to guilty, the judges have agreed to
give each of them a five-year sentence." He smiled and
added, "Four years of which will be suspended. In reality they will not have to serve more than six months."
He turned to Larry. "Because you are an American,
Mr. Douglas, you will be deported. You will never be
permitted to return to Greece."

Larry nodded, his body flooding with relief.

Chotas turned back to Noelle. "This was not an easy
thing to accomplish. I must tell you in all honesty that

the primary reason for the leniency of the Court is the interest of your—er—patron. They feel he has already suffered unduly because of all this publicity, and they are anxious to see it ended."

"I understand," Noelle said.

Napoleon Chotas hesitated in embarrassment. "There is one more condition."

She looked at him. "Yes?"

"Your passport will be taken away. You will never be permitted to leave Greece. You will remain here under the protection of your friend."

So it had been done.

Constantin Demiris had kept his bargain. Noelle did not for a moment believe that the judges were being lenient because they were concerned about Demiris' being subjected to unpleasant publicity. No, he had had to pay a price for her freedom, and Noelle knew that it must have been a heavy one. But in return Demiris was getting her back and arranging it so that she could never leave him. Or see Larry again. She turned to Larry and read the relief in his face. He was going to be set free, and that was all he cared about. There was no regret about losing her and about what had happened. But Noelle understood it because she understood Larry, for he was her alter ego, her *Doppelgänger,* and they both had the same reckless zest for life, the same insatiable appetites. They were kindred spirits beyond mortality, beyond laws they had never made and never lived by. In her way Noelle would miss Larry very much, and when he left, a part of her would go with him. But she knew now how precious her life was to her and how terrified she had been of losing it. And so on balance it was a very good bargain, and she accepted it gratefully. She turned to Chotas and said, "That is satisfactory."

Chotas looked at her, and there was a sadness in his eyes as well as the satisfaction. Noelle understood that, too. He was in love with her and had had to use all his skill to save her for another man. Noelle had deliberately encouraged Chotas to fall in love with her because she needed him, needed to make sure that he would stop at nothing to save her. And everything had worked out.

"I think it's absolutely marvelous," Frederick Stavros was babbling. "Absolutely marvelous."

In truth Stavros felt that it was a miracle, nearly as good as an acquittal, and while it was true that Napoleon Chotas would reap most of the benefit from it, the peripheral fallout would still be tremendous. From this moment on Stavros would have his choice of clients, and each time he told the story of the trial, his role in it would get bigger and bigger.

"It sounds like a good deal," Larry was saying. "The only thing is, we're not guilty. We didn't kill Catherine."

Frederick Stavros turned on him in a fury. "Who gives a damn whether you're guilty or not?" he shouted. "We're making you a present of your life." He shot a quick glance at Chotas to see if he had reacted to the "we" but the lawyer was listening, his attitude one of aloof neutrality.

"I want you to understand," Chotas said to Stavros, "that I am only advising *my* client. Your client is free to make his own decision."

"What would have happened to us without this deal?" Larry asked.

"The jury would have—" Frederick Stavros began.

"I want to hear it from *him*," Larry interrupted, curtly. He turned to Chotas.

"In a trial, Mr. Douglas," Chotas replied, "the most important factor is not innocence or guilt, but the *impression* of innocence or guilt. There is no absolute truth, there is only the interpretation of truth. In this case it does not matter whether you are innocent of murder, the jury has the *impression* of guilt. That is what you would have been convicted for, and in the end you would have been just as dead."

Larry looked at him for a long moment, then nodded. "OK," he said. "Let's get it over with."

Fifteen minutes later the two defendants stood before the judges' bench. The President of the Court was seated in the center, flanked by the two justices. Napoleon Chotas stood next to Noelle Page and Frederick Stavros stood at the side of Larry Douglas. The courtroom was charged with an electric tension, for word had flashed about the room that a dramatic development was about to take place. But when it came, it caught everyone completely off guard. In a formal, pedantic voice, as though he had not just made a secret bargain with the three jurists on the bench, Napoleon Chotas said, "Mr. President, Your Honors, my client wishes to change her plea from *not guilty* to *guilty.*"

The President of the Court leaned back in his chair and stared at Chotas in surprise, as though he were hearing the news for the first time.

He's playing it to the hilt, Noelle thought. *He wants to earn his money, or whatever it is Demiris is paying him off with.*

The President leaned forward and consulted with the other justices in a flurry of whispers. They nodded and the President looked down at Noelle and said, "Do you wish to change your plea to guilty?"

Noelle nodded and said firmly, "I do."

Frederick Stavros spoke up quickly, as though afraid of being left out of the procedure. "Your Honors, my client wishes to change his plea from not guilty to guilty."

The President turned to regard Larry. "Do you wish to change your plea to guilty?"

Larry glanced at Chotas and then nodded. "Yes."

The President studied the two prisoners, his face grave. "Have your attorneys advised you that under Greek law the penalty for the crime of premeditated murder is execution?"

"Yes, Your Honor." Noelle's voice was strong and clear.

The President turned to look at Larry.

"Yes, sir," he said.

There was another whispered consultation among the judges. The President of the Court turned to Demonides. "Does the Prosecutor for the State have any objections to the change of plea?"

Demonides looked at Chotas a long moment, then said, "None."

Noelle wondered if he were in on the payoff also, or whether he was simply being used as a pawn.

"Very well," the President said. "This Court has no choice but to accept the change of plea." He turned to the jury. "Gentlemen, in view of this new development, you are herewith released from your duties as jurymen. In effect the trial has come to an end. The Court will pass sentence. Thank you for your services and for your cooperation. The Court will recess for two hours."

In the next moment the reporters began to tumble out of the room, racing to their telephones and teletype machines to report the latest sensational development in the murder trial of Noelle Page and Larry Douglas.

Two hours later the courtroom was packed to overflowing as the Court was reconvened. Noelle glanced around the courtroom at the faces of the spectators. They were watching her with expressions of eager expectation, and it was all Noelle could do to keep from laughing aloud at their naïveté. These were the common people, the masses, and they really believed that justice was meted out fairly, that under a democracy all men were created equal, that a poor man had the same rights and privileges as a rich man.

"Will the defendants now rise and approach the bench?"

Gracefully Noelle rose to her feet and moved toward

the bench, Chotas at her side. Out of the corner of her eye she saw Larry and Stavros stepping forward.

The President of the Court spoke. "This has been a long and difficult trial," he began. "In capital cases where there is a reasonable doubt of guilt, the Court is always inclined to let the accused have the benefit of the doubt. I must admit that in this case we felt that there existed such a doubt. The fact that the State was unable to produce a *corpus delicti* was a very strong point in favor of the defendants." He turned to look at Napoleon Chotas. "I am sure that the able counsel for the defense is well aware that the Greek Courts have never given the death penalty in a case where a murder has not been definitely proven to have been committed."

A faint sense of unease was beginning to brush Noelle, nothing alarming yet, just the merest whisper, the slightest hint. The President was going on.

"My colleagues and I were, for that reason, frankly surprised when the defendants decided to change their pleas to guilty, in mid-trial."

The feeling was in the pit of Noelle's stomach now, growing, moving upward, beginning to constrict her throat, so that she was suddenly finding it difficult to breathe. Larry was staring at the judge, not fully comprehending yet what was happening.

"We appreciate the agonizing soul-searching that must have taken place before the defendants decided to confess their guilt before this Court and before the world. However, the easing of their consciences cannot be accepted as atonement for the terrible crime they have admitted committing, the cold-blooded murder of a helpless, defenseless woman."

It was at that moment that Noelle knew, with a sudden, mind-smashing certainty that she had been tricked. Demiris had set up a charade to lull her into a feeling of false security so that he could do this to her. This was his game, this was the trap he had baited. He

had known how terrified she was of dying, so he had
held out the hope of life to her and she had accepted it,
had believed him, and he had outwitted her. Demiris
had wanted his vengeance *now,* not later. Her life
could have been saved. Of course Chotas had known
that she would not get the death penalty unless a
corpse was produced. He had made no deal with the
judges. Chotas had rigged this whole defense to lure
Noelle to her death. She turned to look at him. He
looked up to meet her gaze, and his eyes were filled
with a genuine sadness. He loved her and he had murdered her, and if he had it to do over again, he would
do the same thing, for in the end he was Demiris' man,
just as she was Demiris' woman, and neither of them
could fight his power.

The President was speaking. ". . . and so under the
powers invested in me by the State, and in accord with
its laws, I pronounce that the sentence on the two defendants, Noelle Page and Lawrence Douglas shall be
execution by a firing squad. . . . the sentence to be
carried out within ninety days from this date."

The Court was in pandemonium, but Noelle neither
heard nor saw it. Something had made her turn
around. The vacant seat was no longer empty. Constantin Demiris sat in it. He was freshly shaved and
barbered. He was dressed in a blue raw-silk suit,
flawlessly tailored, a light blue shirt, and a foulard tie.
His olive black eyes were bright and alive. There was
no sign of the defeated, crumbling man who had come
to visit her in prison, because that man had never existed.

Constantin Demiris had come to watch Noelle in the
moment of her defeat, savoring the terror in her. His
black eyes were locked on hers and for one split instant
she saw in them a deep, malevolent satisfaction. And
there was something else. Regret, perhaps, but it was
gone before she could capture it, and it was all too late
now anyway.

The chess game was finally over.

Larry had listened to the President's last words in shocked disbelief, and when a bailiff stepped forward and took him by the arm, Larry shook loose and turned back to the bench.

"Wait a minute!" he yelled. "I didn't kill her! They framed me!"

Another bailiff hurried forward and the two men held Larry. One of them pulled out a pair of handcuffs.

"No!" Larry was screaming. "Listen to me! I didn't kill her!"

He tried to jerk away from the bailiffs, but the handcuffs snapped on his wrists and he was yanked away, out of the room.

Noelle felt a pressure on her arm. A matron was waiting there to escort her out of the courtroom.

"They're waiting for you, Miss Page."

It was like a theater call. *They're waiting for you, Miss Page.* Only this time when the curtain went down, it would never rise again. The realization hit Noelle that this was the last time in her life that she would ever be in public, the last time that she would be around other people, uncaged. This was her farewell appearance, this dirty, dreary Greek courtroom, her final theater. *Well,* she thought defiantly, *at least I have a good house.* She looked around the packed courtroom for the last time. She saw Armand Gautier staring at her in stunned silence, shaken for once out of his cynicism.

There was Philippe Sorel, his rugged face trying hard for an encouraging smile and not quite managing it.

Across the room was Israel Katz, his eyes closed and his lips moving as though in silent prayer. Noelle remembered the night she had smuggled him into the trunk of the General's car, under the nose of the albino Gestapo officer, and the fear that had been in her then.

But it was nothing to the terror that was possessing her now.

Noelle's eyes moved across the room and rested on the face of Auguste Lanchon, the shopkeeper. She could not recall his name, but she remembered his porcine face and his gross squat body and the dreary hotel room in Vienne. When he saw her looking at him, he blinked and lowered his eyes.

A tall, attractive, gray-haired American-looking man was standing up staring at her as though wanting to tell her something. Noelle had no idea who he was.

The matron was tugging at her arm now, saying, "Come along, Miss Page. . . ."

Frederick Stavros was in a state of shock. He had not only been a witness to a cold-blooded frame-up; he had been a party to it. He could go to the President of the Court and tell him what had happened: what Chotas had promised. But would they believe him? Would they take his word against the word of Napoleon Chotas? It really didn't matter, Stavros thought bitterly. After this he would be finished as a lawyer. No one would ever hire him again. Someone spoke his name and he turned and Chotas was standing there saying, "If you're free tomorrow, why don't you come and have lunch with me, Frederick? I'd like you to meet my partners. I think you have a very promising future."

Over Chotas' shoulder, Frederick Stavros could see the President of the Court exiting through the door that led to his private chambers. Now would be the time to talk to him, to explain what had happened. Stavros turned back to Napoleon Chotas, his mind still filled with the horror of what this man had done, and he heard himself saying, "That's very kind of you, sir. What would be a convenient time . . . ?"

By Greek law executions take place on the little island of Ageana, an hour out of the port of Piraeus. A special government boat transports condemned prisoners to the island. A series of small gray cliffs leads to the harbor itself and high on a hill is a lighthouse built on an outcropping of rock. The prison on Ageana is on the north side of the island, out of sight of the little harbor where excursion boats regularly disgorge excited tourists for an hour or two of shopping and sightseeing before sailing on to the next island. The prison is not on the sightseeing schedule, and no one approaches it except on official business.

It was 4:00 A.M. on a Saturday morning. Noelle's execution was scheduled to take place at 6:00 A.M.

They had brought Noelle her favorite dress to wear, a wine-red, brushed-wool Dior, and matching red suede shoes. She had all new silk handstitched lingerie and a white jabot of Venetian lace for her throat. Constantin Demiris had sent Noelle's regular hairdresser to do her hair. It was as though Noelle were preparing to go to a party.

Intellectually Noelle knew that there would be no last-minute reprieve, that in a little while her body was going to be brutally violated and her blood spilled upon the ground. And yet emotionally she could not keep from hoping that Constantin Demiris would make a miracle and spare her life. It would not even have to be a miracle—it only needed a phone call, a word, a wave of his golden hand. If he spared her now, she would make it up to him. She would do anything. If she could only see him, she would tell him she would never look at another man, that she would devote herself to making him happy for the rest of his life. But she knew that it would do no good to beg. If Demiris came to her, yes. If she had to go to him, no.

There were still two hours.

Larry Douglas was in another part of the prison. Since his conviction, his mail had increased tenfold. Letters poured in from women in all parts of the world, and the warden, who considered himself a sophisticated man, was shocked by some of them.

Larry Douglas would probably have enjoyed them if he had known of them. But he was in a drugged world of half-twilight where nothing touched him. During his first few days on the island, he had been in a state of violence, screaming day and night that he was innocent and demanding a new trial. The prison doctor had finally ordered that he be kept on tranquilizers.

At ten minutes before five A.M., when the prison warden and four guards came to Larry Douglas' cell, he was seated on his bunk, quiet and withdrawn. The warden had to speak his name twice before Larry was aware that they had come for him. He rose to his feet, his movements dreamlike and lethargic.

The warden led him out to the corridor, and they walked in a slow procession toward a guarded door at the far end of the corridor. As they reached the door, the guard opened it and they were outside in a walled courtyard. The predawn air was chilly and Larry shivered as he stepped through the door. There was a full moon in the sky and bright stars. It reminded him of the mornings in the South Pacific islands when the pilots left their warm bunks and gathered under the chilly stars for a last minute briefing before takeoff. He could hear the sound of the sea in the distance, and he tried to remember which island he was on and what his mission was. Some men led him to a post in front of a wall and tied his arms behind his back.

There was no anger in him now, only a kind of drowsy wonder about the way the briefing was being handled. He was filled with a deep lassitude but he knew he must not fall asleep because he had to lead the mission. He raised his head and saw men in uniform lined up. They were aiming guns at him. Old, buried instincts began to take over. They would attack from different directions and try to separate him from the rest of his squadron, because they were afraid of him. He saw a movement at three o'clock low and knew they were coming for him. They would expect him to bank out of range, but instead he shoved the stick all the way forward and went into an outside loop that nearly tore the wings off his plane. He pulled out at the bottom of the dive and executed a snap roll to the left. There was no sign of them. He had outmaneuvered them. He began to climb, and below him he saw a Zero. He laughed aloud and gave his plane right stick and rudder until the Zero was centered in his gunsights. Then he swooped down like an avenging angel, closing the distance with dizzying speed. His finger began to tighten on the trigger button when a sudden excruciating pain smashed through his body. And another. And another. He could feel his flesh tearing and his guts spilling out, and he thought, *Oh, my God, where did he come from? . . . There's a better pilot than me . . . I wonder who he is . . .*

And then he began spinning abruptly into space and everything grew dark and silent.

In her cell Noelle's hair was being coifed when she heard a volley of thunder outside.

"Is it going to rain?" she asked.

The hairdresser looked at her strangely for a moment and saw that she really did not know what the sound was. "No," she said quietly, "it is going to be a beautiful day."

And then Noelle knew.

And she was next.

At five-thirty A.M., thirty minutes before her execution was scheduled, Noelle heard footsteps approaching her cell. Her heart gave an involuntary leap. She had been sure that Constantin Demiris would want to see her. She knew that she had never looked more beautiful, and perhaps when he saw her . . . perhaps . . . The prison warden appeared, accompanied by a guard and a nurse carrying a black medical bag. Noelle looked behind them for Demiris. The corridor was empty. The guard opened the cell door, and the

warden and nurse entered. Noelle found that her heart
was pounding, the wave of fear beginning to lap at her
again, drowning out the faint hope that had been stirring.

"It isn't time yet, is it?" Noelle asked.

The warden looked uncomfortable. "No, Miss Page.
The nurse is here to give you an enema."

She looked at him, not understanding. "I don't want
an enema."

He looked even more uncomfortable. "It will save
you being—embarrassed."

And then Noelle understood. And her fear turned
into a roaring agony, tearing at her stomach. She nodded her head and the warden turned and left the cell.
The guard locked the door and tactfully walked down
the corridor out of sight.

"We don't want to spoil that pretty dress," the nurse
was cooing. "Why don't we just slip it off and you lie
down right there? This will only take a minute."

The nurse began to work on her, but Noelle felt
nothing.

She was with her father and he was saying, *Look at
her, a stranger could tell she was of royal blood,* and
people were fighting to pick her up in their arms and
hold her. A priest was in the room and he said,
"Would you like to make your confession to God, my
child?" but she shook her head impatiently because her
father was talking and she wanted to hear what he was
saying. *You were born a princess and this is your kingdom. When you grow up, you're going to marry a
handsome prince and live in a grand palace.*

She was walking down a long corridor with some
men and someone opened a door and she was outside
in a cold courtyard. Her father was holding her up to a
window and she could see the tall masts of ships bobbing on the water.

The men led her to a post in front of a wall and fastened her hands behind her and tied her waist to the
post and her father said, *Do you see those ships, Prin-*

cess? That's your fleet. One day they'll carry you to all the magic places in the world. And he held her close and she felt safe. She could not remember why, but he had been angry with her, but now everything was all right, and he loved her again, and she turned to him but his face was a blur, and she could not recall what he looked like. She could not remember her father's face.

She was filled with an overwhelming sadness, as though she had lost something precious, and she knew that she had to remember him or she would die, and she began to concentrate very hard, but before she could see it, there was a sudden roaring sound and a thousand knives of agony tore into her flesh and her mind screamed, *No! Not yet! Let me see my father's face!*

But it was lost forever in the darkness.

EPILOGUE

The man and woman moved through the cemetery, their faces dappled by the shadows of the tall, graceful cypresses that lined the path. They walked slowly in the shimmering heat of the noonday sun.

Sister Theresa said, "I wish to tell you again how grateful we are for your generosity. I do not know what we would have done without you."

Constantin Demiris waved a deprecating hand. "*Arkayto,*" he said. "It is nothing, Sister."

But Sister Theresa knew that without this savior the nunnery would have had to close down years ago. And surely it was a sign from Heaven that now she had been able to repay him in some measure. It was a *thri-amvos,* a triumph. She thanked Saint Dionysius again that the Sisters had been permitted to rescue the American friend of Demiris' from the waters of the lake on that terrible night of the storm. True, something had happened to the woman's mind and she was like a child, but she would be cared for. Mr. Demiris had asked Sister Theresa to keep the woman here within these walls, sheltered and protected from the outside world for the rest of her life. He was such a good and kind man.

They had reached the end of the cemetery. A path wound down to a promontory where the woman stood, staring out at the calm, emerald lake below.

"There she is," Sister Theresa said. "I will leave you now. *Hayretay.*"

Demiris watched Sister Theresa start back toward

the nunnery, then he walked down the path to where the woman stood.

"Good morning," he said, gently.

She turned around slowly and looked at him. Her eyes were dull and vacant and there was no recognition on her face.

"I brought you something," Constantin Demiris said.

He pulled a small jewelry box out of his pocket and held it out to her. She stared at it like a small child.

"Go on, take it."

Slowly she reached out and took the box. She lifted the lid, and inside, nested in cotton, was a miniature, exquisitely made gold bird with ruby eyes and outstretched wings poised for flight. Demiris watched as the child-woman removed it from the box and held it up. The bright sun caught the gleam of its gold and the sparkle of its ruby eyes and sent tiny rainbows flashing through the air. She turned it from side to side, watching the lights dancing around her head.

"I will not be seeing you again," Demiris said, "but you won't have to worry. No one will harm you now. The wicked people are dead."

As he spoke, her face happened to be turned toward him, and for one frozen instant in time it seemed to him that a gleam of intelligence, a look of joy came into her eyes, but a moment later it was gone and there was only the vacant, mindless stare. It could have been an illusion, a trick of the sunlight reflecting the sparkle of the golden bird across her eyes.

He thought about it as he walked slowly up the hill and out the huge stone gate of the nunnery to where his limousine was waiting to drive him back to Athens.

Chicago
London
Paris
Athens
Ioannina
Los Angeles

BESTSELLERS
FROM DELL

fiction

- ☐ EAGLE IN THE SKY by Wilbur Smith....... $1.95 (4592-06)
- ☐ MARATHON MAN by William Goldman..... $1.95 (5502-02)
- ☐ THE OTHER SIDE OF MIDNIGHT
  by Sidney Sheldon......................... $1.75 (6067-07)
- ☐ DOG DAY AFTERNOON by Patrick Mann $1.50 (4519-06)
- ☐ THE RHINEMANN EXCHANGE
  by Robert Ludlum........................ $1.95 (5079-13)
- ☐ THE LONG DARK NIGHT by Joseph Hayes ... $1.95 (4824-06)
- ☐ THE NAKED FACE by Sidney Sheldon $1.50 (5921-13)
- ☐ THREE DAYS OF THE CONDOR
  by James Grady $1.50 (7570-13)
- ☐ CROSS-COUNTRY by Herbert Kastle........ $1.95 (4585-05)

non-fiction

- ☐ TM by Harold H. Bloomfield, M.D.,
  Michael Peter Cain,
  Dennis T. Jaffe and Robert B. Kory $1.95 (6048-01)
- ☐ ERIC by Doris Lund...................... $1.75 (4586-04)
- ☐ MORRIS by Mary Daniels................. $1.50 (5673-05)
- ☐ THE ULTRA SECRET by F. W. Winterbotham .. $1.95 (9061-07)
- ☐ DON'T SAY YES WHEN YOU WANT TO
  SAY NO by Herbert Fensterheim, Ph.D. and
  Jean Baer............................... $1.95 (5413-00)
- ☐ MIKE ROY'S CROCK COOKERY by Mike Roy . $1.25 (5617-04)
- ☐ THE JAWS LOG by Carl Gottlieb $1.50 (4689-00)
- ☐ MILTON BERLE: An Autobiography......... $1.95 (5626-11)

At your local bookstore or use this handy coupon for ordering:

| Dell | **DELL BOOKS** **P.O. BOX 1000, PINEBROOK, N.J. 07058** |

Please send me the books I have checked above. I am enclosing $_____
(please add 35¢ per copy to cover postage and handling). Send check or money
order—no cash or C.O.D.'s.

Mr/Mrs/Miss_____

Address_____

City_____ State/Zip_____

offer expires 4/77